TurnAbout

Doug Booth

TurnAbout

TurnAbout

Part One
1

Jacques Lebeau was born and grew up poor in the Louisiana bayou, the unfortunate consequence of another sweltering summer evening with nothing much else for folks to do than tolerate the misfortunes of their lives by chilling the man's home brew with ice shavings from the kitchen box and visit the wife once the clay pipe was smoked cold.

Jacques was the youngest of twelve. His first taste of milk that he couldn't remember came from his young mother's already weary breasts, the last he could remember was what he squirted secretly from the warm teats of his papa's only cow into a canteen that he hid under his mat.

Until he was three he ran about naked from when he woke till he was tucked in the same condition by a sister into a drawer stuffed with a thin cotton blanket, while the others, his six brothers and the five girls, chased their narrow dreams lying together on straw-stuffed mats in a room with no door.

By the time he started his lessons in a shack a mile or more down the road, the two oldest boys had left for whatever work they might find in Lafayette and Baton Rouge at sixteen or thereabouts, and a girl at fifteen had taken a widowed neighbour's hand till death soon after claimed her soul in childbirth. Names he would not remember as one by one the sisters left for the drudgery and toil of marriage and the brothers for more difficult and tedious work on boats and in the fields; their mats each time devoured by flames making more room for those yet left behind.

He didn't remember the excitement that came with his first pair of dungarees passed down, or that until the inauspicious day he would perforce wear hand-me-down shorts and singlets, rubber boots a size too big with bare feet and a cap that was years older than him.

He didn't often go into town; there wasn't much need or much for him to see or do. Besides which, after his reading, writing and numbers, he had chores that would make him a strong and worthwhile man, earn him a good and steady wage one day, "Car, mon ti-Jacq, mieux d'avoir le dos et les mains très forts que le coeur désappointé avec trop de rèves écervelés. Non?"

No. That couldn't be true.

Jacques didn't so much drop out from school after his seventh grade as stop his lessons when there wasn't much else for him to learn. The other school was miles farther down twisting dirt roads too difficult for his bare feet and boots and his papa had better use of the truck than consuming his time for what wasn't the least bit useful in a man's life.

Instead he bided his time, leaving home two years later at age fourteen, slipping from his straw-filled mat with his canteen on a night that was plenty dark enough; he was done with gators and slithering black moccasins, leaving his dreamless and childless parents sleeping in their bed.

He never did believe his papa. His hands and back were strong enough, except when his hands were scraped and bleeding and his back ached so badly he couldn't sleep at night. Nor would he ever see them or his siblings again, because his father was wrong. That's what he knew in his heart filled with scatterbrain dreams. He also knew he would never disappoint himself or his young heart. He would become someone important, someone who would always make his dreams come true and make a difference. "N'est pas, père? Alors!" He would for sure be a better man than his papa.

He wasn't the best educated man, that he would not deny. But he was far from the stupidest. He had a bright and quick mind; he was good with numbers, big for his age, strong and unafraid, and wouldn't let anyone get the better or the best of him.

*

Evenings were never pretty in the bayou with picturesque golden sunsets, never romantic with silvery moons and starlit skies. The very worst of what the swamp held by day, the incongruous little that was curiously to some wondrous and exotic, were at night unnerving and menacing. The once bright green and majestic cypresses, perches for aristocratic blue herons and cloaked in white moss during muted daylight, were at night towering and ominous shadows draped with dark curtains alive with poisonous black widow spiders and others with fangs no less lethal. Venomous cottonmouth and copperhead serpents, invisible by night, would rest lurking in pits underfoot or instantly fall upon the least disturbance from branches overhead inflicting a horrible death with a single puncture.

The journey into daylight was a perilous one indeed for the boy who didn't cease praying in whispers that his dead grandmama's amulet at his neck and clutched tightly in his hand would keep him from danger and death. Not that he believed in the gris-gris of nocturnal spirits or that he would go mad if he fell asleep in the moonlight; he was fourteen with a vivid imagination.

Happily though, breathing a sigh of relief, Jacques finally did make daybreak and wisely quickened his pace for distance and safety. He would pause for a taste of warm milk when the day's already insufferable heat was at its peak, certain no one would come chasing after him now that papa had only his wife to feed.

His trek was taking him eastward, not from the bayou but far enough from the life he felt in his heart was not his. Where his brothers had sought improved and separate lives in Baton Rouge and Lafayette, ti-Jacq would not. He was making his way toward Dulac, 150 miles from where his mat smouldered in the yard, a good enough place he learned about in school where a boat's captain would care about his arms and his back, not his age.

He would get hired onto a crab boat, for sure he would; someone would hire him despite not being fully grown.

He got into the town of 1800 souls, give or take, given a few were nearly dead and a few were nearly born, two days later with the help of kindly folks travelling the same road, letting the boy snooze partway in the back of their wagons. Back then no one troubled over how many folks lived thereabouts cause all were acquainted, all worked together and married each other's sisters. That was their life, but no one was hiring. Times were tough, most folks just getting by. Until fate walked him into Lamonte Jaloux's gutting shed.

Jaloux was a bear of a man, burnt from the sun with black eyes and blacker hair, with arms the width of ti-Jacq's legs and fists the boy was pretty sure didn't get anywhere near that scarred on a crabber, but he wasn't taking on crew either. With a deep chortle answering "Ah! Petit chéri, que t'es réellement drôle," especially not little pink white boys, the roar and a tight grip on his neck practically making ti-Jacq soil his britches, swinging him around and propelling the kid through wide doors onto the dock.

Not me, the bear told him, "Mais ouais, mon frère Félix à Chauvin il cherche un tel petit merde comme toi. Viens, ti-gars. Saute!"

So he did, for the first time in his life leaping aboard a swaying boat, by some miracle or his grandmama's amulet not landing on his knees, though quickly bracing himself against what he learned was a gunwale, elated and beaming when they got underway and the good Captain Lamonte who would become a good friend invited him to take the helm.

Together they steered through shallow creeks and marsh, making unhurried passage through to where the brother's forty-foot crabber in Chauvin was docking with a full load, where with glassy wide eyes the comical little pink shit gave back the helm and began his new life.

*

Four years later young Jacques Lebeau was captain of his own crabber, renting dockage and shed space from his former boss. At twenty he owned another, hiring on Félix Jaloux's youngest son as captain and a stout Florida runaway as second mate, which gave him pause, which developed into a meeting with the brothers one August evening over several glasses of their finest clear brew.

Crabbing was dangerous, thankless and backbreaking labour which he proposed was too much work for too little gain, always returning after days in the Gulf with full loads. But full loads of what? Waste. Crab and prawn they would process in their sheds while losing precious time at sea. But what if? From which point he and the brothers quickly refitted their vessels into floating processing plants, spending more time harvesting that meant heavier and more lucrative payloads ready for market, better wages and more capital.

He was successful with impressive thousands in the bank, known and respected in town, but he wasn't happy. He rented a humble home and Félix had given him driving lessons years back and a truck for exactly what it was worth: Nothing. Thing is, he had no life, nor friends other than the brothers who were tiring of their difficult lives at sea and preparing to hand over their helms to their sons.

The other problem was ti-Jacq, a Cajun white boy with Cajun blood and a Cajun mouth in a Cajun village that was fast becoming a trap, waking one morning realizing he would never be better than he was if he didn't get out, if he didn't very soon transmute ti-Jacq into the man he dreamed of becoming.

He spent the day pondering and planning not what he should

do, but when, driving the next morning into New Orleans for yet another meeting with the bank, deciding he would stay the night for what had become a monthly diversion since sleeping with any of the village girls would certainly cause catastrophic repercussions he was not ready for. Better he should pay the ten dollars, justifying that he wasn't actually whoring since he would always enrich the same young and lovely girl. Francine Leclerc, if that was actually her name.

The next day he was back in Chauvin by noon, calling the brothers by radio, requesting a meeting that night, promising he would not waste their time, and by week's end Jacques Lebeau owned six boats, a few docks, and was employing eleven fishermen.

On his twenty-first birthday, celebrating the previous evening with the brothers and their families, he drove into the Big Easy where he purchased a new car and visited the state building where he filed an application before driving to Gulfport where he stayed several days meeting with banks and interviewing fishermen. A few weeks later Mr. Jack Fox enhanced his Chauvin businesses with four new boats on the Mississippi Gulf Coast, several new hires and private dockage that came with a processing plant. A success he repeated within the same year on the Florida Gulf Coast while building his new home in the exclusive Upper Garden District of New Orleans.

The construction lasted several months, the pièce de résistance a study that overtime would boast several hundred academic publications, encyclopedias, literary masterpieces and souvenirs from around the globe.

He hired an elocution teacher, emerging from his home a year later as a fully bilingual and articulate Jack Fox, kissing ti-Jacq a fond farewell with his grandmama's amulet pressed to his lips.

He replaced his coveralls and boots with tailored suits and shirts; one Jaloux clapping his hands together with pride, the other erupting in raucous laughter, telling the Cajon boy he would always and forever be ti-Jacq, the little pink shit who almost soiled his britches. Then he hugged his good friend and got royally pissed with him. Misère de mon Dieu!

Despite which, the good Lord visiting the misery of throbbing temples upon them the following morning, Jack Fox declared he would do something good later that day as atonement. He would take a young and deserving young woman off the street, Lamonte declaring good for him. Misère!

A man of his word he rented and furnished an astonished Francine a comfortable flat; he put her through secretarial school and, once she graduated with warm tears in her eyes, gave her a job in his modest office on Canal Street, never again speaking of their past.

By thirty he owned a fleet of several dozen boats in the Gulf and several more plants. He paid himself as president of Fox Fisheries, his office girl was now Office Manager on the tenth floor of a tower, and he was not looking back. He was Jack Fox, member in good standing at the city's Board of Trade, member of a prestigious Gulfport yacht club, owner of a forty-foot Bertram, and an eligible bachelor sought after by the daughters of the city's most influential families.

Causing him at thirty-one to make his first tragic mistake in life. He married, for no better reason than people were talking. Something that made Francine Leclerc privately giggle. Not that he cared, but then again he could no longer stop at street corners, or invite higher quality ladies into his home, and his self-motivated vacations in Cuba and Haiti were as ephemeral as they were difficult to extricate from.

She was five years younger, attractive and preppy and capricious and hadn't worked a day in her life. But she could dance and sing and she loved her daddy who gave her a million-dollar dowry which Jack overtly refused telling the old man over cognacs that dowry meant warranty and that nothing in life was guaranteed. Instead he produced a document the girl would sign agreeing that what was his—etcetera.

They divorced three years later, days after the birth of her first child, Jack Fox claiming in court that the little mulatto girl was good enough reason.

*

By forty Jack owned the industry; he was the industry. He operated three popular restaurants on paper and upgraded to a fifty-foot Grand Banks. He was godfather to the recently wed Francine Duval's son, had stood with his face streaked with tears at Félix's funeral, and Lamonte was again standing at his side as best man tugging at the tight collar of his unfamiliar morning suit.

She was thirty-six from old money, a socialite and champion of the poor which, it turned out, meant serving meals at the mission at Christmas dressed in silk finery alongside Francine who had years earlier eaten at the food kitchen too many times.

For that and countless other reasons, like extravagant living and reckless spending, constant whining and dedication to fine scotch when she didn't get her way, Jack inadvertently seeing her with her feet wide apart while accommodating some happy fellow and kicking the bedroom air, the marriage lasted three tortuous months.

He returned her to daddy that evening, one day later in the week lamenting with a smile in his fifteenth floor office that he should have married his first true love. Water under the bridge. Instead he made her Vice-president of Fox Fisheries and sent her home with an extra ten grand a year and a luxury vacation on the chic and sophisticated Côte d'Azur.

He was ready for a reprieve. He was done with women forever, cheating wives anyway. He called his dear friend, thinking he would suggest a Caribbean cruise for the sole purpose of whoring with wild abandon and drunkenness. Or, if that would be problematic, Lamonte could bring along his wife of fifty years. Instead he shuddered with cold and wept. The bear was dead. Lamonte Jaloux had crossed over peacefully in his sleep the night before.

*

Not long after the funeral, when he was certain Lamonte's wife was in the loving care of her sons, he sailed alone from Gulfport, navigating a course that would put him first in Miami then Cuba and the Bahamas, Haiti and Jamaica, the Cayman Islands and Cozumel, before returning home several months later skirting the Gulf Coast.

And for the next six years he was fine, content with his solitary existence.

He travelled abroad when Francine told him he should, often inviting her and the family onboard for weekend cruises and celebrated his fiftieth with them by smashing a champagne bottle against the bow of a sixty-foot Grand Banks. Yet he wasn't so tired of women that he was averse to hiring a crew of very pretty college girls, outfitting them in trendy short skirts and blouses for nighttime and string bikinis for the daytime rigours of serving his guests fine meals and booze onboard the luxurious Crabby Missus. Something the Duval men viewed as liberal and progressive, if not the family matriarch.

At fifty-three he wasn't at all certain what else he could achieve in life. He was beyond filthy rich with a limo and chauffeur, his home library was one of the finest in the city in a mansion boasting every possible amenity. He owned six fine-dining establishments whose chefs were renowned and he slept alone in his bed as much to his chagrin as Francine Duval's who began admonishing him for being overly blasé about life. He was not getting any younger.

He was aware of that, thanking her. He'd been married three plus years of the past twenty-two, not the best track record. Not that he'd become a monk throughout his tenure as a sought-after bachelor, meaning he was far better at meeting women than keeping them, although he was seeing a particular woman somewhat regularly.

Still he wasn't sure, very mindful of the perilous distinction between dinner dates at any of his establishments and serving her breakfast in his kitchen.

She was forty-two, divorced, a corporate attorney without family obligations and decidedly attractive. She was trim and fashionably au courant, the envy of most women when she lay on the foredeck of the Crabby Missus at the marina or when dropping anchor by one of the Gulf's many sandbars.

So what was his problem?

He didn't know, possibly fearing the loneliness of his later years, until one August evening at dinner she said "Yes, darling. I will."

The next morning they ate breakfast by the pool and in early September he took her on a magical four-week European honeymoon that over seven years deteriorated into a friendly divorce, an amicable last dinner together and a prenup settlement cheque for one million slid across the table in lieu of an affectionate embrace.

They liked each other; she simply loved her job more, frequently away or working long hours—and what exactly was the point? They were both pragmatic, of course, and unemotional. They were married to their careers; he was spending more time on the yacht alone, realizing he had never told her he loved her. And worse, or equally lamentable, he couldn't recall ever hearing her speak the words onboard the yacht, at any of a hundred candlelight dinners, or at the very height of their infrequent lovemaking which was increasingly the case since she was increasingly not sleeping in his bed.

The next day in his office he promptly cautioned his dearest friend and VP with a threatening finger an inch from her nose. "Tais-toi, ma petite. Not a word or I assure you I will invite your loving husband on a long and carefree Caribbean cruise. I am at last contentedly done with your troublesome species...and at a very reasonable price."

Francine patted his cheek, commiserating with a pouty frown, leaving him in his melancholy state with a girlish giggle. "Si pathé-tique. So sad, mon ti-Jacq."

As a man of his word Jack reached for the phone, seconds later greeting Charlie Duval with a very loud and resounding "Hey, Chuck!"

2

He was sixty going on thirty, possibly forty. He hadn't put on a pound in years, maintaining a daily regimen and occasionally trading tailor-made suits for coveralls when he would climb onboard unannounced and take orders from any one of his captains as a means of staying level and never forgetting his beginnings with Félix and Lamonte.

He had not the slightest hint of silver strands streaking his dark hair, not the slightest hint of ennui in his bright eyes, attributing the few hairline creases, that he insisted merely enhanced his already charming disposition, to the female participants in three failed marriages more than his harsh life on the sea.

He was without sufficient warning sixty and didn't know why or how, thankful Francine was such an integral part of his life. He couldn't imagine a better VP or friend, despite Chuck flatly declining his offer months earlier that made her despicably smug.

Seems some people actually loved each other.

He was leaving on vacation, an extended cruise on the Crabby Missus with his crew that now comprised a cute college sophomore who would certainly enhance the yachting experience in her short skirts and bikinis on the port side and a testosterone college clone with chiselled abs on the starboard. A vacation, he insisted. A well-earned absence from her and from the office, nothing more. "Comprends-tu, fille?"

She shrugged. Of course she understood, hugging him tightly before shooing him from the building and beginning a payday pool with her entire female staff that would last a full six weeks. Bien que oui, she understood. Silly man.

He charted a course that would put him first in Miami, then Jacksonville and Savannah, Charleston and Wilmington before challenging the open Atlantic: Destination Bermuda where he gave the cutie and the clone a surprise week-long furlough at the Harmony Hall Resort without the boss. He remained onboard enjoying the tranquility of sun-filled days and peaceful nights before returning to Wilmington, North Carolina where the kids went clubbing and whatever else might happen without their captain who went for a quiet drink at Stan's Bar & Grill. Because when you owned six fine restaurants, eating a burger and fries with a glass of passable house wine was a treat most would not comprehend.

The atmosphere was laidback; the lighting was dim, the music low, the waitresses all young and attractive. What more did a man need other than good food and a pretty girl serving him? A very pretty girl serving him a Johnnie Walker Red since Stan wasn't exactly a must-do for the Blue crowd.

Her name was Courtney Flanders. She was twenty-one, a college dropout who was married at nineteen of Southern necessity, working nights at Stan's after eight hours as a drugstore cashier because hubby couldn't find steady work.

"Anything else?"

"Yes. The seafood platter and a glass of your Cabernet-Sauvignon would be delightful."

"Got it. The platter and a Cab."

She turned, halting at the "And perhaps a small serving of smiles would be very nice as well. Thank you."

Asshole. "Smiles. Got it."

When she came back she was smiling, grinning from ear-to-ear, her bright teeth practically leaping out at him, though he could tell she was being a tad snarly, not the least sincere. Possibly having arrived at her monthly inconvenience, not that he was familiar with the particularly distasteful mood.

"Thank you, Courtney."

She ignored him, walking away, halting again. "What now?"

"Thank you, for the smile." His lips curved into one that was genuine. "At least I believe you were smiling and, if I may say, you are a captivating young woman. A very pleasant vision that will endure as an equally agreeable memory. Thank you."

With that Jack Fox began his dinner. When he was finished he declined a coffee: the ruination of any good meal. Instead he thanked her, waiting until she took away a full tray before adding a fifty-dollar gratuity into the leather folder with thirty for the meal. Then he walked out.

He spent the evening onboard wondering about her, the next day strolling along the white sandy shore of Wrightsville Beach wondering about her, wondering whether she was angry or sad or plainly fed-up with her life. She was not in any way his business, or remotely his problem. Yet somehow, for some reason, he liked her. A natural consequence of which was succumbing to a craving for another platter and Cab that evening, requesting a table in her zone.

Minutes after being seated: "You want a Johnnie Red, mister?"

"I would indeed. Thank you."

"Anything else?"

"Last night's special, which I see is also this night's special." He handed her the menu. "And a smile, of course."

She walked away, pausing, turning. "Hey, thanks…for the fifty bucks. Was that a mistake or something?"

He shook his head, grinning. "No mistake. In fact, Courtney, if you would consider favouring me this evening with another disarming smile, I'll leave you a thousand."

She blurted a high-pitched laugh. "Yeah, right. Good one."

Though two hours later Courtney clapped a hand over her mouth, stifling a gasp, staring the crisp hundreds and three tens, her heart racing as she unfolded the note:

*

My name is Jack Fox, Courtney.
Please join me for cocktails at the marina lounge this evening.
I am not a creep, a stalker, or a miscreant old man. I am simply
on vacation and would expressly enjoy the company of a remarkably
lovely young woman.
The place is swarming with all manner of security and you shall be
perfectly safe. I assure you.
Regards, Jack.

*

No way. Was he kidding? He was what, fifty? Someone's father,
granddad? Shit! No way!

Stan's closed at midnight, Courtney Flanders standing alone in
the dark at the door of her twelve-year Datsun that was faded from
the glaring sun and rusted from the salty coastal air.

The guy gave her a grand. Like, what the hell? Who would do
that? Why would he do that? A scream threatening to burst past her
quivering lips. She was going insane, clenching her teeth and
groaning. There was nothing and no one waiting for her at home,
nothing but a deadbeat drunk, an incurable loser and her one-time
frat house mistake who couldn't hold a job longer than a week.

So why couldn't she? Why wouldn't she sit with the guy, have
a few drinks somewhere she could never afford on her own, for a
little while pretending she actually had a life worth living?

Yes! She would. And did, arriving at the marina's gatehouse at
quarter-past the hour. She was on the list. She was expected; Mr.
Jack Fox would greet her at the lounge where she was driven by an
attendant in a canopied trolley completely in awe.

She had seen the sailboats and yachts many times from the
beach on her days off, but never this close, like gliding between
glistening fibreglass castles. What was she doing! The Fox guy

15

was standing at the curb by the door, waiting, smiling, thanking the attendant with a discreet exchange of palms before holding out his hand for hers. What was she doing! Fuck!

The lounge was dimly lit, the quiet conversations barely audible, though she immediately felt ill; like she didn't belong. Everyone was elegantly attired in white: White slacks and sweaters, white shorts and skirts and blouses. The "in" people, the shits who never saw people like her. She was wearing a tight and short black leather skirt and a polyester black blouse, feeling trapped and vulnerable. She did not belong in soft leather armchairs, her knees inches apart from some rich guy.

"You seem perplexed, Courtney. May I enquire for what reason?"

"Are you kidding me? You left me a freaking grand, I bet that's not a JW Red you're putting back, and I'm sitting here looking like I've come from giving BJs in some back alley. I do not belong here."

"You look like no such thing. You look divine and you belong wherever you believe you should be."

"Says you."

"Yes, precisely. Says me. A questionable aspect of my life, I suppose." He paused a moment, pondering as the lady replied "A Chardonnay" and the gentleman indicated another J W Blue. He did not intend embarrassing the girl who was clearly feeling uneasy, out of her element. "May I suggest, Courtney, a peaceful stroll on the wharf with our cocktails instead?"

"Yeah, I think so. Thanks."

Outside moments later with their drinks in hand, "May I carry your shoes, Courtney?"

"Say what?"

"Solely for the sake of safety and quiet. An unfortunate sprained ankle would understandably provoke a piercing shriek and we yachtsmen sleep lightly."

She hesitated a moment, staring at the dock. The guy was too much. "Okay. I guess so. But first turn away. I cannot ruin these stockings."

He acknowledged the seriousness of the issue, taking her shoes, her glass, and giving her a few moments of privacy until hearing "I'll take my wine now."

They strolled for half an hour, illuminated by towering bright lights, stopping when Courtney was curious about a particular yacht, each one suitably praised with a whispered "Wow" or "No shit," stopping at one where she erupted into a fit of giggles.

"That's funny."

"I don't see the humour."

"The name. Think the wife's a bitch?"

Jack Fox snorted, peering into the empty old-fashioned. "Well, the first two were. The third simply wasn't a good fit. Metaphorically speaking."

"What? This thing is yours?"

"Yes, this thing is mine." He stepped onto the transom, reaching for her hand. "May I offer you a tour of the thing and perhaps another Chardonnay?"

"You serious?"

He was, Courtney Flanders taking his hand, stepping onto a magnificent yacht and into a never-dreamed-of nirvana. The tour lasted fifteen minutes, Jack suggesting the upper bridge would lend a perfect-perfect setting given the full moon and glittering sea.

For Courtney, holding back tears was difficult because she didn't know. She didn't know what would happen when she returned home and she didn't know why this old guy was even bothering with her.

"Have to say, I wouldn't mind a job like that, spending all my time on this thing in a bikini."

"Not all their time. Weekends and holidays. They're full-time students." He sipped his scotch. "Now tell me about Courtney

Flanders, a disarming girl with a disarming smile."

Yeah, like he cared. She shrugged, gazing at her mostly bare legs. Shit! The guy was big-time wealthy; he was educated and classy. She was nothing.

"The Coles version? I dropped out in my second year. I got seriously pissed and laid at a frat party. He got me pregnant, we got married and I miscarried. Now I work days in a drugstore and nights with Stan making ends meet because he can't find work. I live in a shithole and drive an ancient rust bucket with a cracked windshield and a missing doorhandle. I haven't seen my family in a couple of years and my life sucks big time. Seems the miscarriage thing was my penance for being a teenage whore." She paused for a moment, leaning into him."I was never like that. I was a virgin, pure as snow. And why am I even telling you this shit?"

"They're religious, your parents?"

"They're full of shit. My real penance was them making me marry the guy who got me drunk and screwed me." She sipped her Chardonnay. "Did he ever, because I would have graduated this year."

He snorted a burst of air, grinning. "I went as far as grade seven. I ran away at fourteen and began all that you're seeing and more by gutting crabs on a rusty boat because fate put me in the hands of very good people. Because this thing we're floating on reflects what was and what is my destiny." He put aside his glass. "More importantly, what do you believe is the destiny of one Courtney Flanders? Now, please finish your story. I can't for a moment believe you're finished. You're far too delightful and intriguing."

"Yeah, real intringuing. How much did that sweater set you back?"

"Three hundred, maybe four. Why?"

She pinched the hem of her skirt. "This thing cost twenty and the blouse was fifteen on sale. That's why. That's my destiny. Pure shit." She glanced at her plastic watch. "I should go. He's a real asshole when I get home late."

"He abuses you?"

"No. He rants because I won't give him any. Not ever, though most nights he's too pissed anyway." Her lips curled into a smirk. "Not even on my honeymoon because I didn't have a honeymoon."

"I should think the requisite solution would be divorce. You have no child, no obvious reason for enduring further misery. You're clearly unhappy. Get rid of him and continue your education, Courtney. Graduate and become the woman you truly are."

"Yeah, right. College. Good one. Then what?"

"Whatever you want...simply put." He stood, refilling his glass. He had a gut feeling, the same gut feeling that made him wealthy, successful at whatever he wanted or touched. "Or, you know, as you people say, thinking out loud, because I have been thinking about you all day, stay here this evening. Let me help you. Let me help you become someone, Courtney. Let me help you be you."

What! That wouldn't fucking happen. "Fuck that deal. I'm out of here, Jack. Nice try. Thanks for the wine. So do I scream, or what?"

"Please do, if that's what you wish. Although I would prefer escorting you to your vehicle. I would mention first, however, that I am president of Fox Fisheries, as in the seafood on the platter you served me earlier. That's me. I am what I said I am. I have no intention of hurting you or ever becoming involved again for that matter. However, I am apparently in need of female companionship, for the sound purpose of assuaging a persistently annoying friend and colleague of mine."

"Companion? Like what, a fuck-friend? Good luck with that." She stood. "I'm gone. That is fucking sick."

Jack remained as he was, unmoved. "I'm not familiar with the term."

"Yeah, well, this whole night is kind of weird. And sorry. You're not exactly twenty, pops."

"A keen observation. And don't for a moment be sorry, as I would suggest propitious more than weird. Simply put, I don't believe in anything greater than myself or my dear friends, but I stand here believing I should for good reason believe in you. As I said, I find you intriguing and, all day and all last night, found myself eager for my seafood platter at Stan's...for you. What I'm proposing is a friend, you, who after a few more years of education might actually graduate with a more gracious lexicon. An educated friend who will afford me the prestige of youthful beauty by my side for as long as we might endure. You see, I do not need, want, or see value in pursuing a fourth and loving wife. I have been there and I have done that, as they say. I'm also pragmatic. Cheating is as intrinsic to any form of marriage as monotony, particularly in view of such an age disparity as you very kindly pointed out. But you are lovely and young and would suit my need as much as my vanity in every regard."

"I'm not getting this. So you won't jump me. That's nice; you're a gentleman. Good for you." Courtney Flanders held out her glass. "Okay, so what are we doing here...rich fish guy? Because nothing but shit comes free in this life. I know that much."

"Help from a good friend is always free." He refilled her wine. "What I'm proposing is you living with me, finding you a more suitable vehicle with a working doorhandle, and getting you an education during which time you will enjoy a generous allowance, your own quarters, travel and luxury, as well as many occasions onboard this thing clad in a bikini while I do my utmost to transform you into a refined young lady. Which presumably will require a considerable number of years together, in return for which I would expect commitment and success on your part."

"Oh, yeah. That's right, and me in your big bed."

"Well I daresay that experience would be exceptionally and delightfully gratifying, were my heart sufficiently strong, though not uppermost on my mind. Did I not moments ago mention your own private quarters?" He sipped his Blue. "Nor will I at any time obstruct or question a young woman's inherent need to fraternize within her own demographic, with the obvious caveat that you must never import such dalliances into my home. You also will never act excessively in a way that will dampen my expectations for you or become reckless. In other very clear words, Courtney, my home is not a family dwelling or frat house."

"You're joking, right? Tell me you are fucking joking."

"I never joke about such matters. Nor do I often curse, young lady. In fact, should you agree by morning, my lawyers will prepare a contract protecting each of us, a sort of prenup if you will. That said, I will depart the marina tomorrow with you either at home, onboard, or on the dock. Fully your decision."

She gulped her wine, collapsing onto the wraparound seating. Shit! "Yeah, except one thing. I'm married. Remember?"

He took that as a definite yes, holding out his Blue in a nonchalant toast. "Correction. You were married."

3

A short while later an excited and confused Courtney met the crew who came onboard dressed like spoiled preppies, except they weren't. The young guy gave his captain a thumbs-up which, in turn, earned him a stern look and a harmless warning finger. And the girl escorted Courtney to her private berth with questions and giggles and found her something to sleep in. Which was wholly unnecessary because she wouldn't be sleeping.

The cutie explained the head and shower and when she would serve breakfast that came quickly, this time Courtney being served, feeling awkward in yesterday's outfit when the kids as young as her were attired in flawless white.

Jack Fox was not. He was dressed for business in tan pants, a blue blazer, a navy tie and crisp Mediterranean blue shirt, advising they would depart for Jacksonville early afternoon. Then he gave the cute and bubbly half of the yacht's complement a credit card, instructing her to assist their guest in selecting outfits appropriate for a four-day cruise and return by noon, telling the ready and able young clone that he should learn to live with life's disappointments.

Then he left, taking a taxi elsewhere that was not their affair.

When he returned onboard he scarcely recognized her; the girl had done a stupendous job, feeling quite proud of herself and not the least bit timid about saying so, receiving due praise. He wasn't seeing Courtney Flanders of the previous evening or that morning. She was stunning. Her eyes were brighter and happier, her smile real as the girl guided her into a tight pirouette.

Yet an element was missing; the plastic watch simply would not do onboard the Crabby Missus, as the crew was well aware. Inviting her onto the bridge for a private few moments he gave her a small box wrapped in pink foil, pouring chilled Chardonnays into crystal goblets while she tore at the box and gasped at the delicate Lady Rolex.

But her day was not done, not by a long shot. Delaying lunch he drove her, disregarding her chorus of plaintive protests, and in her rusted-out Datsun, to her low-rent apartment where the dead-beat husband was already slouched on a kitchen chair on the first-floor balcony and well into the several beers in his cooler.

Inside the apartment Courtney knew what was expected of her, while Jack went onto the balcony looking down at the poor semblance of a man making things clear—as clear as possible.

"The girl is leaving with me, Flanders. No arguments and no fuss. Unless you are entirely dissatisfied with the current condition of your teeth and your sloppy jaw. Within a very few days you will receive divorce papers in person and you will sign those papers without question or delay. In return for which you will be rewarded with a cheque for ten thousand, which I suppose is a veritable fortune given your current circumstances. Be sure that you do, Flanders, or I shall happily and quickly revisit you." He stepped inside, locking Flanders out, feeling elated. "Are we ready, Courtney?"

"Shit, Jack." She wanted to, she didn't know, kiss him—hug him or do something. "I mean, really, holy shit!"

He snorted, smiling, seeing her standing there looking perfect, except she had nothing in her hands. "Do you require more time?"

"No. I'm done, Jack. I am fucking done." She beamed, caressing her new designer Carolina Herrera handbag. "It's all in here, all the papers. Everything."

"Then, the soon-to-be Ms. Courtney Fox, I believe you and I have a rendezvous with the high seas and the exotic City of New

Orleans."

"Jack, he's locked outside."

"Where he belongs, Courtney. Precisely where he belongs."

*

En route to the tenement building, still very much in a dream-state, a tearful Courtney had asked what she hoped was a simple question. "Jack, I was a virgin then. I swear that's true. That's why now I want my own name. Not his, and no way the man's who called his daughter a whore. Can I do that, can I change my name?"

"Without question you can. Do you have one in mind?"

"Yeah, I do. A really good one and I won't ever let you down, Jack."

"I believe you. Enough said."

However Flanders' Datsun would remain under the No Parking sign, albeit not very long, Jack believing a taxi was more in keeping with their day, the odd couple strolling silently side by side a very short while before Courtney slipped her arm into his for several blocks until a passing cab acknowledged his signal. She had to tell him thank-you somehow.

Then en route to the marina she resigned from the drugstore, for the first time in her young life igniting envy in other women's eyes. At Stan's she got tight hugs and tears from the other girls, her ex-boss remembering the man who had left the thousand dollars, accepting at face value that the head of Fox Fisheries was a good and honest man with no hidden agenda that would hurt the girl.

Later that afternoon, watching from on high as the crew worked at freeing their lines from the dock's cleats, Courtney wasn't sure whether she needed one or not. How would she? Instead she told Jack she did not need a life jacket. She had already been saved. Then, as the Crabby Missus altered course from the IntraCoastal into a calm and open sea, she sat in a corner of the bridge where he let her privately weep with her hair blowing in the warm breeze.

They arrived in port near midnight, casting off after breakfast and arriving in Key West for dinner, docking the third day in Clearwater and spending the afternoon on a bright white sandy beach while the Crabby Missus floated at dock being maintained from stem to stern. Then too soon came Friday, arriving late into Gulfport where the cutie and the clone stayed over and the captain drove home with his guest cum whatever she was or might one day become.

Arriving at the main entrance Courtney remained strapped in her seat, gawking at the huge and glossy black doors, suspended somewhere between anxiety and exhilaration, shocked into reality when Jack swung open her door and took her hand.

The grand tour lasted longer than her first incredible night onboard. Her new designer kitchen came first before the solarium and gymnasium, which she understood she would use each day. As was his own custom, which didn't surprise her. Not since seeing him on the beach in Clearwater when he explained with a burst of laughter that staying in reasonable shape was a requisite means of avoiding endless jibes from his younger crab boat crews, thanking her for the compliment.

The living room was understated, contemporary elegance more than stuffy or magnificent, as were his study and bedroom, his ensuite and his wardrobe. Although she couldn't help staring at the bed, her expression speaking volumes, but the tour wasn't finished. At the far end of the second floor was her bedroom where she went into first, sucking a gasp of air into her already overworked lungs.

"This is mine, really?"

"Yes, really. And the lock on the door is as real as it is imaginary. Let us not have any more difficult moments of undue alarm."

She knew that; she hoped that. Despite which he recognized the invisible sigh of relief.

"Wow. This is gorgeous."

She went through the cavernous wardrobe into the ensuite, gaping with wide-open eyes, slender fingers instinctively pressing against her glossy and widely parted lips, examining the shower and the soaker, her vanity and—and what?

Jack was leaning against the doorframe, grinning, enjoying the moment. "Yes, that would be a sauna. As for the empty wardrobe, we'll address that deficiency beginning tomorrow. Or you will. I believe a dear friend of mine will gladly take up the female cause with you. Then Monday we'll start on terminating one Courtney and making another in keeping with your wishes. In the meantime unpack and join me at the pool for cocktails before we leave for dinner at Le Renard." He shook his head, walking toward her door. "Cute, but certainly not my idea. Francine's. I'm the fox." He paused, glancing over his shoulder. "As are you now, I suppose. Welcome home, Ms. Courtney Fox."

*

Saturday Francine did take up the female cause, doing her best at reducing Jack Fox to a state of penury.

By the time the ladies were done, ready for dinner with Jack and Chuck, Courtney was even more impressed and amazed by the man; confiding that—Francine bursting into laughter that her ti-Jacq could ever in anyone's world be an asshole. It seems the ladies would have their secrets, one assuring the other that Jack Fox, above all, was a gentleman beyond reproach.

By month's end her wardrobe was complete for the season, she was driving an entry level Infiniti and was pre-registered as a third-year Fine Arts student at Tulane. She was formally divorced and Ms. Courtney Fox was having her passport stamped in Cancun where they would vacation for several days at a complex of private villas.

Some twenty months later she graduated with a Fine Arts degree, opening Fox Galleries on Royal Street a few weeks before a successful Christmas season, welcoming Jack and the Duvals as her first clients.

Throughout her college years he never once put a hand to her bedroom door, Courtney too busy with academia and becoming a proper lady to romantically share her body with anyone. Or possibly that her learned purveyors of knowledge and enlightenment were either too infatuated with themselves, or bald, or rotund, or possibly not at all like Jack. And the college jocks were just that: Jerks who would just as quickly grab for a tissue when she was living with one of the city's foremost influential and sophisticated men.

Then, of course, the gallery consumed most of her time and energy.

Until at twenty-five she began accepting invitations for dinner, occasionally returning home the next morning from evenings that never blossomed into a relationship, never being asked or justifying where and why. They adored each other, a tender closeness juxtaposed with fulfilling and separate lives, though never sleeping together.

Still, they continued travelling the world and yachting as anyone would believe was a happy couple, holding hands and being affectionate. Until one Sunday weeks after her thirtieth and his sixty-ninth celebration, after a relaxed weekend at the pool with him, the disparity somehow no longer seemed as vast, telling him with a casual shrug before pressing her lips to his in a not so platonic kiss and sauntering away tugging at her bikini strings that he wasn't a day over sixty.

That evening she prepared dinner wearing silky flounced panties and matching camisole, which for years had been the weekend dinner and breakfast dress code since they were sharing such close quarters. She was comfortable with him, and not doing so somehow seemed foolish; particularly since she was young and beautiful and had gradually and naturally adapted to thongs and sunbathing topless at the pool or on exotic beaches.

Later, sitting quietly with cocktails on the patio, mesmerized by the pool's aquamarine glow, a silvery moon and black sky blanketed with glittering stars, she felt no qualm or uncertainty whatsoever. Without the slightest inhibition she stood facing him, pressing a fingertip to her lips, her eyes twinkling as slender hands guided her panties seductively past her ankles.

Tossing them onto his lap she turned a full circle with enticing precision, scarcely moving her feet, leaning into him, piercing his quizzical eyes with hers, tugging the camisole over her head and flinging that into his lap.

Padding nonchalantly to the diving board she stood at the edge glancing over her shoulder,
diving into the warm water and swimming for several minutes ignoring him because, of more telling importance, he hadn't for a nanosecond taken his eyes from her, studying every inch of her as she stepped out glistening and dripping: a shimmering and exotic nude.

Towelling herself dry, bending over and tousling her wet tresses into damp curls, she sauntered toward him swaying her hips, taking his hand and guiding him inside, climbing the staircase ahead of him with a cunning purpose and wicked grin he couldn't see; didn't care about seeing.

In his darkened bedroom she threw back the duvet, and herself onto satin sheets where she didn't wait long lying on her side propped onto an elbow, waking in his arms the next morning as she would many more weekend evenings. Still, she continued selectively accepting occasional dinner invitations, returning home the next day after essentially cheating with his full permission. In particular the times he was away on business or was alone on the Crabby Missus sipping his preferred JW Blue from the day he and Francine together transferred the helm of Fox Fisheries into the hands of her eldest son and daughter. He was seventy, a still vital Francine decidedly not, though they had done their time and would forever remain the best of friends with a long-held secret buried deep in their hearts.

Until one bright and warm Saturday afternoon in early April seven years later when Courtney arrived home early from the gallery, finding Jack lounging contentedly on the patio wearing a blue blazer and winter-white trousers with a crisp cream-coloured shirt and ascot. Urbane and elegant. He blew her a kiss, raising his Blue in a toast, telling her in a clear voice that "You are the rarest of alluring and exquisite creatures, my dear. I fear I do truly love you."

Strange, she thought. Words he had never spoken, words they had once agreed they would never speak, halting Courtney where she stood though lighting her eyes with a whimsical gleam. Besides, the day was lovely, the water inviting. What more reason did she need after a hectic day?

She put down her handbag, blowing him a kiss across the warm air, beginning a sultrily coquettish striptease from her blouse to her garters, dropping each designer piece onto the deck in turn, diving into the heated water and doing laps for several minutes. A nightly event that had become Jack's favourite pastime.

When she climbed out, glistening in the sun, she towelled herself while telling him he was handsome and debonair and dinner was on her that evening. They were dining out.

"Did you hear me, darling? I said dinner's on me this evening." She went to him, sitting by his side, poking him. Nothing. "Hello? Naked lady…dinner? Something wrong in there?"

She poked him again, slipping his dark Serengetis from his face, intuitively recoiling. Jack Fox was dead, his lips glistening with Blue curved into a thin contented smile.

Her tears were real and copious, clasping his cool hands in hers for endless minutes, at last retrieving her clothes, never taking her eyes from him. He might well have been studying her, watching her dress, sitting peacefully with his legs crossed and the crystal glass by his side, as though he had willingly and serenely transitioned from one world into wherever he might have been carried tag

by caring angels.

She called Francine Duval who came at once with Chuck, giving them time together before the police arrived with an ambulance because Jack Fox had earlier stipulated very clearly that no one would ever stare down at him lying in a silk-lined mahogany box. That indignity would never happen. Instead she respected his wishes, laying him to rest in a calm sea three days later after ti-Jacq's final cruise at the head of Fox Fisheries' entire fleet and a farewell concert of cacophonous horns.

By month's end his final wishes were honoured. All his worldly possessions were by then Courtney's who, apart from his considerable Fox Fisheries shares, received as well a one-time transfer payment of fifty-two million dollars. As did Francine, both women speechless with tears at his final and most manifest act of love.

She put the Crabby Missus in the hands of a broker, trading the sixty-footer that was outside her comfort zone for a current forty-foot SeaRay; La Renarde, however, was a vixen she could easily manage on her own. Even so, now she had a serious problem, fifty-two of them. She was never interested in anything long-term or anyone who wasn't as good or impossibly better than Jack Fox, marriage or babies. She was her own woman; always would be, independent and successful. She adored Jack and yachting, her gallery and world travel. But much of that life was gone.

She spent the entire month of May between her gallery and the mansion, occasionally dining with Francine and Chuck with whom she would always remain good and close friends, Francine each time telling her she should get on with life. She was young, attractive, and it's what ti-Jacq would want for her. She knew that.

Yes, she did know that, and Jack Fox always did get what he wanted.

*

The previous several weeks weren't particularly lonely for Courtney. She kept longer hours at the gallery and more weekend hours onboard La Renard at dock, avoiding teary condolences and regrets from well-meaning dock acquaintances who were his friends, not hers. Yet not a day went by that he wasn't vividly present in her thoughts and her dreams. But somehow, for some reason, June began as a difficult time.

Her seventeen years with Jack, apart from being a successful social ruse, kept from Francine as well for the sake of her reputation, and eventually evolving into a more corporeal comfort zone, were irreplaceable; Courtney very aware that, despite everyone having a supposed double somewhere, Jack Fox was unique in her life and that the best she could ever hope or wish for was the occasional and disposable stand-in when the need or desire arose.

Over those years she had favoured several selective one-night lovers for a singularly selfish and self-serving purpose: She wanted and needed the touch of a caring man's hands caressing her soft and warm flesh; sadly believing for too long that Jack was too old while wishing he was not, regretting that illusion from his very first and delicate probe eight years earlier.

Each of them was as eager as they were exceedingly unexceptional and lacklustre, all of them sharing a hunger for more of her. Though not one succeeded at raising the bar, at winning her charms or capturing her heart, Jack all the while insisting that she was young and vibrant and that one day true love would find her, that one day he would proudly walk her down the aisle. As though there was any chance in hell that would ever happen again, which he very well knew.

No way would she ever again commit such a catastrophic and ruinous blunder in her life. Déjà-vu, as Jack would say.

Been there, done that. Never again, deciding she was in no real hurry, deciding as well she would put his small fleet of sleek and pristine rides worth a million or more on the auction block and negotiate reasonable terms with her six chefs. Not that she needed the money, maintaining her housekeeper a few mornings each week and the weekly grounds keeper who knew nothing about maintaining her in-ground pool or patio, which was becoming exceedingly perplexing.

Students needing money while afflicted by severe memory loss and chronic fatigue, arriving with wide-open mouths yawning, red eyes from partying, and forgetting by noon they were being paid for cleaning the pool and deck, not for wading in it or staring at it while leaning on the skimmer and vacuum.

Nor was she alone in her search, which made the few best an elite and costly commodity, Courtney finally placing a terse ad in the widely read Saturday newspaper fully expecting that every high school and college jock would be calling.

*

Part-time Pool Guy Required
Must Be Twenty-Something
Must Be Physically Fit
Available Evenings/Weekends

*

She wasn't wrong. Her phone did not stop ringing. The girls all too young or too stupid, speaking like displaced West Coast Valley Girls; the younger boys no better, to a clone all of them wanting like a cool summer job or whatever. The freshman types, particularly the Jocks and the Barbies, all of them still pampered and cared for by mommy, expecting the kind of money she never in her life saw until she served Jack his own Fox Fisheries seafood that fateful second evening.

Good luck with that, kiddies; she didn't think so. She wasn't hiring a COO, dammit, deciding she would run the same ad the following Saturday with no great hope of success, admonishing Jack Fox with a warm smile that he should have lived longer, that there was so much more for him to teach her.

"You really fucked me up big time, Jack," she murmured, revisiting a formerly inherent and charming vernacular, "leaving me the way you did. I mean, shit! Why did you do that to me, darling? You really should have taught me that and so much more."

Then, overcome with grief and self-pity that first Saturday evening in June, asking him why he'd left her so early, she laid her head upon folded arms and wept until her quiet sobs became the muted purrs of peaceful sleep.

4

Saturday the first of October, two years and uncounted days after his fundamental life-change, Braxton Miles was on the phone speaking for the last time with his only friend in life, making sure things would go according to his most fervent wish.

They hadn't spoken in all that time, Miles believing he had disappointed his friend, a man who didn't view disappointment with any degree of compassion or understanding. Hence, neither would he ever disappoint, assuring Miles that what would be would be at 11:50 AM precisely. As promised.

They had little else worth saying. Meaningless and shallow words when they had done their time together, had good history together. But all good things—Cody Jones disconnecting without a single fond wish or a simple good-bye.

Outside the morning was dark and grey with heavy relentless rains silently slashing at thick stone walls and barred windows; endless bolts of lightning scarcely lit the sky, the never-ending concert of thunderous rumbles scarcely felt.

Braxton Miles snorted, dropping the receiver into its cradle, peering through a dark space at the end of the corridor that was a window, at the dull bursts of light he was waddling toward. He could not have wished for a better backdrop to his day of atonement. And if not exactly classic with the melodrama of gallows, hoods, and a hangman's knot, at least he wouldn't jerk or gasp or piss himself dangling at the end of a rope.

Stepping into his temporary cell where one of God's lesser dignitaries was eagerly waiting, he was sure, to make the execution seem more like his resurrection, like a treat, where the guards were again securing his feet and hands in place, the clock in the corridor read 10:01 AM.

Inside the ten-by-ten occasional confessional Braxton quickly made clear that God was not uppermost on his mind, that he viewed his final two hours more as his time of need and would have preferred one of those hours with something younger and shapelier, insatiable, naked and warm. Someone like Courtney Fox. No offence, Preacher.

Moments later, moments into the good reverend's mounting dismay and reluctant intrigue, Braxton Miles chuckled, shaking his head.

"Yeah, the ad. That sure was a game changer. Still, truth be told, she was the absolute best. Molten hot. Truly the best T and A. Even had her own face once I stopped seeing Blaire in her. Should have stayed with her and not fucked-up the way I did. But we are talking destiny here: Mine, yours, hers. She was in the courtroom the last day not looking a day older. Came all that way to gloat. Didn't smile or shed a single tear. Nothing, sitting poised and perfect beside her teary-eyed rich-bitch girlfriend, staring, scarcely blinking, probably thinking but for the grace of God go I. That sound about right, Preacher? Do you think? Or by that same divine grace was she complicit in putting me here at the gates of your heavenly kingdom?"

The old man stared into his lap, forlorn, his grim expression making his creased face appear all the more sallow under the glaring overhead light, his boney and spotted hands loosely clasped between the folds of his dated and faded black soutane that, like him, was no longer relevant.

He didn't know what else he should say, or why he was even there, a narrow steel table and chains separating him from a man he had never before set eyes upon, a man who had not once set foot inside his humble chapel so that he might be given the absolution that would calm his soul.

What could he say that he himself would believe, that would comfort one man while infusing the other with renewed purpose? Nothing, he was certain. Not anymore. And for what reason? To comfort and console a cruel and unrepentant man such as Braxton Miles, a man whose feet were shackled to a steel chair, whose hands were shackled without the slightest freedom of movement to the table; a dangerous and unfeeling man who, judging from his insouciant demeanour, might well have been sitting peacefully in a corner café waiting for his latte and Danish and not in a guarded cell awaiting his deserved death?

The preacher inhaled an invisible deep breath; for he truly believed in the Lord, if not his own failed existence.

"You must be strong in your body and in your mind, my son, for God will have mercy on your soul. He will receive you into His arms with love and compassion and forgive all that you have done. A child once lost, you will soon and at last be reborn and made free. Truly this is a time for wonder and hope, for anticipation and the redemption awaiting you at the end of your journey."

Righteous and believing, for that was his entire life, he glanced for as long as he dared into Miles' ice-blue eyes that were glistening and bright with impious indifference, resolute and unblinking eyes unblemished by the least remorse or trepidation. An instant when Reverend Emery Prisby felt a deep and unnerving chill infuse his weakening soul, raising a hand he pressed to the gold-plated crucifix at his chest and lowering his gaze once again in despair.

Braxton Miles remained as he was, chained, believing the aging servant of God was likely more distressed by virtue of his own mortality and unremarkable existence as a prison chaplain, and likely more fearful of his own fast approaching ascent into that supposed heavenly court with more to atone for than a few purposeful murders. Likely as not.

The clock outside, that would mock him through the plexiglass peephole for the next eighty-nine minutes, read 10:21 AM. Then a solemn cortège of guards, the warden and Miles' pious devotee would lead him in shackles into a room that was as yet a mystery to him: His final mile that was, in fact, less than a hundred feet from where he sat feeling sorry for the diminutive and frail shell of a man. At least he'd be dead in one hour and forty-six minutes.

The preacher, he wasn't as fortunate.

"Reborn and free, wonder and hope. Really, Preacher? You believe that, do you?"

Emery Prisby raised his head, nodding mutely, pausing for a moment in silent prayer that he might find the right words.

"I do, my son. I must. You will soon embark on a wondrous journey, as shall we all one day, for which I envy you. Which does not mean I do not wholly understand and commiserate with your fears. I do. The dark and the unknown understandably afflict us with apprehension and fear."

Miles chortled softly; he was neither a loud nor officious man. He had no need to prove himself. He stood an even six-feet, when he could stand, weighing in at 260 despite a slim build. He was athletic, lean and hard, his mind no less conditioned. He was, in a word, no one to cross paths with.

"Well, Preacher, I'm far from being a child and I have never in my life been lost. Meaning let's stop with all this son talk. And if we must sit here with one another until the warden comes banging on the door, let's you and me get away from God. Again no offence, but the way I see things that wondrous journey is yours to long for, not mine. Mine's a little more expedient and possibly a little less enviable. Such is life, or the end of it. As for the unknown, fearing whatever that might be is futile."

"We can pray, Braxton, and together find peace in your final hour."

Doug Booth

Miles shook his head in a gentle, exaggerated sway. The old preacher wasn't cluing in, not much different from those relentless Bible-Belt Witnesses knocking on the door at dinnertime in their black pants and crisp white shirts with the hope of recruiting yet another disciple.

"I fell asleep last night, Preacher, without the slightest worry or regret. You know, thinking back on life. The thing is, I didn't realize I had fallen asleep until the moment I woke. I simply did, fall asleep, without fear, without apprehension, into the dark and the unknown. And this thing I'm walking into, this execution, is no different, discounting the needle, the audience and the warden's parting words." He snickered, curling his lips into a smirk. "One part barbiturate that'll put me into la-la land within twenty seconds, give or take; one part something called pancuronium bromide that'll relax my muscles, stop me jerking I suppose; and one part potassium chloride that'll stop my heart. Five minutes of peaceful oblivion because I'm sleeping and then, two minutes later, give or take, I'm pronounced dead. And a few hours after that I'll be grey ash on a tray and forgotten. That's my journey, Preacher. End of story and not a really big deal; the end of a destiny, not the beginning of life ever after trapped in some celestial nirvana. Like the man said, "Here for a good time, not a long time. And I did have a very good time." He chuckled. "Not that I couldn't have done with maybe another exquisite wife or two."

The pious Emery Prisby ignored the heartless humour. "Pray with me, Braxton. I implore you in these your final moments. Let us together redeem your soul and free you from the guilt of taking another's life, the one who cherished and adored you above all others. And for the other who, so dearly loved by the first and consumed by such hatred, desperately forsook her already tormented young life so that you might perish for your sins and dwell forever in purgatory. That you do not believe does not change what exists in the universe. What you did will follow you throughout time

38

everlasting. This I know."

Miles thought for a moment, remembering her. Brenda. Vibrant, wealthy and breathtaking despite being several years older. And, yes, she did love and cherish him. She absolutely did. The preacher wasn't wrong, but that deep devotion was essential to the plan and that the marriage hadn't lasted beyond their second year was nothing personal. In fact, her death was not wholly of his doing. Merely simple and inescapable fate: Her destiny as much as his was a three-step clinical execution that, although not always inevitable, was certainly a possible eventuality which he understood and accepted prior to going forward.

He peered through the slot at the clock, pondering, deciding why not? He had never in his life seen inside a church, let alone a confessional. Why anyone would willingly divulge their sins and immoralities to a stranger cloaked by darkness and presuming himself superior, sins that for the most part are commonplace, was beyond him. The irrational and willingly embraced subjugation of the weak-minded. Particularly when the darkened stranger no doubt has sufficient sins of his own to relish or regret, if not living life vicariously through the sins of others.

But this would be different; this would be fun, ending his life on a high note the very way he lived his life until the night some two years earlier that didn't exactly go as planned, when all that was wonderful in his life unexpectedly was not, which he took in stride.

They were so incredibly self-satisfied back then, the cops, the DA, and her, especially her—unbelievably smug and self-righteous, the judge and the jury no better. He had scarcely uttered a word throughout the week-long trial. Five days despite his immediate admission that "In a way, yes I killed her. That was part of the greater plan, Judge. Though now I suppose I should have stayed put in New Orleans. Don't you think?"

An entire week of self-satisfied smirks and hers was the widest;

her brown eyes drilling into his back, unblinking each time he turned, winking, smiling, making the most of his time with her, staring him down as though she would make the judge's final pronouncement more dreadful, more haunting. It didn't.

Of course he was guilty, on the first count, freely and falsely admitting to his guilt on the second because they had royally fucked him up. And he was good with that. He simply returned the cold glare, the frozen smirk, particularly since his part in the trial was decidedly minor and of little interest. What was done was done; what would be would be.

Of that he was certain, relishing a recurring dream, reliving his one regret of being forever deprived of pushing her head into a sink or a toilet until the bubbles stopped, until the kicking and the jerking stopped. Because killing her would have been like killing the other bitch twice for what she had done.

He really did not like her; she was calculating and cold, worse than he could ever be, like the sick bitch who wilfully and joyously let herself be killed for no better reason than bringing the man who murdered her best friend years earlier to justice. How depraved and hateful was that?

Death by lethal injection. He was good with that, he knew about that. Then came the victim impact statement, read by the tearful and self-satisfied bitch who wasn't a victim at all. Never was. If anything he was the victim, purgatory clearly and deservedly hers to dwell in for what she did, the entire courtroom wondering at his quiet chuckles. All of them too smug and gloating over their supposed triumph to understand why.

10:27 AM.

One hour and twenty-three minutes remaining before the warden would come calling, Miles again facing the chaplain, expelling a deep breath, wishing he could rub his face hard and feel the warmth of his hands.

"Brenda was a sweetheart, Preacher. That's true enough and,

giving credit where due, she went peacefully without the slightest fear, without a whisper or a tear. She simply passed over, as you might say. I did that for her, because I did like her. I liked her very much, until the night I got home after the last one." He chuckled, remembering the moment. "Have to say, that was one very unexpected brain-fuck. That woman was carved from stone. That's how she went down as quick as she did. Cold as ice. And an accomplished thespian? Well I guess she was. No shit. As good-looking as she was hot in bed, at first, until she turned. Though all the while frosty and single-minded, literally fucking me over to put me here with you. If that's not a bitch, what is? Truth be told, had I known, had I even suspected, I would have done them both that night with equal pleasure after enduring two miserable years of hell on earth."

"In which case, Braxton, I thank the dear Lord for intervening, for at least saving the embittered young woman whose rancour toward you is deserved and understandable."

"Yeah, well, a snare is a snare, Preacher. When I might have divorced her instead. Talk about ill intent. I must admit though, as she was going down, she did seem as though she was on her way to that glorious kingdom of yours. Content, unafraid, completely and diabolically pleased with herself knowing this day would soon come. Either way, like Brenda, she went quickly and quietly. I can still see those dark brown eyes, unblinking, staring up at me till she disappeared."

The chaplain crossed himself, pressing his lips to the simple crucifix. "A remarkable woman. One can scarcely imagine the depth of her courage, the strength of her resolve."

"Well the depth was four hundred, Preacher," Miles added glibly, "and not her resolve. No. I would suggest more like pure hatred, the peculiar kind of spite particular to womankind, abruptly ending a brief and regrettable chapter in my life. I mean, talk about twisted fate." Miles coughed a laugh. "Clearly Bryce Madison should have gone elsewhere, and he probably would have if Charleston wasn't such an alluring city, the women entirely enchanting." He shrugged, his chest heaving with a deep breath, his lips tightly pursed. "What the hell, Preacher? We each have our destiny. We can't ever escape who we truly are. I suppose, thinking back, I should have taken Brandon Michaels along a much different path those many years ago. But then who would be here with you in my place? Who would have done what I was chosen to do with the charming Miss Brenda and the other one?"

The chaplain shook his head gravely. " No, my son. We are never chosen to do evil. Was he a friend of yours, this Mr. Michaels?"

"More than a friend, Preacher. My mentor, I suppose. He taught me in a very dark moment what I was capable of achieving. You might say he infused me with inner strength. In fact he did. He's the very reason you and I are here today. If not for Brandon Michaels I would never have met Brent Mason or Bradley McGuire. Both of them fine upstanding gentlemen of means and deeply devoted husbands, Preacher. As was, for what it matters at this late hour, Bryce Madison."

The old chaplain jerked forward, bracing himself against the edge of the steel table between them, an icy chill coursing through his slight body, his weary eyes instantly bright and alive with dread. "Braxton, my son, what horrible thing are you telling me?"

Prisoner Miles shifted his weight, leaning closer to his ad hoc confessor. Clasping his hands, resting his forearms on the table, he peered unperturbed through the slot at the clock, piercing the old man's frighted eyes with his own that were bright with a disquieting child-like glee.

10:32 AM.

Time enough, he supposed, for a bedtime story.

TurnAbout

5

From his first breath Bill Michaels' destiny was one of chronic failure. Throughout his preschool years he was an unpleasant and difficult child, a character trait that manifested itself increasingly each year until dropping out after failing his ninth grade mid-term a month before his nineteenth birthday, by which time he was viewed by his teachers as an underachiever and, by his peers, as a bully constantly threatening their peace of mind.

Sent the next day to an army recruitment office by his hard-fisted father who put in long and hard days labouring as a steve-dore on the Savannah docks, seeing no other way for his son to one day become a worthwhile man, Bill was summarily ordered from the building. They needed fit and better educated young men, not what they saw in him.

Spurned and sent home he several weeks later found work at the mill as a casual labourer, sweeping floors and cleaning wash-rooms, spending as many nights at a local watering hole as in the drunk tank for brawling and disorderly conduct, nevertheless man-aging for better or worse to marry and make a home with Bella Simpson two years later without much choice in the matter.

Bill was her deserved punishment for being naïve, for believing he was more than he ever could be, for believing she was old enough, that she could do whatever she wanted, for going with him one Saturday night to a motel with a single purpose, giving wantonly and freely of herself without the least restraint or feigned diffi-dence.

She was a year younger, trapped in a small town on the out-skirts of Savannah. Georgia. He was effectively her first; she was the last of many, young and distraught, disowned by virtuous and decent Baptist parents, one clear and oppressive July morning delivering his son Brandon into the world as Bill sat sprawled on the kitchen floor too drunk to stand and too short of money to afford another bottle until week's end.

And nothing in his life would change.

*

Bella was no one's dream-girl. She was curiously pretty with freckles and a button nose, wide eyes, full lips and two rows of unremarkable teeth that seemed like dentures made a size too small. Conversely, her flawless 5'7" body from her slender shoulders to her perfect toes made ample amends for the perceived shortcomings, throughout high school and long summer days at the beach inspiring countless dreams. Problem was, she deflated as many egos. She knew the boys didn't want her for a friend or their girlfriend, which didn't in any way bother her. She had something much better; she had her purity when, what they wanted, each of them, was being her first and claiming that elusive victory. She wasn't the prettiest girl in school, just the most sought after, though not a single aspirant in those four years scored even a minor victory.

She wasn't interested. She wasn't like those other girls; she was saving herself for the man of her dreams, which didn't necessarily mean husband.

Neither was Michaels remotely handsome in any girl's mind. In fact, if not for his inherently belligerent nature he would walk through life unnoticed. He was 5'10" and heavyset with curly red hair, dull eyes and, when he smiled, which wasn't often, chipped and yellowed front teeth. And for a Georgia boy he was unusually pale for never being in the sun, with good reason. He never had a girlfriend to sit with on her veranda and sip lemonade, or frolic with at the beach. He was a loner by virtue of public opinion; he had no choice in the matter. And, by virtue of being born, he was a loser.

Before Bill, before the worst mistake of her life, Bella worked at her first job as a cocktail waitress in a fancy upscale Savannah lounge against her parents' wishes, rightfully suspecting she was hired on the spot because of her body and secretly thrilled that the requisite uniform was a short satin skirt that would display the entire length of her shapely legs, and often a bit more. The complementing three-quarter satin bra for several nights after keeping her father in a rage and her mother in tears.

She was instantly popular for the same reason, often saying 'no' with a coquettish smile, disappointing hopeful men who likely had teenage daughters of their own at home. Until the Friday evening an account executive from up north came in late for a few drinks to end his week. He was very handsome, impeccably dressed and well-spoken with an easy manner, a captivating smile and would be in town for another week of meetings.

The man was immediately taken with her, engaging her with innocent conversation the more the lounge emptied, finally suggesting that she join him for drinks in the exclusive Concierge Club of his five-star hotel that never closed to their most privileged guests. One drink, perhaps a second, before he would send her safely home in a taxi as he fervently wished he might do the next evening after an elegant evening of dinner and clubbing.

And she did, finding herself completely smitten in seventh heaven within the hour. He was twenty-seven, a bachelor, and charming.

She had never in her life felt as mature or feminine, had never been treated so much like a lady. He adored her. He was attentive, hanging on her every word. And he was affectionate, often touching her hands and her shoulders as they laughed and talked. Until her fourth drink when she didn't mind at all that his hand was probing under her skirt or that his lips were pressed hard against hers. No one had ever kissed her, let alone as ardently, or squeezed her young flesh as tenderly; Bella not the least bit wary when he stood, taking her hands and guiding her to his room where he would call for a taxi.

Instead, not many hours later, she woke alone in his bed, gulping air and shrieking into the mirror. She was a dishevelled nightmare, her mascara smeared into a frightful mask; her lips and her cheeks were smudged with gloss and she was naked, reeking of sweat.

She clutched her throat, resisting the urge to vomit, too devastated to cry. Her youthful breasts and her thighs were discoloured with bruises; though, what was much worse, what made her tenderly cup a warm palm over the throbbing pain, was the stain.

Worse yet, she couldn't remember a thing and the guy was gone. The thirty-nine-year-old sales rep from New Jersey was already in the air flying toward a life he'd begun loathing, a job he needed more than he wanted, a wife he was stuck with and kids he wouldn't be rid of anytime soon. In fact, if not for willing and stupid young girls like Bella Simpson who would frequently brighten his travels, he had no real purpose in life other than sustaining the selfish lives he was seldom a part of. Something Bella would never know, or even think about.

She had more pressing concerns.

Easing from the damp bed she padded into the bathroom, into a steaming shower, scrubbing away the pungent smell and all traces of the man until her skin was a deep pink and prickled, shampooing her blonde tresses until they squeaked as she pulled them into a matted tail.

Stepping out she towelled herself dry, scanning the small space, peering into the wastebasket at the empty vodka bottle and nothing else, which was neither a good thing nor a surprise. She was not a stupid or bad girl. She was not. She would think things through.

She would create a believable excuse and, most importantly, plan for a worst case scenario. Because, whoever the guy was, he was her first and cared nothing about her. That was pretty obvious and she wasn't about to ruin her life because of a single mistake, because she was better than those other girls.

She dropped her panties and bra in the basket and dressed. She sat on the bed and called her mother, explaining how she was staying the weekend with a girl from work and how terribly sorry she was for not calling earlier.

Next she called her boss, explaining how she was feeling ill and needed a sick-day. Then, feeling more sanguine than cruelly violated, putting her future ahead of her past, she took the guy's room key that made her a privileged guest and went to the Concierge Club, believing after a few glasses of wine that she had things figured out.

*

She spent much of the afternoon shopping for new ensembles, each one very short and very sexy, tossing the sweater, skirt and nylons soiled by his touch into a trashcan before leaving the mall.

The fashion had become her signature style since her first evening on the job and of an age that would for a long time pit a daughter's right equally against an indignant father's sense of morality. Her proven rationale being that, being proud of her perfect and alluring body, that in no way was flaunting her charms, she would detract attention from what she believed were her far less attractive features.

She didn't want or need a higher education; girls didn't do that in the day. Neither did she intend atrophying into the obedient housewife she saw in her mother. And for that matter, neither did she want a family. She wanted—she didn't know—a fun job that was anything but boring and paid good money. She wanted exotic travel and being with a good man who would love her and see her as beguiling. That was her dream.

She checked in to a hotel she could afford for the first time in her life, where she continued perfecting her plan with a carafe of mediocre house wine. Though, still hurting and angry for putting herself so willingly in harm's way, she was at the same time disappointed that she would never have that most special moment in her life to fondly remember and share. She wasn't certain, because she had no barometer, but the guy must have had a really good time with her. Something she would never let happen again.

After dinner alone, dressed in the simple yet daring outfit that would guarantee success, that her mother would never approve, and that her father would never forbid because he would never see her wearing it; though pleased by the women she shocked and elated by the men she openly delighted, she stepped onto the street where she hailed a cab.

She went to a popular bar where she recognized many of the regulars from school and her neighbourhood, many of them already married and pregnant, which wasn't surprising because in any Little Town, America if you weren't dating or sleeping with someone else's sister, someone was dating or sleeping with yours. The very reason she was there.

Others, the smarter ones preserving their freedom, or the outright losers, would be in a row hunched over their beers on barstools bird-dogging predictably amenable girls for the night. Or, better said, to-die-for bodies for the night and Bella was both. And she wasn't particular, more interested in a name than a boyfriend. She was also aware she wouldn't be the first camp's first choice; she wasn't a total picture, which should have been a red flag the previous night and not a red stain on her thighs and the crumpled sheet that morning.

She wasn't wrong and she didn't wait long. The college guys were holding out for something better, despite her enticingly short dress leaving very little to their imaginations; the others, she could tell, were weighing the odds until all but one were again reconfirmed as habitual losers.

She knew the guy walking toward her, carrying his beer, sort of. She remembered seeing him at school in her final year. And, dressed as she was, he very quickly remembered her.

He asked if he could join her, Bella waving him into the chair beside her. He was average at best and about her age, dressed well enough in jeans and a denim shirt, which didn't mean much. Not in Little Town, USA. Although his boots were polished and he wasn't wearing a hillbilly ball cap.

He was a foreman at the mill, heading a crew of a dozen men, responsible for maintaining critical equipment and day-to-day operations despite his young age. He was going places. Damn straight he was. Because he had a natural inclination toward all things mechanical, working his way toward management. And she believed him, to the extent that she cared. More importantly, he would very shortly be her eager and willing precaution against any future dilemma that might present itself.

They spent the evening talking across from each other, since Bill Michaels' idea of urbanity and flirting with any girl was buying more rounds and getting her in the back of his car. This one however he wasn't sure about. She was half-good-looking, with super nice tits and killer legs, even if she wasn't giving off vibes. Nothing. Sitting there listening, sipping her wine, and he was running out of wonderful things to say about himself.

Which she understood, letting him suffer and the conversation wane until Bella, her mind fortified by purpose, her body by wine, altered her future that otherwise would have been much less devastating than she imagined.

"Bill, I really like you. And I think you like me. So I'm thinking if you have money for a room we should go somewhere together. You and me, right now. Let's do it. Let's you and me have some real fun." She leaned into him, placing a hand over his, moistening her lips the way she had practiced with the tip of her tongue. "I mean right now, Bill. I won't ask you twice."

The stunned disbelief lighting his dull eyes was instantaneous, in a blink transfiguring into undisguised and palpable desire. She could easily have laughed; he was that obvious, no doubt better acquainted with drunken women years older and less shapely that he wouldn't ever drink pretty by dawn.

"Ya mean…?"

"Yes, Bill. That is exactly what I mean. Unless, of course, you would rather not get me into a bed. Tonight."

Michaels practically toppled his chair, hurrying to settle his tab at the bar.

Minutes later at the table Bella stood on her own, sauntering ahead of him, pushing her way first into the night air, in the parking lot opening the door of the decommissioned and rusted-out taxicab, grimacing, regretting her killer dress wasn't a good bit longer. Then, too soon, she was waiting alone with her head down under a green neon sign flashing 'Vacancy' as if desperately entreating weary travellers or the abjectly pathetic like the clumsy bumpkin rushing inside to fork out forty bucks for the best lay of his life.

Stepping out minutes later, again without a gentleman's hand to assist her, the vinyl seat cover pulling at the bare flesh between her stockings and her silk hem, she followed him into a room that at once made her feel cheap and dirty. At least this time she'd be conscious and leave when he was finished, as soon as he finished.

She could have done worse, possibly, telling herself that Michaels was strictly a means to an end, her solution as much as her due punishment for being incredibly naïve and impetuous. She accepted that; she would focus on that.

She had always imagined candles and wine, a proposal at dinner, a diamond ring that would legitimize her first taste of true romance. He was forever in her dreams handsome and debonair, attentive and adoring, a sophisticated and adept lover. When what she got was pasty white skin loosely covering a limp and shapeless body standing by the bed in cotton boxers anxious to see her naked when they hadn't been in the room five minutes and he had already been in the bathroom relieving himself without first closing the door.

Instead she turned and went herself into the bathroom where she unstrapped her low-heeled pumps before shimmying from her ruffle dress that scarcely touched the lacy tops of her stay-ups that she rolled to her feet and tugged away, focusing. Seeing herself in the mirror, studying her face and her body, she caressed her arms, cupping her breasts and inhaling a deep breath before pressing her warm palms against her sculpted belly and squirming from her lace thong, dimming the light as she stepped out.

A signal, she supposed, that caused Michaels to push his shorts to the floor and stand gaping at her instead of looking into her eyes and telling her how exquisite and flawlessly smooth she was, that he had never seen any woman more perfect. Which would have been true, which would not happen, which she did not expect, given that he had come to her from the row designated for losers.

She'd seen pictures, of course, and she knew how the things worked. But never a real one up close, including the one from the previous night that put her in this predicament, determined she wouldn't touch this one either. The thing looked ridiculous peeking out from a prickly orange bush like a purple thimble stuck in a ball of coarse wool, Bella thinking her thumb was bigger, and more useful, his balls hanging there dotted with a brown wart the size of her polished nail.   That he would touch her was bad enough, worse than bad. Then she would run. She wouldn't stay a second longer, and he could do whatever.

Strangely, being naked in front of a man—him anyway—consciously for the first time, she didn't feel at all embarrassed or vulnerable because she knew that part of her was awesome. She was feeling cheated, thinking that the Friday guy must have had something a whole lot bigger and better. Because what she was seeing, the tiny thing peeking at her, couldn't possibly ravage her the way Friday's did no matter how hard it got. Not that she needed more pain. But, shit.

Startled, she looked up. "What?"

"I said, turn yerself fer me. I wanna see yer curvaceous butt."

"No."

Drawing back the thin quilted cover she crawled under the sheet, laying on her back with her arms by her side. Not surprised that a second later he was beside her, pushing apart her legs and sucking on one bruised breast as though her tender nipple was the neck of a beer bottle, mauling her other as though desperate for a souvenir. Then he was clambering between her legs, rudely spreading her wider, staring as if he had never seen a naked girl, at last pushing the thing into her after several failed jabs an instant before he began jerking and pounding, crushing her under his weight.

She closed her eyes, imagining her debonair lover, creating in her mind a romance that was heated with passion and desire that she would make herself believe, not the frantic hammering reigniting her sore wounds or the smell of his breath and sweat. She wanted to shove him away, believing she would vomit, swearing never again. But she couldn't. His head was cradled between her head and her shoulders, his hands clutching and groping her buttocks, each painful thrust bringing with it a sickening groan.

Then without warning he shuddered and twisted, expelling a guttural hot breath into her ear as though he was the one being damaged and bruised. What's more he pulled away without the slightest emotion, making a repulsive wet sucking sound and a mess on her legs, collapsing onto his back, panting heavily and staring dumbly at the ceiling without covering himself or her, without caressing her or smiling at her in a way that would make her feel less like a common street slut.

She turned away from him, loathing herself, propping her

weight onto an elbow, in the same instant discovering to what extent. Instinctively reaching for the clock-radio she screamed a silent "What!" She was stunned, seething, in that same instant absolutely feeling like a whore and not wasting a second more hesitating, deciding what she should do. Shit! Fourteen minutes since walking into the dank room.

She kicked the sheet away from her feet, swung them onto the threadbare carpet and strode with a purpose into the bathroom fully aware he was ogling her. She didn't care. Good for him. She did what she had to, not denying a deepening regret for allowing her most special dream to be taken from her by a rapist and, because of him, purposely debauching and degrading herself with a tactless village idiot with a thimble for a dick.

As much as she hated the other guy for spoiling and hurting her, she hated Michaels more for not making their minutes the least bit pleasurable, for not saying she was sexy or warm or soft or any of that. She just did, despise him.

At eighteen minutes she had peed him into the toilet without touching the seat, had cleaned him from her legs as best she could, and was at the door dressed with her stockings in her purse.

"No way! Are ya kiddin' me?" Michaels scrambled to his knees. "Bella, what's up? What're ya doin? C'mon, the night's young. Git yer butt back here. I ain't done with ya."

He was clownish swaying with his knees spread wide apart, taking up most of the narrow bed with his hands outstretched, little Dick secreting itself into the glistening orange bush.

"Not going to happen. What is, is me going back to my hotel room that doesn't stink like a brothel for a very long shower and a serious douching. Then I'll do myself the way you should have. So thanks for nothing. You go ahead and have a good time doing whatever with that little thing. Just do not bother dreaming about doing this again, asshole."

With that she walked out, closing the door behind her. She

called a cab from the lobby and forgot him. He was just too repulsive for words.

In her hotel room she dropped her outfit to the floor and went into the bathroom where she stood under a steaming torrent until she felt clean, sitting on the toilet reading instructions on the box she'd bought earlier at the drugstore.

When she was finished, satisfied she was one-hundred percent sanitized, she crawled into bed and cried herself to sleep.

6

December 31st Bella Simpson came home from work feeling exhilarated, eager for the evening and thankful her parents were asleep in their bed. She was excited, too excited for sleep. Her dream was coming true, becoming more real each day.

The week since Christmas was her best ever at the lounge and, for the first time in her life, she was going alone in March on a Caribbean all-inclusive vacation. In view of which, keeping the breaking news from her mother and father, she was smarter than ever. She was on the Pill, deciding she was ready to get serious. Or pragmatically amenable by conscious choice and not liquor-induced poor judgement until whenever something serious or exciting might happen.

She hadn't thought of Michaels or the Friday guy since waking that Sunday morning, when with a new day came a new girl dressed in a midnight blue panty and bra set, a navy blue suede skirt that wasn't much longer than the belt was wide, a sheer dark blue blouse that would cause her father to convulse, and mid-calf suede boots. The new leather bomber would stay in the bag. She didn't care, let him vent and fume. If they couldn't love her for who she was, their problem.   From then on she would be the woman she dreamed of one day being, the woman she had already become.

After a lunch on historic River Street lined with bistros and galleries, enjoying the early autumn warmth and being noticed, openly admired and envied, most of all adoring herself, she sat through a movie killing time before going home to the usual parental inquisition and a grown daughter's usual creative replies. The time had clearly arrived for her to move out and by spring she would have enough saved for a downpayment on a home and car.

She began working six-day weeks, committed to making that happen, at the same time starting with weekly spa treatments that by Christmas had considerably faded her freckles. She was not the same woman and very much on track, incrementally preparing them for the day she would leave. Until late afternoon New Year's Eve as she was leaving for work, when dad and daughter were cast even farther apart as though a rogue wave had, without warning, swept divisively through their living room.

The paster and his wife were invited for turkey dinner the next day, in light of which she would please dress for the occasion in proper slacks and an appropriately loose-fitting sweater since she seemed not to own any decent dresses or skirts. A man she hadn't seen in over a year. Not since the Sunday after her first evening at the lounge when she argued bluntly that sleep was preferable to raising her voice in joyful song and that she could feign prayer as easily and effectively in her bed.

Believing the matter was closed she was taken aback by the pastor's unexpected appearance at that Sunday dinner, scarcely believing his gall, or her parents' quiet superciliousness as he began chiding her for being disrespectful of them and forsaking the Lord and the purity of her soul by putting herself so indecently clothed amongst men of ill will.

When he finished she thanked him for his concern and left the table. And now she couldn't imagine the impending joy—because it wouldn't happen. Not a chance. Instead she calmly packed a small suitcase in her room and walked out, leaving mom and dad beside themselves in a living room decorated with a fake tree glittering with lights, a fake fireplace sparkling with flames as real as Christmas was with uninspired gifts and eggnog made with powdered eggs, powdered milk and precisely measured brandy.

Yeah, time to get out.

*

At the lounge her priority was getting a room, calling a dozen hotels before finally booking a room for a couple of nights that apparently no one else wanted at double the usual rate. Two nights because she needed space and time from her high-minded father and his docile wife who each day was less of a mother and more judgemental.

The last call came an hour later than the usual 1:00 AM, all the girls collapsing onto sofas and kicking off their stilettos when the doors closed promptly at 3:00, massaging each other's feet and relishing the quiet as the boss was serving them for a change. He was also sending them home in taxis, after the requisite hugging and kissing and heartfelt wishes, taking care of them.

Bella got to the hotel near four in the morning, exhausted and not feeling very well. A malaise she attributed to the smoke-filled air and din at the bar, the champagne she wasn't accustomed to and the hour. In spite of which she was particularly pleased she had put her father in his rightful place, making a point that she was her own person. Not his child any longer.

Forgoing her usual shower, her skin and her hair heavily scented with the fumes of cigars and cigarettes, she fell into bed and woke ten hours later Thursday afternoon fully dressed and moist with sweat.

Nothing came off easily. Her sweater got stuck in her barrette that tore at her hair, the difficult clasps on her bra evoking rare expletives; the nylon zipper on her skirt seized, making her twist and squirm, pushing the thing to the carpet and tearing the seam. Then trying to do the same with her stockings she stumbled backward onto the bed, tugging them from flailing legs and putting runs in both.

Struggling to her feet she tied them in a knot, whipping them into the air, tripping forward onto the carpet and landing hard on all fours with her thong taut between an ankle and the neighbouring knee when the delicate piece should have come away easily. But it didn't, "because of that fucking pastor!"

Plodding her way into the bathroom, bracing her arms against the vanity, she stared at herself, gulping air, bringing a hand to her throat and leaning closer to her reflection. She didn't utter a word, staring, looking like shit. Of course she did. Because she felt like shit, tears and plaintive groans erupting in concert, dropping to her knees seconds before emptying her stomach violently into the bowl.

When she finished she crawled over the tub, gripping the edge tightly. She ran a shower and sat under the comforting rain with her knees hugged to her chest until the convulsive shivering subsided, when she stood still feeling nauseous and gently patted herself dry.

She lay in bed for what remained of the afternoon under the covers in a guest robe with her head wrapped in a turban, believing she hadn't felt as nauseous a day in her life, thankful her boss had given the girls the day off to spend with family and friends. Everyone except her.

She ordered an in-room dinner; her first-ever New Year's dinner alone that came with milk, with the first mouthful rushing to the bathroom wondering what the hell was happening, afraid of what was happening, exhausted yet resisting sleep for fear she would not wake. Yet she did sleep, albeit in torment, waking several times curled into herself, her flushed cheeks damp with tears, until once again sleep enveloped her.

When she finally remained awake Friday morning, in a room flooded with bright daylight, no longer afflicted with nausea, she sat in bed hugging herself with her chin on her knees, pondering when the day would come that she would wake with the one who would love and comfort and cherish her the way she longed for and deserved. She'd never had a boyfriend, had never been kissed or invited to a dance or a party. Yet she had been raped and laid, and how sick was that? Worse, she mused, what kind of terrible secret was that to bear?

Easing from the bed, her mouth sour with bile, her throat raw, she shrugged the robe from her shoulders and padded to the bathroom, emerging half an hour later after concurring with a more agreeable reflection that she wasn't that curiously pretty girl; she was beautiful, as close to beautiful as she would ever be. She was that total picture and one day soon someone would see her that way and want her.

She ate lunch at the hotel, checked-out, hailed a cab and went to the clinic. She wasn't going home, not then. She wasn't ready for them. In fact, she was more likely finished with them and their medieval Bible Belt mentality.

She asked for a female doctor and waited, led an hour later into a stark office where an unsmiling woman decades older with a stethoscope hanging from her shoulders waved Bella into a seat.

"What can I do for you," she glanced at the sheet on her desk, "Miss Simpson?"

"I came home from work after New Year's and woke up puking, feeling really awful until this morning."

"From partying, perhaps a little too much alcohol?"

"No. I'm a cocktail waitress. I don't party and I never get sick."

"Any idea why?"

"No. Like I said, I never get sick."

"A girl who never gets sick, for no reason vomiting and feeling not so good. I would call that strange, wouldn't you?" Bella shook her head, agreeing in a mournful whisper; the doctor pointed to the examination table. "Off with the fancy blouse and your back to the wall."

She obeyed the curt instruction, unwrapping her tie-side top, laying it to one side and shifting her weight onto the faux-leather padding.

Joining her, the doctor mechanically wrapped a blood pressure cuff tightly around her arm, slipping in the stethoscope's diaphragm over her brachial artery and pumping until she seemed satisfied. Removing the thing she blinded Bella with an otoscope, first one eye, then the other before seeing how clean and healthy the ears were without so much as a hmm.

"Lay on your back, legs flat."

She did, cold fingers pressing and prodding into the warm flesh between her belt and her bra before the stethoscope's cold diaphragm made her jerk. A moment later she was dressing while the doctor returned to her desk, reached for pad and began scribbling.

"That's all, you're finished?"

"Yes, we're finished. What you have, Miss Simpson, is very common. I'll write you a prescription that will ease the morning sickness."

The frank diagnosis took a second to reach and penetrate Bella's conscious mind, another for the horrific words to infuse her with panic. That was months ago. "What! No!"

"You're pregnant, Miss Simpson. Strange for a girl who doesn't party." She pointed to the chair. "When somebody certainly did. My best guess would be three months, give or take. Any ideas about that?"

"It wasn't a party and this cannot happen to me. Not now, not ever." She leaned forward. "I'll have an abortion. I can do that, I've got the money."

The doctor shook her head. "This is 1975, Miss Simpson, and you are in the Deep South. You are not having an abortion. You are having a baby." She slid the prescription across her desk. "I presume you know the father."

Bella hesitated. "Yes, I know the father. But..." She stared blankly into her lap, clasping her hands. "Shit."

"But what, Miss Simpson?"

7

But—she didn't know who he was or where he lived and she hadn't bothered taking note of the room number.

She would not have dared ask the desk clerk for the name of the man she had spent the night with. Besides, she had no reason because no one would possibly take her side. No one would believe she was raped when she willingly went to his hotel at two in the morning for drinks and then to his room for what, a taxi?

What they would believe, what she would make them believe, was her time with Michaels, a few beers and a stupid mistake. Who wouldn't believe she was drunk? That would be a given and precisely what she wanted, making an unforgivable worst case scenario believable by demeaning and humiliating herself with a repulsive cretin. Though what she didn't consider for a moment was the blind morality of the Deep South that at first filled her with dread.

So what? She didn't care. She would survive the coming days, survive her father, the rebukes and the shame because her life was her own, her body was her body, a detail she would make very clear. And with that resolve she went to work later that afternoon thankful for the distraction, thankful she wouldn't be facing her priggish parents until the next morning at breakfast, with no doubt in her mind how her day would begin and end.

Her father would lose his cool, exploding into a rage, her mother would be utterly mortified and sit weeping into her hanky, and Bill Michaels would call her a liar. He would say no such thing ever happened, or that she made him do it, that she made him take her to a motel and spend the entire night in bed with her. That it was all her fault. As though anyone would believe him, particularly since those two nights, since her weekly spa treatments, she was that total picture.   Yeah, so what were the odds? Good luck with that, Billy Wart.

What he would do instead is admit being with her, simply because he had no choice. That was her trump card. Then she would have Friday's kid and put it up for adoption unless Michaels wanted it free and clear, because she certainly didn't. She had no intention of becoming a mother trapped in a continuum of monotony.

She would move out, go on that vacation, buy that car, and begin a real life.

*

She arrived home near 3:00 Saturday morning, took her usual shower and laid out her clothes for the day. She couldn't see that tights and a short skirt, or anything else in her wardrobe, would make her day any better or worse. So she made it better for herself, pulling on tights without a skirt and a raglan sweater loosely cinched at her waist that was sufficiently long, though not very, to appease the delicate Baptist sense of decency. Excepting loving husbands with acquaintances on the side or mothers like hers who should have something on the side that would make their lives tolerable if not purely exciting.

At seven o'clock she went into the kitchen, making coffee fifteen minutes before the worst storm yet would rip through her home, when mother and father wrapped in flannel pyjamas and plaid robes for breakfast would show surprise at seeing her up that early and at once start with the interrogation.

Until then, until zero hour, however, she sat quietly letting her mind wander, imagining who she would meet on her first real vacation that would of necessity be delayed several months. She wasn't thinking of her parents, a baby or Michaels. Nor did she whisper a single word or script a single thought that would seem practiced and come off as defensive.

Hearing the muffled footfalls of their slippers, she refilled her mug with steady hands. She was ready. Sitting down looking up, purposely putting herself in a weaker position, as though guilty and begging forgiveness, would not happen; she would meet them eye to eye. It was her body, not his. She was no longer a schoolgirl; she was a woman and would be treated as one.   Because serious shit would most definitely hit the fan when any hope of warm embraces and understanding was futile.

"Goodness gracious, dear, you're up unusually early," Dora Simpson started. "And where, may I ask, is your skirt?"

"It's a look, mother. Very European and very artsy."

The older woman shook her head. "And very sultry, dear. I really do wish you wouldn't."

"That's a good thing, mother, being sultry, being attractive. In fact…"

She stopped short. Whatever she might say wouldn't matter. Her mother was well past forty and too far gone. With a makeover, a hairdo that wasn't a throwback to the hairspray fifties, and a wardrobe that didn't scream Matron, she would look and feel years younger and not years older. If she had ever thought to do a mother-daughter shopping and spa day. But she didn't and she never would because of him.

"Not sultry. I believe a more appropriate term would be suggestive or immodest. Good morning, Bella." Simpson never used endearments beyond occasionally addressing the wife as Miss Dora. "I imagine you have something of some importance to tell us this early in your day." He went straight to the coffeemaker without hugging or kissing his daughter, without saying how lovely she was, since they rarely saw each other. "I see in your eyes that something is amiss, girl. Have you lost that job of yours? And what was in your head, leaving this house as rudely as you did, staying away these past nights without calling, putting your poor mother into a state of worry and woe?"

"Good morning, father." She sipped her coffee, deciding she might actually be relishing the moment. "No, I did not lose my job and this is not immodest. It's very current, so get with the living." She put down her mug, not sure how her father would react. "I was staying at a hotel for some space, if you must know. And yesterday I went to a clinic not feeling very well…but it turns out I'm perfectly fine, father. I'm just, well, a little pregnant."

Simpson stayed as he was, reading his daughter. Dora Simpson clapped a hand over her mouth, smothering an anguished wail. Though despite the silence of a few seconds seeming like an eternity, as a respectful and dutiful wife she understood the husband should always speak first.

"No doubt the reason you arrive home at such a late hour each night. I might have expected as much, flaunting yourself the way you do. I can't for a moment pretend the least surprise, daughter. Were you acquainted at least? Do you know the man?"

"No father, we were not acquainted. We happened. We met at a bar and until three months ago I was a virgin. More than you or anyone can say about the other girls at school who started fucking like pros in grade eight. When this happened I was nineteen, so let's not get too bent out of shape here."

"Bella, it was the weekend you stayed with that girl," her mother wept. "Whatever were you thinking? And please do not use such terrible language in your father's home."

Simpson put up a hand, silencing the wife. "Tell me who this man is, Bella. Who did this? Was he married, preying vilely on a naïve young girl? Some miscreant, an older man cajoling you with liquor into such wicked and scandalous behaviour?" Simpson asked flatly, stoically at his wife's side with an expression of—Bella couldn't tell, disappointment, shame? "Surely you must know his name, his whereabouts. And is he aware?"

"He's neither. His name is Bill Michaels. He's twenty, if that matters, and works at the mill as some sort of manager. That's what he told me. Anyway, he was a one-time thing and didn't cajole me into anything. We were drinking and we got drunk. We ended up in bed at a cheap motel and I haven't seen him since. He was a mistake I won't be repeating. I'm moving on."

Simpson's expression didn't change, the eyes did. Repugnance. "Drunk…laying in bed with a complete stranger?"

Bella shrugged, unwavering. "Yes, father. We were drunk and he got into my pants; I got laid and pregnant. End of story."

Silence, father and daughter waiting. Simpson for any sign of remorse or abashment; Bella for a father's understanding and compassion, and possibly his warm embrace she hadn't once in her life felt. She coughed a curt and derisive laugh, in that instant feeling raw contempt for the man, leaning backward against the countertop and crossing her arms. Like that would ever happen, dad. Something she had never in her life called him. Or would.

Yet he was unmoved. "I find myself deeply appalled, Bella. That you lay inebriated with a stranger is despicable enough, thinking so little of your mother and me. But confronting us here as insouciantly as you are, confessing your debauched behaviour without the slightest shame, defies the decent and moral mind."

Dora looked to her husband. "Theadore, whatever shall we do? Our neighbours, the church?"

Bella quickly added, "Oh, yeah, the pastor. He'll really love this one. I can't imagine that sermon, mother. Anyway, here's the thing. I'm putting it up for adoption, since the state does not allow abortions. Then I'm leaving, moving out and moving on. However I might possibly accept dinner invitations on occasion, when convenient, when you two lighten up. Just never with your over-the-top haloed pastor and his angelic wife."

"Not quite, Bella. What you're suggesting is premature and irresponsible in the extreme. What *will* happen, however, is a meet-

ing with this Michaels who has obligations that you have clearly ill-considered, if at all. And for that the courts *will* intercede, I assure you. Then you will have and you will keep this child as your due penance and your possible reawakening." He checked his watch. "I will call this Michaels later today, and his family. He will not get off with simply walking away. Nor, my despoiled daughter, will you. There will be consequences."

"No. I will not do that," she snapped, practically snarling. "I have this worked out and I do not need you telling me what I should do."

"You have nothing worked out, you stupid girl. Working at that place, dressing the way you do in this age of such widespread prurience, you should have better prepared yourself."

The distraught mother tried, "Perhaps the fault is ours, Theodore, for not providing our daughter with the proper guidance."

"The girl has suffered no such neglect, wife, raised by us to one day become a decent and moral woman, not the capricious and decidedly immoral girl defying us here. This entire matter is solely on your daughter, with all her fanciful dreams and talk of waiting for the perfect husband. This is her cross, one she must bear alone, no one else's." He faced Bella who was scarcely breathing. "As for you, girl, I would suggest that until we meet with this Michaels you become a good deal more schooled in becoming a mother, an occupation considerably more demanding of self than laying with strangers in motel beds. Believe me when I say that you are in for a series of very unpleasant discoveries which you will of necessity confront on your own, and for which you are at this moment remarkably unprepared."

Bella was invisibly stunned. She knew her father was a self-righteous and cold, never having learned love and compassion from his father; her grandmother as irrelevant as her mother, their lives revolving around setting a table, keeping a home and bearing their husbands' children. Until, of course, the first child ruins the hopes of a second. Which was not her fault.

But she never believed he was heartless and cruel, retorting in kind. "Thank you, father, for telling your loving daughter she's a whore. I made a mistake, I know that. The way mother did the day she married you. Because you are a total fuck-up. You are the worst father a girl could imagine and the poorest excuse for a husband. And you, mother," Bella facing the older woman clutching her robe as though protecting herself against evil, who could scarcely believe what she was hearing, "you're no better. You're the one who should be ashamed and, really, I feel sorry for you. I do. Because the sad thing, what I really believe, is that with a better man, any man who wouldn't always be such a righteous prick, one you actually would love and not just obey as the servile wife, you would now have those two children to love instead of me to ignore. I mean for Christ's sake, Dora, he calls you wife. How demeaning is that?" She glared at her father, utterly loathing the man. "Enjoy your breakfast, Theodore."

And with those final words she strode to her room ranting silently that she would rather die than sit with Michaels being interrogated.

8

Bella left the house very soon after, taking for granted they would understand the meaning of her suitcase, wondering how she would ever endure another six months with them.

Unfortunately nothing went the way she expected; the good thing being that there was no misunderstanding. She was a disappointment and a whore, her father was a total fuck-up and her mother was a non-person with no past or present or future that wasn't all about him.

She booked a room for that night and Sunday, working Sunday to compensate for the impact on her savings. She didn't need a night off. She needed distraction; she needed people, her kind of people, doing the same the following Friday and Saturday because when she arrived at the house on the Friday morning she saw the scolding note on her bedroom door making her furious.

She would stop being a churlish girl and be home on the Sunday for an afternoon meeting with the Michaels.

She didn't see her father again until then, nine days later, ignoring her disconsolate mother the few times each weekday they came within range of each other, leaving the house shortly after waking each day, preferring lunch, afternoon movies and dinner alone rather than enduring her mother's woeful company. And she was good with that, feeling completely independent and confident. More precisely, since their confrontation, her father's deplorable overreaction and her mother's insensitive concern, not for what and how her daughter was feeling, but for what others would think,

Bella being anything but remote was impossible.

In her mind she was simply no longer their daughter.

Sunday was a far different matter. She had no choice, doing what she could to mitigate the humiliation imposed on her by a thoughtless parent. She would be her own woman, not the least submissive and, if need be, walk out. That was until Sunday morning when, exhausted from a long night and ready for bed, her boss called her into his office.

Julio Vasquez was the very essence of Southern gentility, a strong Latino accent enhancing a magnetic and natural charm. He was refined, respectful of his ladies who loved him not because they were the best paid in Savannah for being as attentive as they were flawless or that he sent them safely home each morning in taxis. They loved him because he was Julio. He ran a class act, catering to the Rolex and Cartier demographic that understood a mandatory dress code of casual elegance. No jeans, no sneakers; no tee-shirts or shorts, even on the steamiest of Georgia nights.

He served premium brands at premium prices in a sophisticated setting where his ladies were an essential part of the experience. And therein lay the problem he did not want and did not need because Bella Simpson was one of his best and most popular girls. She was a draw, good for business, good with the other girls.

"I had a really great night, Julio, really fantastic." She dropped into a leather seat, slouching. "What's up, big guy?"

He leaned forward, planting his forearms on his desk and clasping his hands together, bright fuchsia cuffs pinched together with ruby and silver links peeking out from his ivory tailored suit. His expression was grim, hoping and praying he was wrong.

Then she noticed. "God, Julio, why so serious?"

"Serious, yes. Because I have one simple question for you, Bella. A question that causes me considerable concern."

She straightened. "Sure, anything."

"Good. The questions is, are you pregnant?"

The gasp was spontaneous. "Excuse me? What?"

"Are you pregnant? One of the girls, I will not say who, believes you might be. And this, you must understand, concerns me."

No! A bolt of lightning could not have struck her with a more devastating force. "Yes Julio, I am." She had no choice. "I found out myself a few days ago and, I promise you, this will not affect my work. I promise. I would never do that. I love my job."

"As we all do love you, Bonita." He shook his head at the worst possible news, searching for words. "You are an alluring girl... muy bonita. But our patrons, they do not favour us strictly for our fine spirits and our excellent wines; they honour us also for the pleasure of being with in the company of exquisite young ladies. The men who admire, the women who envy and perhaps luxuriate in their impossible dreams. That is what we do, Bonita. We flirt with their minds as we titillate their palates. Why do you think it is that all my ladies are young and single and lovely? Because they are, as you are, a pleasant illusion. Until you can no longer wear your short skirts and sheer blouses, until you can no longer arouse their imaginations."

"I get where this is going, Julio. Pregnant isn't sexy. I get that. I'm not exactly thrilled about this either, so I'll take a couple of months off near the end without pay. Then I'll be good as new. I promise."

Vasquez shook his head, pursing he lips. "Sweetheart, you promised me also the day we first met. You are single and you live at home. You work nights until early morning. You work when your parents are asleep in their bed, as it should be." He slid an envelope across his desk. "Two thousand, Bella, with a letter of recommendation praising you. I am sorry, and wish all the best for you. The other girls and I, we will all miss you."

"Julio, no. I'll find a way. I promise. In fact I'm giving it up for adoption, I am. Because I couldn't get an abortion. I tried, I swear. The whole thing was a huge mistake, one I will not ruin my life over."

"Do not say such terrible things, Bella. This life you have begun is a blessing. You will see."

He stood, smiling warmly despite the heaviness he felt in his heart, making himself believe she'd be fine. "I am deeply sorry, Bonita. Now please, your taxi is waiting."

Bella stood, feeling completely crushed, reaching for the two grand. "Thank you, Julio. I'm sorry too." Walking toward the door she felt exposed and vulnerable, turning. "Perhaps in July, Julio, when all this is behind me?"

He tilted his head, unsmiling, raising his open palms in a way that told her emphatically not to bother. He was Latino, a devoted husband and doting father. "Perhaps, Bonita."

*

Arriving at the darkened house, since Simpson never left a light on for her, she did her thing and slept until an hour before the parents returned from church, dressing in an outfit she'd bought not for them but for the occasion, the entire ensemble screaming contemporary chic, completing a modern woman and certainly a believable patron of the lounge if no longer a valued employee. Nor would she ever be again. She saw in his sad eyes that July would not happen.

What would most definitely happen was the adoption and her longed-for freedom. Of that she was determined, reluctantly understanding why Julio no longer wanted her. She had broken a promise and would move on, to a place far away from Savannah, to another high-end lounge that would want her. Which would happen one day very soon, a promise she would keep.

Although at that moment she was calmly and disdainfully curious, eager to wipe their bullshit righteousness from their faces, slipping into a navy blazer that completed the cream-coloured silk blouse and camisole, high-waisted navy linen pants, a slim pale blue belt and low-heeled navy pumps.

She was indeed a lovely young lady destined for success.

Thirty minutes after the Simpsons arrived home they called her for Sunday dinner, sitting without her at the table when she didn't answer, not long after insisting she come down that very moment. They were leaving, father and mother visibly stunned by their daughter's undisguised derision as she sauntered quietly through the living room and onto the front porch ignoring them because she knew full well what they were expecting.

Bella, however, was not surprised. Neither did she feel disappointed or hurt. She felt in control.

Her father might have said how lovely she was, or how mature and ladylike; instead he said nothing. And Dora, following her husband's lead, simply told her daughter how Mr. Michaels had suggested a week of getting to the bottom of things, giving them time with their son as they would have time with their daughter that would let the emotions quieten down.

At that Bella swung around, believing she might actually lash out at them, practically hissing, "And when exactly did that happen, Dora?"

The uneasy ride several blocks over into a different world didn't last long, Theodore Simpson blurting "Jesus Christ" when he pulled into the Michaels' driveway and saw them sitting in coveralls and work boots on the veranda, Bill Michaels straddling the railing and swinging his legs as though he was at the county fair playing giddy-up. None of them standing until the Simpsons were at the steps, one family eyeing the other, all three Michaels closely inspecting Bella.

The fathers shook hands, walking first into the house. The mothers followed without the slightest nicety; then Bella went in, feeling ill at seeing him, hating that he was trailing behind recalling every inch of her.

In the parlour tea was offered and declined, the families sat facing each other and Harry Michaels, being the host, began.

"Let's git tuh where we're goin' straightaway, Mr. Simpson. Ain't no use us waistin' time with pleasant talk since y'all ain't sittin' here fer purposes uv congeniality. The boy says he ain't bin with the girl, not ever once. Ain't never spoke with her neither."

"My daughter says otherwise, Mr. Michaels. She claims they were drunk, that your son paid for a room, and here we are. So who do we believe?"

"I can't see, mister, that a girl such as her, lookin' the way she does, would have much use fer the likes uv him. He ain't the brightest bulb on the post, if y'all catch my meanin'. Sides which yer girl seems a good bit prettier'n most he knows."

"If not for the liquor and drunkenness, I would agree. No insult intended, Mrs. Michaels. But strong drink does quickly fog an otherwise clear mind."

The woman simply stared back, unmoved. Dora, sitting no less passively, realizing she hadn't ever in her daughter's life told the girl she was pretty.

"Pa, I'm tellin' ya straight out, I ain't never bin with her. Never once," his boy barked too loudly and too demonstratively, jabbing the air at Bella. "Ain't never bin drunk with her neither, let alone poke her. Sides which, look at her sittin' all superior and smilin'. Why is it yer smilin' all stupid like, Bella? Go ahead, pa. Ask her what fer."

The four parents focused on her, her father asking the question. "Your condition is not in any way amusing, Bella. Please tell us what you believe is so humorous, because quite frankly your casual display shows very poor character."

"Because, father, no one in this room can possibly believe I wasn't stone drunk, a victim. I mean look at him, listen to him. Not only is he a Georgia hillbilly…he's a Georgia hillbilly with a wart on his tiny cock the size of a peach stone. That is why I am smiling."

Dora gasped, pressing a palm to her chest, the other across her mouth; Bette Michaels snapped her head toward her son, her flushed complexion instantly pale. Though while Simpson promptly rebuked his daughter for her foul language and unkind remark, Michaels, a tested man familiar with harsh language and coarse manners, sprang from his seat. He jerked his son to his feet, crashing a steel-hard fist against his jaw that sprawled Bill onto the floor, then sat as calmly as though he had reached for his cider jug.

"Git yer butt back in that seat, boy, with yer lyin' mouth shut tight. Me'n y'all, we ain't nowheres done." He faced Simpson. "The boy's a liar, mister. That's clear nuff. But his bein' so don't make him the source uv yer girl's lamentable condition, leastways not till he's proven. In which case he'll do what's right'n proper by her." He watched his dazed son clamber onto a chair, rubbing his jaw. "I'll make sure uv it. Or he'll be worse off'n a tap on the head that spreads his sorry self across the floor. That's fer damn sure."

"Despite her obvious complicity and indecent behaviour, Mr. Michaels, I must believe this was her first such experience."

Michaels nodded. He understood a father's shame. "Still'n all the situation needs clarifyin', a simple enough test that'll prove what's what, is all."

Simpson studied his daughter, ashamed. The smile was gone, her smugness replaced by what he rightly construed as worry. "I agree. A paternity test within the shortest possible timeframe."

"No!" Bella blurted. "No paternity test. He's the one. And what does it matter anyway? I am not keeping it. Get that through your heads, all of you."

"We're not doubting you, Bella, that he could be the father. However we must also consider that he possibly is not, despite your intimate knowledge. He's clearly one or the other. For which reason the testing will be as much for paternity as for truthfulness since you are both proven liars."

"That's a fact." Michaels agreed. "As well, missy, should the boy be proven the father, y'all won't be tradin' it off or terminatin' its existence. Not if the boy's the father. So y'all git yerself good'n prepared. Cause if yer pa can't force ya, I surely will." Michaels heaved his bulk from the couch, smacking Bill off the head. "Y'all do likewise, boy, less'n y'all want another cuff tuh yer empty head."

The meeting was over.

9

Bella's appointment at the clinic with Bill Michaels came early the next week, by which time she no longer cared how the results might come back, even more put off with her father for making her pay the 400-dollar upfront lab fee herself.

Besides which, he had twice implied she was a whore. Once more wouldn't matter. At worst she would give it to the hillbillies if they wanted it so badly. Though what she truly wanted, what she hoped and prayed for despite the remotest possibility, was a miscarriage that for her would be the ideal solution instead of having her feet in stirrups and a needle through her abdomen that would either prove her father right or put another hillbilly in Georgia. Either way, in six months she would be twenty and gone.

She took the week off work, telling her mother she needed a rest with everything that was happening.

She told her mother how Julio had given her weekdays from lunch until Happy Hour's last call, certain that with her unemployment cheques and her savings she could last that long, when her father's company insurance would finance the unwanted delivery. Until Friday evening, after hearing from the clinic that she had tested positive. Bill Michaels was indeed the father and, as though that wasn't the worst possible result, her father made the sickening revelation even worse.

"No, Bella. Absolutely not. Your insurance ceased when you began working. I would strongly suggest you speak with your boss about that tomorrow."

She dropped onto a couch, stunned, her mind racing. "Shit."

Simpson remained as he was, assuming the worst possible dilemma. "You cannot be serious, Bella. You have no insurance?"

"I did have insurance. Until Julio fired me because of this, because I would not be good for business."

"Wonderful, another lie. One which worsens an existing and grave situation, young lady. One with not many agreeable solutions, I fear. Not the least of which by any measure is bearing the child of that backwoods fellow. That you acted so indecently with the likes of him is beyond my comprehension. A witless fellow of the lowest calibre whose dismal future will never surpass one of brooms and washrags, which unfortunately is your future as well, Bella. A sadly abrupt and regrettable ending to a life you haven't yet begun."

"What are you saying, father?"

"I'm saying your fanciful dreams of gentlemen suitors and exotic travel are things of the past. None of it will happen because you have made very bad choices while blatantly ignoring our wiser advice. Waiting tables indecently clothed until all hours, foolishly putting yourself in bed with the likes of Michaels, that you lied about, then losing your job because of him that you lied about as well."

"You're not getting this, Theodore. I will live that dream. Because I'm giving it up. Because no one has to know about this. My body, remember?"

"What you believe or want doesn't matter a whit. What does is the very harsh reality you recklessly created for yourself, not your fanciful wishes. You did so, no one else. In short, Bella, you are on one-way parallel paths going nowhere. Meaning that in very short order you and Michaels will be formally joined and you *will* be a mother because we simply cannot assist you with the many thousands in expenses, but Michaels' father will no doubt. As willingly as he will block an adoption."

Bella jerked forward, clutching her stomach. "No! No fucking way will I marry that repulsive pig. What is wrong with you, father? I'm your daughter for Christ's sake. You should be helping me."

"You chose this path, Bella, which you will travel without me or your mother who you have deeply injured, for which I will not forgive you. Regrettable? Very, but of your doing. You will however enjoy limited privileges in this home until you become Mrs. William Michaels. Such is the price for your lies, Bella. I will not have our good name sullied by your debauched behaviour or your new name."

"I won't."

"You have no choice. You have no experience beyond that of carrying a tray and when this thing does happen you will have no other home because we will not have any association with that family. You would be an unemployed mother with a large debt living in abject poverty. And once there...," he shook his head, looking at the wife. "You would more fully comprehend what you have done."

"Mother?"

"You really don't have a choice, Bella. For one thing, we cannot possibly have you living here indefinitely with a child. Because, quite frankly, what good and decent man would want you? At least with him your circumstances won't seem as severe."

"I cannot believe you said that. Not as severe, are you kidding me? Mother, you saw him."

Dora replied coolly, her hands clasped in her lap. "I did, and I'm sorry. Yet what you did was very wrong and immoral. You went astray, Bella, and this is your atonement." She glanced at her husband as much for his reassurance as his strength. "Yet very much a wonderful blessing. You will have a child who you will love and adore, if not a loving husband such as mine to care for. That will be your salvation, Bella. You'll see."

Bella sank back onto the couch in a daze, staring at them with wide-eyed disbelief. They were abandoning her, condemning her to live her life trapped in a nightmare she would not let happen. She could never and would never marry anything as vile as Bill Michaels. She wouldn't; she would find a way.

She watched her parents leave the room without another word, without the slightest concern for her welfare. She couldn't imagine not living in a nice home, not wearing her nice clothes, or one day not marrying someone who would give her everything she wanted and deserved in life.

She should have waited and not been so incredibly stupid. That was her real crime, her sin; then none of this would have happened. Or told the truth if need be, that she'd been drugged by an older man and raped in his hotel room. But changing one lie for another now was pointless.

She went to her room and lay on the bed, wondering why him and not the first guy who in a few hours she couldn't remember made her life not worth living. How insane was that?

She punched her pillow, curling into herself and moaning. Her father was right. Michaels would block an adoption and take the kid, leaving her with no money, no home and no job. She would live in a slum and no one would want her; not her parents, not Julio, not anyone. Never again.

But if she kept it she would have a better home because she would find work, nighttime work in a bar because Julio had given her a glowing reference and she was his best. Nighttime work that would keep her away from him and no one said anything about being faithful. That's right. She would have her own money, wear nice clothes and meet people. She would be with people, people like her, and make very sure she would never be stupid again.

*

Waking the next morning Bella lay on her bed musing, making sense of the previous evening, making certain she wasn't making the second worst mistake of her life.

Yes, people would stare at her, gossip about her. Yes, the girls she knew from school would laugh at her, mocking her for getting laid and pregnant by a halfwitted hillbilly.

She coughed a derisive laugh, especially the uglier ones who would know about the wart. But so what? They were no better. After four years of extracurricular fucking, not many outlasting a semester before moving on, having separate locker rooms and washrooms never seemed exactly requisite.

Many of them were married years too early of necessity with unwanted kids, locked into their own hells with store clerks, car salesmen and bookkeepers. At least she would be with better people, men who would see her for what she was, becoming more enchanting and alluring each day. Then, when she was ready, she would leave; she would get away. She would make herself legally free of him and custody of whatever was a non-issue. Nor would her parents who no longer had room for her be an issue, especially a man who could actually believe his daughter was a whore.

She was better than any of that; she was better than all of them.

She waited until her parents were midway through breakfast before joining them, surprised by how she felt when they looked up at her. She didn't feel anything, the same way she felt when no one invited her to school dances or parties. So yeah, she would definitely be leaving mom and daddy dearest behind

She pulled herself onto the kitchen counter dressed in jeans and a sweater, crossing her legs and placing her hands by her side, looking down at them.

"So, Dora, let's be very very clear here. This thing that's happening is not a blessing of any kind and sure as shit is not my salvation. Also, I am not atoning for anything, including what you believe are terrible sins and lies. So this is what actually happened and what will happen because I *will* have that life I want and deserve with the man I deserve. Not your life, and certainly not his."

She snorted, shaking her head, sneering at her father. "That's right, not yours. I could never be that self-righteous. And this," she pressed a palm to her belly, "this is worse than a mistake because it wasn't necessary. The first guy into my panties didn't get me pregnant, which I do not understand because he must have done me a dozen times while I was passed out. That's right, folks, the first guy. A complete stranger the night before I tricked Billy Wart into a motel bed so that Theo here would believe I made a stupid mistake with a hillbilly and not some guy doing me on his expense account. Turns out though, that guy wasn't my mistake. Billy Wart was. And how do you think the pastor'll like that one, Theo?" She raised an open palm, she wasn't interested. "Don't bother. We both made pretty clear what the other is. And fast-forwarding a year or so, this is what will happen. I'm marrying Billy Wart on the first of July at the courthouse and should have the kid a few days after my birthday. Then it'll be split shifts. His days sweeping floors, my nights doing what I like, what I'm very good at. And if he doesn't like it he can fuck off and file for divorce. Because if he doesn't, when I have enough saved, I will."

"Bella, no. You would leave your husband and your baby?"

"Not would, Dora…will. Pretty much the way you and Theo here are leaving me." She creased her brow, smirking. "Really, how can you not find that seriously hypocritical?"

"You're increasingly unspeakable, Bella, becoming worse each day. Tell us, when does all this stop?"

"Survival: 101, Theo. Mine and yours. You don't want me as a daughter, keeping me around strictly for appearances. And I don't want a father who must now believe I'm a slut. As for when, July 01st when Mr. and Mrs. Theodore Simpson will regrettably not be attending their daughter's wedding or the joyous birth of their grand whatever."

10

The six months passed without pretence or civility. The father who remained as Theo, the disrespect festering more with each passing day, never again called the daughter by name. And Dora, who was never again a mother, seldom spoke with the girl who she recognized less with each passing day.

Bella began receiving unemployment cheques that she banked, deciding she would no longer contribute to the house because, well, what would the neighbours and their holier-than-thou congregation think of them putting a vulnerable teenage and pregnant girl on the street? That's right! And a few days after her numbing confession she met with a frantic Bill Michaels on the veranda, setting things straight while Harry and Theo spoke inside.

Harry and the girl would share the cost of delivery, that would deplete her savings by half, and the boy would cover the cost of the civil wedding. And the deal was struck, except that the two men weren't fully aware of Bella's upcoming vows that she was sharing with her distraught fiancé who she would not see or speak with again until her wedding day.

"That's right. Furthermore, on July 01st or any other night, you go get yourself laid. Have a good time with whatever you can afford because you will never again put that thing in me. Nor will you ever sleep in my bed."

"Then what's the point uv this? I mean…fuck."

"That's right, that's the point. Because I am already royally fucked."

"Yer not right in yer head, Bella. It ain't the leastways proper what yer proposin'."

"Not proposing, telling." She gurgled a laugh. "Don't like it, do something about it, Billy Boy, because what I'm saying is perfectly fine. And, believe me, I am doing you a huge favour. One that even you might figure out in time."

Hearing that he had a strong urge to punch her good and hard, like she deserved for her bald-faced lies and cunning ways, which he didn't, fearful of his pa's hard fists, glad when she was gone. Told bluntly when sitting with his pa, bemoaning everything she had said, that he'd be best off finding his sorry balls.

From that day nothing changed but Bella's condition. Theo and Dora showed no interest in her progress into motherhood and Billy Wart was content being away from her. She attended prenatal classes alone, shopped for a maternity wardrobe alone and, the day before her wedding, she packed her belongings into cardboard boxes alone. Except for the quart of Jack Daniels on her dresser.

Then came the day when a hapless groom dressed in jeans, a tee and sneakers came for her with a rented truck, loading her life's possessions and her bed without Theo's help because Theo wasn't around. Neither was Dora on a delightful Saturday not yet oppressive with Savannah's usual midsummer mugginess, instructing the girl before she left to lock the door and leave the key in the mailbox, not hearing the reply that months earlier would have appalled and shaken her.

When he was finished, when she closed the door on her past, the groom didn't bother complimenting her simple dress or her updo, opening her door or helping his pregnant bride into her seat.

In fact he hadn't said a word since arriving, scarcely acknowledging her. He just climbed in beside her and without a word drove to the courthouse where he paid the fee and repeated after the judge before signing the declaration of his failed life. Then he delivered the wife without ceremony or dinner to their first-floor three-room Shangri-La across from the sprawling and busy Savannah port authority where he emptied the truck with more grunts and curses.

Then he left her without having spoken a word, without concern for her condition, though happily in accordance with her previously stated covenant, until early Sunday morning when he arrived home reeking of cheap booze and cheaper perfume.

*

Bella Michaels celebrated her wedding night with her commiserative friend Jack, not thinking as she explored the apartment that she would never again see her parents, understanding intuitively that she would forever loathe them as much as she would her husband.

In the bedroom she separated her comfy queen-size from the double he had bought at a local thrift store along with the dresser she wouldn't put her clothes into until she sanitized the thing. As for the kid, that would go in the kitchen into one of the bigger boxes until something else was needed. She was not needlessly squandering her money when she knew full well that Billy Wart and his progeny were very short-term.

When she finished she commandeered the biggest closet as her own. She hung her wardrobe and sat preparing a list in the living room sitting on a sheet over the couch she would never let touch her bare skin. And on that point, neither would he.

She wanted nice pictures on the walls, new kitchenware, bath towels, a modern stereo and television, throwing all that he had brought from his hillbilly home into an empty box that she put outside the door along with his cheap hi-fi and television; the way she would one day soon put him out.

Then five days later without any fanfare she turned twenty, without a gift or a simple "happy birthday," a phone call from her parents or a special dinner, the week ending as it began. He went to sweep floors and clean toilets while she stayed home alone wondering when she would get her body back, which happened the following Monday when she was rushed to the hospital in an ambulance.

She stayed the night without a single visitor, certain he was out celebrating with something he couldn't drink pretty but could afford. Something Bella wouldn't ask about because she couldn't care less. She hoped that beers and whores would be his weekly reprieve as much as hers from then on, happily discovering the next afternoon that she was absolutely right, arriving home to find him sprawled on the kitchen floor drunk with a beer in his hand and sniffling.

"You took the day off work?"

"Had tuh. Wasn't much good tuh no one."

"You never are. And wait until your mother hears you were out getting laid when you should have called her. I don't suppose your daddy'll be pleased with you either, when he hears how you're piss drunk and snivelling."

He clambered to his feet, dragging himself up by the countertop while Bella laid the tightly swaddled newborn in its box, stepping aside as he stumbled into the living room without the slightest interest in the kid, demanding his supper and mumbling about the TV and stereo as he collapsed onto the couch where he sat flipping channels.

"It's a boy, by the way. Brandon Michaels and tomorrow I'm joining a gym. I'm getting my body back and finding that lounge job."

He put a fist to his mouth, chuckling. "Ain't no one near ready fer hirin' the likes uv y'all, Bella. Y'all look wore out'n haggard, not givin' no thought tuh that there thing."

"Not for long and remember what I told you on the porch. You're the father as much as I'm the mother. That there is yours as much as mine, so wake up and get real about this. And one more thing, that'll be a nightclub job which means your fuck night will be the night I'm off."

"Yer job is right here, Bella. Yer the wife. Yer the one needin' wakin' up. That there thing, it ain't a man's job."

"Perhaps not a man's, but it is yours because I won't waste my evenings trapped here with you when I can be out with real people having a good time and making money, money you won't see. Any night for that matter, meaning you'll likely be making Sunday your dirty night. Unless, of course, grandpa should hear about you neglecting his grandson."

He waved her away, reaching for his beer. "We'll see what's what, wife. Could be yer in fer a real shock, is what I'm thinkin'. Them tits won't never again be perky, not once y'all start with puttin' that there thing on 'em. Won't be many runnin' tuh take a gander tween them previous enthrallin' fine legs neither."

"I'll do fine, very fine. Better than you."

*

The next day she left Brandon in the box once the kid was sleeping and went out, returning an hour later from the mall with a k'tan, not because she wanted him close, because she would rather carry him than pay hundreds more for a stroller someone else would soon push. Then she went to a popular gym, paying upfront for a ten-week special, two outfits and the nursery.

She was determined, devoting six gruelling mornings each week and walking several miles every afternoon with her ankles weighted and the kid on her chest. So that by the fourth week Bella not only got her body back, she was more shapely than ever. She was the envy of all the other women and ready for work.

That Saturday afternoon she left the kid at the nursery, dressed for interviews at the four nightclubs she was confident would give her a chance; she didn't bother with the fourth, taking an offer she couldn't refuse once the owner read Julio's reference while imagining the little of Bella he couldn't see.

At home that night she lied, telling her husband she'd be earning eight grand, two more than him, not the twelve she would pull in before her tips serving cocktails in a posh club to an urbane crowd wearing a sequinned bra and a scanty thong under glittering tassels.

She maintained her regimen six more weeks, motivated, letting Bill fend for himself, feeding and cleaning her son before leaving him alone for an hour each day at 5:00 and again when she arrived home near three until she was showered and ready for bed after a few hits of Jack Daniel.

That much she could manage in the short-term, asleep when he left for work, gone when he came home and her Sunday nights alone. Three months tops, not day longer, especially with her tips practically doubling her salary. Then she would go for good and good riddance.

She would have the home she deserved and the car she wanted. And yeah, she would begin selectively saying "yes." Though what she didn't count on, what she never expected, was the first Saturday in October midway through her shift when she practically tripped in her heels at seeing her husband arguing at the door and pointing at her. He was piss drunk and making a spectacle of himself, dressed in his work coveralls when everyone else in the club personified Southern elegance and poise.

He wasn't getting in and didn't stay long, ushered out politely, and likely with an ultimatum, by a tuxedoed doorman cum bouncer within seconds of walking through the door, yelling out that it "ain't in noways proper, a decent man's wife servin' liquor with less'n a stitch concealin' her secret parts. There'd be hell tuh pay, sure nuff."

She was mortified, managing a smile as she placed cocktails onto her customers' table, the woman commenting with a hand on Bella's arm that both she and her outfit were delightful; the bartender saying as much when she went to refill her tray.

The manager however was more pragmatic, asking if Bella needed a hotel room for the night, or perhaps a capable escort who would first make certain all was fine on the home front. She didn't, thanking him. She'd be fine.

*

When she did arrive home, stepping from the taxi, she noticed the lights were on in her living room.

Inhaling a deep breath, whispering "twelve more weeks," she swung open the door, climbed the steps and stood waiting in the hallway. Twelve more weeks; she'd be gone by Christmas. A day she couldn't possibly imagine, not anymore, not until she found a real man.

She went in thinking he'd be in front of the television watching porn as usual, since he wasn't working Sunday and wouldn't need his limited senses until the following night when and if he could find something still standing that he could afford.

She wasn't wrong. Except this time he wasn't tugging at his sweats. He was pushing his weight from the seat, staggering toward her, right away punching her chest, slamming her against the door, his other hand viciously snapping her head sideways.

"Ya can't fuckin' be serious, doin' what yer doin' with yer tits practically fallin' out'n yer butt bare as can be fer all tuh gawk at." He wasn't yelling, he was snarling, waiting, smacking her other cheek when she straightened. "Ya can't fuckin' be serious. What kinda whore does that?"

"The kind that makes a shitload more money than you, asshole."

She dropped her purse, clenching her hands together and driving them into his soft gut, a burst of air escaping her mouth an instant later as she buckled over before another savage blow to her face slammed her head against the door. Then she was stumbling, dragged into the living room and flung, crashing between the coffee table and couch.

He stood by his seat, swaying, sneering down at her. "Yer the wife, nothin' more'n that. Ain't nothin' special bout ya and yer gonna start respectin' and payin' yer fair share."

The "Go fuck yourself," earned her brutal kicks that would leave her even more bruised in the morning. Still, she wouldn't give him the satisfaction of seeing her cry.

"That's not what I got swirlin' in my head. It's y'all I'll be fuckin' from here on in. Like the wife y'all should be. Ain't right the way y'all bin actin', leavin' me here with that there thing while y'all go flauntin' yerself, showin' more'n I seen since first pokin' ya."

"That won't happen, because if you do I'll bash in your face when you're sleeping." She propped herself onto an elbow, smiling as though she hadn't just been brutally attacked. "Don't believe me? Try me. Because of you I don't have a family and I live in a shithole with a drunken janitor. So yeah, try me. And let's not forget the very big guy at the bar, the one you called a butthole. Think he wouldn't like a few minutes here with you?"

"A man's wife, is a man's wife. Not the concern uv no one else."

She dragged herself onto the couch, adjusting her skirt. "Unless he's a dumbass hillbilly who thinks he can rape and beat women."

"Teachin' respect. Teachin' what is, is all. Sides which yer duty-bound, Bella. Ain't no one sayin' nothin' bout rape or beatin' ya."

"Think he won't believe me? Think he won't teach you a lesson?" She stood, pausing until the dizziness passed. "Finish your porn and don't even think of doing anything stupid, because I swear. Touch me again, hurt me like this again, and he will come."

She crossed the room, checking on the kid that was sleeping, deciding it could wait until noon. Sleep was more important.

In the bathroom she locked the door and showered, grimacing as the steaming torrent stung her face and arms.

Stepping out, patting herself dry as gently as she possibly could, she slipped into briefs and plain sweats eager for the day she could wear silk and satin without provoking a diseased mind. She wasn't surprised her legs were bruised, though turning to the sink she gasped at what she saw in the mirror: the severe bruising on both sides of her face, the bluish tinge marring her chest, her arms that were black-and-blue and chafed from colliding with the edge of the table.

Twelve weeks. Pulling on a plain brassiere and fleecy top she walked out, pausing at the bedroom door. "You know what, Billy Boy? I really believe you're already in *the* deepest shit. And the money? Good luck with that."

11

Sunday Bella woke near 11:00, lying in bed listening, not turning until she was absolutely certain she was alone.

She rummaged through the dresser for jeans and a sweater, panties and a bra that were much more her. Then she walked out scanning the living room and kitchen, ignoring the wails of an unhappy Brandon.

He was gone, a half-dozen beer bottles littering the floor by his seat. Still, she locked herself in the bathroom before stripping away her clothes, aching everywhere, standing by the mirror naked and shocked despite expecting the worst. Her entire face, her arms and her legs were a hideous bluish-yellow, her arms reddened with painful scrapes and the marring on her chest had spread to the swell of her breasts.

Dressed with no way to mitigate her pain or soothe her body, she cared for the kid because she didn't have a choice. Her single solace from abject misery being that, as thoroughly as she despised Dora and Theo, they were right for disparaging the hillbilly Michaels from on high. The hillbillies hadn't shown a speck of interest in her or their grandson. Not even a phone call that she knew about, which for her was very much a non-issue.

She put him in the k'tan and left, spending the afternoon at the park, letting her mind wander when she wasn't answering predictable baby questions, each of the passersby shocked by her face though happy she hadn't broken any bones when tumbling down the stairs.

Certain that Billy Wart would stay out until finding some pathetic girl or bargaining with some down and desperate hooker, she went back but didn't stay long. She couldn't; she hated the place. She hated the second-hand furniture, the green paint on the bare walls that would remain bare, the breadline neighbours and the low-rent neighbourhood. Instead she did what was needed by the kid, put him in his box and went to the cineplex, relieved when she got home that her husband wasn't there.

Nor was he when she woke the next day, lying in her bed thinking she should put eighty-two Xs on her wall, wondering how she would possibly endure the hillbilly or his kid that many days, filling her mind with all but the most crucial issue, not feeling good about the way her day would end.

She went for a walk in the park with her weights and the kid on her chest, clearing her mind rather than brooding over the inevitable that she was certain would be short-lived, suddenly aware she hadn't thought of her parents since leaving the hospital, chuckling at the thought of the Michaels finding a baby on their doorstep. A baby she had never kissed or hugged or even cooed at because the notion of her ever being a mother was absurd.

Back in the apartment she spent an hour walking in circles with a Jack Daniels in her hand, checking herself in the mirror before leaving and, at the club thirty minutes later, she went directly into the manager's office.

"I'm sorry, Max, for the other night."

He stood, eyeing her. "What happened, Bella?"

"There's more, Max." She shrugged off her leather bomber, undoing the tie of her wrap skirt and letting it fall, standing in her thong and bra which didn't bother her or raise an eyebrow since she was pretty much in costume. "Saturday, when I got home. He was pretty drunk."

"That is not a good reason, Bella." He stepped closer, taking her hands. "And since?"

"Nothing. He stays out Sundays. We have an agreement."

He tilted his head. "More like a serious disagreement. Bella, my girls are mostly single or divorced and not one of them will be here in five years. The married ones, they're a different breed whose husbands know this place is class act." He helped her into her jacket, stooping for her skirt. "Your guy's a loose cannon with a big esteem problem. That's not good." He waved her into a seat, filling two old-fashioned an inch deep with his finest Hennessy Paradis. "Bella, I am straight out giving you three months. This, what he did, will certainly happen again with you working here. Or any place like this. Guys like that, they don't change. They're inferior and they know it." He sipped the cognac. "I must say, I was surprised when I saw him. He wasn't at all what I would have imagined and I very much regret not sending Tommy home with you."

Bella believed her heart would stop beating. She loved her job, losing out for the second time because of someone she loathed.

"I'm sorry, Max. He's a janitor going nowhere at the mill. It's complicated."

"Perhaps so, but you shouldn't be going nowhere with him. Get out, Bella. Just walk. And when you do, come see me."

"I will, Max. Thank you." She stood, putting her drink on his desk, wrapping herself in her skirt and zipping her bomber. "I will come see you."

He put up a hand, pressing a button on his desk. A moment later a 6'3" Tommy ambled in, at once creasing his brow. "Sweetheart, that husband of yours do this?"

She nodded. "Yeah, but never again. I sort of worked that out."

Tommy turned to Max. "Boss? You good with that?"

"Not entirely. By which I mean you need time away from this lowlife, Bella. I'm putting you in a hotel for a few nights. No argument. Tommy here will get you there and settled in. As for your clothes, you may find something more suitable in your locker until tomorrow when you'll be safe packing some things. I assure you, he will not be there."

"Thank you, Max." She hugged him tightly. "And thank you, Tommy."

"Okay, we're done here. And Tommy, once Bella is taken care of, you call me."

*

Tommy and Bella left the office, Tommy waiting outside the girls' dressing room while Bella cleared out her locker and put on a sweater before kissing and hugging the girls on her way out, thankful the lounge was dimly lit.

When she was safely in her room Tommy called his boss from the lobby, hearing that at such times an ounce of prevention like a few nights away was never better than a lasting pound of cure. And when the brief conversation ended with a "You got it, boss," he put the receiver in its cradle and walked out onto the street with an address and a very broad smile. He adored that little girl.

Not long after he was parked outside Bella's apartment leaning against the car, giving the place a once-over, shaking his head, wondering why in the hell a lovely and smart girl like Bella would live in such a dump with deadbeat good-for-nothing.

Fitting his hands into leather gloves as he went in, making his way to the first floor, he knocked on the door. Then he knocked twice and a third time, waiting until Billy Wart stood facing him with not enough time to blink let alone think before a fist crashed into his chest and Tommy stepped inside the apartment.

He picked Michaels up by his shirt, this time ramming a fist into his face and letting him fall, repeating the process a few times until he saw blood and a bent nose in serious need of attention. Then he went into the kitchen, finding the perfect utensil, several seconds later pounding the thick edge of a cast-iron skillet against Michaels' arms until he was satisfied, finally addressing the issue of Bella's bruised legs in a way that left Michaels curled into a ball and blubbering.

"That's it, big man. I'm done here, unless I hear you've done that girl wrong any which way. And tomorrow you stay out. Do not be here. Not for any reason. You got that?" He slammed a foot into Michaels' back. "I said, you got that?"

Michaels nodded, holding his head in his hands.

Tommy kicked him again, for Bella. "You sure you got that?"

Hearing Michaels sputter something sounding like a "Yes" he went into the kitchen with the skillet. The place was a mess, but he understood. Bella was leaving, she wanted out. And so did he; his work was done, thinking it strange that Michaels wouldn't have taken the box of trash to the outside dumpster because whatever was inside was ripe.

He walked out, deciding he wouldn't worsen Michaels condition with a few strategic kicks for making Bella's life unbearable. Though unfortunately for Bella, had Tommy stayed those few moments longer, had he heard a baby cry, Bill Michaels would never have killed his wife.

*

However Child Services would never hear of the baby in a box, the next day Bella hurrying to the apartment, opening the windows and grinning at the smeared blood on the floor.

When she was finished with the kid she packed for her time away and sat in the living room debating what she should do. That Michaels was a borderline moron was a given. Without being told he would likely not feed the kid and keeping it clean was a distinct impossibility, finally taking it with her and, at the hotel, putting it in the tub with pillows.

Four days later she returned home, unaware that Tommy had called the apartment the night before refreshing Michaels' memory. Though from then on Bella's nights were never the same, save Sundays.

Her bruises lasted several more weeks, by which time she was ready for work. Yet sadly for her the two clubs she'd previously turned down no longer wanted her, the one she hadn't tried wasn't hiring and by week's end she'd gone through a jug of Jack Daniels surviving her evenings.

She spent the next several weeks walking in and out of doors with her references and little else. She had no experience except as a waitress and the other clubs wanted her stripping and dancing as well as serving.

She didn't think so, finally hired some weeks later at a diner where the pale blue frocks, hairnets and sneakers weren't as appealing as lacy thongs, push-up bras and high heels. Neither was the pay at seven K and ten-cent tips. Even worse was the forty-hour workweek, putting the kid in daycare that made working somewhat counterproductive, and her evenings trapped in an apartment with seemingly less money each month.

By Christmas nothing had changed. They had no tree, didn't exchange gifts and the kid didn't know the difference. Then came New Year's when Bella stayed home with Jack and Bill went out wearing his best slacks and sweater for a reasonable and amenable facsimile of the wife.

By Brandon's first birthday without presents or cake Bella still worked at the diner, putting in overtime when she could, as much for the extra money as for the reprieve. She was also drinking more, her only solace. She hadn't seen her parents in a year and the few times the Michaels did come by she went out alone. She had no friends because the high-end girls at Julio's and Max's had forgotten her, the women at the diner were all much older with their own problems, and the neighbours were clones of her husband.

By his second birthday she realized she would never see Max or Tommy again. She was twenty-two, her stunning body was becoming softer and she hadn't worn makeup or styled her hair since leaving them. Nor would she ever see her parents who now never crossed her mind.

Tommy, though, did continue being a looming threat each time Billy Wart peered into the mirror at his crooked nose, not once straying from his bed into hers in a smaller room where Brandon now occupied an open suitcase in the corner.

When the kid was three they moved because he needed a proper bed, into a small shack of a place on the outskirts of Savannah, an expense that forever destroyed Bill's dream of a Mustang convertible.

At four he left daycare, ready for preschool, and at five he was dressed for the first time in clothes she hadn't bought at the thrift store. He had no concept of love, or hugs or goodnight kisses after a bedtime story. Though Bella was now speaking with him without saying very much because she had never gone anywhere or done anything worth talking about.

She no longer wore flimsy blouses, short skirts and sexy lingerie because she never went clubbing or dining out and now passersby and customers hardly noticed her. She had become singularly ordinary, nevertheless locking the door whenever she changed or showered, sleeping in her childhood bed always fully clothed in drab sweats and sensible underwear.

Throughout elementary Brandon didn't interact well. He didn't know how. He was amiable enough in a shy way, always smiling; he just preferred his own company, hurting a girl's feelings in eighth grade when she invited him to a Sadie Hawkins dance. And that summer, as with all others, he spent his days in the backyard alone throwing rocks at birds when he wasn't reading while other boys were at the lake showing off for the girls.

In grade nine another girl tried and failed at Christmas because he couldn't dance. His mother had never taught him; she was always too busy or too tired whenever he asked. And by then he understood she wasn't really tired.

He didn't remember his early years, the box or his year in a suitcase. Christmas was always just another day and New Year's was a night without a father who often shoved or smacked him when his chores weren't properly or quickly enough done for the man's frequently dulled mind. He never had friends over because he was ashamed of practically everything in the house, including the man he never called dad or father who always went Sundays to late-night meetings, when Brandon would sit quietly reading with his mother wondering how she could completely ignore him. Until one Sunday evening when he was fourteen, when he sat beside her.

"Mom, where'd he go? And why doesn't he ever take you?"

Bella was as shocked by the question as by the boy who, for no reason, was sitting close to her. What she wanted was a quiet evening and a few too many drinks. She didn't need or want a confused and curious kid.

"He went out celebrating with friends."

Brandon furrowed his brow, thinking. "Like he always does. So why don't you ever go with him? Why don't you have friends?"

"Because there's no money. Going out's expensive and the people around here aren't the friends I want. "

Brandon put down his book, placing a hand on his mother's thigh, feeling her warmth for the first time. "Why don't you ever touch me, mom? I don't remember you ever touching me. And why don't you ever sit close with him?"

Shit! "Isn't it obvious? Because we don't like each other. He thinks I'm a bitch and he knows I see him as a failure because he is one."

"That's why you never talk or look at him, the way he never talks or looks at me. Is it because of me? Is that why you never touch me, because I'm a failure too?"

Bella put down her drink. She didn't need this shit. "Listen, you'll be gone from here in three years when you're finished with school. Be grateful for that, look forward to that. Because when you're gone you'll never come back. He's an unhappy man and won't ever be better than he is. So, yeah. As soon as you can you will leave here and become better than him despite having his blood."

"That's all? He's unhappy? Mom, he's always drunk. I'm afraid one day he'll do something really bad."

God! She was not ready for this. "No. He won't because he's afraid. The one thing keeping him from being worse than he is, is fear. He's a coward. Once, a long time ago, he did something very bad and men I knew then took care of business. They took real good care of him for hurting me and, deep inside, he's still very afraid of those men."

"Then why did you marry him?"

"My parents and his forced me. I didn't want to, but I had no choice." She sipped her whisky. "What can I say? Shit happens, kid."

"Because of me."

"Yes, because of you."

"And now you won't touch me." He took away his hand. "That's not fair, mom. I never hurt you."

She knew the kid was right. She never did touch her son because touching him would be like touching her husband. Something she would never do.

"You're right, Brandon. I know that and I'm very sorry. The simple truth is you should never have happened. You should never have been born."

"I was what, an accident? That's what you're saying?"

"No, not an accident, a criminal act. He got me very drunk one night. He did things to me while I was passed out, and now you're here. End of story."

"Shit, mom. You mean like he raped you?"

She inhaled a deep breath. "Yeah, he raped me. It's the reason he goes out, because I won't let him touch me. I won't ever let him touch me. Or see me. So he goes looking for other women. And yeah, he's the reason I never touch you. I never wanted children. Never." She sipped more whisky, rubbing the chilled glass across her forehead. She couldn't feel sorry for the kid because she didn't feel anything for him; he was a constant reminder. She felt sorry for herself because once free of them her life would still be shit because of them. Shit would always happen for no good reason. "The truth is, I wanted an abortion. But then abortions were illegal and his father blocked your adoption. So here we are, you and me. Stuck with each other."

"Then I'm sorry."

"For what?"

"You know, that you couldn't get rid of me. Because then you'd be happy somewhere else and not with him or me."

"Yeah, well, in three years I will be."

It wasn't what he wanted to hear, moving away, watching her put the glass to her lips. "Do you need that, mom, all the time? You do that because of him?"

"Yeah. Because of him and for me. I was attractive before him, good at what I did. I had a good life, money, nice clothes and I was going somewhere. Now I'm thirty-four going on forty and feeling like fifty because of him. Because of you. This gets me through and will until the day you're gone. Then I'm done. Because the day you leave, I'll be gone as quickly and as far. Three years. Until then we're stuck here, you and me, with him and each other."

Brandon stood, watching his mother gaze into an empty glass. "At least now I know why you can't ever love me or touch me. And I won't ever blame you, mom; I won't ever let him hurt you again. I promise."

With that Brandon turned and went into his room.

*

By Brandon's fifteenth birthday nothing had changed except that Harry Michaels was dead and buried, his wife Bette weeping alone at the grave. Bill wasn't much interested, not seeing what difference his being there would make, surprised at the door a few days later when his mother's neighbour showed up with Harry's long gun which he had no particular use for.

The kid had two years left, too busy with his studies to contemplate where he might go or what he might do once they threw him out. He was as tall as Bill with dark red hair and enviable good-looks that were his mother's only gift, already understanding the meaning of being poor, believing it best that he didn't have a girl-friend because he couldn't afford one.

He hadn't asked his mother a single question in the year since his rude awakening, deciding on his own that he should get a summer job, spending those weeks stocking shelves at the local drugstore, told by his father that from then on he'd bear the cost of his own clothes. Nor did he ask his mother about her heated argument with his father on December 24th, the day Michaels was sent home with his slip for drinking on the job. And from then on things worsened with each company that turned him down.

No one needed a man whose sole skillset relied on brooms and toilet brushes. He began cashing his assistance cheques at the beer store and spending his days lamenting life, when Brandon worked after school and weekends at the drugstore and Bella asked her boss for more hours.

He put on weight that made his Sunday night clothes a size too tight, over the following year finding himself downgraded from desperate and drunk women near his age to much older and more desperate women. Until finally no one wanted him and he landed one summer night in jail for public intoxication, for cursing at something miserable in her fifties that wasn't yet drunk enough, and a few days later Brandon's sixteenth birthday came and went like any other day.

He didn't expect a gift and he didn't get one. Such was the norm, but now he had clothes that didn't come from a thrift store and that was better than any gift.

TurnAbout

In September he was about the only kid in eleventh grade without a girlfriend, without ever kissing one or seeing one naked, when most other boys were regularly getting lucky with theirs.

He didn't care about girls. He cared about leaving home in nine months, about how better his life would be living on his own. Because he would be better than a pathetic drunk. He would. He just could not foresee that his liberation day would come as it did on a starlit December 29th.

12

He was in a mood with his bottle near empty.

He ain't had no Sunday spree in months. Wasn't no one lookin' fer his kind neither and his weekly source uv revenu would soon nuff run dry, and the woman sittin' across in her frock drinkin' booze when beer was good nuff didn't give no shit neither. That there was the ferever problem. Her. Always was, alway would be cause here he was, denied all these years, his natural yearnin' fermentin', havin' tuh put up with her all these years, her sittin' smug as can be, sayin' not a word, sleepin' nights in her fancy bed all wrapped up tight when a man had his rights the way the wife had her obligations. Damn straight!

She sure nuff weren't the prettiest thing no more, still'n all she was fit nuff fer the chore.

With that blurred thought in his head Bill Michaels did a very stupid thing. He stumbled his way toward her, smacking the glass from her hands, jerking her to her feet and ripping open her frock, tearing away her brassiere and smacking her. He pushed her backward onto the couch, pressing a knee into her stomach, tearing away her underwear before smacking her into wifely obedience a second time good and hard.

He stood back guffawing, pleased with himself. "Sixteen years, Bella. And these past months of privation. Yer in fer a good one, missus. So git yer legs wide apart."

He pushed his stained sweats to the floor, then his stained shorts, pulling a shapeless tee-shirt over his head, swaying. But

Bella had just come home from the diner, on her first drink, and the instant he was blind and vulnerable she kicked him viciously in the balls, sending him sprawling with all her strength across the floor.

She ran into the kitchen searching for whatever she could find, reaching into a drawer for a iron skillet that would abruptly put an end to his evening and his bullshit, turning a second too late.

She didn't feel her head being bashed repeatedly and violently into the wall, stunned by the first impact of his clenched fist crashing against her temple. She didn't feel herself collapsing onto the floor or see the blood trickling from her ears and her nose. She simply lay twisted at his feet, expelling a puff of breath when he stomped on her chest.

He leaned forward, swaying, bracing himself on unsteady knees, studying her, kicking her again, slipping and falling, and cursing her.

"Y'all can lie passed out all ya want with yer face all plastered. But yer the wife, goddammit, and I mean tuh have ya well and good in yer bed or here on the floor. Ain't no never mind tuh me."

He clambered ontuh his hands and knees, steadyin' himself against the counter, thinkin' things through, pullin' himself tuh his feet'n reachin' fer a half-filled bottle afore staggerin' intuh the livin' room, fumblin' intuh his shorts'n sittin' there mumblin' tween his gulpin'n belchin' fer her tuh stop her poutin'n "git yer lazy self off the damn floor afore y'all need more convincin'."

Then Bill Michaels did something very good. He fell into a comatose sleep, aided by her whisky and his beer.

*

About an hour later Brandon walked into the kitchen through the backdoor for dinner, shutting out the Savannah twilight on a pleasant winter's evening.

The kid was instantly jolted, his entire body convulsing with a cold chill at seeing his naked mother lying dead and bloodied at his feet, fear screaming from her gaping eyes, the terror of being brutally murdered trapped in her wide-open mouth.

The house was eerily quiet, the son lost in time staring trans-fixed at the mother, her tortured face tasseled with matted hair; the contours and details of her body giving her the aspect of a broken and frightening mannequin, not his mother, her naturally milky skin more pallid, her once full and pink lips tinged with a purplish blue hue.

He rubbed his face hard with one hand, clenching the other into a fist, slowly turning a full three-sixty. He wasn't certain what he should do, thinking the man who killed her was still in the house. Then he noticed the bloody damage on the wall mixed with strands of blonde hair, and the skillet that within a second was gripped in his hands. He wasn't afraid of the man. He was taller than Bill, in better shape and stronger. Neither was he drunk, Brandon knowing full well the man was.

He went as stealthily as he could into the living room, the anxi-ety and tension wracking his body and mind gradually subsiding, standing for a few minutes watching the man slouched in his seat, seeing his mother's ruined clothes on the floor, the cans and the empty bottle, looking at the skillet and recreating the violent scene while intuitively resolving that he would never live alone with the man.

Again in the kitchen he stood by his mother, studying her, thinking how peculiar she seemed in her socks, angry with himself for not protecting her the way he had promised. He felt helpless, incensed by the man blacked out in the other room who had years earlier raped and now killed his mother, who made a mother de-spise her only son, seized in the moment by a peculiar image flash-ing across his tormented mind.

He remembered the shed where he went in a hurry, reaching for the loaded Winchester rifle laying on the top shelf covered with rags. Fleeting moments later, again in the living room, before the least sense of self-doubt or guilt would take hold of his mind and reason, he put the man's legs on a worn footstool while keeping the skillet within easy reach—in case.

He cocked the gun's lever calmly and matter-of-factly, laying the stock between the man's legs and the barrel over his scarcely heaving chest, nestling the muzzle under his chin. Next he took Michaels' limp right hand, carefully inserting the forefinger into the trigger guard, pausing. Something wasn't right; he was doing this all wrong, stepping away several feet where, without taking his eyes from the man for an instant, he stripped away his shoes and socks, his jeans, his tee-shirt and jacket.

Now he was ready, determined he would make things right for his mother and, in a way, keep his promise.

"This is for mom, for making her be the way she was. And for me, for all the pushing and the shoving when I couldn't fight back. But now I can."

With that he put his finger against Michaels', pulling back gently, killing the man who was never a father or much of anything else in life.

Leaving the body with the rifle in place, pleased it hadn't done more than twitch a bit, he hurried into the bathroom checking himself in the mirror, telling his splattered reflection "No big deal" and hurrying outside, tossing the rag into the shed as he ran toward the rain barrel.

Clambering in, his knees and shoulders scraping the sides, agitating the water the best way he could, he cupped the cold water in his hands and scrubbed his face to a renewed innocence.

Gripping the edge he hauled himself out. He combed a curtain of water through his hair, stripping from his briefs, rubbing himself dry with a towel from the line and draping both to dry before rushing breathless into the kitchen where he kneeled by his mother, studying her, losing track of time until realizing they were naked together.

He had never seen a naked girl. Though some boys at school

had, some of them sometimes telling him about how easy the girls were, how they liked their tits being squeezed and rubbed hard between their legs. The best of them even taking off their underpants for the boys to get a better look-see, the older ones almost always eager for a poke.

He sat cross-legged gazing at her, musing, lost in time, leaning forward, pressing a fingertip to a breast, cupping the cool contours, deciding she could have been pretty long ago. But now she smelled, her private pale hair glistening with the piss puddled around her legs, Brandon pretty certain leaning closer, studying the darker folds and the split between them, that he could imagine how a boy might poke a girl, deciding he wouldn't touch them, feeling sorry for her.

"Thanks, mom. And what now for me? You should've run away when you could. You know, with me, taken me far away with you. But now you're dead and what about me? Because I killed him, mom. I did that for you and because you left me alone. Now what about me?"

He sat awhile longer, not thinking that he should or shouldn't. No longer curious about her body he was being smart because he was smart, smarter than him, smarter than everyone in his class. And besides, he already knew. That's why he killed him the way he should have, the way he promised his mom, the way he did because he was smart. Because he already knew.

What he didn't know was, what now? Which he determined meant leaving her, going outside for another towel that would give her dignity, and making sure of his own proper appearance in the bathroom mirror. That's what.

And with that done he dressed in the living room, ignoring the man but inhaling several deep and calming breaths before the moment of truth, before he called 9-1-1 from the kitchen that brought cops screeching into the driveway within minutes, cops who naturally assumed the boy sitting quietly on the front stoop was in shock.

Everything Brandon told them and what they saw substantiated the murder-suicide: The lost job and the drinking, the separate beds and why, a Christmas tree that was not standing in the living room all aglow, and the colourful gifts that had never been bought. However when they asked his age he answered with a straight face that he was nineteen and worked at the drugstore, because no way was he going into a foster home. If anyone would even want a kid who in his appearance was fully an adult.

And at 6' 0" and 235 they believed him.

He also came off as a going-nowhere kid who would work in a drugstore, for the rest of his life, suggesting they help him inform the grandparents, Brandon firmly insisting he was fine. He would tell them his own way after the bodies were taken away, when the Simpsons would then help him through the difficult days ahead.

Except no such thing would happen and when they were gone after dozens of photographs, bagging evidence and more family details peppered with fiction, Brandon sat on his bed without a single tear dampening his cheeks marvelling at how easily he had gotten away with killing the man. Albeit, in his mind, justifiably.

He didn't care about Bette Michaels or the Simpsons he'd never met. They could hear about the horrific domestic tragedy on the inflated late news and wouldn't care. Besides, he had no idea where they lived.

More importantly his mother had lived from paycheque to paycheque with not a penny in the bank, the man was as useless as teats on a bull, no insurance was coming his way, and the house was far from being paid for. All Brandon had was the several hundred in his bank account and the clothes in his closet, hardly enough to get by on till school was over, which was the other problem, the real dilemma: School. They knew his age, which wasn't good. But much worse was that for the coming six months they would all point fingers and gawk; issues he quickly resolved.

He woke the next morning propped against the wall by his pillow as though the night before had been a surreal dream sequence, except for his mother's blood in the kitchen where he sat on the counter drinking a glass of milk, and the man's brown blood staining much of the seat in the living room with a .22 calibre bullet hole in it where Brandon leaned against the doorway feeling he had done something good.

When he was dressed for the first day of a new life he rummaged through his mother's purse, taking the few bills. He went to the bank withdrawing his small fortune, and the drugstore for his pay, sadly explaining that he'd be living with his grandparents across town. Then leaving with heartfelt sympathies he bought a cheap watch and a backpack that he stuffed with clothes he'd recently bought, the cash and his mid-term report card, leaving the house unlocked and Savannah far behind for good.

At the bus station he had no clue whatsoever. He'd never seen such a place with all the hustle and bustle. He'd never been anywhere, so he didn't know, believing anyplace north would be a huge mistake. Like Chicago or New York that were piled high with icy cold snow half the year, where a Georgia country boy would surely stick out worse than a sore thumb and likely not endure very long.

At least in the South he knew the way folks were; he would fit in better. The weather was always more pleasant and the beaches would be a far better place for sleeping under the stars whenever his money might run low until he could find work and settle down.

Above all he wanted out, the quicker the better, standing in front of the Destination screen at 12:05. Miami would depart at half-past the hour, New Orleans at quarter-past that would get him into The Big Easy late New Year's Eve morning via Montgomery, his youthful rationale being that, given his limited savings, big and easy sounded more inviting than some magic city despite the extra 100 miles and forty-five dollars.

*

He ordered beans and franks with a slice of bread for dipping and a Coke for dinner within minutes of arriving in Montgomery. His first meal of the day, spending the next few hours sitting on the tiled floor in a corner of the station until his eyes shut out other indigent travellers who couldn't afford proper rooms.

At 6:00 he was one of many in the men's room splashing their stubbled faces, rubbing them dry with coarse paper towels, coughing and hawking into perpetually spotted and sticky sinks.
Others were behind closed doors sitting in comfort, effecting the common noises of their class while others drained themselves with long sighs into urine-puddled urinals with their feet spread wide apart while gazing at the ceiling as though in prayer or fearing that something might come loose and fall.

On the quarter-hour he was in the diner sitting at the counter on a vinyl stool hunched over his plate wolfing down the Big Man's special for a mere 12.99, plus the tip he was again blindly remiss about since he'd never eaten in a diner, let alone a fancy place; not appreciating the sad correlation between that particular inexperience and the privation of his mother's love.

He hadn't yet begun his steep learning curve that would kick in on overdrive within hours and come from the street well before any further formal education, opposites that together would in the not very distant future lure him into a world he could not have previously imagined and a life he would one day casually embrace as his destiny.

At 7:00 AM he boarded the New Orleans-bound bus, thankful he commandeered the window seat first, spending the next five hours with his forehead pressed against the glass.

He was intrigued and excited. He was free and on his own, his mother creeping into his thoughts for the first time in thirty-six hours. He'd been too busy, too enthralled by all he was seeing and doing to remember or mourn her; the way she was always too busy or too drunk to care anything about him. But she was right, really, when he was fourteen, the day she made very clear what was.

"Yeah, mom. We finally got free of him, you and me. And we will never go back."

With those caustic words, his warm breath fogging the window, Brandon Michaels coughed a jaundiced laugh, putting his past exactly where it rightfully belonged.

13

The forever disadvantaged, the impoverished and the beggarly, recognize their own kind.

They recognize how they got where they are and, with no small degree of resentment, they inevitably blame others for their woes and their misery. In particular ruined young women who as teenagers run from lovingly strict parents and comfortable middle-class homes, their comfy bedrooms and their dolls, into a fanciful better life on the street, somehow seeing in their myopic juvenile minds that begging for loose change and sleeping wherever with whomever is way better than living another day of their oppressive and smothered existences. There joined on the crowded curb by less privileged girls breaking away from the hopelessness and hardship of the ghetto, who truly do not see any other escape, any better future than the street.

The critical difference being that those pitiable young girls are a far different breed, often abused and already streetwise with nothing to lose or give up; the two unwittingly bringing with them to the street and their respective corners their disparate social baggage.

Enter the first guy who sees her and waits for her because, if not him, someone else as smooth and as practiced will find her and tell her all the right things, all the same things: She is so young and like really fucking beautiful. Yeah, no shit her parents are stupid and abusive and like really fucking blind. School is bullshit; he knows, cause he's like doing really fucking good on his own without it. He don't need that shit cause he's got the smarts. He knows what is. Like he even has his own place, shacked up with friends and life is like really fucking good. But, hey, listen. Does she have like a place to stay, or what?

No, she doesn't, taking his hand. They both do, the abused and the pouty. In fact they all do cause he cares about them. He wants to take care of them.

Thing is, middle-class boys, they're different; they aren't at all like their naïve little sisters, lost and vulnerable. Not them. They're cool, hanging out with guys from the other side, guys who know a shitload more about life than they do. Until the night they get the crap kicked out of them, or get busted cause they don't know shit, or take one snort too many ending up face down in a ditch or in some morgue. And no one cares.

Or too late they cry out for their mommies. They want to come home. Please! They're sorry. They want their spoiled life back, they want the keys to dad's Beamer and, like, everything. The thing is, mommy's pissed. She's had all she can take. She's done with him; she's fed up with all his bullshit.

"You dropped out, living on the street, doing God knows what for one year, for two years. Now it's too late. You cannot go back, you cannot ever go back. And, what's worse, you're the weakest of the lost litter, an endangered species surviving the only way you can, degrading into the lowest of your breed until one day you're found dead in some alley. Sorry, but we simply cannot love you anymore. We don't want you anymore. We're moving on without you."

Which isn't at all the same for the poor kids, the ghetto kids, the street-smart kids. Cause I ain't got no otha option yo. Cause, know what? The old man? He a drunk mutherfucka and the bitch wife, she ain't no betta. That what is yo. Ain't no way I gonna be the way they is yo. Cause me, I got me some real good shit goin on yo.

114

*

Enter Cody Jones sitting and patiently waiting at the New Orleans bus station, watching. Because he knows. He knows that whether they're spoiled brats from upper suburbia or ghetto runaways, New Year's is prime time for fresh recruits: spoon-fed deserters and those who, since birth, have no possible chance in life.

Every bit as promising as Thanksgiving and Christmas because those are wonderful times of year, times of rejoicing and loving thy neighbour. Except for the poor who can't afford a turkey dinner or putting gifts under the tree. Except for kids whose middle-class parents confuse over-the-top gifts with love and caring, clasping their hands together in prayer at the table as dad self-absolves for doing the neighbour's wife and mom warmly recalls a year of special 'girls' nights' that he actually believes were all about shopping. All the while believing the kids don't know.

Well, they do know.

Then comes New Year's, a festive time for inviting in neighbours and wives, light-hearted resolutions and furtive side glances for one demographic and the grim spectre of scarcity and privation heralding another long and miserable year for the other. When the neglected and never-wanted children of both find themselves lost and alone in the nation's bus stations and streets and into the arms of the nation's Cody Joneses.

*

Bus stations nation-wide are invariably found at the intersections of Indigence and Commerce, and New Orleans is no exception.

Precisely on schedule the Greyhound coach pulled into the Loyola Street station that Brandon did not understand was on the undesirable side of Canal, the city's main business corridor, and dangerously situated north of Rampart where honest and decent folks wisely feared to tread.

Neither did he realize that he shouldn't be the last one stepping from a bus in a strange city whose cops are very often the bad guys, looking as though he's lost and can't find his mommy, which was somewhat incongruous given his tall and straight stature.

Cody Jones couldn't miss him through the windowed wall, thinking something wasn't right with the guy, following his path through the doors and onto the street where the guy's head pivoted from left to right several times personifying the quintessential runaway. The question was, from what?

CJ was a self-styled entrepreneur. He did not have a formal education; nor was he a member in good standing of any business association or possess a formal collection of accomplishments. In fact his one real accomplishment was anonymity. Unless you were well-placed, filthy rich and in need of his discreet services, you wouldn't know him.

He was continually on the lookout for new acquisitions that would ensure his clients coming back because careers at Nightlife, as most knew him, were by their nature short-lived, save certain rare exceptions, keeping his nose on his face and out of all business that was not his.

There were established parameters, of course. His ladies were all top-of-the-scale desirable, college educated with flourishing daytime careers who shared the heavy burden of college debt as much as they did the excitement and intrigue of being the city's most elite ladies of the night.

Until things would invariably change, until dating and marriage and babies somehow seemed more glamorous through the hue of rose-coloured glasses, though the stream of willing and eager college grads never ran dry.

However certain other job descriptions required a lesser criteria, for which reason he would be there waiting and watching those special times of year when the most deserving of families would surely be ripped asunder by neglect and deep hurt, real or imagined.

He was thirty. He wore signature black suits, white button-down shirts and polished black boots. He never wore jewellery, excepting a Submariner Rolex. His wavy black hair was neither long nor short with never an errant strand, his caramel skin always smooth and clean; his dark eyes always crystal clear and searching. He didn't do hard booze, smoke or do drugs; he didn't carry a weapon or speak that AAVE shit or confuse his topnotch working girls with his uptown lady friends. All that was purely business, not who he was or had become.

From anyone's casual perspective he was a young and respectable New Orleans businessman who faithfully watched CNN and the morning anchors, copying their styles and mimicking their eloquence.

He stood behind the guy shaking his head, thinking Hicksville, Alabama or someplace not far removed. The guy hadn't bothered checking his back in a town swarming with pickpockets and muggers. Still, he could fit the bill, CJ thinking he might be of some use once dressed-up and put straight: moulded to do whatever. Useable and disposable. And if not, no big deal. The stream of lost and wandering souls into the city was endless.

"You, there…white boy. You waiting on someone? A girlfriend, a boyfriend?"

Brandon Michaels swung around, staring at the black guy several feet behind him.

"Huh?"

"I'm guessing somewhere like Shitsville, Alabama." CJ took a step closer, closing the gap between them. "You coming here from Shitsville, white boy?" As though he didn't know by the beige windbreaker and yellow shirt, the brown Dockers and brown laced shoes over yellow socks.

"No, sir. I'm from Savannah. That's a place in Georgia."

Bright kid. "Somebody meeting you?"

"No, sir. I'm here on my own…looking for work. You know, after I get myself settled in at a hotel or something."

"Is that a fact? Looking for work at New Year's? Well good luck with that, kid, and the hotel. How old are you?"

"Nineteen."

"Nineteen. Well now that's a pure lie." Another step closer, CJ sizing up the runaway. "You have clearly made one very huge error in judgement, kid. Cause no one in this town wants you. You're not a day past seventeen and whatever you have in that backpack will not be yours within ten minutes of you and me going our separate ways. Including whatever money you stole from your mama before running." CJ held out a hand. "Cody Jones…Now let's you and me get real about this lamentable situation of yours. You are a runner and I'm thinking there's not enough in that bag of yours for one night, let alone a week or more."

"Okay, I'm sixteen. So what? I'm practically seventeen and I'm not going back. Not ever."

CJ was wholly aware of that, taking back his hand. "Then the best you can do, kid, is find yourself a street corner that isn't someone else's and hope you're still alive in a week. Cause this is New Orleans and things here will not turn out well for you."

"You a cop or something?"

"I'm a businessman who sees an opportunity, when others would see an angry boy running from his mama and send you home. Unless you're already dead. Unless you listen up and start being smart real fast…kid."

"Meaning what? You're giving me a job, or what?"

"I'm buying you lunch. That is, if you're interested in hearing my offer. If not, go find that street corner." He waited while Brandon's head pivoted once, twice. "So, you hungry? You interested in hearing my offer, kid?"

"Yeah, I'm hungry. And, yeah, I'm interested. Because I'm here and I'm not going back."

Brandon Michaels had never seen a Jaguar, let alone sit in one, CJ pulling the luxury ride to the curb in front of a diner several minutes later. Somehow he didn't believe the kid was ready for a real restaurant, curious whether he could actually use a knife and fork, fully expecting the Georgia boy would stuff his napkin into his yellow shirt collar and slurp from the plate.

The kid needed grooming, no question, CJ recognizing a very faint flicker of promise in him.

Cody Jones operated differently from other dealers and certainly wasn't a street-corner pimp. He was a provider of high-end services, a sort of personal concierge catering to a privileged clientele. He didn't sell cut drugs on the street, supplying desperate addicts, or put his high-end girls on dimly lit corners serving up ten-dollar BJs in micro skirts and sheer blouses through car windows.

His weed and coke clients were regulars with standing orders delivered weekly, high-level businessmen and women who understood the value of discretion. As well, those same clients, their referred out-of-town guests and others requiring attention of a more intimate nature, were regularly entertained by his ladies in their homes at ten C-notes a pop for the night.

Life was good with a 60/40 split and simple rules: No drugs, period; no hard booze weekdays on or off the job; a five-client cap each week and regular gym time; stay clean and don't ever get personal or curious. Above all, do not disappoint. His ladies were young and attractive, eager and expert in their unique craft, one in particular when she wasn't teaching at Tulane, living in well-appointed luxury condos owned by Cody in separate high-rises across town for the client's peace of mind and the lady's increased anonymity.

He knew people and, if he didn't know you, given that you mattered at all, he knew someone who did. He collected favours, never putting himself in similar debt, quite certain the kid would work out.

Brandon Michaels listened intently, more eager with each smooth word.

"That's it, kid. You make the deliveries when and where you're told, mostly small packages, and each morning you'll bring me envelopes from the ladies in a way that will not disturb them."

"What do I get, you know, for money?"

"Two grand each month, upfront starting now, an apartment and a few suits. Very definitely a few suits." Cody waved a hand across the space between them. "This country cousin vogue does not work for me. So one of my ladies will take you shopping; she'll also teach you some proper manners cause you're a little rough around the edges. You good with all that?"

Hell yes, he was good with all that. "What about tonight? Do I crash with you somewhere?"

Cody snorted. "No. I'll put you up in a hotel and not a five-star, where you'll stay put till the second. Let's not get too spoiled too quick. But hear this, kid. You stick around, you don't in any way mess this up, and your life will be good…very good."

14

Brandon Michaels spent New Year's Eve alone in a fourth-floor room counting and recounting his two grand.

He'd hit pay dirt big time, ordering room-service pizza for dinner the way CJ had explained in detail including the requisite gratuity. He lay on the bed flipping channels, not believing his incredible good fortune until he came across something called Pay-Per-View, quickly deciding he would spend the rest of his evening sitting at the foot of the bed, mesmerized by Linda Lovely and Delectable Deena until his glazed eyes and boggled mind betrayed him and he fell backward into a deep sleep.

On the first he woke late, throwing the clothes he was wearing into the garbage per his instructions and showered. He went for breakfast to the hotel's adjoining flapjack joint, staying inside the way he was told.

From the menu he ordered the daily special: two eggs, two strips of bacon, two sausages, two French toast slices, two buttermilk pancakes, a large juice and milk; surprising the waitress when he was done with an order of sweet strawberry cream crêpes. In the smoke shop off the lobby he bought magazines and books about the The Big Easy, spending the rest of his day reading in his room and flipping channels, ordering in lunch and supper before sharing his late-night hours with more breathtaking girls like Linda and Deena

Late morning on the second Cody Jones arrived unannounced with a drop-dead gorgeous young woman Brandon would never know anything about apart from her name, an address that might not be hers, and a box number. She was one of CJ's girls, one of his best about five-ten in low-heeled boots and twenty-seven. She was a full professor at Tulane, happily unattached with no student debt and legs to her neck that she crowned with an enticingly short leather skirt, the swell of her smooth and delightful breasts framed with silk lapels and fur-lined cardigan.

He believed she must be the most beautiful woman in the entire world, as magnificent naked as the girls on the television. She was Blaire; she was perfect with a voice that would melt butter and eyes—

"Okay, kid. Eyes back in the head. Blaire is your shadow this week. That means your handler. You do what she says. You do everything she says. You got that? You understand that?"

He nodded, feeling stupid or clumsy. Or something. He hadn't ever in his entire life seen such a sensational girl—woman. Now he'd be spending the week with her. "Yes, sir. I do."

"She has free rein. You will not argue, talk back, or give her grief. You got that?"

He nodded again. "Yes, sir."

"Good." CJ scanned the room. "Sweetheart, let's upgrade this white boy…somewhat. Nothing that'll spoil him but somewhere in the Quarter. And next time I see him I want him dressed and acting like he might possibly belong with us, not like some country cousin who's never seen a city girl."

"You won't recognize him, CJ. Promise. And we'll get along just fine. Won't we, Braxton?"

"Yes, ma'am, we will. But…"

"Good. I'll be in the lobby." She paused, pointing at the backpack by the unmade double bed. "Don't bother with any of that. Just take your money because you will not come back here and whatever is in that is no longer you."

Then smiling at her boss she strode toward the door and walked out, fully aware the Georgia boy was in love.

"Wow. She's wonderful."

"Yes, she is. And a whole lot smarter than you will ever be. Meaning you will listen and learn from everything she tells you. Everything. You got that?"

"Yeah, I got that. But she called me Braxton. Who's Braxton?"

"You are. Or you very soon will be. Cause I'm thinking you're not running away, you're running from and I do not want or need some Brandon Michaels raining grief down upon me. Also, you being sixteen is a big problem. Thing is, when that girl is finished with you, you will look every bit of nineteen." He put up a hand. "I believe you'll work out, kid. I have a good feeling. Either way, by Friday you will be Braxton Miles, nineteen from Virginia. That's what your birth certificate will show. You graduated high school with a GPA that'll get you into most universities whenever, if ever. You will have a driver's permit which you will not use until I say you can and, with that particular ID, you will not drink until I say you can. You will also have a passport once we've got that pretty Virginia mug shot." He grinned. "On the downside your new parents are dead. Died some years ago. Sorry about that."

"And me, my name? What happens to me, who I am?"

"You got anything in this room that proves who you are, anything at all?"

"A report card. You know, from school."

"Get rid of it, kid. That and anything else. Cause, wherever you come from, you have done some very bad shit that I will not step into and for that you are for evermore Mr. Braxton Miles."

Brandon stared past the window into the parking lot. "There's no shit anywhere, sir. The man I lived with at home with my mom, he killed her a few nights back. So, you know, I killed him. Sort of in a daze; know what I mean?" No reply. "But there isn't any worry. None. Because I did everything right before I called the cops. They believe he killed himself." He turned, facing CJ. "When they left I didn't hang around."

Cody Jones showed no surprise, studying the kid. "Good. That's good. What you did, that took real guts. Tells me I was right about you. And let me assure you that Brandon Michaels is dead and gone forever. He will never again resurface to rain grief down upon Braxton Miles or me. But understand something here, kid. All this, the newly born Braxton Miles and his newly acquired good fortune, this all comes at a price and I am not talking two grand a month. That's salary, living expenses. I'm talking about favours. This here, what we're doing, is all about owing a favour. You got that? You understand that?"

He didn't really, but he didn't see that he had much choice in the matter. "Yes, sir. I know about favours."

Though what mattered more was that he was free. He would finally wear nice clothes, earn good money, live in a nice place on his own and he was only—nineteen. He snorted, reaching for the backpack, grinning at his saviour. How cool was that?

When CJ left him with a simple "You treat that young lady kindly," the new Braxton Miles stuffed the Dockers he was wearing with the two grand and Brandon Michaels' Georgia savings. He tore the high school mid-term report into tiny pieces, flushing the last vestige of his past without a glimmer of regret and hurried to spend his day with Blaire

*

Blaire Fortune was a class act, with not the least intention of lunching with a goofy six-foot kid in a chequered short-sleeve shirt and windbreaker that by day's end would hang in a thrift store. Wouldn't happen. Instead she drove him to Jackson Square where he discovered Louisiana's must-do Po' Boys, beignets and napkins, eating on a park bench and watching the girls go by.

She opted for an ice tea, looking several steps above her companion.

By the same token, dressing Braxton in expensive woollen suits and 100-dollar shirts was a ridiculous notion. That wouldn't happen either. So while he was chewing down the food stuffed in his cheeks she studied him, deciding on the high side of mid-range at the Lakeside Mall, leaving the menswear boutique several hours later with CJ owing her a few thousand on her American Express.

Filling the trunk of her Mercedes with the several bags, she took him next for a hair styling and manicure at an exclusive salon for men, dropping another hundred plus forty for his and her gratuities. She booked Mr. Miles into the elegant Maison Dupuy in the Quarter because she knew CJ wouldn't mind. He was a good guy, a good boss who treated his people right. And Braxton was people, or soon would be.

With him in his room she showed Braxton how a gentleman hangs his shirts and his suits, how he folds his ties and his personal items and rolls his socks, educating him as she worked that gentlemen do not wear anything intimate twice and that suits, with their ties and their pocket hankies, must always be alternated and as widely separated as possible. And that, distinguishing oneself from the pedestrian devotees of flip-flops and sneakers, a gentleman's shoes must always gleam softly.

She snapped her fingers, an instant later tossing his watch into the garbage, telling him that fashion faux-pas would be corrected the next morning, taking him for a casual dinner in the hotel's Bistreaux dressed as he was in a navy blue suit, a salmon-coloured shirt with French cuffs linked with sapphire studs, a salmon-coloured silk hanky and oxblood loafers. Despite which, the metamorphosis from backwoods to urbanity was far from complete, Blaire thanking the waiter as he draped the linen napkin across her lap.

Ladies were alway seated first. Why? Because gentlemen assisted them into their seats, on occasion yielding to an attentive server, though never the waitress. Ladies always ordered first, uninhibited by the gentleman's selection or the condition of his wallet; whereas, taking the lady's tastes into account, the gentleman would naturally select the appropriate wine. And so went the etiquette lecture.

"Which in your case, Braxton, is soda water."

"Yes, ma'am. I'm really curious, though. You know, why me? Why all this, the fancy clothes and you? Me being here with you? No one ever showed me this much kindness. Not ever in my life."

"We are what we are, Braxton. Still, the lucky ones, like you, like me, we don't get there on our own. Now you, you'll be with him a good while. Two years, three, possibly more before he cuts you loose. Who knows?" She paused, waving away the crystal water goblet, ordering for the first and last time, prefacing her selections with a soda and lemon for monsieur and a half-bottle of the house Chardonnay for herself. "Be smart about all this, Braxton, and you will come out on top. You'll have money and street smarts; just do not disappoint him. He has high expectations and you are not here with me tonight for any other reason than he believes you will fit in. Otherwise you would be sleeping in an alley for the second night, if not in a mission with the disenfranchised, a hospital bed or cold storage."

"I know that, ma'am. I do. And thank you. You know, for all this." Braxton felt, he didn't know what—strange, nervous being with such a perfect woman who he suspected knew pretty much everything about him. "Did he do this for you, too? Did he help you this way?"

She nodded. "First off, it's Blaire. And yes, six years ago when I made a conscious decision I have never regretted. I like my life, I enjoy what I do and my greater plan is on track. I live two lives, one necessarily exclusive of the other. One by day, the other by night. Enough said. That's all you get."

"Will I ever see you after this week, Blaire?"

"Nope. Doesn't work that way. I'm your tutor, Braxton. Nothing more." She smiled at the server. "Now let's eat, starting with the small fork on the outside left and please remove your elbow from the table."

During the Romaine-Roquefort salad he learned about the soup spoon on the right, the dinner knife and fork; Blaire discreetly reminding him seconds into the third course that the filet mignon was already dead, guiding him next to the bread plate and butter knife that was intended for spreading, not hacking.

For dessert she ordered the Italian Cream Cake, this time leading by example, pleased when he took up the small fork. He was doing alright for a backwoods Georgia boy, she mused sipping her coffee.

"What now, Blaire? Can we go for a walk or something?"

"No, we cannot. You're getting a good night's sleep and remember what I said about alternating. That, what you're wearing, that is not for tomorrow. And, please, no more one-hand romance with the late-night girls. That is totally disgusting and expensive. You'll have the real thing soon enough."

At that he chuckled. "Do you think that maybe, could be I'll need a lesson?"

"No, I do not think." She signalled the waiter for the bill. "And you don't think about it either. Because that would put you very quickly in a body cast."

She processed her card, explaining the concept and mathematics of gratuities when the man was gone, Braxton surprising her when he stood first to assist the lady from her seat. He was catching on.

In the lobby he extended a hand. "Thank you, Blaire. Thank you for all this."

"You are entirely welcome. But it's CJ you're thanking, not me. And you're on your own for breakfast. I'll be here at nine sharp."

15

On the third Blaire was waiting when her protégé ambled into the lobby on time, dressed in designer jeans and boots, a turtleneck and leather jacket. Some of the backwoods veneer showing signs of peeling.

The first stop was her favourite Canal Street jeweller for a single sterling silver signet ring that would lend a much-needed air of masculine je-ne-sais-quoi, personalized with a *BM* by the time he left the store with mirrored Ray-Bans over his eyes and a stylish stainless steel watch on his wrist that didn't look like some sort of wafer device monitoring his vitals. Vitals that were way off the chart; the kid not yet fully aware that unabashedly gawking at a lady's spectacularly smooth and long legs, although possibly flattering when done discreetly, was ungallant.

After lunch they drove into the Garden District, checking an address Blaire had circled in her morning paper. The apartment was the unfurnished second floor of a duplex: ideal for an up and coming nineties something or other. Something or other because Braxton Miles wasn't at all certain what he was or where he was going, nodding dumbly when Blaire suggested a100-dollar deposit that would secure the apartment until the next day when her cousin's first paycheque would be deposited into his bank account.

When they left the property they went shopping for furniture, Braxton deferring to Blaire's superior sense of absolutely everything, though disappointed when she graciously turned down his dinner invitation. She was a tutor, not a nursemaid and certainly not a date.

The next day at Maison Dupuy she met him in the Bistreaux for lunch, pleasantly surprised at seeing a glass of Chardonnay waiting for her and the newly created Braxton Miles standing with a beaming smile as she sauntered through the doorway. She let him help with her coat and pull out her seat, thanking him with a discreet chuckle when next he draped the linen napkin across the hem of her stunning sweater dress—fairly certain the thoughtful gesture wasn't necessarily all about gallantry.

"Thank you, Braxton. All this is very thoughtful. A definite A-plus on your report card."

"I'm paying too, Blaire. This is my treat."

She suppressed that giggle behind disarming eyes. "Thank you. That's very kind, Braxton. Very gentlemanly." She signalled the waiter, not bothering with the menu, waiting until he was gone before reaching into her handbag. "I have something for you, Braxton. I met this morning with CJ."

"What?"

She sipped her wine, complimenting his exquisite taste, naturally suspecting the waiter had played some minor role. Then, framed by her place setting, she put several envelopes in front of her. "This is pretty exciting, Braxton. And oh, by the way, happy belated birthday."

"What?"

"Not what. No more whats. From now on it's excuse me." She passed him the largest of the envelopes. "This is your birth certificate...and it's legitimate. Braxton Miles was born January 01st, 1973. A document no one will ever dispute. Congratulations. Unfortunately we cannot properly toast the occasion for another two years. Because, like I told you, do not disappoint him. The others are your parents' death certificates and will. They were buried a few weeks ago in Virginia, leaving you not very much to get by on until you find yourself. Sorry about that."

Braxton snorted. "Yeah, really sad. But Blaire, no way will I disappoint him." He inhaled a deep breath. Wow, everything he promised. This is too unreal."

"Yes, very unreal, and there's more wow." She passed him a second large envelope. "Your academic record, which I must say is very impressive. It's also very fake, meaning you should start reading a few good books and don't wait too long before deciding what you should do with it. Like making it real. You're in for a good ride, Braxton, but he will cut you loose one day. It's what he does and you must be ready for that."

The third envelope was smaller. "That's your driver's permit. Your first lesson is tomorrow morning, not that you'll have a car anytime soon." She slid the fourth across the table. "This one is your SS card, your bank card, a credit card with a five K limit and a safety deposit key. Something we all have since bank accounts are sometimes somewhat of an inconvenience."

"I don't understand."

"Well, simply put, I don't need CJ. None of his girls do. We all do perfectly well on our own. It's what sets us apart. We're not with him for the money, money that is extremely good; far better than lower suburbia and stretch marks, money we couldn't possibly explain…like your twenty-four K which you will not let go to your empty teenage head. Which is why this Monday you're launching your career as a freelance executive go-boy doing messages for downtown business types and there are plenty of them. That's your income until you figure out where else you're going, which I suggest you do very soon. Do you understand me?"

*

After lunch, which the gentleman paid for with his credit card, they drove to the Lower Garden District home. He signed the lease with three months down and then she did something she wasn't at all sure about. Still she liked the kid, against her better judgement deciding he needed big-time help. She saw in his eyes a glimmer of something she recognized as intelligence. She also understood that, as much as Cody Jones was a good guy treating his people well, he was a businessman not a big brother or babysitter.

She was a professor, an exquisite example of femininity, held advanced degrees, and had 700 K evenly divided between her off-shore account and her safety deposit portfolio. She was the quintessential successful woman who didn't want marriage or kids; she wanted the company of elegant gentlemen, the special kind of intimacy that comes without real desire, long-term commitment or obsession. When they left her, whether at midnight or soon after waking, she felt whole—whole and, at week's end, a whole lot richer than spending her weekdays lecturing from a podium with a microphone and laser pointer.

Her clients weren't simply out for a quick release and ephemeral escape from whatever they lacked or regretted; they wanted youthful vitality and the fantasy of a second home, conversation that wasn't the mundanity that evolves from too many years with the same spoiled women whose lives revolved around luncheons, shopping sprees and charity benefits. They wanted the flawless body and rapt mind of a caring and attentive Blaire Fortune without knowing that, the few times she did date, which were usually on vacations, she was actually Professor Angie Wilson.

She drove him through the city's worst projects, pointing out prostitutes and the homeless, druggies and their dealers. Not one of them remotely resembling Cody Jones or Blaire Fortune. They were the diseased, the infected and the infectious, bottom feeders scarcely surviving off each other until one day they were killed or otherwise found dead on a sidewalk.

"I am none of those women, Braxton, and they will never be who I am. They'll be dead in five, ten years and I'll be going strong on my own or with CJ. By forty I'll have serious millions in the bank; I'll continue being the respectable daytime citizen I am now and will not waste a second of my life thinking of you. Because I don't believe you do understand me. That guy on the corner, the asshole who thinks he's cool all dressed up in black leather and ten pounds of gold around his neck, that's you not long after CJ cuts you loose: A junked-up pimp dealing cut shit. That's you unless you do something smart right now, before you get too full of yourself. Because twenty-four a year only sounds like big money. It is not. I made that much in Christmas gifts last month, ten times that much last year, because the daytime me is very highly regarded in her milieu and the nighttime me is the absolute best at what she does. I'm their dream girl, the one they wish they married, with pretty much the same admirers since my first night." She chuckled. "A good bit busier than my high school and college years and very definitely more rewarding." She leaned into him. "Are you getting this?"

"Yeah, you're angry with me. What I don't know is why."

"I'm not angry. I'm making a point, meaning that I am light years beyond your sad pay grade. Why? Because I'm educated and what I do on my own time is fun for me. My life is exciting, which is what I want for you. Why? Don't ask, because I don't have the faintest idea. Because after Sunday I won't know you, Braxton. In fact if I ever see you I'll walk on by because you won't be worth my time. The way that now you're probably not worth my effort. That go-boy thing you'll be doing, that'll put you one step above that cretin over there. You'll be delivering drugs to unhappy rich guys who will shut you out the moment CJ drops you. Then you'll be the one dealing cut shit on a street corner because that's all you'll know. Shit."

She put the car in drive, fifteen minutes later driving onto the grounds of the University of New Orleans where she often lectured as a guest speaker. Climbing out she let him follow, telling herself she didn't care, the ensuing tour of the grounds thick with an uneasy silence. She'd said enough and, strangely, she did feel angry walking past countless students, all of them engaged in some socio-political conversation or other, or being hit-on, holding hands or embracing a cluster of books, all of them going somewhere a whole lot better than mid-city projects.

He was clearly bedazzled, which she believed was a good thing, often glancing back over his shoulders at college girls years older than him in short skirts and sweaters or braving winter's balmy sixty degrees in cut-offs and tee-shirts.

She halted him at the Admissions building, telling him he should stay put and not be pitifully obvious gawking with wide-eyed wonder. They were girls, very smart girls who would never be interested in a high school dropout drug courier. So stop the dreaming. Won't happen.

With that off her chest she turned on her heels and disappeared into the building, coming out fifteen minutes later with yet another large envelope that she practically slammed into his chest.

"What is this?"

God, hopefully not a waste of my time. "No. Not what is this? It's 'Thank you, Blaire, for caring about me.' It's a booklet of academic programmes." She grimaced, shaking her head. "Subjects you can study here at university, given that you're accepted. There's also a copy of this year's SAT that will either boast or betray the size of your underdeveloped teenage brain. Care to hazard a guess?"

He tucked the package under arm, smirking, Blaire thinking she was about ready to smack him.

"Thank you, Blaire, for caring about me. You're like, you know, a big sister or something."

"I'm no one's sister. Besides which, like these girls you haven't stopped gawking at and stripping inside that little head, no brother of mine would ever drop out. So whether you're seventeen or twenty this time next year, you make very sure you get your ass inside one of these hallowed halls. I will help you do that, Braxton, which effectively is cheating, but once you're in you are on your own because no one here will ever care about you." She began walking away, pausing. "I'll be busy this evening having that fun I was talking about, while you have your face in that prospectus. So start making some smart choices that you will tell me about tomorrow while we're dining at Antoine's...for which you will please wear a suit and tie and be ready at seven."

He rolled his eyes. "Okay, mom."

*

Saturday Braxton checked out at 10:00, met on time by his instructor who opened the trunk with a relaxed New Orleans flair, watching and waiting as his student tossed in several suitcases and bags.

The morning was Braxton's first time ever behind a steering wheel and if he was expecting accolades and praises for a job well done, he didn't show his disappointment. Possibly because he was far more eager for his evening with Blaire and more of her subliminal tutoring.

Braxton ended his hour of "do this, do that—turn right, turn left" at the Garden District apartment, the instructor suggesting as his student was placing his worldly possessions on the sidewalk that an additional five or six hours would be a wise investment. They agreed on the following Saturday, same time. Braxton had more on his mind than a permit he wouldn't use anytime soon, feeling as though he was breaking and entering as he stepped into the vacant space with its gleaming floors and bright picture windows looking out onto a wide avenue made private with a wall of towering and gnarled decades-old live oaks.

He wasn't sure what he felt, except that he was not sixteen anymore.

An hour later his bedroom, living room and complete kitchen were delivered, telling the men wherever. He didn't care. He'd never had a real bedroom or living room, a bathroom of his own and things in the kitchen he had no idea about, thinking everything was kind of okay where it was.

Besides, that's why he had Blaire; his Blaire would help him. She would come over the next day and take him for groceries. She would stay for lunch and perhaps supper because she *would* see him again, lots of times because she liked him and he positively liked her. What she did with those other guys didn't matter. He liked her and why would CJ care?

She was wonderful. That's why she was angry with him. Because she was wonderful and she liked him.

He forgot his new surroundings, digging into a suitcase for the prospectus he'd perused the night before, his introspection and self-doubt frequently interrupted with vivid images of Blaire.

She was smart and she was sexy. Whatever she did during the day, at night she was with men having sex and making tons of money for herself. And she was happy; she was always smiling except at the school when she was a little pissed with him.

He wasn't sure what he could do, but he knew what he could not do, putting Xs through the subjects he would fail, putting more Xs through what would very soon disappoint Blaire and not leaving himself many choices. He didn't care about helping people, the way no one ever helped him. He hated arithmetic and math and sitting in a classroom, not understanding why anyone would study for years toward a boring nine-to-five job like teaching or working in an office for the rest of their lives. That was not who he was; he wanted to be like Blaire, doing what would always make him happy and rich—really rich.

He determined that he would ask her, because she would know best. He had an idea, thinking that by the time he was twenty-something, if he was smart enough, he would have a degree like Blaire, tons of money from working with CJ, and he could meet people. If he was right.

*

Blaire arrived promptly at 7:00, conceding as her charge swaggered toward the Mercedes that his transition from backwoods Georgia into the preliminary stages of New Orleans respectability was taking shape. Slowly, but perceptibly.

En route to the restaurant she gave him a refresher, coaching him on what he should and should not do. She was talking; he was keeping his eyes from wandering, deciding he could as easily imagine what he couldn't see of her as he was listening and learning. Now that he had a clue.

Stepping from the car, Blaire gave her hand to the valet. Braxton stepped out on his own, waiting for his date cum mom cum tutor cum wet dream fantasy on the curb, smiling as the lady in a short and silky skater dress and wrap took his arm. He opened the door, stepping back. And once inside he took her shawl, draping the woollen square over his arm. At the lectern they were the Miles party of two and, at their table, he remained standing while the host assisted the young lady with her seat.

When the man was gone, noting the lady's choice of wine and the gentleman's preference for soda water, Braxton Miles continued doing his best.

"You're very pretty this evening, Blaire. Really, you know... wow."

She thought for a moment. "Only this evening, Braxton?"

Shit, no! "No. Every time I see you. Every time anyone sees you. You're, you know, really fabulous."

"Thank you. I was teasing you. So how's your new place?"

"It's nice, thank you. I've never lived in a nice home."

"Good. And you're doing very well this evening. One thing though, a gentleman always compliments a lady's outfit. That particular neglect is a major breach of good manners." She put up a delicate hand. "You're forgiven this one time." She waited as the waiter served the wine and soda, suggesting he would give them a few moments. "Now what about your academic future, any firm ideas?"

"A lot of that stuff isn't for me, Blaire. Like chemistry and math, engineering, and all that social and health stuff. I'm not interested in that. I was thinking, you know, about you. About what you do at night with those guys for all that money."

She cut him off. "Tread lightly, kid. You're one punch in the face away from calling me something I am not. I do what I do because it's me. That I get paid for having a good time is a bonus and I would really hate putting you on your hillbilly ass in the middle of this restaurant. Because I can, and I will. Meaning you be real careful."

"No. That's not what I meant. I would never hurt you. I mean, I was thinking…about perhaps languages, about learning languages. That way I could be like you. You know, sophisticated. I could have a good job somewhere, like a travel agent or something, and do my own thing at night like you. I could never work in a place like this, or in any office. I want what you have."

"Let me get this straight. You want to study languages, by some miracle evolving into some semblance of a gentleman and make being a male escort your life's greatest accomplishment. Is that about right?"

"Not now or tomorrow. I mean when I'm finished, when I know things like you."

What she was hearing was too much. She sipped her wine, raising her open palm again at seeing the waiter coming toward them. Once she ordered, letting the kid manage on his own, she sat studying him while sipping more wine.

He was right, of course, in his own artless fashion.

After a few years with CJ he could never work in an office, apart from declaring on his otherwise blank CV that throughout college he couriered drugs. He would never be a cop or a doctor or build bridges. Wherever he truly came from, whatever the reason he ran, whatever had caused his world to implode, the kid had secrets, big secrets that would no doubt ostracize him from the mainstream. And working for Cody Jones was merely the beginning, an apprenticeship toward bigger and better things. Just not anything very legal or very moral.

She swirled her wine, putting down the crystal goblet. He *was* right, which was possibly partly her fault, the very way she wouldn't survive teaching without her nighttime distractions. The fact was, given his current and slanted reality that would endure until CJ would set him free, the one way higher education would serve any real purpose in his life was possibly making him smarter and more prepared for that life on the fringe.

"Which languages?"

He shrugged. "I don't know. I was kind of hoping you would tell me."

"Well that's a no-brainer. French and Spanish because they're romance languages that will instill culture and tradition and get you places." She chuckled. "Perhaps even help mould you into a quintessential inamorato if that's where your head is."

"How do you know that?"

"Because I do."

"Because of your day job. Are you a teacher or something?"

"The daytime me is not your business. Nothing about me is your business." Blaire put up her hand, waiting as their crawfish soup and gumbo were served and the waiter refreshed her wine. "Did you bring the SAT?"

He reached into his jacket, passing her the folded document that she slipped into her handbag. "I did the best I could for you, Blaire. Almost five hours."

She shook her head. "That's nowhere near good enough because they'll give you three hours-forty minutes. That's it. And they will not care." She reached for her spoon. "What?"

"Do you know what I did, why I ran away? Did he tell you?"

"He did not. Nor do I have any such desire. That he brought you in is good enough for me."

Her trout pecanière sprinkled with roasted pecans and drizzled with Creole meunière sauce was exceptional; his barbecued spareribs, he discovered, was a regrettable choice. Her pots de crème served chilled in hand-painted porcelain cups melted in her mouth; his ball of frozen yogurt sprinkled with sugared strawberries and drizzled with wine sauce a much wiser decision on his part. Then too soon for Braxton dinner was over and he was standing by her side waiting to drape her shawl over her shoulders.

The night air was pleasantly cool and calm for January, Blaire suggesting an evening stroll along Bourbon peering into storefronts, Braxton understanding as they walked what streets he must never cross, where he did not belong. Did he understand? Yes he did, mom. Did he also now understand that sauce-laden ribs were intended for children and not an aspiring gentleman? Yes mom, he did. The wannabe gentleman thrilled that mom's arm was entwined with his. Like how cool was that? Then strolling along Royal they visited art galleries and a book store he could never have imagined before Blaire drove him home.

Climbing onto the curb he paused for a moment, getting things straight in his head before tapping on her window. Peering in, seeing her sitting there waiting, his head was a teenage testosterone junkyard. He was way out of her league. She was the most beautiful woman in the entire world.

"Thank you, Blaire. You know, for everything. You were more than pretty tonight, you were   really hot and your dress is very nice. I won't ever make that mistake again."

"Well thank you, Braxton." And thank you for not too obviously ogling my legs. Now go inside. "I'll see you tomorrow…noonish."

She didn't add and then we'll be done. Permanently, kid.

16

At home alone for what remained of her Saturday evening, Blaire Fortune changed into a silk slip and bootie slippers. She poured a Courvoisier into a crystal snifter, warming the amber liquid between her hands as she sat reviewing and grading the Scholastic Assessment Test.

An hour later she needed another nightcap, padding into her dining room for a refill, amazed by the unbiased score she'd given him that was way beyond her expectation. The kid did have a brain. One clearly not accustomed to exertion or exercise and in dire need of attention before atrophying from neglect, but worth the effort.

He would never be welcomed into the aristocratic Mensa circle, that was a given. Yet he was certainly college material and therein lay a very unfortunate twofold problem: Her and Braxton himself. She could not and she would not help him beyond the next day. CJ had given her until the coming Monday to shape him into less of a Georgia backwoods Neanderthal, as well as compensating her for lost evenings, which by some insane miracle she had managed.

Lying in bed curled into her pillow she couldn't help thinking about him, shaking her head, pursing her lips. Absolutely amazing. Both his score and that, with a higher education that would open countless intriguing doors, his singular ambition was to become an escort. A teenage virgin dream: Endless pussy. Except in his case with women decades older and desperate. Not at all the same as entertaining privileged gentlemen after a thankless day as Angie

Wilson lecturing dozens or hundreds of Psych undergrads far more concerned about getting laid than the complexities of the human condition. Which, in fact, was the chronic undergraduate condition.

She snorted a puff of air wanting to smile, but she couldn't. He was a kid with a ridiculous dream and a brain on the verge of collapse. The most she could hope for, and soon forget, was that his ambitions would grow in accordance with his mind. Though, in his favour, he would be the youngest undergrad at UNO and that was exceptional. Exceptional, contrived, and no one would ever care. Pay the tuition, go into debt, excel or fail, and no one would care. Such was university; such was life and she didn't trust him to understand or deal with that.

Either way, the following afternoon she would turn her back on him and walk away. She had no choice.

*

Sunday morning Blaire Fortune lingered in her soaker, most of her flawless and smooth five feet and nine inches submerged under a playful cloud of scented white foam, formulating a plan. She wasn't tired despite at most having slept a few minutes each hour since midnight, which she deservedly blamed on the kid from Georgia.

Towelling herself dry, she sat at her vanity styling her lustrous and long auburn tresses over one shoulder. She dressed in black tights, a short rust-coloured suede skirt with a zippered front and a thick cable-knit beige sweater, adding tan suede mid-calf boots to the mix. Satisfied with the chic result she went into her pantry, scrunching her face into a frustrated mask and cursing, going instead into the dining room for an unusually early hit of over-the-top expensive Rémy Martin.

Why?

"Really? You're asking me why? Because a hopelessly dumb-ass Georgia hillbilly won't stand a snowball's chance without me. That's why!" She stamped her foot, groaning. "Do you have a really big issue with that?"

The facsimile of a lovely and distraught young woman in her eighteenth-floor picture window overlooking the city had no opinion, simply scowling back at Blaire, which somehow made her even angrier. She needed someone's intervention, someone to tell her she was being irrational, stupid, that he was not her business. Not worth her time or her worry. Fuck! She was not his big sister, not remotely his friend. She was his short-term tutor making him ready for a job that would likely lead him into the darkest places where he did not belong. Shit! Where he would never belong.

She gulped back the cognac, coughing a spray of expensive booze into the air and pressing a hand to her chest, feeling a single tear moisten her eyes as she stared at her phone. Gulping air she reached for the receiver, certain he would understand. Hoping. He was a decent man, understanding and kind. He cared about his people. He would understand.

She dialled the unlisted number, her heart pounding more rapidly with each timeless second.

Then: "Good morning, Angie. I trust all is well with Blaire and our mutual acquaintance."

"No, Cody. I don't believe anything is well. Which is why I really need you to listen."

*

Blaire left her one-woman Shangri-La bordello on a mission, arriving hours later at Braxton's feeling not the slightest guilt for being late or for grimacing at the three slices of cold pizza and Coke he had waiting for her. She didn't think so. Instead she reached into her handbag for the '82 Paulliac and corkscrew, asking if he had clean glasses.

He did, practically bolting into the kitchen.

"This is not happening. You understand that, junior?" She passed him a half-full tumbler. "And please do not gulp that. We sip, we appreciate, we savour. We do not ever slurp or make noises."

Braxton sipped the wine, smiling. He liked it. She didn't care and he wasn't getting anymore.

"Your score was good and you are going to college because I will help you get there. That's the easy part. The hard part is graduating with a more developed brain, for which reason you've got me on your back until April when you ace the real test. What you will not do is waste my time. Do you understand?"

She gave him the requisite dictionaries she'd bought and the first-year textbooks that would cover the SAT, raising her tumbler in a toast, telling him she expected incremental results until his D-Day that would come all too soon. It did not mean seeing her every day or evening, but once each month on her days off with a single agenda that did not mean they were becoming friends.

That was the agreement, that's what CJ would allow. Not one day more. He would also get a club membership and work on conditioning his body in keeping with his new age. No college girl would want—him. Someone's unfortunate country cousin. And for pity's sake get a burn on.

A girlish giggle erupted without warning, a delicate hand and fluttering fingers waving the air between them. "Besides which, junior, those pampered and spoiled housewives twice your age, and they'll be the young ones, pay big bucks for romance book-cover six-pack physiques." She jabbed the air. "Not this. So you've got a busy few months coming your way."

"I'm ready for all that, Blaire. I won't disappoint you or CJ."

"Think so?" He shook his head yes; she stared at an infatuated—. She didn't know, which didn't matter. What did matter was distancing herself, which was not her decision. "Yeah well, think again, Einstein. You're taking a quantum leap years too soon into something you don't know squat about. The good thing is, CJ has an exclusive clientele. No street vermin, no dirty cops, which doesn't mean you're not doing something illegal. Because you are."

"For a while, maybe. Till I'm smart like you. You know, edu-cated. Because I've got really big plans."

Yeah, screwing old ladies. She let that one go; she didn't care about his mercurial fantasies. She was more concerned about the month of April when she would tell CJ she hadn't wasted her time, that Braxton Miles could well become another resource worth keeping and shaping. The wide-eyed kid sipping expensive French wine would understand soon enough that all he had was a grand and change, a heretofore unchallenged mind filled with questions and awe, and the considerably more advanced intellect of Professor Angie Wilson surreptitiously on loan until Easter when she would see and think the last of him.

That's precisely what she was, a loan who was living a perfect-ly happy and wonderful life without family or the pressures and stresses of invasive relationships, meaning she did not need or want an adopted baby brother-drug courier.

Together they spent the afternoon organizing the apartment while Blaire dictated a list of missing essentials, making the point that girlie magazines was not one of them. She inspected his clos-ets and drawers while dictating a grocery list and requisite sun-dries, delighting in her final few sips of exquisite wine in a tumbler before taking him to the supermarket where she lectured him on Groceries 101: Basic Survival. After which she left him at his door without waiting for a tap on her window, eager for a quiet evening at home.

*

Monday an anxious and excited Braxton Miles met with his boss at a Canal Street diner for a late backroom breakfast, hearing in more detail what was expected of him.

"You're looking good, kid. Blaire's done excellent work. I hardly recognized you."

"She's really nice, really special."

"That she is. She also made a heartfelt pitch about you. She believes you're worth extra time, extra effort." Cody Jones reached for his coffee. "University, good for you. That being your world, not mine. Maybe we'll work out, or not. More likely I'll drop you when we've had our time. Who knows, kid? You work out, you do good things, we'll talk."

"Thanks CJ, for everything. You know, for helping me disappear."

"Well, you work out, next year I'll kick you up a notch to thirty K. After that it's on you. You got that?" He ignored the bobbing head, sliding an envelope across the table. "Ten addresses, box numbers and keys. Monday through Friday you collect envelopes from two of these addresses by bus. Never the same two on the same day. Then you meet me or whoever wherever you're told, when we'll give you envelopes and packages for delivery by cab that same afternoon. You do whatever. UNO, wherever. Don't care. Just stay clean, get the job done on time, go home by bus, and do not ever let me hear of you messing with Blaire Fortune. That would not be a good thing, kid. And this nighttime boy-toy notion you've got swirling in that head, you hold off on that until I say so. You got all that?"

The piercing eyes weren't asking for a dashboard nod.

"Yes, sir."

*

By Friday Braxton had collected thirty K in envelopes from ten prestigious condo complexes and had been into several downtown office buildings delivering padded envelopes in exchange for smaller envelopes that he would transfer the following mornings along with the day's mailbox receipts. He had things down pat, the ladies' addresses by heart, and his "I have an urgent and personal delivery for Mr. or Ms. Whomever" perfected. The way CJ told him, the way he was never to reinvent because CJ did not need his clients experiencing panic attacks.

Yeah, he got that.

His evenings and weekends were his own: Cody Jones' concept of a normal life for his people while keeping himself and others under anyone's radar with nine-to-five weekdays and weekend dinners with mom. Something Braxton Miles would never think about or do.

Friday evening he was sitting at his kitchen table eating a burnt pizza that an hour earlier was frozen, wondering at the afternoon envelopes he would keep safe until Monday at noon or whenever, wondering if CJ was testing him, wondering which condo building was Blaire's. He'd already read a chapter from each book each night, pretty certain he understood most of it, and by the twenty-eighth he'd be finished, ready for his next test and dinner with Blaire.

He missed her. He couldn't stop thinking about her. But he got that too. She was too busy and way too sensational to think about him. He was like part of her job with CJ or something, which didn't stop him from ending his evening with Blaire playfully teasing him in his bed.

Saturday he woke determined that he would not disappoint her. He perused the Yellow Pages phoning several gyms, deciding on the closest and least expensive where he went that afternoon and Sunday because without Blaire he was alone with nothing except his books.

Which one day soon would change. He knew he was too young and too stupid for dating older women who would gladly pay him, which didn't mean he couldn't plan for the day or that the women wouldn't sometimes be younger. In a couple of years he would be twenty-one; he'd be that much smarter and Blaire would teach him everything about women. Because she couldn't be serious about never seeing him again.

17

Sunday evening he read more chapters. He crawled into bed early and gingerly, every newfound muscle aching, soon falling asleep without spending precious moments with Blaire in some quixotic utopia.

Monday he woke, showered, dressed for work, ate his second wholegrain breakfast with skim milk, waited for the 9:00 AM phone call and left for his first pick-up. At 11:30 the guy whose name he would never know arrived on cue, waving Braxton into a nondescript Buick and dropping him off three right turns later with a small package and a few padded envelopes for his PM deliveries in different cabs.

Then he went home, changing into his tracksuit for two hours of grunts and groans so that Blaire would see him differently and maybe not disappoint him. That was his week and his life until the twenty-eighth when she came by after doing a girls' lunch in the Quarter with a fellow professor.

He spent the entire morning preparing, combing his hair a dozen or more times, slapping his face with cologne; matching his socks with his cords and sweater, his belt with his loafers. In front of the bathroom mirror he was sure she would see a difference. His trainer did. Even the women at the gym, the ones wearing what his trainer called tights and halters were always smiling at him. That must mean something, but he wouldn't ask her until he was ready, not until April after he passed the test and made her proud.

She arrived at three with another SAT instead of wine, sitting him at the kitchen table with a pencil and a four-hour timeframe. Though she did notice a difference, acknowledging the effort, the casual elegance and cologne, quietly puzzled that he hadn't asphyxiated himself.

She left at 7:15, staying long enough for Braxton to absorb the nylon-covered legs, the short skirt, the black-on-black sheer blouse and three-quarter bra into his brain. And as much as she did appreciate the dinner invitation for burgers with mac and cheese or potatoes or something, she was unfortunately pressed for time and grading his test was more important.

Instead she asked for a rain check she would never cash. Despite which, remaining true to her word, they were together twice more before Easter Sunday, a day like most other holidays that didn't mean much. She didn't have family; she was utterly apathetic toward any philosophical discussion regarding the existence of some phantasmic higher power in the universe since she had no faith to defend and hadn't received any dinner invitations. So she decided she would test and grade Braxton as he wrote, obviating a thumb-twiddling four hours and the need for further contact. His score had improved on each subsequent test, proving her right. He would ace the actual test in a week's time, making further contact unnecessary and pointless.

She was cutting him loose, sending him on his own the way CJ eventually would. Such was life, nothing personal. Nothing lasted forever including life itself, precisely the reason, a reason, she had become Blaire Fortune.

*

Stepping in she immediately saw all that he'd done with framed images on the wall, a collection of books on the stereo cabinet, black leather pants, boots and a fitted tee against a pale tan à la Cody Jones. The kid was coming along on schedule, showing more promise than she could have hoped for; visibly leaner, more sculpted than he was in March with stylishly longer hair.

For his part, whatever he might have created in his mind and hoped for, he opened the door to a living fantasy in spring sandals, high-waisted flared shorts, legs shimmering in clear nylons, a wide-lapel blazer tied with a single large button, and a new Easter bonnet because the day was wonderfully bright and warm and she was in every way a Southern lady.

"Wow!"

"Wow? Really, Braxton? Wow? That's all I get? Not Blaire, you are positively stunning? Or, Blaire, how incredibly delightful you are? How disappointing."

"I'm sorry. That's what I meant. All of that and totally amazing."

"And I meant you. You're disappointing."

'A' for effort, though moments too late. She stepped past him at 1:19, checking her watch, dropping her handbag and briefcase onto the sofa. "You've been busy, Braxton. Very nice."

"I did everything you said." He came closer, reaching out. "Can I take your jacket, your hat?"

She placed her hat by her handbag. "No. You certainly may not take my blazer. And a more attentive gentleman would certainly understand why not."

He shrugged. "Want a Coke?"

"Thank you. I brought wine, for me." She reached into her briefcase. "This, on the other hand, is for you. Starting on the half-hour and I want you finished before five with a near-perfect score. Understood?"

He decided he wouldn't tell her about the ham sandwiches with mayo and pickles. Instead he took the infamous exam and went into the kitchen. She followed with an extremely drinkable '78 Saint-Émilion, reaching into a cupboard for a tumbler she judged was the cleanest, leaving him with a pencil and five forty-minute tests, collecting his work each time without a moment's grace and refreshing her wine, admonishing him that washrooms would not always be conveniently accessible. Sorry.

Despite which, he finished at 4:42: a personal record.

She joined him in the kitchen near 5:00, smiling. "Ya did good, kid. You do this well next week and you are in."

"Thanks, Blaire. You did this. You and CJ."

She sipped her wine, studying him. Something was coming her way. How many times had she seen that look? I'm really sorry, Professor. I don't have my completed paper. The library was closed. My dog ate it and died. My car went over a cliff. Boohoo.

"Okay, what now?"

"I was thinking, I don't know, maybe supper. I bought some stuff. I was thinking, you know, we could cook something."

Shit! She did not need this. "No, Braxton, I do not know. What you're thinking is against the rules."

"What I think is that you must be a teacher because you know about tests and things. I was thinking I could ask about things. You know, like girls. Doing things with girls. I've never had girlfriend or seen one that way."

She grimaced. She did not need to hear this shit. "And what way would that be, exactly?"

"You know, without their clothes."

He had to be kidding. "You're sixteen, Braxton. Believe me, you'll figure things out. It is not complicated."

"Maybe. Thing is, now I'm nineteen. Right? I should know things already. Who do you think'll pay me if I don't? That isn't complicated either."

She snorted, holding back the raucous laughter because she wasn't hearing anything amusing. She couldn't believe where this was going.

"Let's get real here, kid. No college girl will ever pay you. No girl anywhere will pay you or simply get naked for you. That is not how the game works. They're girls, Braxton. Slim and cute or big-boned and pimple-faced, they're all in high demand and they are fickle. They will come and they will go, never content, always out there. Lots and lots of girls away from home, unleashed and competing for the best deal. So, in words that even you will fathom, the guy pays. The guy always pays one way or another."

"But…"

"But nothing. The day you see me naked is the day you're forty-something in a tailored suit, a hundred-dollar wine in your hands, and a grand in your pockets that you think is loose change. You got that?" She glared at him. "Jesus H. I cannot believe you thought I would do that. That is utterly sick."

He shrugged, feeling his face flush, frustrated things weren't going his way. "I don't see the difference. You're always naked with those other guys, always doing things with them. So why can't I see you? I mean, what's the big deal? I don't know, maybe a few minutes or something?"

Seriously? She was a nanosecond from smacking him. "Don't be asinine. I don't do amateur nights for repressed boys and I certainly don't do freebies. That's what college is for: Playtime. Meaning that for the next five months you might consider those girlie magazines and not go anywhere near those street-corner girls in platforms and mesh stockings unless you want serious shit with CJ. Do you understand me?"

He did. "Yeah. You're angry again and I didn't do anything."

"You did. You insulted me and disappointed me. So here is one last piece of advice. Not a single party or sleep-over will happen here until you are done with CJ. Do whoever she is in her dorm or some motel. She won't care. But you will keep your mouth shut tight about what you do. College girls are curious and they are conniving. They want bragging rights. They'll want in on this place and your twenty-four K which will not happen because that will get you seriously hurt, like the do not fuck with Cody Jones kind of hurt."

She was disappointed and insulted? What about him? What

about his feelings? "Do you mean you're not staying for supper?"

"That is precisely what I mean."

The "Blaire, I'm sorry" was plaintive and pathetic. "I didn't mean anything bad. I thought you wouldn't mind. Like it would be okay. You know, like natural for you."

"Well you were wrong." She reached for her hat and handbag. "Goodbye, Mr. Miles. We are done here and I sincerely hope you have not wasted my time, for your sake. Because if you do not make the grade next week, if you royally fuck this up, you will degrade into that asshole on the corner and forever be royally screwed. That is a given." She strode toward the door, halting. "Oh, one final note of caution. Blaire Fortune does not exist. Understand that. She has never existed except in your juvenile imagination that I strongly recommend you purge sooner than later."

With that she was gone, disappearing into the stairway, free of guilt for the final and harsh lecture, for shaking the love-sick puppy from her leg, driving off without pausing in doubt or glancing over her shoulder at a disconsolate Braxton Miles gazing down in disbelief from his balcony.

Blaire Fortune had done her absolute best preparing him for his time with Cody Jones, as did Professor Angie Wilson for whatever might come after.

18

10:38 AM.

The good reverend's expression was priceless.

"Like I said, Preacher, Brandon Michaels at the time was indeed a mentor. He came through for me when I most needed him."

Prisby raised the crucifix from his sunken chest to his lips, his sallow complexion blanched with undisguised incredulity. "Braxton, my son, so many lies and deceptions. How is it possible that you sit here with me untroubled and calm at the very precipice of your final judgement?"

"Not lies, Preacher. Secrets." The smirk was unnerving. "Dark secrets, admittedly, but I never said those things never happened. No one ever asked."

"Braxton, you killed your own flesh and blood, the father who gave you life."

At that Braxton Miles straightened, chuckling. "Destiny, Preacher. Seriously thinking your God will forgive me that one. I can still see my mother after all these years lying dead on the floor with her head bashed in. Some imagery never fades. Though, truth be told, she wasn't much better, never much of a mother whose story I eventually believed was purely fiction: The rape, the forced marriage. Nothing she told me made sense. The man was a hillbilly of the lowest order, a failure pissed with life. He always was. Not someone any girl would hike her skirt for."

"I can scarcely imagine your confusion and terror at such a young age. Surely the authorities would have understood a child's tormented mind; surely they would have embraced you with succour and compassion."

"Not tormented, determined. I couldn't bring her back and didn't want her back. Killing him was spontaneous and self-serving, not some unhinged kid's knee-jerk revenge. I wanted out and internally I realized he was the ticket. I did not need anyone's succour or compassion. I needed Cody Jones and Blaire Fortune. End of story."

Prisby bowed his head. In all his years as a failed man of God, as a prison chaplain, he had never come across a man as cold and empty as the one sitting there grinning at him. He was almost afraid to ask, ashamed of himself for wanting the man's final few minutes of life to pass quickly.

"What did become of Miss Fortune, Braxton? Please tell me nothing terrible for the life she lived."

"She was a fleeting moment, Preacher, and very much an everlasting dream. In fact she'll be my last and pleasant thought when the needle goes in. And Courtney, naturally, who very nicely put a body to her face. Still, whatever she was during the day, she was a well-paid and stunning whore after the sun went down. A rose by any other name I never asked about. So whether she was a teacher, who knows? She left Cody on her forty-fifth, which speaks volumes, about the same time I stepped into the deepest shit with Samantha. Cody never did tell me who Blaire really is. Now I suppose she's alone and happy somewhere on a deserted beach or in some classroom gazing at the clock, remembering, counting down without the faintest inkling that she directly influenced Brandon Michaels' destiny. Her and Courtney together. Talk about a fantasy." For an instant his expression was melancholy, his clear blue eyes betraying a deep yearning. "I put their faces on a lot of bodies over the years, ravishing and lithe bodies; though not a single one anywhere near as seductive and captivating as those ladies. The cold reality being that, even when I did have the grand in my pockets, I would have seen in Blaire's bewitching eyes that she was fucking that repressed kid."

Prisby ignored the harsh choice of words, unaffected by prison parlance. "And this Cody Jones? Whatever became of him?"

Braxton Miles coughed a laugh. "Like the lady said, Preacher, the product of a juvenile mind, very much like Brandon Michaels who happily died those many years ago. Now if such a person as CJ ever did exist, he would have remained a good and reliable friend. If, like Blaire, he ever existed."

10:39 AM.

19

Angie Wilson learned from CJ the following Friday evening, a short time before her alter ego
invited a man whose company she particularly enjoyed into her Shangri-La and bed, that Braxton Miles would attend UNO in September. She was happy for him, certain he would do well once he got real and stopped with the puerile fantasies.

She understood that Cody Jones regarded himself as a facilitator, giving kids new to the street a jump-start in life, always cutting them loose before they might become too familiar or careless; either liability placing the man in jeopardy. The problem was that Braxton Miles was different from most others. He was unique. No recruit had ever landed on Cody's doorstep in desperate need of a new identity, which clearly meant the kid had put himself in shit that was serious and deep.

Nonetheless, she believed he had potential. She believed he was destined for better things with or without CJ, a calculated risk Cody had confided could be worth taking, the way Blaire Fortune was worth keeping. Because she was no less an anomaly. She wasn't with him simply for the big bucks; she loved what she did, as though being Blaire Fortune gave her life and her clients thoroughly adored her. Time would tell, she supposed.

Something Angie Wilson would never learn or ponder. Braxton Miles seldom leaked his way into her reveries after that evening, until eventually she forgot him completely, never thinking to enquire of CJ about his short-term and disposable courier whose sole and callow ambition was one day enrapturing wealthy women twice his age.

*

Braxton Miles began his freshman year in leathers and boots, an immediate hit with the young and impressionable female contingent.

By his twentieth birthday he'd done well on his mid-terms, he had a girlfriend who was seventeen and tickled pink that her 'older guy' had given two years of his amazing life serving his country.

He began most evenings in her bed, his curiosity about the particularities of the female nude fully sated and replaced by frequent bursts of heated passion before he would reluctantly leave her to work as a security guard at the mall. Before going home where he would study into the early hours and wake sleep deprived, always heeding CJ's twofold warning that "you should have a good time, kid. Get yourself out there. Mount the entire herd, but do not ever get tight with them. And be smart about it. When not appropriately dressed for the event, deprive yourself. You were given a chance at a better life, you're going places. You do not need more grief raining down upon Braxton Miles. You got that?"

He did, loud and clear. Though through to his first-year finals he brought her most Saturdays to his brother's Garden District home where she stayed over for pizza and wine, empty bottles he would leave with Sunday afternoon on the off chance that CJ might drop by.

The brother worked off-shore on the rigs, letting Braxton crash at the apartment and use his bed except during his seven-day furloughs when Braxton was downgraded onto the living room couch, which the girl thought was totally awesome. Until late June when she left the Swamp for a cooler summer with her parents in Mississippi and he forgot her, never returning her letters or phone calls, recalling what Blaire had said about clingy girls never letting go once hooking their talons into unsuspecting prey.

In September they scarcely recognized each other, Braxton swaggering away as coolly as Blaire had from him seventeen months earlier, after telling her he was currently hooked-up with someone more to his liking. Sure he liked her, but you know... whatever.

His second girlfriend was as good-looking and shapely as girl number one. With thirty grand a year in his pockets he could easily afford the best of the sophomore herd, the shapeliest and the most amenable bodies. He didn't much care about her history. She was short-term, convenient, and disposable. A collegiate life amenity, as was he. Neither one's first, neither one's last. And more importantly she was voracious, always eager and often daring, as inventive as she was tireless: A research project he would study and learn from, who stayed with him through the two semesters, believing the same story until the last Friday in May when he received his grades placing him near the top of his class.

The problem was she wouldn't stop talking about spending the entire summer with him at the apartment, about meeting his brother, about him meeting her hoity-toity parents. Like that would happen, the terse "do not ever get tight with them" resounding in his head. He didn't want or need her intruding into his valuable summer reprieve from long days and longer nights. He was too focused on his third-year plan still lingering in its infancy, doing a good job for Cody Jones, and the personal ads which were the basis of his uncertain epiphany.

He found her in the shade under an ancient oak tree, hissing a curse. She could not be fucking serious.

"Brax, sweetheart, why have you kept me waiting you naughty boy? Come to me." She was beaming and gleeful, prancing and twirling and naked, letting her open shirt dress flutter to the ground, easing seductively onto her knees and teasing him, spreading the flimsy material into a delicate blanket, lying back propped onto her elbows completely oblivious. "There isn't anyone around.

Hurry, sweetheart. Please hurry."

"Stop that shit!" He might as well have hurled a brick at her, freezing her. "And get up. You look ridiculous."

What? "Sweetheart..."

"Listen, let's do this real quick. We've had fun. I had a good time with you, but it was just a fun thing. Besides, I cannot get tied down. Got too many things going on and it's time to get myself clean."

"What did you say?" She didn't believe what was happening, what she was hearing. In an instant she was on her feet. "Are you fucking joking? You're ditching me? You fucking bastard. My parents are coming tomorrow, you fucked me a thousand times, and now you're ditching me?"

"What can I say? Shit happens." He stepped back, just not far enough. "You know, like I said, we had fun. But you're into this thing way more than me. You know, parents and everything, my brother. I'm not good with that, not ready for that. Besides, with that killer bod of yours, the way you put out like you're keeping yourself alive, you'll hookup fast enough." He pointed past the tree, smirking. "I'd say in about thirty seconds."

She glanced over her shoulder. So what? She was a flawless vision, drop-dead gorgeous and comfortable with every inch of her body. She was 5'11", a Phys Ed major, and she adored being admired. She was athletic and sculpted; she also had a purple belt in Jujitsu and put him on his ass in a blur before he realized he was staring up at her in a daze, before her foot crashing into his chest sprawled him across the soft grass.

Stepping over him, daring him while giving him the finger, she blew the three-guy audience a whimsical kiss. She curtsied at the applause and twirled, bending from the hip with a slow and deliberate stretch for her dress, her sandals and panties, draping her dress nonchalantly over her arm and sashaying toward the parking lot beaming.

No shit they loved her.

*

Despite his deeply wounded pride and bruises accompanied with jeers and mocking laughter, her carefree improv performance that earned her cheers and whooping, he soon forgot her. He had more important issues. He was twenty-one, too mature for capricious teenage girls. He was ready for his third year and hopefully something older off-campus, something like Blaire, curious why CJ had not yet mentioned cutting him loose or giving him more meaningful responsibilities.

His French was good, his Spanish was better, though by graduation he would be fluent in each. He thanked Blaire for that, if not for discarding him, and Cody for taking him in.

He would forever be grateful, never disappointing the man despite his furtive weekend study of increasingly fine wines that he justified was an essential part of his future. In spite of which he would not be fully rounded for some time, realizing that a good education was not exclusively about university and diplomas.

He needed more preparation, more exposure he would never get with promiscuously rampant college girls, spending the first week of June tanning on his balcony, reading the Classifieds and making notes when he wasn't working, circling what he hoped would be ideal on the second Saturday.

*

Part-time Pool Guy Required
Must Be Twenty-Something
Must Be Physically Fit
Available Evenings/Weekends

*

He was available weekends and evenings. He was fit, no longer the kid who ran away, and ready for bigger and better things. He was moving on, going places like the man said.

Rolling from the lounger he went inside, dialling the number with no idea what he would say, crossing his fingers that C. Fox was a woman.

Doug Booth

Part Two
20

She was thirty-nine, though anyone seeing her, anyone capable of admiring a truly enchanting young woman, would easily believe she was more like twenty-something. She was educated, cosmopolitan and wealthy, over the past several weeks becoming acutely aware of the peculiar juxtaposition of being rich and a widow.

Excepting Francine and Chuck she was being excluded from social circles and functions unless generous contributions were a factor, deciding she wouldn't bother with dinner invitations for Jack's sake. He was dead and she loved him, but she didn't need the bullshit of anyone's polite and empty regrets, amusedly cognizant of even cheating wives being jealously fearful of someone much younger, much more alluring, and a shitload richer dethroning them.

Their very tragic loss. She didn't need or want them. She had become the lady Jack had envisioned and shaped; she was also a fabulous hostess, queen of her designer kitchen with the talent of a Michelin chef and a penchant for creating epicurean delights. However she was not in the least way interested in the requisite and mundane tasks required for maintaining a mansion. The resultant consequence being that finding an adept keeper of her pool was a frustrating and time-consuming effort and the second Saturday in June was no exception.

Plagued with another stream of giddy young girls and pubescent boys, college jocks and their nubile counterparts, she was fed up, completely discouraged by mid-afternoon, expecting the same babble: They wanted like mornings or afternoons instead, but not like on weekends or anything. Could they have like a week off or whatever? Was that like all she was paying? Could they like bring a friend or something or whatever? She answered anyway. What the hell? One more braindead teenager with a reading disability.

Instead they spoke for several minutes, the guy answering more questions than he asked, describing himself in the best light which of course she expected.

He was upfront about having no experience, suggesting in the same confident breath that cleaning a pool and deck furniture couldn't be very difficult. Besides, he was a quick study with good grades, working summer days as a courier in the business district. Evenings and weekends would never be an issue. He did not drink or do drugs or have a girlfriend, truly excited about the opportunity if she would simply give him a chance.

Which she did, without expectations or promises. The interview would continue in person at six that evening and he should dress appropriately for an evening thick with humidity, a heat index stable at a sweltering 125°, and he could possibly be cleaning a pool.

*

Once hearing the woman's address Braxton was even more curious. He knew about the Upper Garden District, remembering how Blaire Fortune had told him he did not belong there and wouldn't for a very long time.

He spent the remainder of his day hiding from the glaring sun, deciding he would look more the part in his tracksuit and sneakers, foregoing wine with an early supper and leaving for the bus stop near 5:00. He would not be late, regardless of the upper and lower districts being separated by richesse and grandeur far more than distance.

The Upper Garden District was majestic with the natural splendour of magnolia trees, live oaks and all manner of colourful local flora lining the avenues and vibrant façades of stately and gated mansions, manicured lawns and lavish fountains gurgling streams of glistening water from the mouths of marble cherubs.

He was impressed and nervous, until he arrived at the wrought-iron gate, staring through the bars like a village idiot without a clue about the carriage home with its tall curtained windows and faux-balconies, the bright white painted walls, the glossy-black shutters and door. Until his daze was broken by the barrier magically swinging open as some disembodied voice instructed that he should "wait at the main entrance and please do not stomp across the grass."

She kept him waiting several minutes; she was studying him, appraising him. He seemed in good enough shape, lean and tall, but he wasn't a city boy. Not by a long shot unless he came from the projects. He was too, she wasn't sure, enchanted.

Swinging back the door she stepped out barefoot under the elaborate portico. "You're either Braxton Miles or you've wandered into the wrong part of town. Which is it?"

"Braxton Miles, ma'am," and Holy shit!

Courtney Fox was 5'9, give or take, slim and tight with straight and long bronzy hair tied in a tail. Her lips were glossed and glistening like Blaire's, staring at him through bronze-tinted glasses. She was richly tanned, Braxton thinking her skin must be really smooth, very small and yellow triangles barely covering what he couldn't help but see were perfect breasts. Holy shit.

"Thank you for coming, Braxton."

She shook his hand, believing he would fit the bill, do perfectly fine. She turned and went in, telling him to follow and close the door. He did, practically lurching forward, accepting that he would experience a fatal seizure or stroke at any moment.

He didn't see the foyer or kitchen, the gymnasium or solarium, before stepping behind her onto the expansive patio and pool area, the thin yellow strings under the sheer coverup framing the most wonderful ass he'd ever set eyes on. Yeah, and she knew it. The job was his; he knew that too. She was teasing him, flirting with him.

"This is it, Braxton. Your job. You keep everything looking good for the next day, two hours each evening and whenever I need you on the weekends. Day or night at fifty an hour. Are you good with that? Think you can handle all this without drowning?"

"Yes, ma'am. I can. I'm a good swimmer. Don't think I'll need that many hours though. You know, being honest."

She chortled, reaching for a fluted glass of chilled and effervescing champagne. "Being honest, good." She sat, stretching out. "Now show me you're worth fifty an hour. Start with the pool because that track outfit was a very poor choice. Whatever were you thinking?"

He didn't hesitate, toeing off the sneakers and stripping away his jacket, pushing the nylon pants to his ankles. She was right. He needed into the cool water.

Then: "Excuse me, what is that?" She jabbed the air, shaking her head. "What are those things, exactly?"

"My trunks, ma'am, for swimming."

"No. That definitely does not work for me. Next time, if there is a next time, I'll be expecting something that won't cause a drowning in my pool."

"Yes, ma'am. I will."

She shooed him away. "Go. Do something, after you shower. Rule number one: My pool is not your bathtub."

He walked toward the outdoor sauna, stepping under the rainhead, turning a full circle under the rush of cold water and stepping out. He took a leaf skimmer from its rack, circling the pool before following her instructions for attaching the vacuum and spending

166

an hour sweeping the bottom. Then he followed her instructions for mixing and adding chemicals, wondering why she needed a pool boy if she could do everything herself.

"Stop now, Braxton. Come sit with me." She waved him onto a chaise-longue. "Let's you and me have a little one-on-one."

"Yes, ma'am."

"Do you have a mommy or daddy somewhere paying your way?"

"No ma'am, they're dead. Killed by a drunk driver a few years ago. They're the reason I don't drink." He paused, wishing she would face away. She was without question the hottest thing since Blaire. A real woman and practically naked. "Maybe a beer on occasion, but never real booze."

"That's a tough break. So now you get by on this delivery job thing? Life insurance? What?"

"A bit of both. It's not a big deal. In a couple of years I'll be working at a real job."

"You want a beer?"

He did. "Yes, ma'am. Thank you."

She pushed herself from the lounger, padded into her kitchen through another door, and came out moments later smiling. She liked him; she could definitely see things working out. They spoke for an hour about school and his summer job, about where he lived and what she expected.

She would allow one beer and one dip in the pool each night and weekends when she would also offer him lunch. He would call her Courtney and stop with the contrived "ma'am."

"Ma'am?" The slip was intentional. "Courtney?"

"You're hired, provisionally. Though if we do get along, and I suspect we will, it could be a year-round thing. The pool's heated." She swung her feet onto the deck, facing away. "Now get those things off, put on your clothes, and get out of here."

That one came from nowhere. He stood, staring down at her, at her strings and the curves of her ass, stripping off the wet cargos, tugging at his track pants and jacket.

"It's okay, I'm decent."

She turned, lounging. "Be here tomorrow at noon, Braxton. I believe two hours should do nicely and make the day worthwhile."

"Thank you, Courtney. And for the beer. Have a nice evening."

She stayed as she was, musing that her evening was decidedly the nicest in several long weeks. Cheating on Jack with his full and loving consent was one thing, if not at first somewhat bizarre, not at all the same as searching for love and devotion as a young and grieving widow.   She pointed at the solarium. "Show yourself out, Braxton, and don't forget. Leave those things at home tomorrow or throw them out. They look ridiculous and please do not stand at the gate like you want out instead of in. Press the intercom. Goodnight."

He would, he promised, glancing over his shoulder at the door, thinking he should perhaps thank her again, cement a good impression. Instead, for as long as he dared, he stood gazing at an exquisite Courtney Fox sauntering toward the diving board minus her coverup.

21

Sunday Braxton woke early for an hour at the gym focused on strength training, stopping at the boutique for a swimsuit he hoped Courtney would approve. At the apartment he got ready for her with sport shorts and tank top, the forecast promising a day muggier than Saturday, curious how he would spend two hours cleaning a pool that was pristine and crystal clear, while she was wiggling her way from her bed, making her way sleepily onto the patio and plunging herself into the deep end for an instant wake-up.

She did laps, letting herself drip-dry with the sun's early warmth before a naked hour in the gymnasium until she was breathless, bracing her arms on her knees, asking her panting reflection on the mirrored wall why staying in shape and hypnotic in the eyes of all men who passed her couldn't take a little less work.

She didn't get an answer. Instead she went inside and brewed coffee, microwaved danishes and lay basking under a morning sun pondering what she would wear for the desired effect, deciding on her favourite high-rise one-piece thong and tasseled coverup combo. After all, it was her home, her yacht he'd be maintaining when he wasn't working on the pool. It's who she was, the woman Jack Fox helped reinvent and mould, quite certain Braxton would not have an issue.

She wanted her life back, if only for a few months flirting with a kid practically half her age. She wanted the playful days and romantic nights onboard her yacht she had never known with Jack; she wanted candlelight dinners in restaurants without being gawked at for sitting with her grandfather, or hit on the way she was all too familiar with by socially inept dregs who couldn't afford a glass of wine let alone the bottle.

So yes, she hoped he would work out for the summer as an innocent flirtation. Then? She didn't know. Maybe she would sell the mansion and gallery, move to Florida and start over with a man she could actually love and live with without expectations, who had millions of his own.   She snorted, smirking. Why not? Really, why not? Maybe she would keep him, train him to become an ardent lover and refined gentleman. Déjà-vu. Why not? Then show the world, show the two-faced bitches who were snubbing her.

She pushed herself from the chaise-longue at 11:00, a burst of warm air parting her soft and full lips. She was being stupid, which didn't mean she couldn't enjoy the summer. What was the harm? And the evenings, she supposed, when she would have worn silk and satin after doing titillating laps for herself as much as for Jack, would either unfold naturally or by design. She didn't care which because despite loving and missing Jack, she wasn't quite as pristine as her new boat.

*

Braxton arrived on time, passing through the gates into a life he would not have believed had he somehow peered into his future.

Courtney was at the door waiting in a bright orange one-piece that perfectly complemented her tan, guiding him through the house onto the patio where she had left her practically useless coverup. She saw no point in false modesty since he'd be cleaning the pool and she would be swimming in it behind mirrored glasses watching him watch her. If he didn't, which was absurd, too bad; if he did, she'd put him in her bed Monday night as either a precursor of a very pleasant summer tryst or his immediate 100-dollar severance.

At the solarium he held the door for her, not wasting time once on the deck stripping to his microfibre straight-backs that she ap-

170

proved with a nod before easing onto her chaise-longue where she stayed until the half-hour when she began the barbecue and went inside for burgers with a revised plan. Saturday would be the better evening and the floating La Renarde the ideal venue.

At noon she called him over. She served him a burger, pointed to the salad she had prepared and gave him a beer believing he would do as well as any of her previous diversions.

She padded to the diving board with her burger and wine, letting Braxton trail behind, very pleased with her choice of outfit, very pleased with him and eager for Saturday. He was doing his best at acting blasé, and failing miserably. A condition that would soon and agreeably worsen once she got the thing wet.

"Braxton, let's do the same hours tomorrow and weeknights be here at seven, while its still light."

"Sure. That works for me."

"And Friday come with an overnight bag and a change of clothes. We'll be spending the weekend in Gulfport onboard my yacht. I'd like you to maintain her as well. You do like boats, don't you?"

He shrugged. "I've never been on one."

"Then I'm sure you will." She sipped her wine. "Same hours, same conditions apply. Three hundred for the weekend plus the hotel where I'm sure you'll find fun company at the pool." Unless you would prefer doing me. "Unless you would prefer staying onboard for some day cruising."

"Cruising sounds good, I guess. Thanks."

When lunch was over he went for the vacuum, Courtney went into the kitchen. When she came out she went straight into the water where she waded and swam and floated until the top of the hour when she climbed out and lay face down on her lounger while he began sweeping the deck and cleaning the furniture.

He was thankful for the relative privacy, even more thankful she was paying him easy money for watching her get off on being beautiful and one transparent layer from completely naked, wondering what Monday would bring. Because she was clearly playing the game.

At 1:30 she stood, suggesting he should take a shower or have a swim, and leave anytime after. But she wouldn't join him, she was saving that for the coming Saturday. Instead she poured a chilled Chardonnay, circled the pool once, and went inside where she showered and changed into gauze loungewear, watching him from her bedroom window until he left precisely at 2:00.

*

Monday she arrived home near 6:00 after a full day at her gallery, eager for a dip in the cool water.

On the patio she laid her clothes neatly on a footstool by the diving board, pondering how even on the steamiest days of the year New Orleans' proper ladies would not dream of being seen in public without their stockings. Or without loaded derringers in their purses for that matter.

She waded and did laps until quarter-past, rinsing her body by the sauna and drip-drying with a glass of Pinot Grigio before going inside for a light dinner salad after changing into a lacy white thong and white muslin coverup. He wasn't like her other men across seventeen years. In the beginning they were her age and, if nothing else, obsessed. But as she got older men her age wanted younger women and being that younger woman meant dating older men, the last one being on the very wrong side of forty and unforgivably unremarkable in bed.

Braxton was in far better shape and, from what she'd seen while studying Sunday's security videos of him more acutely studying her, he would not be a hard sell. Not after seeing her in sheer muslin and gauze outfits, or her micro bikinis, or any other daring delight du jour she would numb his brain with through the week.

She was done with older men. She was filthy rich and why not?

So what if love's ephemeral facsimile came at a price? Whenever in history did it not?

He arrived precisely 7:00 when Courtney greeted him at the door, guiding him through her home, telling him she wanted the pool's chrome work polished first.

Fine. Whatever.

At the patio he went one way; she went the other, lounging on a chaise-longue with a novel.

He stripped to his straight-backs by the diving board, thinking she must be a clean freak or needed the company. Either way, seven bills each week for cleaning clear water and polishing already shiny fixtures was a good deal. Then he paused and she smiled, engrossed in her book. Good. Exactly what she was hoping for, a still-enchanted Braxton transfixed by her panties and garter laying atop her stockings and dress. Very good.

At 8:00 she called out asking if he wanted a beer. He did and she went inside telling him she would be a few minutes, climbing the stairway to her bedroom window where she sat on the sill observing him, giggling like an excited schoolgirl when she saw him reach out quickly for her panties.

He left at 9:00, as he would through Thursday, Courtney sitting in her cinema room each evening watching him leering at her, never disappointing her. Or the inverse each night with a new and more daring outfit, deciding she would wait for him Friday outside by her creamy-white Vantage convertible in flared retro shorts, a cotton blouse knotted under her otherwise bare breasts, and three-inch sandals looking in no way like some Barbie college girl.

She was musing, watching him come through the gate, that apart from Jack's last words that shocked her, she couldn't recall anyone saying they loved her. The first in her queue of hotel guests, either young husbands or altar-fearing boyfriends, were all about pounding her as hard as they possibly could without breaking the thing. No better than Flanders his one time at the head of the line, digging into her as though he'd never seen a naked girl or never would again.

Then slowly they deteriorated into older cheating husbands whose blind or indifferent wives required them home from the office or a week away by eleven, twelve latest. Very few stayed for room-service breakfasts and none ever said they loved her. Or were given a second chance. Only Jack that one time, making her wonder if the kid would either say something stupid Saturday evening or give her a three-minute college pounding that would get him sent home on a bus.

She did the drive along the I-10 and Beach Boulevard in an hour with the top down because she didn't want conversation; she wanted intrigue and expectation, arriving at the marina and gleaming white yacht well before sunset.

"It's a boat, Braxton, close your mouth. The people at this end are not good with gawkers and gapers. They're at the other end, which is admittedly a little aristocratic but an essential element in the yachting world."

"That is big. You drive that thing?"

"The word is pilot or steer and not a thing. This is a yacht and a she. Your first lesson." She stepped onto the transom, unzipping the clear vinyl. "She's also an overheated bitch most evenings until her top comes off. Which means get your ass onboard and do some work."

With the top stowed she showed him his private berth and head, her private stateroom and the galley for a chilled Chardonnay and cold beer before they unpacked and met on the foredeck, happy that her closest neighbours had not yet returned to dock.

"Tomorrow we'll head early to Dauphin Island. Two, three hours depending. The place is popular with lots of white sand and great swimming."

"I bought more swimsuits."

She raised her glass in a casual toast, looking out over the Gulf.

"Good. And, while we're on the subject, some ladies tomorrow will be swimming and sunning sans their tops. And when the sun sets, if we stay at anchor, most won't wear anything. The rule being: The less you gape the more you see. Understood? No gawking at the pretty naked ladies. And remember that you're also here to put in your hours each day, which means not falling overboard when you do see something nice and not drowning when you're scrubbing the hull."

He promised he wouldn't, not asking the obvious question. He didn't see any point. She was being deliberately obvious, getting off on teasing him. All week she strutted around in clothes he could see her underwear through when she wasn't lying practically naked in tiny bikinis, the second night leaving her clothes where he could see them and the evening before lying on her lounger with her top undone and her ass bare. So yeah, the way she was speaking, not looking at him, she was big-time priming him for something super good coming his way Saturday.

And he was ready.

"What say another round then bed, Braxton? Early tomorrow means seven AM at the gas dock."

"I'll go."

"Thank you. And you might get out of those jeans. I think your Lycras are a little more in keeping with a 30° evening. I'll do likewise and remind me to give you an extra few hundred for some proper yachting attire." She slipped her feet into the open space between them. "My personal escape hatch. Great for late-night stars and spectacular sunrises."

In her stateroom, hearing his footfalls inch along the port side walkway, she tugged away her 50's ensemble and stood in the dim light selecting a fitted white cotton thong and tank top. She posed for the mirror, nodded her approval, and pulled herself onto the deck a few minutes ahead of Braxton who found her at the bow bathed in a golden sunset.

Definitely in for something good.

"Oh, thank you, Braxton." She sipped the wine, savouring the crisp richness. "Listen, I hope you don't mind me, hmmm, dressing like this. I suppose one could call it yachting casual, something you'll see often around here." She giggled. "There isn't much the neighbours don't see or know."

"No, I don't mind. And, hey, lucky neighbours. Right?" And lucky me.

That's right. Lucky neighbours and lucky you. "Well, thank you, Braxton." A very lucky you.

They spoke for an hour, mostly about the morning cruise and what she expected of him. He was ready. Big-time ready. Then she suggested a dockside shower, leading him aft, showing him how the thing worked and sitting on the gunwale with her wine watching him hose down and towel off.

She thanked him, but she didn't believe her already damp loungewear was hose-approved. Besides, she always dipped into the Gulf once in deeper and bluer water.

Instead she refilled her wine. She wished him goodnight and pleasant dreams, dreams every bit as pleasant as watching her step onto the gunwale and leisurely disappear onto the foredeck where she remained until midnight when the marina was calm and quiet and the lights were dimmed, dropping her panties and top into her stateroom and lying on a soft sun pad counting the stars. Something Jack had once assured and cautioned her would kill him long before anything else. Truer words.

She turned onto her front, resting her head and long tresses on folded arms, sighing, drifting into a deep sleep blanketed with the warm night air.

22

Courtney woke at six, greeting a warm sunny day and calm sea, her body taut and quivering with an early morning stretch, reaching into the hatch for her thong and top, dressing while she scanned the half-empty marina.

In the galley she brewed coffee, beginning her weekend as usual on the dock admiring her pride and joy, thinking how far she had come in life: Her degree and the gallery, world travel and La Renarde that was gleaming in the sunlight. And her pool boy who would without question require as much care and polish as her yacht, onboard dreaming of getting lucky or seeing more of her than she regularly and teasingly allowed. She knew that; she had planned that, which did not mean he was a shoo-in. As much as she abhorred the notion of a future with a recovering divorcé or widower, or getting dismally laid by anymore cheating strangers in five-star bedrooms, she did not need spastics his age convulsing on her young and lovely body for all of three minutes.

"Oh, good morning, Braxton." More microfibre. Good. He was adjusting. "Sleep well?"

"Morning, Courtney." Holy shit. Way better in the daylight. "Yeah, I did."

She passed him her mug. "Get some coffees. Then come join me."

When he stepped into the galley she went into her stateroom for a change of clothes. Out on the afterdeck she stripped away the thong and top, dropping them onto the wraparound seating where he would see them, tying herself in no great hurry into a red micro-bikini and triangles. And when he came out she was on the dock coating her body with SPF, facing away for maximum effect. Yet very aware.

Braxton stood for long seconds gaping. This he could not believe, like he was in some sort of heaven. A dream coming true. Blaire and so much more. "Coffee." What else could he say? She was his boss, sort of.

She turned, smiling. "Thank you, Braxton. We'll castoff in fifteen, put in some gas and get there about nine on a nicely calm sea, like floating on a cloud." If you're not already. She passed him the SPF. "We'll be doing forty with the top down."

As she was sipping her coffee she gave him precise instructions on freeing the yacht from the slips while she was at the helm and what exactly the dockhands would expect of him at the pumps. He would not disappoint her, Courtney replying "This is not a dinghy" when he asked about his lifejacket or something.

*

He did good, she told him when underway.

The conditions were ideal for skimming the glassy surface at the maximum cruising RPM, though several miles out she cut the engines, drifting a few minutes letting the wake settle. Then she jumped overboard and circled La Renarde twice before climbing onto the transom and telling him where he would find shampoo in her private head. A minute later she was lathered from head to toe, dripping with foamy suds and plunging again into the Gulf's warm waters.

"Come on, try it. Jump in."

He shook his head. He could barely see land. "I don't see that happening."

Whatever. She swam to the transom, climbing the ladder. Not bothering with a towel she pointed him into the galley for more coffee and danishes and by the time he came out La Renarde was again at maximum RPM. ETA: 9:15.

With breakfast served, the captain standing at the helm, her hair fluttering in the wind, her creamy smooth skin dried by the sun, he sat back taking in the exquisite surroundings.

She gave him an hour, occasionally smiling at him over her shoulder before giving him the wheel on a straight course until they were a few miles out from Dauphin and the glistening blue water dotted with little boats and big boats and, as they idled closer, bodies splashing in the water and strewn along the white sandy shoreline.

When they were anchored, sitting on the foredeck scanning the nautical parking lot, Courtney asked not as a question but as a precondition, "So Braxton, how do you like boating?"

"I like it, Courtney. Really cool."

"That's good." The first passing grade, though more tests were scheduled. "I was hoping you would."

As much as he would need some fine-tuning, she wanted more than a passable pool boy and one-man crew who was clearly fixated on her spectacular ass and perfect breasts that perfectly complemented her sculpted body, although he was somewhat less obvious when facing her.

She wanted and needed someone in her bed who would prove as skillfully pleasing as Jack but each time making her body slippery and pungent with melded sweat without treating her vagina as a mortar for his selfish pestle-dick. She needed a true lover, a man who would never confuse fucking with fucking-up, until whenever, because no man would ever truly replace Jack. But in the short-term, why not have fun?

"So, what now?"

"We dive in, of course. We swim to the beach and we show off. Another essential element, we show off. The older ones with their yachts and Rolexes, the younger ones with tight bodies, bikinis and six-pack abs." She stepped over the bow rail. "We'll do fine. I have the yacht, you've got the abs."

"Yeah, but somehow I don't think they'll be checking my abs, Courtney. Not with that bikini. Sorry, but you're really, you know, really very hot." He shrugged. "I think I needed to say that. I'm glad I said that."

Yes, I am. The second passing grade. "Thank you, Braxton. That is very sweet of you," and you're doing very well, better than expected. Just please do not fuck-up tonight. Please.

Then she stepped into the air, spearing the ten-foot depth with scarcely a splash, touching the bottom and springing to the surface, fanning the clear water with her arms and waiting, not expecting the double backward flip favoured by smart-ass jocks that she would excuse for the time being.

*

At the beach Braxton's prophecy quickly proved correct, as she expected. He was invisible; she was the centre of everyone's shameless attention as they ambled by. She always was, proud of what she was and how they saw her: Beautiful. She forever would be since learning from Jack that vanity was not the essence of one's beauty, but the assurance of one's continued allure.

Though while others frolicked in shallow water, or strolled along holding hands, or lazed on the white sand getting a burn on, they could not.

"I've decided, Braxton, that we'll get along very well and that, if you wish, the job is yours for the coming year. Quit anytime, just do not take me for granted or get lazy. Understood?"

"I won't get lazy, Courtney. I like working for you. Thank you."

"Good. I'm also doing a week in the Bahamas in August. Think you can work that out with the courier people? I would appreciate the company on such an extended cruise, by which time you'll be more adept onboard. You'll be paid, of course."

"It'll work out. If not, I'll quit."

Though he was sure CJ would cut him some slack, certain he could manage the two jobs and college without much worry.

"Excellent. Now why don't you swim out and get us some beers before we melt? Can you do that without drowning?"

Sure he could, wading into waist-deep water before launching himself forward, certain she was watching him until he hauled himself onto the transom where he stood searching for her, shrugging, wondering how she must feel being practically naked. Other women were skimpy, but nothing like that. Then he committed a major faux-pas, taking her binoculars from the helm and crouching, making himself less conspicuous. He could not believe the dozens of women lying on their decks or dangling from anchor lines topless, on a few of the bigger boats completely naked. Courtney was right. Absolutely incredible.

Clearing his head, replacing the binoculars, he went for the beer, passing her open stateroom and noticing her handbag on the bed, hesitating, telling himself he might never have another chance, going in without the slightest guilt.

He found the wallet laying near the top, working quickly. Shit! No way! She was thirty-nine when he'd been guessing, he didn't know, late twenties or something. But twice his age? How sick was that?

Leaving everything as he found it, he hurried into the galley. He grabbed the beer and flung himself into the Gulf, doing a one-arm breaststroke until he collided with the sandy bottom.

Clambering to his feet, he searched the crowded beach. Nothing, nowhere. He couldn't see her.

"Were you brewing them, or what?"

He did a one-eighty, smiling despite feeling stunned. "Sorry, I needed the bathroom."

"The head, really?" She blurted a girlish chuckle. "Braxton, FYI. You're standing in it." She took a bottle, twisting the cap. "Come. Let's strut our stuff. Let's do a little showing off."

They walked for an hour, swimming back for a lunch onboard when the sun was at its zenith. He could not believe what he was seeing, sitting on the afterdeck putting back a beer while she strutted around concocting a meal and sipping her wine with an eye patch between her tanned legs and two more scarcely covering her fantastic tits. She was awesome. Why should he care about her age? No way did she look that old.

Bringing out plates stacked with crudités, a cheese dip and her Po' Boy 'dressed' with lettuce, tomato and mayo, Courtney sat straddling the gunwale and swinging legs in a way that was either obviating the need for the red patch or enhancing the appeal. He couldn't decide which, or care.

"I'm staying onboard this afternoon, Braxton. The beach is getting crowded and I could use some downtime at the bow. You can do whatever. Enjoy. No timeframe for dinner."

"Mind if I stay? I won't get in the way. Besides, I should be putting in some hours. You know, swabbing the deck or something."

"You know, I actually forgot that. You're right, of course. Just not all afternoon and maybe another beer first." She held out her empty glass and when he came back she was leaning against the gunwale with her feet parted for balance on a calm sea, pointing at panels on the deck. "Whatever you'll need is down there."

With lunch and drinks finished he went into the galley; she went into her stateroom where she changed into another micro, this one green, and that the patch was sheer was inconsequential given the nubile attractions on many of the flotilla's decks. Inconsequential and habitual since she'd been sunning that way for years at dock and at anchor, being who she was and not some pathetic cockteaser.

*

Braxton began with the transom and afterdeck, taking his time, giving her space while very eager to clean and polish that space, not certain what he should do with the galley that was her domain or the heads that he decided were clean enough. An hour into it he made his way with his work pail and brushes onto the foredeck where he found her lying braced on her elbows, reading her novel, all the more naked and irresistible without her top. He could not imagine the Bahamas.

She didn't acknowledge him, nor did Braxton interrupt her precious leisure time as he went about polishing the brightwork with ample time and opportunity to absorb what he was seeing. What he realized she wanted him seeing and adoring, when somehow his second hour had elapsed and he was done, ready for a rewarding plunge into the Gulf. Until she stopped him.

"Braxton, good job. Now why don't you get a beer, get wet, and walk the beach or whatever. I'll find you wherever in an hour. And no more backflips. This is not a kiddie boat."

In other words, get lost. "A beer and the beach sound good. Thanks. I could use a dunk. And no more flips. Got it." Just you flipping over.

When he was gone she stood. Tugging at the side-ties she dropped her thong by the triangles, stepped over the railing and sprang from the bow, surfacing at the anchor line and kicking her way aft.

Climbing the ladder she combed her hair into a damp tail, letting her body drip-dry quite unabashedly while studying whichever of the thousand bodies at the beach might be Braxton, wondering how many binoculars from shore or other boats were checking her out. Wondering how many Braxton had zoomed in on while he was supposedly in the head. Like she believed that one.

Pouring a chilled Grigio, she slipped into the Gulf from the transom, kicking on her back into chest-deep water. Nighttime skinny dips were fun; daytime nudie wades were exhilarating. She didn't need a watch, swimming back when her glass was empty, drip-drying and refilling her glass before floating back into shallow waters for a more even and sensual tan.

How often had she done that for Jack? How often would she wade naked in turquoise seas for someone else? And when?

With the Grigio finished she swam back to La Renarde, tied herself into the red micro and jumped from the bow, meeting Braxton a few strokes later who was waiting for her in waist-deep water, which prompted a mischievous smirk.

They strolled for an hour meandering between smaller craft and stepping over the lines of larger yachts, Courtney suggesting a shampoo shower and a few cocktails before dinner. She understood the booze thing. But, hello? A little wine never killed anyone.

Onboard he showered first in his straight-backs, drying with the sun—waiting. Except that wasn't about to happen. Not his way. She suggested Chardonnays on the foredeck, waiting until he was changing into shorts and a tee, dropping her bikini beside her morning ensemble before leisurely soaping and rinsing, combing her hair into straight strands and wrapping herself in a towel.

Besides, if he did see her, good for him. He had all day and a little extra peep show was no big deal. He would see a whole lot more of her later that evening in the water and in her bed.

In her stateroom she laid out a metallic silver suspender thong and tasseled coverup she would wear for dinner on the afterdeck, hauling herself onto the foredeck in her towel through the hatch, smirking at seeing him smiling down at her.

"That was quick, Braxton." She took her glass, easing onto a sun pad with her back against the windshield. "Thank you." She patted the other cushion. "Sit." Tell me how you enjoyed the show.

No shit! A towel. She was jerking his chain big time. Fucking with his brain. Something was definitely in her head that was not about cleaning her boat—or her pool. No way. She had a thing for young guys. Thirty-nine and pissed about getting old. "Thanks. This is weird though. You know, me up here with you. Do crew guys always get wine and beer?"

"Mine do." She touched the rim of her glass to his. "How was the gawking through those RayBans?"

"You said I shouldn't. That way I would see more."

"I bet you didn't."

"I guess I did. Women don't do that where I come from."

"Boaters do. Doesn't matter where you're from." She sipped her wine. "Ever skinny dip where you come from? That a thing for little country girls?" She didn't believe him. "Well that's something else boaters do, something of a time-honoured after-dark tradition that does not allow for gawking."

"Do you?"

"Yes, I do. I always have because it's fun."

"Is that why you're wearing a towel? Should I stay up here?"

"Stay wherever you want. Or jump in. Your call."

"You're my boss. Isn't that a little weird?"

"No. Besides, I like you and what's the difference between you not looking and me wearing a bikini? It's not like I was wrapped in a blanket all day. Like I said, no gawking. Eyes forward at all times. After we enjoy dinner below."

He wasn't sure. However he did like the Chardonnay and she sent him for refills while she stood, dropped her towel through the hatch, tousled her damp hair into flighty curls and slipped into her stateroom tempting fate or designing it.

Either way, when she pulled herself through the hatch she was wearing the suspender. Twin silver strips from her shoulders to the apex of her firm and tanned thighs, aptly reading his mind behind her mirrored glasses. He was thinking holy shit, why bother? He was thinking he would not have a problem being naked with her under the cover of night. Or coating her with sweat on deck or in her bed, his not fully developed brain assuring him he could do her better and harder than anyone. She hoped.

But for Courtney that conversation was over. She would not press; she would not be pathetic, particularly since he would watch

her showering or changing. She knew that. And good for him because she'd done all she could, but he was too young and stupid to
man-up.

He would or he wouldn't and with the wine finished she let him
quietly trail her onto the afterdeck, Braxton deciding that, yeah, he
would get naked with her because watching her all that week, being with her, was like living his dream with Blaire. He would at
last be fucking Blaire. That is what they both wanted.

She spent the next hour in the galley preparing dinner, foregoing the tassels as a dispassionate last ditch effort, setting the mood
with easy listening music while he set the table and sat musing,
weighing the pros and cons.

When dinner was over she relaxed on the aft's contoured seating, watching the sun sink into the Gulf while he washed the dishes
and secured the aft anchor according to his captain's instructions.

23

The sun disappeared below the horizon at 8:52, the Gulf's pink-gold glimmer becoming silver under a bright moon near quarter-past illuminating a hundred or more gleaming pleasure boats.

He wasn't nervous, he was curious. Curious about her body, about how much of her he would see, how much she would let him see; expecting total darkness, not the entire boat, all the boats, shining under dazzling white lights.

"Three-sixties, Braxton. They keep us from crashing into each other, not intended as aids for juvenile peeking which is entirely against code."

"Code?"

"The nudie code. Nautical nighttime decorum." Courtney put down her wine, stepping onto the transom, sitting sidesaddle. "Some dangle from ladders or lines, others get waist-deep or lie at the shore with a glass of wine gazing at the moon while the harder core stroll the beach or get busy, everyone in their own private world. Not an ideal time for making friends."

"Which one are you? I'm guessing waist-deep."

"I suppose mostly near the shore. I mean, where's the thrill in dangling when the whole idea is having fun, being a little titillating and sexy?"

He shrugged. "Yeah, I guess."

She stood facing the shore, nonchalantly slipping from the suspender, glancing over her shoulder with a playful "Bye for now," and taking a single wide step, quickly surfacing and swimming into dark and shallow water.

Braxton remained as he was, stunned, studying the thong, amazed by how much more naked she seemed without it, how vulnerable and young she seemed for that split second suspended in midair. Everything she wore was silk or satin, provocative or daring. He wore cotton briefs that came in five-packs. She was wealthy, drop-dead gorgeous and successful; he was a second-year college drug courier and working girls' go-between living on the edge.

Still, she didn't have a problem getting naked or fucking with his brain all day, or doing that towel thing. And it wasn't like he needed the job. What he wanted was her, or someone like her. Someone like Blaire and who cared if she was twenty and not ten years older? She was there, she was ready, and she was hot. She was Blaire hot. So grow the fuck up. Why not? And, yeah, she was wealthy. She was really wealthy and she liked him, taking him for a week in the Bahamas.

He could not fuck this up. He tore away his tee, stripping off his shorts, stuffing a pocket with his cotton briefs and took the plunge. A minute later he found her alone and smiling, wading in waist-deep water.

"Alright, I was hoping you would. Thank you." She giggled. "A girl can get lonely out here."

"I convinced myself. Does feel weird though, seeing you like this."

"They're breasts, Braxton. Not a big deal. Something I won't bother with going forward with you. I mean, wouldn't that be incredibly silly? You are okay with that, I hope."

"Sure."

They waded and swam for over an hour, Courtney several times venturing into knee-deep water, twirling and splashing. An intriguing silhouette for distant boaters, though for Braxton Miles a clear and exceptional nude in the moonlight making him in that instant fully devoted to her every whim and his dutiful service.

At La Renarde she climbed the ladder first, letting the warm air dry her while she straddled the gunwale unabashedly watching him towel off, convinced he would do perfectly well with his callow bullshit no longer an impediment, until possibly her age might one day slip out or he would more likely disenchant her, which wasn't at that particular moment.

When he finished she swung her feet onto the deck, pleased with her day. She poured a crisp and clear '88 Pouilly-Fuissé, a grand vin de Bourgogne, telling him to do likewise and join her up front in a dry towel where the deck was shaded from the yacht's nighttime navigation light.

He found her lounging on a sun pad, propped against the windshield, too enticing for words, words not yet his because he was a stunned teenager playing pretend.

*

She woke spooned into him under the morning's warm sun. If not exactly her dream come true he was the best she'd had since her first time with Jack, more athletic and perhaps too eager but never rough or hectic, pacing himself, studying every inch of her, exploring and probing her as though in another place. Above all, pleasing her.

She sat gazing out over the Gulf, content, pressing slender fingers against her pulsating labia, relishing the heat, the longed-for tingling, the sticky sheen coating her thighs and pungent smell of their melded sweat.

She eased into the stateroom yanking a sheet from her bed. Young and naked ladies sleeping on deck at sunrise were always a pleasant surprise, not the men. A definite contravention of code and decorum, leaving him covered and sleeping, brewing coffee while she dipped into the Gulf with a dozen other early risers before enjoying a leisurely shampoo shower on the transom.

Towelling herself, combing out her hair, she squirted SPF into a cupped hand, beginning with one arm then the other, hearing from behind "Hey, let me do that."

From then on they were frequent lovers. Braxton honed his amorous skills with each tender caress before going home each weeknight after dinner and heated romance, though spending his weekends with her, showing promise for the coming months and years with no further need of college girls. The triangles and thongs were gone as well, excepting yachting weekends, and by the time they set sail for the Bahamas with CJ's blessing Courtney had sold off Le Renard and Jack's five other restaurants at fair-market value that added substantially to her millions.

His fleet of exclusive rides went as well, except the Porsche she was keeping for Braxton once his classes began because taking buses when she was filthy rich was completely unseemly, not understanding at all why a courier service would not allow cars. Furthermore, why did he bother? She was paying him close to forty K tax free for cleaning her pool and yacht which was now essentially an allowance. Why was he delivering packages?

Because he had a work ethic and needed his independence until graduating, was the short answer and smooth lie.

The Bahamas cruise took three days over calm seas with stopovers in St. Pete and Key Largo, Braxton learning more each day about yachting and navigation and, at night, dining in marinas or lounging onboard with her sipping expensive wines dressed like a yachtsman. Not considering for a moment that he might be seen in the eyes of others as the rich lady's toy boy, while the lady was the clear envy of women her age and older whose yachtsmen husbands were paunchy, bald and viewing her from an entirely different perspective.

They stayed in the Bahamas three days, port hopping before returning home one week before registration tanned and satiated, Braxton calling CJ for an unavoidable meeting his first morning back on the job, worried he would disappoint the man because the vacation had also been one of discovery beyond the enchantment of exotic shores.

He discovered Courtney was no longer content with evenings and weekends. She wanted him full time or not at all, which made him realize that, with the burden of college looming, she was exactly right. The mathematics of time and demand did not add up, did not make sense, and time was not on his side.

He discovered that he wanted the combined seventy K a year, that he wanted Courtney, her Upper District home, the Porsche and her yacht. He discovered he could not give up all that he had won over the summer simply by being exceptional in her bed or anywhere else the mood struck her.

*

"You're looking good, kid. You find a beach somewhere?"

"Yeah, I did." He got right to it. "And more than a beach, CJ. A woman."

"You found a woman, not a girl. What kind of woman?"

"A rich one, a widow. She lives in the Upper District. We did the Bahamas on her boat."

The man's good humour transmuted into a furrowed brow and piercing eyes. "How old is this rich widow on a boat and since when?"

"Touching forty, going on late twenties or something, and sexy. Really sexy. I met her a few weeks ago. She was looking for a pool boy weekends and evenings. I thought it would be fun. You know, the pool and everything. Like I said, she's hot."

"A pool boy. I give you thirty K net and you're out cleaning pools?" Cody Jones leaned onto his elbows. "You doing anything else with this aging rich widow, kid, after you clean her pool?"

"That's the problem. She's got this crazy thing about young guys. So yeah, for a few weeks now. But I never had her over, CJ. Not once. I go there, most times for dinner. The thing is, she wants me living with her, moving in. Says she doesn't feel right me leaving each time. Guess it's a female thing. You know, getting old. But it's totally physical, CJ. I swear. Nothing serious. I mean, shit, forty. So I'm thinking, you know, take it while I can. Have some fun with her if I can."

"Now this is where you tell me she doesn't know, kid. That said, and taken for granted, what exactly does she know?"

"Nothing about before I came here, nothing about you and me. I'm a student, twenty-one with no family, no girlfriend, and a courier for a downtown company that doesn't have cars. She's giving me a Porsche for school…or wants to anyway. She doesn't want me taking buses, which is your call, CJ. I'm being straight with you. I like her, she's fun, but you're the one who saved me. You tell me whatever, that's what I'll do."

"She paying you, kid, apart from meals and giving you lubes?"

"Yeah, seven a week. Another reason I want to keep her. That's good money for a kid my age, CJ. I'll be set when I graduate. Thing is, I'm really stretched here. You know, with school."

Cody pushed back into his seat. "Thirty-five K for cleaning a pool and the honey jar? You got a little black in your history, kid?" He put up a hand, the question was rhetorical. "Let me get this very straight. You fell on this hot old widow by chance, she's good money, she knows nothing, and you figure you can play her for two years and seventy K. Is that what I'm hearing here?"

"Not playing her, CJ. More like a win-win: She gets what she needs and wants, I get what I need and want. That's fair."

"Who is this woman, this rich old lady?"

"Her name's Courtney, she owns an art gallery on Royal."

Cody practically catapulted against his desk. "You're telling me you're doing Courtney Fox, Jack Fox's girl?"

"Yeah, I guess. Courtney Fox."

"You look around this office, kid. Take a good look. All that, that's Fox Gallery. Goddamn. I like that girl. She is one lovely lady and smart. I've entertained a few pleasant thoughts myself over the years. That said, what in this miserable world can she see in a poor white boy like you?" Another rhetorical question. "Not a week goes by I don't visit one of those restaurants. Won't ever be the same though. Not with Jack gone."

"She's into young guys, CJ. I think the Jack guy was pretty old. She doesn't talk about him."

"Goddamn. Courtney Fox." Cody rubbed his face hard, breaking into a chorus of chuckles. "I do not see it, kid. I do not. That is one very classy and pretty little thing. She's been places, seen and done things. You and her, you're from different solar systems and what you've done is land in hers on a visitor's pass. No offence, but do not get your sorry ass too comfortable in her life. What she's doing is finding herself; she is not looking to take up with any Braxton Miles. You got that? You understand that, kid?"

"Meaning what, CJ?"

"Meaning she must truly be lonely after Jack. I knew the man; he was good people. Thing is, that kind of money can ruin folks, especially women, pretty girls like Courtney. They can't ever be sure, can't ever trust what they see or hear."

"You're saying I can live with her?"

"I'm saying you be smart about things. You and me, we're good. So do not mess with the status quo. Move in, take the car and have a good time. But you will keep the apartment where you will begin each day and park your fancy car each day until your work is done. Because you will continue taking buses. What you will not do is ever invite that lovely girl into your private space and world. You got that, kid? You understand me loud and clear?"

He was elated. Courtney would be elated. "I do. Thanks, CJ. I mean, really, thank you."

Doug Booth

24

Monday evening Braxton walked home from the bus stop in a suit and into a mansion carrying a suitcase, telling her with a beaming smile that he'd paid the three-month penalty and given up his apartment. He was being foolish; he positively hated leaving her each night, hurting her when he without question wanted more time with her. He would bring the rest of his clothes and books the next day after work if he could borrow the Porsche.

Instead she gave him the keys, asked how much he paid for the suit and tie, shook her head and threw the suitcase in the trash bin.

The next morning he woke beside his de facto wife, showered with her, ate breakfast with her and left her with passionate kisses. He drove downtown in a gleaming red Porsche that moments later he parked in his Lower District driveway before answering his phone for the coordinates that day and taking a bus to his first high-rise mailbox.

That evening he returned home to her with his academic library and a passable wardrobe he would sacrifice each night through the weekend, explaining how he had left his furniture for the landlady.

Friday he registered for his first third-year semester; Saturday she took him shopping for a complete wardrobe more in keeping with his current address and the fashionable Courtney Fox. Sunday she took him for dinner in public for the first time at Le Renard where, by the most delightful of coincidences, a dignified client of the Fox Gallery happened by with his wife who Courtney introduced as Mr. and Mrs. Jones.

194

A week later he attended his first class, again the youngest in the room; the youngest in her bed that night. His mid-year finals were impressive, rewarded with Christmas in Monaco à la Français that he believed impressed her. They celebrated his birthday and New Year's in the Big Apple with a Rolex when Courtney increased his weekly allowance to 1500, that with CJ's current thirty-five would add eighty grand after expenses to the paltry fifty lining his safety deposit box.

He was living the good life, his previous private study of fine wines on hold since Courtney's cellar would be the envy of any wine snob, at times surprising her with his relative mastery of the subject. He was learning about theatre, art and music, learning that not all dancing required flailing one's arms and legs.

At Easter they vacationed in Costa Rica, in May dedicating their weekends to making La Renarde ready for spring and summer cruising. Although she was quietly disappointed. They wouldn't be spending the time onboard they'd planned and charted, island hopping to the Virgin Islands. He had landed a real job in a language school teaching linguistically stunted business types. Of course he was disappointed too, but more importantly he needed her respect as much as he wanted his summer with her, which would never sit well with Cody Jones.

Sorry, sweetheart.

Instead he gave her a week with CJ's OK before registering for his fourth and final year. They did the Texas coast, spending Christmas in Barcelona where she understood nothing he said, and New Year's in chilly London where he turned twenty-three with five months remaining before graduating with a meagre 170 K in the box because she wasn't increasing his allowance, figuring he would spend the summer planning how he would terminate his four years with CJ and what he should do about her who was turning forty-one in April and not real happy about it.

A week after Easter he gave her a weekend in the joie de vivre of Montreal, of fine dining and dancing, the theatre and sex that for her were still bouts of intense passion but that for him had waned into an obligation to meet or surpass her high expectations.

Despite never in their two years hearing that she loved him, never a whispered slip while she was grinding and groaning, tears often dripping from her eyes as she shuddered and twisted on him or under him. Never a cutesy name except an occasional bland 'sweetheart' like he was some neighbour's teenage son and not the urbane man graduating May 31st, fifty-three months after coolly murdering Bill Michaels a day too late.

She gave him a titanium pen and pencil set with matching latest-edition silver-embossed dictionaries and dinner at Le Renard before a weekend on La Renarde anchored off the shores of Dauphin, Courtney a little pissed she wouldn't have more time with him before another summer teaching job. Moreover she was completely pissed that he had not yet decided on a career path, or hadn't made a bigger deal of her birthday, especially the more significant fortieth a year earlier that reignited her darkening mood, or that he never reached for the bill or put gas in her boat.

He was too comfortable, too smug about life, about her, and that would change very soon.

Monday, June 03rd, Braxton's Lower District phone rang at 9:00 sharp. This time however Cody Jones was calling and not with coordinates. No mailbox retrievals. They met instead for an early and quick lunch.

"Two years with our Miss Courtney. Must admit that's impressive, kid. You sure you don't have some black blood in those white veins?"

"I'm pretty sure, Cody."

CJ slid an envelope across the table. "Anyway, congratulations. That's ten K. Five for making it all the way, five for me cutting you loose. With that degree of yours you'll have a tough time not earning a real paycheque. You just remember a simple fact: Favours, they do not go away; they do not fade with time. You got that?"

"I do. But CJ, I wasn't expecting this. She thinks I'll be teaching. I mean, shit. Can't we hold out a few weeks."

"We're done, kid. Good things never last, can't last. That's what makes them good, like you and Courtney who likely will be a little put off with you losing your job on the first day."

"She's already there. She's been a little cool lately."

"Then you might well muse on that a good while, kid. Like I said, she is one smart lady." He chuckled, dropping a fifty on the table, pushing his way from the booth. "A whole lot smarter than a dumbass hillbilly like you leastways, white boy, who might well think on buying the lady some posies." He squeezed Braxton's shoulder. "You take care, kid."

Then he was gone, leaving Braxton feeling strangely disconnected.

*

He spent the afternoon in his apartment taking CJ's advice, mentally scripting plausible reasons and credible excuses while emptying a twenty-year grand cru. He was not ready to leave her or give up the mansion and the yacht he could now steer as well as her. He needed more time, more preparation, his allowance and more cashflow in the box, which meant getting her warm, putting her back on track and treating her as though she was young and vibrant. Maybe even love her, say the words. Why not? No harm done.

At the mansion Courtney was at the pool looking fantastic, dressed for a sunset barbecue in a pink gauze jumpsuit, a deep-red silk thong and red satin slippers, believing she would slap his head from his neck when he stepped onto the patio with a dozen carnations wearing a ridiculous grin. She did not give a good shit about his day, he hadn't once bought her flowers, and she about had enough.

He couldn't deny she was gorgeous, as tight as ever, sexy and looking more like thirty. She was all that and more. Problem was, at fifty he'd be thirty-two and that would not happen. Like the man said, good things cannot last.

"Flowers, Braxton?" She stopped several feet from him. "Why?"

"Because it's what I should do, what I should have done sooner. And we're doing the Virgins, the way we planned. They wanted me teaching Saturdays and nights, which wouldn't happen. I could never do that to you. In other words I quit, which gives us the entire summer together."

She was not thrilled. She was not smiling and she had not budged and inch with her arms crossed. "A three-week cruise is not an entire summer, Braxton." Her voice was flat, devoid of emotion. "And quitting one job before finding another is not real brilliant."

"That's the other thing, something I've been thinking about. I can't work for anyone. I mean, how do I fit into a junior level anywhere when I wear thousand-dollar suits and live with you in a mansion? I can't. So I'm doing my own thing. When we get back I'll work on a business plan while being with you. Talk about a win-win."

"Business? What business?"

"I'm thinking a freelance translating service. You know, for companies, the big guys, perhaps even book publishers."

Her mood softened. She took the flowers and went for a vase, suggesting that he dress for dinner. When she came out he was on the patio dressed in white linen slacks and a polo.

"Thank you, Braxton. They are lovely." When I absolutely loathe carnations. Why don't you know that? "And I believe your vision is a wonderful idea. Of course I'll help you with the plan, help you select a location and put ten K toward start-up costs. However, effective immediately I am cutting your allowance, otherwise you will never succeed. Businesses do not survive without purpose."

*

He was dumbstruck. He couldn't believe what she was saying, that she could be so heartless after all he'd done for her. She almost seemed pleased with herself, as though mommy was teaching little Braxton a lesson, lifting her puppy's paws from the floor.

She was blasé through dinner, asking questions that prompted impulsive answers, taking a moonlit dip in a one-piece thong without him, needing the space, pondering what was true and what was fiction, later in bed claiming exhaustion after her demanding day. She had clearly startled him with her terse FYI, Courtney more curious than disappointed about the obviously concocted career choice that she would make happen. However he had come up with that one.

She rolled onto her side, propped on her elbow. "I've decided we'll castoff for the Virgins this Saturday and that you should be job hunting while we work on getting you established in business. A fallback, Braxton, with August 31st as a reasonable target date." Because if you don't have a job or tax number by then, you won't be sleeping in my bed that night. Something I am fully aware will happen eventually anyway. Because forty is a memory and I have no illusions. "Goodnight, sweetheart."

She put a hand to his cheek and turned out the light.

*

Saturday morning La Renarde departed the gas dock a few minutes past 7:00, Courtney deciding on breakfast while underway. They spent seven days marina hopping toward Tortola, the BVI's capital island, a lush green thumbprint in the Caribbean surrounded by white sand and turquoise water. Seven evenings spent in the company of other well-heeled aficionados because she wanted distance from him, a solitude that came more easily with strangers.

Tortola was a paradise, her dream come true, Courtney believing she could live on the island forever. She spent the cooler mornings touring the island on mopeds, some days without him, spending the severely hot afternoons swimming in secluded coves, sunning on private sand and sipping chilled wine on deck; some days probing deeper into Braxton's career plan with an open mind, other days quietly absorbed in the reality that he was a hanger-on.

Seven more evenings spent at dock in light muslin dresses, gauze rompers and eye-catching silk thongs, dining in town before ending her days over nightcaps with neighbours; Braxton enduring unwanted career advice from men three times his age who didn't know shit, amusing their chubby wives with his languages while the nearly-dead salivated over his ravishing woman.

And finally her last day had come too quickly for Courtney, sitting pensively on the gunwale mid-afternoon in a monokini savouring her final few hours before heading home the next morning. Then somehow she wasn't on the gunwale sipping wine, she was flailing in the water, dazed and gasping for air, clutching her head, a thin stream of blood trickling from her hairline tinting the turquoise sea.

The shock on his face screamed "No!" as loudly as the panic in his voice. He hoped as much anyway. He'd practiced in his mind for the last few hours.

"Courtney, I'm sorry. You okay?"

She didn't answer. Teetering from the searing pain she grabbed for a fender, feeling nauseous, her mind a kaleidoscope of flaring sparks, confusion and anger.

"It was an accident. I was having fun with you. Come on. Talk to me. Tell me you're okay."

It was an accident. Sure he pushed her over, playfully. He wasn't thinking she would smash her head on a cleat. Not that she hadn't been a completely cold bitch since he quit his job for her—and she wasn't exactly drowning.

He jumped into the water from the transom, taking her by the shoulders, not expecting her fists would crash into his chest. "Fuck off, Braxton. I mean, really, fuck off. What are you, ten?"

"Hey, this is our last day. I was playing, joking around. It's called having fun, Courtney. I said I'm sorry."

She ignored him, splashing water onto her face, guiding herself along the hull toward the ladder, thinking how Jack would never have done such a stupid thing and, if she had hurt herself, how he would have rushed to her without asking stupid questions.

Her vacation was over, the swelling and unsightly bruising spreading out from the stinging wound precluding dinner in town, for one of them, and nightcaps on deck before retiring. The mood was broken, Courtney deciding as she bandaged her forehead that she would do the return cruise at maximum RPM in five days throughout which they would seldom speak.

She castoff early each day, arriving late, eating breakfasts and lunches at the helm with a single purpose and preparing onboard dinners when her focus was his business plan, increasingly nettled by his lax attitude. He wasn't taking his future seriously, questioning why he even needed an office, why he couldn't turn one of their rooms into an office and work from home. Courtney explaining how there was no 'their' room, that a downtown office would lend credibility and perhaps restore that modicum of self-respect he had apparently misplaced.

He understood. He understood she was serious about the business concept he had no real idea about, at one point during their final night onboard suggesting he might continue into a master's programme that would in a few years lend even more credibility. She agreed wholeheartedly. He could certainly study for a master's at night while growing his client base.

Moreover he understood arriving home late Friday that by Monday she expected an initial blueprint of a workable plan transcribed from his brain onto paper, surprised when Saturday he left for the day, hearing over dinner that he'd been at Audubon Park where he could think things through and would do the same Sunday.

She didn't believe him, turning her back to him in bed, leaving home before him Sunday for a day at the gallery. Though she wasn't greatly surprised when he drove past the park, her mind flooding with questions when he stepped from the Porsche at his previous Lower Garden District apartment that he went into with a key and where he remained several hours.

At dinner she asked about his day at the park, telling him she was expecting a delivery the next day but that she also had pressing business at the gallery, suggesting he use the extra time to review his strategy. When in fact she had a strategy of her own.

After dinner when he asked whether she was dipping into the pool, she was not. As well, after dressing alone in her bathroom for bed in a slip and panties, which she seldom did, she suggested as a command that he sleep in the guest room. She was not feeling at all well and in the morning she locked her safe before leaving.

*

When the lady answered her door, Courtney greeted her with a pleasant smile.

"Good morning, I have a package for a Mr. Fox. I tried his bell, but he's not answering."

The woman was very sorry. The address was correct, but "There is no Mr. Fox upstairs. That gentleman's name is Mr. Miles, Mr. Braxton Miles."

"Oh, my. Then did Mr. Fox recently move out? Did he leave his forwarding address?"

"No. Mr. Braxton's been with us coming on five years now. There was never a Mr. Fox."

Courtney inhaled a deep breath, seemingly disappointed. "Well, thank you. I'll check back with my HO. I'm sorry for the disruption."

Which was quite fine. Everything was quite fine in the genteel South.

Next Courtney went to her bank's personal investment manager who'd known her for years. They had history. She was depositing a

gift of ten thousand into the account of Braxton Miles. A graduation surprise.

"Miss Courtney, Braxton doesn't have an account with us. He
never has."

"He must. He receives a very generous weekly allowance. He
has credit cards."

"I'm afraid I really can't discuss him."

She wasn't in the mood. "Meaning what exactly? Investments,
what?"

"I'm very sorry."

"Francis, I don't have time for this shit. You're wasting my day.
At least until end of business he and I share an address, you and I
share several tens of millions. Get the picture?"

He did, succinctly. "Let me say, Miss Courtney, that if he does
have funds with us they would currently be in a non-taxable, non-
accruing investment portfolio to which only he has access."

"A safety deposit box?" She could feel her face burning.
"That's what you're saying? He's got a fucking box?"

"That would seem a reasonable conclusion. As for the cards, he
never exceeds his limit and settles each monthly balance in cash."

She thanked him and left, having learned from Jack to act
quickly and decisively when need be. She returned to his apartment, apologizing, telling the lady the package was indeed for Mr.
Miles, a graduation gift from a C. Fox who wished to remain
anonymous. Could she please call him at once, and not spoil the
surprise?

Courtney walked into her home stone-faced after dining at Le
Renard, planning her evening, several minutes after driving
through her gate, telling him the delivery would be coming the
next day, and not the least surprised that something unexpected had
come up. He wouldn't be long.

She didn't care; she had a more important errand for him. The
wine store was closing in an hour, Braxton leaving in a hurry with

a very extensive list of wines she wanted for her cellar that she would reimburse later. Then when he rushed in moments after, flustered by the Porsche's flat tire, asking for her keys to the Vantage, she didn't think so. Instead she called for a taxi and took his set of keys for the roadside service guys.

When he was gone, when he was not coming back, she boxed his collection of books and personal effects; she bagged his entire wardrobe that she had paid for and drove to the Mission House. When she returned she changed her gate code as an additional precaution, went inside, poured a glass of exquisite wine and flushed him from her mind where he would not resurface for another sixteen years when her best friend and lover would weep quietly in a Charleston, South Carolina courtroom at the thought of her precious Courtney being heartlessly hurled from her own yacht by the cold-blooded killer.

Which wasn't the case for Braxton Miles who would remember Courtney Fox as often as he would Blaire Fortune, who all but flew through the wine store that night, sharing the extensive list with eager staff.

For whatever reason she was pissed with him he would not make her anymore sour than she was, would not jeopardize the ten grand coming his way. The taxi's meter was running and whatever urgent thing was waiting for him at the apartment, which he believed must be from Cody Jones, could wait an hour longer.

When he did get there, bounding up the stairs into the apartment, into the kitchen where the thoughtful landlady had left the package, eager for what CJ was giving him, he froze at seeing the *C. Fox* in thick black letters across the envelope.

Inside the message was concise and telling:

Got Ya!

Wine is so much more delicious when we actually pay for it! Sorry about that! Not!

You'll find your books and clothes at the Mission House, re-

duced for a quick sale!
    Salut and Adios! Asshole!
    Ms. Courtney Fox (who you shall not fuck with)!

25

11:05 AM.

"The vindictive bitch screwed me over for five grand, dumping another twenty into a junk bin for the city's lost and lonely. Go figure. I took the woman at her word and she screwed me, a distempered female being the worst of any herd. Of course, you wouldn't know that. Fact is, Preacher, Blaire and Courtney each put out for fun and profit. Both as tight as a beggar's grip on a dollar. Anyhow that's how Blaire was the first few times I was doing Courtney, the difference being that Blaire was never a hedonistic and selfish bitch. She was straight up. She knew what was and got paid upfront while the biggest cockteaser on the planet bided her time until the old coot passed on. For a prostitute is a deep pit; an adulteress is a narrow well. That would be Proverbs 23:27, Preacher. If you're not aware. Which clearly begs the question: How was she not a whore? For our Ms. Courtney Fox was indeed very deep and she was indeed very narrow. Probably still is. And rich."

The chaplain grimaced. He wanted out. He wanted his mind and soul cleansed of the impious and impenitent man. "I am happy for Miss Fox, Braxton, that she survived you. Yet she was very wealthy and comely with no one in her life but you. Why then did you not kill her, my son?"

Miles chuckled. "She was forty-one, Preacher. Forty-one. When you're twenty that is ancient, despite her body and insatiable appetite. And she was using me for a single purpose, the very way I used her for mine. Fair is fair, though arguably one major fuck-up on my part, I suppose. Don't you think?"

"Possibly if you had treated her with genuine kindness and love you would be with her now, and not here with me."

"That was not my destiny, or hers. You should know that. She had me on demand, on a string. I was her living add-on to her top dresser drawer and getting especially well laid while I doubled my income with her easy money. Until the vacation, until that day. And truthfully, you know, before God," he checked the time through the slot, "and particularly with our time closing in on us here, what I did was truly a playful accident. Nothing else. Albeit an unfortunate turning point by which time she had no doubt decided I was persona non-grata in her sad life anyway. Shit does happen, Preacher, to the best of us. Like CJ once warned me, I got too comfortable with her and she saw that. We just were not destined for anything longer or more meaningful. Was not in the cards. Karma. Imagine, a star character witness sitting in the courtroom and not a single one of those smug cretins had a clue. I mean, who else but Courtney could have spoken better of me since I never hurt her? Not once." He snickered. "Excepting those frequent demands, naturally." He twisted his palms outward inside the tight steel restraints, hunching his shoulders and smirking, his eyes bright and glistening. "All I ever did was make her feel young and happy. Truth is…not killing her wasn't my choice. She was not meant to die, not by my hand. Was not her time. She was simply a means, an inescapable gateway into all that would come after, every one of my breaths since guiding me to this my final hour with you."

"Breaths that altered countless destinies, my son."

Miles shook his head. "Ensuring those destinies, Preacher. Big difference. One might even say doing God's work. Don't you think? Did take a few months, though, developing a workable plan."

11:08 AM.

26

At twenty-three Braxton Miles knew no other home. He had travelled, had been places, but the Swamp was home, the Lower Garden District familiar and friendly.

He didn't want three wasted years attending classes with children simply for a master's that would ensure Professor Miles spending his life in the same classroom day after day dying a slow and agonizing death. He was above and beyond all that. How could he when he was better than them, working harder and more deserving? They were average; whereas he was clearly in a class of his own, intended for bigger and better things after all he had done with CJ, had accomplished with her.

He had lived two years in a mansion earning every penny, had a fabulous yacht and a luxury ride. He was educated, smoother than any college jock and street-smart, which, in fact, was the workable plan he would begin nurturing and one day make real.

July in the Swamp was always the worst hell with daily indexes often surpassing 100° F and torrential midday downpours bringing with them suffocating humidity and dense clouds of steam wafting from streets and sidewalks.

Braxton passed the entire month brooding at home, drowning in self-pity while drinking 100-dollar wines. The Lower District apartment was okay, comfortable, but he missed the patio and pool, the Porsche, the fine restaurants and his tailored wardrobe.

Of course the translation thing was doable. He had the credentials; yet the inescapable reality was that spending his days shut in doing mundane work alone for fifty a year when he had too easily adopted her lifestyle and richesse as his own would never endure. He knew full well he had become too quickly enamoured of the good life, her good life. And he needed more. Above all he needed more money, more of everything she once gave him on a silver platter.

He had no friends, and certainly no social circle from college; the two girls whose clinginess he terminated with guiltless ease, and the many willing aspirants to the Porsche he'd snubbed, each despising him for different reasons. Which he was good with, particularly the jocks still living with mom and dad while he was drinking richly flavoured Bordeaux believing his two years with her must have had some meaning, some real purpose. Fate. Whatever. Something he could fall back on—cash in on. He needed to get real.

Throughout the month he began of necessity relearning Survival 101: Groceries and basic math, recalling Blaire's wisdom about taking things slow, about fitting in and never attracting unwanted attention. He figured with an entry-level Beamer and his apartment, a decent wardrobe and vacations, other sundry expenses like women his age who wouldn't come cheap or last very long, that, more importantly, his cash would for about three years. Ample time for devising and realizing a sustainable career strategy, by month's end Braxton rationalizing that he could never regain his previous charmed life by beguiling and mounting a herd of older women who would never be Blaires or Courtneys. Nor would younger and more eager-to-please females on the hunt fitting his criteria ever deem to pay for his faux-tendresse and disingenuous blandishments. Not a chance. A completely ridiculous notion contravening natural law that he would honour and obey.

The problem was that by the following summer, satiated with the flavourful monthly nuances of several young and amenable huntresses, honing his skills by way of their nubile bodies before returning each one to the dating auction block, he'd gone well over budget with perhaps a year at best left in his box. Which he didn't construe for an instant as excess or failure, not for a moment neglecting his plan. He had a concept, one he'd been exploring for a good while, one that would significantly increase his net worth.

To a girl they were instantly enthralled by him, by the car, the well-appointed apartment, the wine and the candles, the sweaty and breathtaking romance, by her reverie of marrying the man of her naïve dreams. Each nubile incumbent skillfully seduced in under a month, each breathing life into Blaire Fortune's warm flesh and urgent whispers of warning.

The girls were an ongoing course study helping him prepare for a deservedly better existence, in return for which he was helping them become more gifted and desirable girlfriends and wives. Though he did believe his time in New Orleans was closing in on him, that he should be moving on after five years and not get trapped in the Swamp where indulgence and excess were rampant, where he would never stand out in any meaningful way.

He was thinking Charleston, another new beginning and once again getting paid for what he did best, which was not cleaning pools. He was thinking a master's and becoming that respected Professor Miles on his terms, thinking Cody Jones who he hadn't seen in a year, too preoccupied with pretty and compliant girls to remember his indebtedness, not expecting that providence would take his hand that very afternoon.

CJ was calling, the private number flashing on his cell sending a chill down Braxton's spine. One year without a single word. Shit! CJ was calling in the favour and that could not be good.

Neither was Cody Jones good with small talk, the medium of dull and unchallenged minds. They would meet by chance the next day in Jackson Square for an outdoor Po' Boy lunch attired appropriately for business. Goodbye, kid.

By chance? Outside? A Po' Boy in the park? No way could that be good, not when CJ's idea of a quick bite in public was his corner table at Le Renard, the rest of Braxton's day spent in a daze, his sleepless night fraught with anguish and fanciful worst-case scenarios. Despite which he was standing on the less travelled corner of Decatur and St. Peter at noon under the shade of an oak when he was pleasantly surprised by a smiling and familiar face he'd never forgotten.

*

"Heard you and Courtney went your separate ways, kid."

"I messed up." Braxton sipped his beer. "What can I say? Life goes on. How's she doing?"

"Like anyone else with that kind of bankroll. Happy one day, lonely the next."

"And Blaire?"

"Who?"

"Got it." He gave the man a once-over. "How can you do that, CJ, wear black all the time?"

The man snickered. "Black on black. What's your point, kid?" He pointed with his bottled water down St. Peter, suggesting the white boy would appreciate the shade. "You still good, kid? Still keeping up?"

"She put me into a bit of a dead-end. Been working on some plans though."

"That would be a no. We don't plan for a year, kid. Not with that fancy diploma of yours. You get things done."

"That's what I'm doing. That's why I was going to call you, ask a favour."

CJ listened until Braxton finished detailing his blueprint for success without displaying the least surprise, offering no opinion since "Every man must make his own way, kid. Or not. Walk his own path alone. That said, if that's what you want, I can certainly help get you there. With one very big consideration."

"Which is?"

"Thirty grand upfront. You got that much cash after losing one very pretty lady and wasting an entire year?"

"It'd wipe me out and really fuck with my plan, CJ. I need that money."

Cody shook his head. "Which is on you, kid, for not taking things seriously. These situations don't come cheap. You should know that, like Braxton Miles who was also an expensive favour. One you have clearly wasted and not yet repaid…until now. A debt I need settled sooner than later."

"Anything, CJ. I knew that when you called."

"Good. That's good because I need a man dealt with."

"Meaning?"

"Meaning killed."

Braxton froze. He stopped breathing, feeling his blood turn cold. "You're joking, right?"

"He beat on one of my girls. Saw something young and pretty strolling by, thought he'd have a real good time in the park, and put her in the ER by the time he was done. Caused a shitstorm of undue grief to rain down upon me. Thing is, my girls are smart. She photoed his tag before he drove off when, somehow, she saw nothing else. Go figure." He coughed a curt laugh. "No doubt he saw the flash. Probably thinks the cops are coming. But they are not coming. You are."

"Killing a guy? Shit. No way."

"More like putting down vermin and not the first time for you, kid. Albeit every bit as righteous. Believe me, you'll be doing the city a favour, doing any stray girl a favour." CJ tossed his bottle into a trash can. "No different than that and just as easy when you do as you're told like old times. Then we can talk about that thirty grand…after this gets done."

"No way, CJ. That's prison for murder and this shithole state's got the death penalty."

"Won't happen. The ones in prison, they killed folk they have

212

history with, not strangers. In prison as much for being stupid as killing. The pros, they don't get caught. They do things right."

He wasn't convinced. "Shit."

"You'll do fine, kid. This is a community service. One you will not have a problem with once you see him."

"Who is this guy?"

"Wally Bunker. Single, fifty, five-seven, 170. Rents a room on Marais Street. Spends his days washing dishes and his nights seeking to hurt innocent ladies. More importantly he is no one's loss. You remember that. No one will lament his passing or think of him."

"Is she okay, your girl?"

"Vacationing, taking things easy."

"Shit, CJ."

"That girl was every bit as pretty as the one you knew for a short while, kid. Real pretty. Now she's mending, having a tough time, and we're making things right for her. You and me."

"Okay, so when am I doing this? And how? I mean, shit, that first time just kind of happened. This is way different."

"Tonight."

"What?"

"No time like the present, kid. At his bus stop when he gets off work. Eleven-fifteen. Unless you get company, which you will not. Not midweek. You will be met and given a gun you will not shoot yourself with. You will be dropped off nearby, you will do the job as you are instructed by someone you will not ask about, and you will leave with the gun."

Braxton rubbed his face damp with the midday heat, wondering how the man could look as cool and be as calm as he was. "Okay, CJ. I'll kill the guy. I will, the way you say. I owe you."

"Good. That's good. And, kid, no booze. Not a drop till this is over. Then you stay up as late as you want."

27

For the rest of the day the blueprint for a meaningful life was the farthest thing from his mind.

The well-dressed businessmen parted company with hand-shakes, Braxton first spending time at the gym working up a sweat before doing a five K run around Audubon Park until he could practically hear his heart beating. In the apartment by 6:00 Wednesday evening he stood under a cool shower controlling his breathing, wishing CJ had met him for dinner instead, spending the few and interminable hours remaining pacing in circles before leaving at 10:30 dressed like a thousand other New Orleanians in crisp Dockers, penny loafers and blue denim.

He walked three blocks, stopping where the nondescript brown sedan was parked, waved in by the driver who began a casual crash course in murder as though talking about the weather before driving toward Mid-City. Listening the way he was told, not seeing the man the way he was told.

The nine-millimetre fifteen-round Q4 TAC was heavy in his hands, somehow more ominous with the suppressor attached. But he liked the feel; he liked the sensation of the cool black metal.

"That ain't no toy, kid. Ain't no girl either. Meanin' y'all don't go gettin' yourself all hard over this. This ain't no game."

"I know that. Just never held one before."

He showed Braxton a clear photograph. "One fat fuck, this Bunker guy. Ugly as yesterday's shit to boot. Kill the fucker my-self in a blink if not for CJ's conflictin' wishes."

"You do this often, kill people?"

"I do what CJ wants, like y'all. Now shut your hole'n listen. He'll cross the street, sit his ass down beside y'all'n surely wonder what the fuck. Y'all be ready for that. He ain't much accustomed to company takin' up space on his bench. Meanwhile y'all are countin' down from ten, keepin' your head straight. Then y'all stand. Y'all shoot the fucker first in the chest, then in the head. Y'all bury the gun in the satchel, walk east down Banks like y'all are doin' just fine'n dandy, out for a late stroll'n we are done. Y'all got that?"

"Yeah. I can do this."

He handed Braxton a canvas satchel. "Good. That's good. Cause, y'all don't, I will. Then guess what comes after?"

With that encouragement they drove to Banks Street, Braxton climbing out a few blocks from the diner once the eleven o'clock bus passed them. Countdown. Until like clockwork Wally Bunker waddled across the street, sat his ass down at the far edge as expected, and studied the stranger from the corner of his eye, making his killer seethe. Bunker was indeed a loathsome troll. That he could wash anyone's dishes was difficult enough to fathom, but the way he was made his vicious crime against CJ's girl all the more repulsive. Vermin? No shit.

Ten, nine, eight—the way he was told. Then he stood, reaching into the satchel, sneering at the loud gasp, the wide-open mouth and eyes. He couldn't help himself. He needed the man to understand and be afraid.

"You've got that about right, asshole. You are dead. This is for the girl you attacked last week. She has people who care." A round went into Bunker's chest, Braxton scarcely realizing he'd pulled back on the trigger, Bunker staring dumbly at the stain as though he had messed himself with hot sauce. "I wish I could stay longer. I do, for the girl. Instead this one's for Blaire, who you will never hurt."

He stood amazed at how violently the head snapped back, at the loud thwacking sound of the forehead shattering, at how he didn't feel a thing. CJ was right. The vermin was dead and the city was a safer and cleaner place, if the Swamp could ever be safe or clean. Then he walked away burying the gun in the satchel and strolling east the way he was told until the brown four-door pulled in to the curb.

*

From noon until the moment he saw Bunker hobbling toward him, obese and stubble-faced in baggy jeans and a tent-size tee-shirt, until he saw the gaping toothless mouth and the yellowed blood-shot eyes screaming silent fear, Braxton thought he would spend the aftermath on his knees racked with guilt and puking. Instead he went home, poured a glass of wine, and slept peacefully because killing Bunker was not a big deal. In fact he enjoyed the moment, the adrenaline rush.

Thursday he did an hour at the gym, did a run, and went home preoccupied with his plan, thinking about Courtney and her boat, about the day she glared up at him entirely pissed with blood trickling down her cheek—thinking what if? What if he'd stuck around and been smarter? What if she'd been younger? What if they had been married and the water deeper? What if he could work something out with CJ? What if?

Mid-afternoon his phone chimed. Cody Jones was returning his call. They were meeting for late-night drinks at the Doubletree in Metairie.

*

Walking into the lounge Braxton felt peculiar. While driving there he'd listened to how the city's eighty-fifth victim was an ongoing investigation, likely a random shooting with no apparent motive. He felt peculiar because there was a very clear motive and Cody Jones was sitting in a corner smiling, raising his wine glass.

"Good job, kid." He waved Braxton into an armchair. "You

okay?"

"Yeah, no problem. Like you said, as soon as I saw him he was a community service." He reached for his glass, swirling, inhaling the aroma. "This sort of thing happen often, CJ?"

"Circumstances are usually different. Last night should not have happened. Fortunately the girl had her head on straight. Helped us get things done."

"Does she know?"

"She knows I took care of business. Period." He sipped his wine. "Now tell me more about Charleston. You serious about that?"

"Yeah, I am. Thing is, I need that thirty K. I got a little too deep into a few things this past year. Things got expensive, but it was all good."

"I can imagine. The question is, apart from the costly euphemism, is this really necessary us sitting here? You need another favour that badly, kid?"

"I've thought a lot about this. A lot of shit's gone down in five years, CJ. A mother I can't get rid of in my dreams, the guy I killed because of her, the lady you tell me I don't know, college, Courtney, that piece of shit last night. Am I sure? No. But I'm not that dumbass hillbilly anymore and, like the man said, I'll be walking my own path alone because normal will not work for me. Killing those guys was easy, CJ. If that's the worst you'll call in, then yeah, I need a favour that badly in case things don't work out, especially since my time with Courtney." Braxton sipped his wine, grinning. "Truth is, there's nowhere else for me, not since her. She's my destiny, whoever she might become."

Several quiet seconds followed, each man studying the other. Braxton sat swirling his wine, waiting; Cody sat with his hands clasped, pressing his forefingers against pursed lips, musing. He liked the kid, he always did. Though whatever was swirling in his head in perfect rhythm with the deep burgundy '84 Nuit Saint-

Georges was nothing he wanted or needed to hear about.

"Then when I call, you come. I don't call, in two years you're in for seventy grand not thirty. You good with that?"

"I'm very good with that." Braxton raised his glass. "How long?"

"A couple of weeks. In the meantime you make peace with the landlady and take a loss on the Beamer. No ties, no connections. Braxton Miles remains in New Orleans in limbo and when all is said and done he will get his white ass to somewhere in Europe one-way and stay there doing good for humanity. Whatever. He does not come home, ever. You got that?"

"Yeah, I do."

"Now, you got a name?"

He put a fingertip to his ring. "Yeah, I do. He is also three years older and a shitload smarter."

TurnAbout

Part Three
28

June in Charleston, South Carolina is mostly pleasant without the dreaded summer heat their southerly neighbours perforce endure. Most days are sunny and bright with cool breezes off the Atlantic, but not Saturday, June 15th, one year earlier as Oliver Holloway was being laid to rest in a private ceremony after a solemn service and bidding his collection of friends, neighbours, associates and sycophants farewell.

The dark sky was suitably ominous, covered with purple-black clouds lit up with abstract spears of blinding white light in concert with resounding thunder that shook the ground and relentless heavy rain that whipped at coattails and slashed at faces already wet with tears.

Oliver Holloway was forty, a pillar in the community; he was successful and respected, wealthy and deeply in love, dead of a careless car accident not of his doing. His adoring wife of nine years was a grieving widow at thirty-three, sobbing as the lacquered black casket assailed with exploding globules of rain laid suspended above his final resting place plaguing her with guilt.

He had taken a detour a week earlier on his way home from his downtown offices, killed minutes after leaving the flower shop with a dozen of her favourite long-stem yellow and red roses. However the couple's best friend and Oliver's corporate attorney didn't see it that way, she and her sister Presley gently guiding

Brenda away with their arms enlaced. Seeing him disappear into the ground would simply worsen the pain.

The three were inseparable throughout their school years and beyond until Presley was hired by a firm in New York where one year later she married the love of her life, two years after that divorcing him and moving to the West Coast where Presley Burke swore off marriage for good while becoming a highly sought-after fashion photographer. Presley Burke because, as much as she hated the domineering prick, she loathed her Sicilian father that much more for what he had once said and done to the girl she loved more than anyone and always would. That was the day she left home, never to see her father or meekly obedient mother again.

Charleston, however, was Priscilla Serra's destiny, as was Brenda Holloway's, often joking that if anything ever happened to Oliver she would marry Brenda, something Oliver was ready and willing to see happening, Brenda reminding them with forlorn sighs that Presley would be her first choice. She was far prettier and, oh yeah, totally hot. Totally yummy and more her type. Something she could definitely see going on. If only she could be a little curious, my darlings. Oh well, leaving Oliver to his own laments. But now the humour was gone.

"Brenda, it's been a year. Oliver would not like this. You know that. He was always so full of life and would not like this at all."

"I haven't dated in ten years, Prissy. Anyway, you should talk."

"Not the same thing."

"Maybe I should try jumping Presley. At least then I wouldn't be cheating."

"That is just too gross, apart from Presley having enough serious heartache; she doesn't need yours. And not cheating. Living. The way Oliver would want."

"With how many before another Mr. Right comes along? I think that's called fucking around. Cheating."

"Or dating until things work out."

"Yeah, the personals. Lonesome and desperate but attractive middle-aged millionaire widow. Only serious suitors apply."

"I was thinking more like exquisitely breathtaking and vital young woman with midnight blue-black hair and hypnotic green eyes who knows shit from sugar seeking a serious Mr. Right. References required."

Brenda curled into her friend with a mischievous grin, linking their arms and kissing her cheek.

"Beautiful, breathtaking and vital. Just not good enough for a dyke with lustrous chocolate brown hair, liquid brown eyes, soft full lips and Southern Belle flawless white skin. Oh, yummy. Muy deliciosa, chica."

"Skinny bitch. I'm being serious here. And the personals are just too creepy. I'm thinking a dating service. Let them sieve through the shit to find the sugar."

*

Priscilla won out. A few days later Brenda signed with an agency. That he would be under forty, in excellent shape and educated was non-negotiable. Nor would he embarrass her in public, belch in restaurants or scratch himself. Nor was she out to get laid, which would not happen until he passed the litmus test.

By the end of August after several first dates and polite dinners, several good-nights on the sidewalk by her GranTurismo MC and late-night talks with Priscilla, she was fed up, tired of making herself desirable for losers. She was done with jerks suggesting they split the bill, the guy who should be working anytime soon, the weekend nudist and the one whose wife was probably in bed bagging some other guy by the time that news flash broke.

In spite of which Priscilla persisted, suggesting she add *Executive* to the preconditions. Which she did, agreeing through the matchmaker that he could call her the Friday of Labour Day weekend when they spoke for an hour before her lesbian soulmate with the lustrous brown hair called for an update.

"The guy sounds too good, Prissy. I mean, really too good. He's in your email. You tell me."

Priscilla reached for her laptop, rating the photographs, a few moments later chuckling into her phone. "Not far from a ten, I suppose. But what's with guys and their abs?"

"That was my idea. The problem is he's twenty-eight."

She ignored the faux-doubt. "He's not bad in a suit either. Does he have a brain or money or both?"

"He's from New Orleans."

"God, he's a hillbilly."

"Not exactly. He graduated from UNO, then moved here a few years ago for a master's when his parents died. He knows about wine, he's travelled, and he's self-made. Paid his way through college by crewing on yachts."

"Does he have one?"

"I didn't ask? We're having dinner tomorrow at L'Etiquette. That's something else, Prissy. He speaks French."

"How would you know?"

"Because, like me, he speaks fluent Spanish mi preciosa lesbiana. That's what he does; he's a private tutor and corporate translator. Something we already have in common."

"Really, a teacher?"

"No, a professor."

"Well, he doesn't look poor. Does this guy have a name? And, yes, thank you. I am gorgeous."

"Brent Mason. Formerly Professor Brent Mason at the U of SC. And kind of dreamy."

29

By mid-August Brent Mason had been in Charleston a year, returning home from a brief stay in Europe after working his way across
the Atlantic on a Panamanian freighter in lieu of paid passage.
Should anyone ever inquire.

He drove a mid-range BMW he paid for with cash and lived in
a tenth-floor condo he furnished with European flair where he tu-
tored private daytime students with failing grades that would keep
the IRS happy at 500 a week.

His evenings were another matter, several times a week escorting young widows, spurned lovers and eager divorcées to the theatre and dinners, earning that much in a night with a loyal clientele
and referrals while honing his skill and urbanity.

He was doing alright with over sixty K in his safety deposit box
and a single deferred debt he had no worries about. Despite which
the escort thing was not intended as a long-term investment strategy or part of his blueprint; they were quick money, but as much
hard work as they were lucrative and pleasingly prurient dates. Of
necessity he was moving on, diversifying, investing in his future
by melding his regulars with on-the-hunt hopefuls fitting his strict
criteria of youthful good looks, reasonable smarts, and her suscep-
tibility to incremental loving devotion. He wasn't wasting time on
sceptics or anyone past her prime.

He'd gone through a half-dozen, each one to-die-for stunning,
each one independently well-off. Just not well-off enough, sending
each disappointment home alone in a taxi from L'Etiquette and

hoping September 01st would reverse the trend, spending the day mastering her profile, studying the notes he scribbled during their Friday conversation. He didn't mind her being thirty-four. He could easily work with that, especially since Blaire was thirty-three, years younger than Courtney, and his regulars were either touching or had arrived on the wrong side of thirty. So no big deal. Not anymore. He was adapting, seemingly having found his niche. Besides, what would he ever accomplish with anyone that much younger? Not a whole lot.

They agreed they would meet at the restaurant at 7:00, Brenda Holloway pleasantly surprised that he was handsomer than in his photographs, that he stood by the table as she came closer, greeting her with a pleasant smile and genteel tilt of his head as the maître d' pulled out her seat. Above all he was there, not making her wait and wonder, looking casual yet debonair in a dark fitted suit that was clearly made for him and a white button-down with French cuffs.

He was confident, clearly his own man who was not the least bit nervous or intimidated, his bright blue eyes telling her he was pleased with what he was seeing. Nor had he ordered a calm-the-nerves cocktail. He didn't need one. Yes! Priscilla would certainly approve.

What Mason saw sauntering toward him was a 5'8" self-assured lady with everything in the right place. The sheen of her perfect legs accentuated a modestly short and silky midnight blue shift dress and shawl the colour of her hair that would have easily set her back a grand or more, her flawless complexion glowing with the hue of a fading tan. Gorgeous and graceful, turning heads and prompting appreciative glances as the tuxedoed gent brought her closer.

"Your guest, Monsieur Mason." The maître d' adding as he drew the lady's napkin across her lap, "Your server will give you a few moments."

"C'est très bien. Merci, Joaquin."

Brent Mason eased into his seat, thinking he had never seen such deep emerald eyes. "I was sitting here a little perplexed thinking 'Good evening' would seem too formal, too serious, and a 'Hi' somewhat too familiar." He grinned, holding out open palms in supplication. "Happily you resolved my dilemma the moment you walked in. Wow. You are completely stunning. I am truly happy I called you, that you allowed me to call you."

Brenda set her clutch on the edge of the table. "Gosh, I'm sorry I caused you such a grave concern. I feel terrible."

"Please don't. My anxiety has completely subsided. I'm fine."

She adjusted her napkin, her smile warm. "Thank you for inviting me. And perhaps stunning is a little overstated."

"Very stunning from where I'm sitting, Brenda. But with that difficult part over they have an extensive cocktail menu and excellent wine list."

"Cîroc on the rocks would be wonderful. And you? A scotch man, maybe single malt neat?"

"I prefer wines. Bordeaux and the Loire mostly, though I do venture elsewhere occasionally."

He signalled the waiter and, naturally, the lady's vodka and the gentleman's Saint-Émilion Grand Cru were excellent choices.

While the man was gone they got the weather out of the way, their day, and the restaurant each had patronized several times; Brenda complimenting the choice, not believing for a moment he was perplexed about anything. That declaration producing a contrite confession.

A discreet time later the waiter highly recommended the consommé aux xérès followed by the haricots verts en salade au gratin and the Châteaubriant for Monsieur et Madame lightly drizzled with a delicate Béarnaise sauce. Et voilà, the sommelier by then well familiar with the gentleman's tastes suggesting a rich and full bodied Santenay-Maladière as the most perfect accompaniment.

She was widowed; he knew that. Her husband was the president and CEO of his electronics firm before he was taken from her and she worked as Chief Administrator at a not-for-profit drop-in centre and was feeling guilty.

He understood about loss, about pain. He earned a master's at the U of SC; she knew that. However the professorship didn't work for him. He wasn't happy, leaving Columbia after a year to do his own thing in Charleston where he could at least be near the sea that he loved so dearly.

Desert was crème brûlée sprinkled with cognac, the meal completed with a sharp Courvoisier for Madame and Rémy Martin for Monsieur, a rare luxury he allowed himself when dining with an enchanting lady.

"Brent, what a lovely evening. Thank you."

"Does that mean dinner and the theatre next Saturday? I have tickets for Les Misérables. Not that I was being presumptuous, more like positive." The ensuing silence seemed like an eternity, Brent raising an open palm. "Please, don't answer. I deserve the torture of waiting, the dread of pending rejection. I'll call you Thursday."

"I completely adore the theatre." She giggled, patting the corner of her prune-coloured lips with her napkin. "Call me anyway for confirmation."

"That's a yes?"

She nodded. "Yes. That is a yes."

*

Mason walked her to her Maserati, an awkward moment obviated with Brenda's sisterly hug. She
 was taking things slow. One pleasant evening did not mean a lifetime. Kissing or anything more promising was not an option. Neither was avoiding Priscilla's post-date inquisition once at home, the gorgeous brunette giving her full approval for a second date.

Thursday evening they learned more about each other. Brenda

listened to how his parents were killed in a terrible tour bus accident while on vacation, horrified when he confessed that one year earlier he was stood up at the altar and that his crushed heart was the real reason he left Columbia and a flourishing academic career. She understood how he must still hurt, telling him how she met Oliver, how he was taken by a Happy Hour miscreant who was sentenced to three years, and how she would always love him.

However, "Yes, Saturday we'll put our personal tragedies aside and enjoy the evening."

Because "Your friend is right, Brenda. You have no reason at all to feel guilty and we both deserve to recapture our happiness. I'll see you Saturday at seven," when Brent Mason turned into her driveway and cemented his destiny from which there was no turning back.

He understood Thursday evening what South of Broad meant, which didn't prepare him. The neighbourhood's pithy designation meant money, big money, the stately Holloway home nestled between hundred-year-old trees on a manicured half-acre, which didn't mean he was getting into her private domain just yet.

The lady was standing at her door, the very picture of elegance and poise, the proper words already forming on his lips.

She was sensational with her black hair twisted into a French braid. The sleeveless olive green choker dress plunged, the swell of her breasts glistening with silver dust, her bare legs no less entrancing from her mid-thighs; the silver strapped stiletto sandals brought her to an even six feet, the matching silk shawl enwrapping her, draped over her arms, and her silver tassel earrings completing the sensual portrait.

Brenda saw a man she pushed from her mind as often as she thought of him, each time telling Oliver's photograph at her bedside she was sorry, explaining that perhaps Priscilla was right. His black suit was tailored and his black shirt did not come from the Apparel Shack. Neither did the perfectly knotted silver tie or the silver pocket hanky. In fact, if she didn't know better—.

Climbing from the candy-apple red cabriolet whose tan top he'd put down for effect, he was beaming. "Brenda, you are sensational. Ravishing. And, being perfectly honest, not letting my eyes wander right now is proving extremely difficult."

"Thank you. Prissy came by today. Her idea. She's very persuasive. I love her deeply, but sometimes…" She nodded at the car. "Nice Beamer. Impressive. And you're very dashing this evening."

"Merci infiniment, madame. Nevertheless, I won't be the one turning heads." He stepped in closer. "May I? A lovely corsage for a very lovely lady."

"How thoughtful, Brent." She held out her wrist, peering over his shoulder at the convertible, scrunching her face. "I'm thinking I should have chosen something a little longer, like slacks."

He glanced down, smirking. "That's one perspective, I suppose."

*

The evening went splendidly and, as previously agreed upon, neither party broached a painful past that for so long had threatened their happiness, Brenda ending the evening on her portico with another hug. And yes, dinner on Saturday before front row seating at the Cirque du Soleil sounded fabulous, except that she was paying for dinner because, unless he was dealing drugs on the side, she didn't know too many rich professors.

Then Brenda stepped inside, poured a nightcap, and reported in to the pushy brunette who listened for an hour about the guy who apparently was doing everything right. She just wasn't ready to invite another man into Oliver's home. Something even Priscilla Serra understood was not up for debate, satisfied that this Brent guy would call Brenda again on Thursday.

Things were looking up.

As they were for Mason. Although he wasn't doing drugs anymore he continued fulfilling the needs of his loyal clientele, albeit taking his chances in public. Things were looking up indeed. The following Saturday at dinner she touched his hand from across the table, slipping her arm through his as they strolled toward the Beamer after the performance. That was a good thing, a very timely thing.

"Brenda, I like you. I like you a lot."

"As do I you, Brent."

"Good. Because I'm thinking Fernandina Beach next weekend. Because at some point, thinking out loud, hoping this thing we have grows into something even more special, we should do something about that. That said, no pressure. Think about it. Saying no won't change what we share now." He paused, peering into her emerald eyes. "Truthfully though, I want much more."

"I will think about it, Brent. Because sleeping with you would change everything and let's not forget...I am older than you. What happens when something younger comes along?"

"Well, whoever she is, she keeps on walking. Because I'm already with someone young and pretty." He chuckled. "Five hours a week and, being positive, I rented a cottage on the beach thinking you would enjoy the space and perhaps want some alone time."

She knew this was coming. Still she was torn between guilt and desire; she didn't know. "Okay. I will think about it, which does not mean yes." But after a quiet ride home and under her portico she kissed his cheek before stepping in, leaning against the door and sighing because she knew exactly what was coming.

"What! He said that?"

"More or less. And he does have a point, Prissy."

"Good. It's time you got laid before you forget how."

"Like you."

"Don't be snide. I get laid just fine. And getting laid doesn't mean a lifetime. It means getting laid, having a good time. We are not talking marriage here."

"The entire weekend. What if there's no connection? That'll be a long drive home."

"Don't start with excuses. Go shopping. Do the garter and lace thing. Remember, I've seen your sweet cheeks and your girls. There's nothing he won't like. And I want the dirty details."

Brenda sighed into the phone. "Shit. I wasn't expecting this, not this soon."

"Soon does not apply here. Go get yourself laid. Have a good time."

"You're so pushy."

"Skinny bitch."

"Pushy bitch."

30

Friday was a superb first day of autumn, bright and warm with a clear pastel blue sky, Mason doing the 220 miles in under four hours with the top down, enjoying the view, enjoying Brenda in a loose-fitting scalloped shift dress and heels.

Wednesday evening she went for dinner and a shopping spree with Priscilla, outfitting herself for the two-night tryst, insisting she would not wear a thong on the beach. Fernandina was not Miami or the Caribbean, Priscilla insisting she would. It's not like the guy wouldn't be seeing her tan lines, or lack of, Priscilla reiterating the dress code as they kissed and hugged before stepping into their respective Maserati and Lexus.

Thursday she took the day off for a full menu of ready-for-romance spa treatments trying not to think of the weekend, failing miserably throughout the day. She was worried. Dating him was one thing, not having sex in over a year and being naked with him after three dinners was very much another. Yet Thursday evening she called him, expecting him by nine the next morning.

She needed the entire day with him first. Arriving late and simply jumping into bed was not an option.

Then she went to bed, phoned Priscilla and endured a wakeful night, deciding she would wear a thong at the beach after all, her reflection in the mirror justifying that Priscilla was right and that giving him a preview of their evenings would make her first night with him somehow easier. Besides she was always backless at exotic resorts with Oliver, many times discreetly sans top on white sandy beaches. Not to mention the playful Spring Breaks and sultry summer days throughout her college years with Priscilla and Presley.

So what was the big deal? She wasn't exactly a cloistered nun, more concerned with looking better than she felt, spending the first few hours of Friday's warm sun lying on her patio absorbing the curative rays, waiting as long as she dared before applying restorative makeup and dressing in something short, strapless, and sensational.

She stepped out onto her portico at 8:55, the red convertible pulling up precisely at 9:00 when Brent Mason was appropriately wide-eyed and effusively gallant.

They arrived at the beach house near 1:00, Mason thinking a Cîroc on the rocks and a chilled Chardonnay on the front porch would help set the mood before the beach towels and SPF, though what impressed Brenda more was the secluded backyard and private walkway at the far end of the beach. He was being thoughtful, giving her the lead. Whenever. Whatever. And however. They were not there to sit on a porch gazing at the horizon while making idle conversation.

She stood, taking the lead, resting her glass on the Adirondack. The whenever was then, the whatever would come in a few minutes when his eyes would speak volumes, the real prelude to their weekend.

"Let's get down there, Brent. The day is too delightful." Padding toward the door in bare and delicate feet, she turned. "Give me some of that alone time first. A couple of minutes."

"Take your time. No hurry."

She wouldn't. In their room she stood staring at the bed, wondering what side he preferred, wondering what else he preferred. Oliver always slept on the right and was never disappointing, Brenda wondering how much longer his photograph would be by her bedside, remembering what he so often said, that "bodies are like rental cars, never the property of the driver. Available for one's pleasure until the lease runs out."

Stepping from the gauzy dress Priscilla had selected with a dual purpose, she was pleased. No marks; her body was flawless. She knew that; Oliver always told her that. Then slipping from one tiny thong into another she paused, thinking how foolish. One had strings, the other did not and the beach was practically deserted. No big deal. She often did that with Oliver on romantic beach vacations, recalling their first Adults Only, wiggling into her top and cupping her breasts, thinking soft and warm and no tan lines, telling herself she was there because she felt good with him and that Priscilla was right.

She was ready. Stepping onto the porch, a sheer coverup knotted at her waist, she inhaled an invisible deep breath. "You're up. I'll meet you at the water and bring the wine."

Mason pushed himself from the uncomfortable must-have seaside wooden seat. "Hello! I cannot stand here and not say anything. I cannot imagine anyone more stunning, more exotic."

"Well you keep thinking that and don't keep me waiting because I'll be the topless girl in a thong." She shrugged. "What the hell? Might as well see what you're in for. Most of me anyway. Bye."

He stood watching her saunter along the walkway, hurrying inside, five minutes later taking her hands and twirling her, studying her. Any pretence of being blasé about her body glistening with lotion under a hot midday sun and beautifully naked but for a patch of red was useless.

"Wow. This I was not expecting. This is way beyond my dreams. Are photos allowed?"

She went to the cooler, squatting, not caring, pouring an ounce of wine from the bottle into a glass into her mouth. She needed moisture urgently.

"No, they are not allowed. Use the memory card in your head

because I'm taking this slow, Brent. You and me. This is how I've always done the beach thing and I didn't see that a few hours would make any difference." She took his hand, walking with him into the ocean. "I don't swim very well, but I do love the ocean and we should start acting like lovers since that is what the weekend is all about. Don't you agree?"

Seeing him at first coming toward her in Spandex and not much of it, Brenda's mouth went dry, gulping for moisture that wasn't there. Without his shirt Brent seemed even younger. Much younger in fact and somehow thinking of him as an academic was comical. A slim and tanned lifeguard maybe, a sculpted personal trainer possibly, but no one's pompous professor. No way.

"I couldn't agree more." He swept her into his arms, striding into deeper water, hurling her back toward the beach, watching her flail and disappear, recalling that afternoon with Courtney.

When she surfaced, sputtering and coughing, her face draped with matted thick hair, she was not impressed. "To be clear, Mr. Mason, I did not like that."

He shrugged. "Standing there all drippy you look like a beguiling sea nymph, a captivating and mythological seraphim sent by Neptune to bedazzle and mesmerize me."

She scrunched her face, leaning forward with her arms akimbo. "What? I'm a nymph and a seraphim? Seriously?"

"Yes. Beguiling and captivating."

He stepped into the danger zone, reaching behind her, gently pressing his hands into mounds of soft flesh and raising her from the ocean's floor, pressing his lips to hers, igniting an eruption neither was expecting.

She acquiesced greedily, wrapping her legs tightly around his waist, her arms clinging to his neck, her breasts pressed hard against his chest. Apparently he was forgiven and the mood was most definitely being set. She was at once excited by the dirty details of Priscilla's Sunday night debriefing and her impending evening that now seemed too many hours away, suddenly needing more, imploring Mason who absolutely wanted more, fevered by her lithe body grinding into him, her urgent groans and his remarkably rapid success.

His life was once again good, and getting a shitload better; her life suddenly wonderful again.

He twirled a full circle tugging at her side-ties, scattered beach roamers too far in the distance for either to care. The lady was naked and the lady was primed.

*

Brenda hung limp in his arms, depleted, thankful for the healing warm water. Until the severity of her emergency dawned on her and she spent the next lifetime of minutes desperately searching in the waist-deep ocean for her thong. She didn't care about his problem.

Though with both issues resolved, sitting on the beach sipping Chardonnay, they held hands and talked. Doing the restaurant thing would be too much like work, too detracting from what had undeniably begun as a perfect weekend. They would order in. Pizza on the front porch Friday watching the sun set, Chinese on Saturday with pastries and coffees from a local shop for breakfast that he would go for while she enjoyed peaceful morning strolls.

Then too soon they were heading north on the I-95, kissing goodbye at her door early in the evening because inviting him in would be anticlimactic. He agreed. He would give her time, call her Thursday and miss her until the weekend.

Inside she went onto her patio with a twenty-year Château de Bouchassy, an empty glass and her phone. Savouring the wine she strolled around her pool, staring at the lifejacket she would always wear, tempted but not convinced. That's why she had a girlfriend.

"What! Seven times?"

"Seven fantastic and breathless times. I haven't been that wet since I can't remember. The first time in the ocean in broad daylight. Can you believe that?"

"The ocean? What, with people?"

"Not many. Some. Things just happened, Prissy."

"I was right, I told you. I'm always right. Thongs and bare girls, what's not to die for? So is this a thing, you and him?"

"Not there yet. I'm getting my head straight. I didn't feel for a moment like I was cheating, more like Oliver was happy for me."

"He is. I am too. So when do I meet this washboard hunk?"

"Sunday. You're invited for dinner," Brenda greeting a ravishing slim brunette dressed in an olive green shirt dress and tan heels with thick lustrous hair bouncing at her shoulders as she strode onto the patio where Mason stood confidently swirling his wine and smirking.

He might as well have waved a red flag.

She simply said "I'm Priscilla Serra, the girlfriend," without shaking his hand.

He returned, "I'm Brent Mason, the boyfriend," remaining as he was without complimenting her dress, a pleased-to-meet-you. Nothing. A major contravention of Southern social decorum.

Four hours and two wine bottles later, a boeuf bourguignon, homemade key lime pie and a cognac, Priscilla smudged her girlfriend's warm cheek with glossy mahogany on the portico, adding that Mason being conspicuous by his absence was a non-issue. Though not really.

Then with the evening at an end she drove home, poured a second cognac and called Presley to keep her current and vent. She disliked Brent Mason instantly, before a single word was spoken, not keeping the distaste from Brenda when she called for a requisite recap the next evening.

"I can't say why. I found him utterly smug and standoffish, as though he was in his house, not yours. His eyes, I don't know. As though he was trying to figure me out, figure out how much of an impediment I would be."

"To what?"

"To you. And please tell me you sent him home."

"I did, and dry. He also knows we're very close, like sisters, and that would never happen."

"That's precisely right. And he's not much of a people person for a professor. During your very sumptuous dinner I had the very distinct impression he was somewhere else. What was up with that?"

"He's had a rough life, Prissy. His parents were killed, a year ago his fiancée didn't show for the wedding and the one before her was doing some other guy he believed was a friend. That's a lot to survive."

"I'm just saying. He put me off."

"Well you were delightful company and," she chuckled, "very yummy in olive and tan."

"Thanks."

"So can we give him a chance?"

Seconds of silence. "Okay. Yes, we'll give him a chance. He was polite enough, I suppose, in a feigned kind of way. But do not expect too much too soon, Brenda. I'm taking things slow with him too and you know why. Remember, I drew it up and was Oliver's executor."

*

Oliver Holloway's will dictated that Brenda was the sole beneficiary of his personal wealth that amounted to twenty-six million in addition to their prestigious home valued at four million that should always remain in her name alone; he further stipulated who would succeed him as interim president and CEO and that Priscilla Serra's enviable top-floor executive post as the firm's legal advisor was lifelong. Furthermore, Brenda should maintain her shares, buy out his fifty-one percent majority, and be particularly wary of future suitors because life does go on. In short, she was a young and wealthy widow with a portfolio approaching forty-two million.

Beware the eager suitor!

One month after his death, her heart still crushed and not tolerating any argument, Brenda gifted the sisters one million each. However what neither Priscilla nor Presley realized was that she had rescripted her will. Upon her death, the sisters would share her wealth equally with or without whomever she might be with. Should anyone else ever happen because she could never love anyone as much as she loved Oliver.

By Christmas Priscilla had lunched with Brenda several times, they had met for dinner and she was staying current. However as in past years she was doing Christmas in San Diego with Presley, promising she would do New Year's with them on condition they celebrate downtown and that she pay her own way.

For his part Mason was expecting a Caribbean Christmas vacation or jewellery or something extravagant, completely taken aback when she told him that she and Oliver would always share the festive day serving meals and giving out donated gifts at the drop-in. They never exchanged gifts under the tree, nor did she want anything from him that year. What was the point when they could do so much more for the less fortunate?

He understood the rationale and generosity entirely, commending her, commending Oliver, not expecting she would corner him. What's worse, he couldn't decline her very clear invitation. There was too much at stake, returning that evening to his rental home entirely pissed with her.

He didn't yet have a key and hadn't yet stayed over. Nor had either one blurted the L word in four months, Brenda conflicted between her cherished memories of Oliver and thinking she should be prepared for the inevitable with a new bed that would not offend those special years. She also worried that if she didn't do something positive soon she would lose him too, greeting him at the door yet again early on New Year's Eve.

"Is she bringing a date?"

"No. She's experiencing a dry spell."

"Too bad for some guy. You'd think with that tight body she'd be big-time busy. Freezer burn maybe?"

"No, not freezer burn. She does alright, believe me, and they are all as spectacular and sexy. She just doesn't want long-term."

Mason's forehead creased. "She's lesbian? Seriously?"

"Yes."

"Holy shit. Why didn't you tell me?"

"Why would I? You're not female so what does it matter? That's sort of how the girly-girly thing works."

He was floored, pausing, a smirk forming on his lips. "Hey, did you guys ever...?"

"No. So get your mind out of the gutter. She'll be here in a few minutes and tonight please be a little more sociable."

*

He was throughout the evening, somewhat, Priscilla clearly recognizing the hypocritical hetero male condition. He knew; she didn't care. Despite which the evening was deemed a moderate success. He danced with his date and Brenda danced with her girlfriend, ringing in a new year and his twenty-ninth birthday with champagne, the girls kissing and hugging in the expansive foyer when Priscilla was ready to leave, when Mason decided he should be somewhere else in the twelve-room home.

Successful except for Priscilla still recognizing something in him she did not like, accepting that Brenda was lonely with her own life to live, agreeing that Valentine's would be as good a time as any and that being worried was probably indicative of something good happening.

Which did not mean doing anything unforgivably foolish like getting all starry-eyed and giving away the family farm, a final goodnight kiss an hour into 1999 without him before she drove home for a nightcap and forgot him.

31

The Sunday one week before Valentine's Brent Mason's phone chimed not long after he walked in from a poolside sunny day of romance, dinner and wine with Brenda. She was calling to say she missed him

Putting down his wine he wasn't surprised reaching for the receiver; she was evolving slowly but surely into the woman he increasingly desired. Instead he froze in time and space, staring at the area code from his past, shivering from the icy chill shooting down his spine. Cody Jones was calling.

"CJ. Wow, hi."

"It's been a while, kid. Tell me, Brent Mason doing well with that plan of his? Good things happening for him over there?"

"Yeah. He's on track. Taking a while, but it's all good." He wet his mouth and throat with wine. Shit! "And you? Everything good in the Swamp?"

Cody Jones chortled. "Well now that depends on who you might be and what you might have done that was for a short while good for you and not particularly good for me. Making your own way down a dark and dangerous path till you see the cul-de-sac sign flashing your name and you hear the footsteps behind you."

He'd almost forgotten. Favours do not go away, do not fade with time. "These footsteps in the dark, that's why you're calling? I'll be taking care of some business?"

"I need your former self here Tuesday evening. A room is reserved and paid for him at the Sheraton. You will fly in Monday as who you are and follow the instructions left for you at the front desk. Clean, easy, and out first thing Wednesday. No fuss, no muss. You got that? You good with that? Or are we now talking a substantial transfer of funds, Professor?"

Mason snorted into the phone, grinning. Like he had a choice, like he cared. He had nowhere near seventy grand in his box, which was on Brenda, keeping up with her, and the only footsteps he was interested in hearing on any dark road were his own.

"Yeah, I'm good with that CJ. Like I told you. So, do we meet after, put down a beer?" "Another time, kid. You just get here with a clear head. No booze. In the meantime, you need me, I'm here. We have good history, you and me."

*

Mason called his affected students, fitting them into the following Saturday. He booked an early evening flight into New Orleans, the first one out Wednesday, and called Brenda because he was missing her and she might worry needlessly when not hearing from him. He would be in Miami three, possibly four days. An important account needed him involved in a meeting with Mexican clients. He would see her on Sunday.

When they disconnected he finished the wine watching mild porn, sometime later in bed drifting into a peaceful slumber without a worry. He had forty-eight hours and no way was he a kid anymore.

Waking to a day shadowed with dark hovering clouds he put in an hour at the gym, did a sixty-minute run, ate breakfast, showered and dressed for travel feeling good except for the negative impact on his resources. Packing as well for the return Wednesday flight, and more in keeping with his adopted lifestyle, he chose his least expensive suit, tie and shirt for Tuesday evening's obligation which would set him back well over two grand. Money he could ill afford, though he would do anything for Cody Jones because they would be seeing each other again.

Before leaving he made a fast snack. A burger and fries. No hurry. No bother, save possibly for the blackening skies. Both airports were passenger-friendly and easily navigated, the ninety-minute flight touching down on schedule at 7:30 Central despite severe crosswinds, driving rain and the electric light show that was more threatening than awesome; one camp of buffeted passengers seemingly acclimated and nonchalant while other heads jerked desperately this way and that searching in vain for an escape into a longer and happier life.

Mason took up with the nonchalant camp. He had no real choice; he was tall and athletic, too debonair and too well-dressed to come unglued, all the while hoping he wouldn't disappoint CJ by screaming his way downward at terminal velocity into a smouldering carnage.

Wasn't his destiny, he supposed, by 8:15 standing in the dark of his hotel room gazing past a window drizzled with ceaseless heavy rain at a cityscape decorated with an amber glow and cars painting red and white jagged streamers along glistening streets while red, yellow and green halos flashed at deserted street corners.

He shrugged, fogging the window with a deep breath. No big deal one month ahead of Mardi Gras, though he felt good being home, musing all the same that the city being so intensely cleansed of its day was a good thing, a timely thing, given that temptation seldom was and seeing her again would serve no purpose, putting from his mind how near and beautiful she was. She was never for a moment his destiny, merely an enticing and hedonistic continuation of his sober and fleeting moments with Blaire.

Flicking the lamp switch he tore open the envelope. The printed instructions were laconic, the last two words a terse: Flush This. At 9:30 precisely he would meet with a nondescript brown sedan on the corner of Canal and Burgundy. Until then he would stay put. That was it. CJ wasn't big on words and the confetti swirled into the drain.

Braxton Miles suspected he would recognize the car, curious what else was coming his way like a name, a description, a gun, and maybe a reason. Or not. Not his business. Nor was staying put a suggestion. That was a clear CJ directive, a precaution which meant in-room meals, a few hours the next morning in the fitness centre, an afternoon lazing by the pool, an early dinner with a delicious club soda and whatever would come next. Like killing some guy. Number three, then who knew?

Do not wonder about what is not your business; do not fret over things you do not care about or cannot manipulate. The wisdom of Cody Jones—and Braxton Miles drifted into a deep sleep waking near 7:00 Tuesday.

He ordered in, doing breakfast in bed with the News Channel before his workout regimen with a rooftop view and the same news faithfully presented verbatim from the same shiny plastic faces, contact-clear eyes and blinding white capped teeth. The real news, the real way, as viewed by a Southern believable Barbie in a designer dress and everyone's credible Ken in a 1000-dollar suit. Good for them. Love me, love you. Mutual adoration and Miles went for the remote, a black screen and solitude.

The day was clear and blue, promising a comfortable 75° rooftop lunch and pool afternoon, which began well. Until his serenity was obliterated by the supercilious housewives vacationing off hubby's expense account thumped onto the deck, their modesty panels floating like lily pads as they waded and fanned the water exchanging exaggerations while a gaggle of blue hairs spent the afternoon carrying on about Ethel and Wilbur disrupting the morning bus tour. Octogenarian androgynes. Old men behaving like old women, old women looking like old men, until en masse the blues tugged each other from their chairs, tottering off to their regenerative naps, the chattering chubbies wrapped in hotel towels following soon after for Happy Hour cocktails.

Miles snorted derisively when they were gone. Not a chance in hell would that ever be him or any woman with him, he mused. Would never happen. Destiny.

He stopped counting after twenty laps, stretched out drying with the warmth of the sun before leaving, ordering-in a burger, fries and more soda, biding his time, dressing for his business meeting in a dark suit, shirt and tie.

At 9:00 PM precisely he left the hotel, walking several blocks north, waiting until he reached the appointed corner to protect his hands and the gun with Italian kid leather moments before the familiar brown sedan slowed to a stop, the passenger door swinging open, Miles stepping in as though he had flagged a cab.

The driver took a slow right onto Burgundy. "Been a while, kid."

"Yeah, a while."

"Looks like life's been good. Y'all find yourself some rich old girl?"

"Something like that. So what's this about? All I know is meeting you here at half-past the hour."

"The guy's name is Vinny Davaux. A real Cajun piece of shit. Dumb as fuck from shitville Lafayette. Brought his good-for-nothin' backwoods runaways with him. All young stuff, pinky white'n freckled. Backseat'n alley girls. Too young'n too stupid for much else. He fucked up, is what. Thought he'd push his way into CJ's domain, the high-end folks, causin' a good man heartache and grief, settin' himself up like he knows shit when he don't. Now y'all are here provin' him wrong." The driver handed Miles a blow-up. "That's him. Creepy little black fuck. Eyes like fuckin' golf balls, more gold in his mouth than his fuckin' fingers."

Miles studied the photo, creasing his brow. "You're shitting me, right? What is he, three feet?"

The driver coughed a laugh. "Ain't no one laughin' here. Like I said, creepy little fuck. Five-five'n a pound of pure Cajun shit." He pulled in at the corner of Burgundy and Conti, pointing at the south-east corner. "That's the place. That's where he's at every night. Nine till ten like clockwork. One dumb Cajun fuck that'll be takin' Conti south onto Bourbon. Always does, walkin' the dog, thinkin' himself well protected cause that there Doberman hangin' on the fence, that's his piece of shit. Meanin' y'all let him walk a ways, keepin' a fair distance." He made a right onto Conti, then another onto Dauphine, pulling in half a block down. "White suit, white hat, red tie in fuckin' February." He reached onto the back-seat for the satchel without turning his head. "A Q4 TAC, kid. Y'all's favourite. Locked, loaded'n quieter'n pissin' in the rain. Now tell me, y'all remember good'n well or y'all need a refresher?"

Miles gave back the photo. "I'm good."

The man nodded. "He ain't the biggest piece of shit, so it's the chest twice'n there ain't no need for talkin'. This ain't about po-liteness. Do the head next, up close'n personal after keepin' the damn dog from gettin' all nasty. Then y'all backtrack'n get your ass in without makin' a scene. I'm thinkin' three, four minutes or y'all did not kill the dog that'll be sorely pissed with y'all." He checked his watch: 9:57. "Y'all are up, kid."

The guy with a one-sided face was right on. At 10:01 Davaux turned onto Conti with the dog on a taut leash, Miles thinking he was about to kill some comic book gnome and its panting beast the closer he got. About all he could see was the suit and the eyeballs; all he could hear was the dog straining against its tether.

Miles stepped onto the street, Vinny Davaux grinning. Proud. "Ain't no cause fer y'all tuh worry, mista. Won't eat nothin' but corn beef hash'n prime rib. Just looks a mite snarly, is all. Sayin' a polite how-do, is all."

Miles chortled. "Didn't mean no offence, mista. Ain't much inta dogs, is all. Not much inta little shits like y'all neitha, upsettin' the status quo'n all." The Q4 TAC came out. "Cody Jones sends his best wishes, asshole."

The first nine-millimetre ripped through Davaux's chest like a cannon ball, the second putting down the confused dog. The third slammed into an already destroyed heart, the fourth exploding yellow and gold teeth onto the sidewalk, effectively and efficiently repaying a debt in full.

The driver was right, and probably very well-paid for doing things right. Miles was back in the sedan inside of four minutes, if not a little breathless. One minute later they were on Canal; a minute after that, Bourbon Street.

"Damn if y'all ain't the best, kid. Anytime y'all figure on leavin' that rich old lady of yours, y'all get your ass back here."

"Thanks. I'll take that under advisement." Miles opened the door. "Hey, listen. Say hi to CJ for me. Tell him thanks for me, for everything. Can you do that?"

The "Yes" was silent, the man putting a hand to Miles' arm. "A job ain't done till it's done, kid. Y'all do things right. Y'all got that?"

"Yeah, I got that. No worries."

"Didn't think so."

Without a handshake or another word Miles lost himself in a milling crowd of drunken male tourists throwing beads at the prettiest girls in hopes of seeing nicely crafted bare titties and as many drunk midwest females baring theirs anyway. Cause ya just can't do such a crazy and outlandish thing back home.

The stench of urine and vomit emanating from the alleys he walked by was as much the fragrance of the Quarter at night as jazz was the culture, casually tossing his gloves into one of them, passing by drunk and disoriented girls with their skirts too short squatting on sidewalks while their young and sober counterparts leaned against corner lampposts ready to hike their short skirts for any reasonable price.

In his room he stripped and showered. He changed into a tracksuit, bagged his business attire, called down for a bottle of their best Bordeaux and spent the next few hours watching pay-per-view porn bemoaning how more rewarding doing Vinny Davaux would have been during Mardi Gras.

Wednesday he woke early, doing breakfast in his room, avoiding the marauding blue hairs in their polyester windbreakers, Dockers and running shoes calling each other 'Dear' and generally annoying everyone else.

At the airport after Brent Mason checked-in his alter ego dropped his suit into one washroom trashcan, his shirt and tie into another. Then he relaxed reading the morning paper while the shoe shine boy cleansed his tasselled loafers of New Orleans.

Back in Charleston by noon he did an hour at the gym, a run, and prepared for Thursday's linguistically challenged kids who by graduation would scarcely have a proper command of English. Though as eager as he was to speak with Brenda, keeping her focused, he decided he would put her off until the following evening.

He wasn't in the mood for her reasonable questions or his requisite bullshit.

32

Mason's present from Cupid was the first of several weekend stay-overs, Brenda's was a gold pendant she didn't need and a dinner reservation since he wasn't as clever or skillful in her designer kitchen as he believed. Weekends at her place making more sense since his tenth-floor cubby hole seemed ridiculous compared to twelve luxurious rooms and a pool anywhere south of Broad.

At Easter they vacationed in Martinique, taking another week in Barcelona as Mason began questioning his summer tutoring schedule and his immediate future. They had been exclusive for eight months, Oliver dead for two years, well and truly time for Mrs. Holloway to get her act together because his resources were taking a serious hit keeping up with her.

He had no idea how much she was worth, nor could he ever ask without putting himself at risk, the arithmetic pretty much a no-brainer. Then came the shockwave from out of the blue once back in Charleston and her damp bed.

"Brent, I love you. I do. I'm sure of that now."

He blew a stream of hot air past his lips. "Wow. You're sure, sweetheart? Not because we're lying here dripping with sweat? You're very sure?"

"I am very, very sure and I'm thinking you should move in. And I mean soon. Our weekends and a few dinners…they don't seem enough anymore. They don't seem right. Do you understand what I mean?"

Well of course he did. "I've wanted to tell you for the longest time how much I love you, how important you are to me. But, you know, once burned," he coughed a laugh, "or twice."

"We should this week, move you in." She rolled onto her side, sitting with her legs crossed, hugging a pillow. "The one possible drawback I can foresee is your tutoring." She shook her head, tousling her hair. "That cannot happen here. We are where we are, making me think you should perhaps sell your condo and rent a small office space or maintain the condo for your students and do your corporate work here. We can set up an office for you."

Neither scenario worked for him, paying a high rent for no reason. "Is Priscilla aware of this? You ladies talk a lot."

"Of course she is. That said, we're testing the water here. Meaning my home office is off limits, Brent. That's my private space, as I'll respect yours. Also, this will be our home but it will always be my house. Not very harsh guidelines, but guidelines nonetheless. Are we agreed?"

He didn't have a choice. "Agreed."

Brenda Holloway reached behind her into her night table drawer, dropping a key on his chest. "Good. Then let's do this thing."

*

Mason moved in his wardrobe, sundries and certain personal effects the following day. His Rolex and whatever else he left in his safe on the tenth floor were not her concern. Never would be.

Throughout the summer he taught days and did non-existent corporate work for an hour each evening, missing the variety and yields of past evenings. But now he was trapped, wondering when, contemplating how, his one freedom being his daily run since Brenda's gym was complete with the best and most expensive equipment.

She loved the pool as much as he loved seeing her naked, compromising, doing the ocean Saturdays, doing the pool Sundays. All the same he was eager for her annual week on the West Coast with her obnoxious girlfriend and the other one who couldn't fly because of some heart condition, the long-awaited freedom finally coming in late May when, back from the airport, he sat by pool making a few calls.

By the pool because he couldn't be certain, for the very reason he would never encroach on her office. More importantly he had a week of license, all but ecstatic when the seven women he called on their private numbers were excited about seeing him again if only for a night while he was in town. Seven, making the most of his week, by Saturday morning adding near four grand to his sadly depleted box without investing a cent, which gave him pause, Saturday throughout the day dialling more unlisted numbers.

Though when he met the ladies at the airport he clearly had missed her terribly, hugging her tightly and kissing her, welcoming Priscilla with a scant smile, asking how she enjoyed her trip in a way that told her he didn't give a good shit. Then later that evening, with wine, candles and soft music setting the mood, he instead sat through a painful hour-long recap.

"I missed you."

"I missed you too. The week was unbearably long."

"The good thing though, you not being here made me think, made me open my eyes and realize things."

"Uh-oh, like what?"

"Like I love you."

"I know you love me."

"Not what I meant. I meant I will forever love you, as in till death do we part. I want to marry you, Brenda, be your adoring husband forever and ever, amen." He pressed a finger gently to her lips. "The big question can wait. First, I'm dropping the kids. They're a lost cause, a waste of my time and expertise, thinking language would be an easy out. Something you well know is not the case, muchacha."

"Sooo? Meaning?"

"Meaning converting my condo into an office, doing strictly

corporate, sweetheart, leaving my evenings free for you. Working here is a real distraction with you so close; whereas working at the condo I can bring in more clients, accomplish much more and actually enjoy what I'm doing with substantially more cashflow so I won't feel so much like a kept man." He raised open palms, making a silent statement. "I figure I can pull in 200 a year once I'm established, which won't take long. That's not chump change and I'm building an impressive list of referrals."

"You're impressive, Brent darling."

"Then becoming Mrs. Brenda Mason sounds good? You'll marry me, make me the happiest man ever?"

She kissed him. "Yes, darling. I'll marry you. Mrs. Brenda Mason sounds very good. But a girl…"

He put a preemptive finger between them, reaching into his coat pocket as he eased from the sofa onto his knees with the open velvet box resting on an open palm. "Brenda Holloway, will you please marry me?"

The titanium band was simple, setting him back not far from a grand, Mason sliding the symbol of his commitment and success onto her finger in concert with her teary-eyed "Yes" that she reaffirmed with a breath-stealing kiss.

*

The prenup was anticipated, Mason shrugging off the formality. His corporate business was flourishing beyond all expectations, pulling in three grand a week with minimal expenses. What did he care about her millions that he estimated at ten, maybe twelve? Unaware that days earlier she had put his name to the 'whomever' in her will.

The simple and civil wedding took place on the first of September, Priscilla Serra standing in as witness. Brenda didn't want the pomp and circumstance of her union with Oliver, a day she would never confuse with any other; Mason's thorough lack of devoutness apart.

She did however engage a videographer. She needed Presley sharing in her special day, the distraught young woman the evening before weeping into her phone, woefully sorry she couldn't be there kissing and hugging them both, Priscilla and the bride constantly gazing at her with adoring smiles through the lens.

Nor did Brenda Mason want a reception. She was not comfortable inviting her close friends and Oliver's former associates into his home, celebrating what was effectively closing that tender chapter in her life, which Priscilla completely understood. Instead she gifted fifty thousand to the drop-in, which Mason quietly understood was completely absurd. Not that he had a voice in the matter or friends of his own. He didn't, not a single one; Brenda appreciating the reticence borne of his traumatic past, Priscilla deeming the social anomaly, particularly for a professor, the result of a severe character flaw.

Instead he took the ladies to dinner, pondering throughout the meal why Priscilla wasn't joining them on the French Côte d'Azur for ten days onboard a twelve-metre Stephens flush deck mahogany cruiser that all but emptied his cashbox; Brenda first posting a two million-dollar surety against all damages, trusting her husband was not the worst yachtsman ever, mildly unsure when he reassured her the chances of drowning in the middle of the Mediterranean were very slight.

Great. Cause of death: Honeymoon. "Thank you, darling."

Though after her first day on the glittering sea topless and naked, leaping from the transom with her lifejacket, speeding circles around the cruiser in the Zodiac, basking in the sun on the foredeck amongst hundreds of other topless and naked sirens of the sea crossing their aimless course, she was hooked.

On the second day she took the helm, throughout her honeymoon eagerly absorbing all she could about charts and terminologies, navigation and the mariner's code of conduct which called for cocktails at two bells in casual white that was an essential part of the yachting experience.

Then too soon on day eleven they flew home, greeted at the airport by the girlfriend, Mason spending Thursday at the condo setting up appointments for the coming week, figuring by year's end the depleted condition of his box would reverse itself by some forty grand, give or take. Not a fortune, but his corporate-only strategy quickly proved lucrative and wise, exceeding the wishful projection by several thousand the week before his Christmas break when even his most ardent and regular devotees would perforce spend time with their families and less-loved ones.

By which time his client list expanded as well with several referrals, his own learning curve teaching him quite by chance that entertaining two pampered friends suffering from the ennui of wealth for the sale price of a thousand on many occasions was also a good business strategy, that he was not merely a gigolo and paid lover but a facilitator of fantasies.

At Christmas no gifts were exchanged, not that morning, Mason hinting that a glittering tree without gifts, surprises and hot toddies was not a tree. Especially one that was sixteen feet, silver with blue lights and made of stainless steel and plastic. Bad enough there was no snow, despite which he quietly endured his day-long servitude smiling and playing Santa before going home fully aware he was not passing through their door but leaping head-first into a shit pond.   Nevertheless he would, Brenda putting down her Cîroc.

"Excuse me. What was that very ridiculous thing you said?"

"New York, New Year's Eve. The two of us...alone."

"And Priscilla? What about Priscilla?"

"What about her? Christ, she's thirty-six. She hasn't been laid or licked or whatever they do in months and she's using you as some sort of, I don't know, a cushion instead of putting herself out there."

"Won't happen. New Year's with her is a tradition since high school."

"Traditions don't exist, merely fabrications that go on longer than they should until fading into oblivion and no one cares."

"I care. And the only way New York will happen is if Priscilla comes with us."

He chuckled, drifting a moment for effect. "How exactly will that work, a threesome with a lesbian? Albeit a hot one and not that I couldn't be convinced. Unfortunately I booked the room a few days after France and we're talking New York here, Time Square. So good luck with her getting a room."

"Then cancel."

"Let's be positive here for a moment. She'll have more quality time with the other one. How can she not want that? And besides, when she does finally snag a woman who might last a year or two, who says they won't want some sort of gay thing at New Year's? These people are big-time cliquish. You know, birds of a feather..."

"Don't be that way. You should try liking her. She's very warm and tender."

"I don't doubt she's warm, with women, which I'm good with. I mean what guy would not want to see that happening? If she didn't have this hate on for me for some reason, like she has this secret thing for you and I'm in the way. Who knows? More precisely she's not my wife. You are, who I would like to celebrate my thirtieth with in Time Square." He put a hand to her cheek. "Sweetheart, call her. Blame me, fuel the smouldering fire. Say whatever. She might even be happily surprised by having an extra couple of days where she is because nothing lasts forever. Nothing."

"I don't like you very much tonight, darling. And let's get something straight here, she does not have a thing for me."

"I don't like myself tonight either, sweetheart. But I do love you, very much. You know that."

Brenda Mason sighed. "On one condition, that going forward you'll be nice to her. And, Brent, the other one is not a her or a she. She's Presley."

33

By Easter he stepped up to a large safety deposit box, Brenda on occasion truly flattered by other women seemingly enchanted by her husband at the grocery store or mall, Mason's natural charm always lighting their faces with demure smiles. Which she understood. Which she believed she understood. She absolutely adored her man, taking him on a pleasant Sunday afternoon in April for a patio lunch at the marina, later sipping a twenty-year Paulliac from plastic goblets as they strolled arm in arm through a maze of boats and yachts big and small.

"What a truly magnificent day, darling."

"What a truly magnificent wife." He paused, kissing her. "Seeing these I'm thinking we should do the Riviera again, sweetheart. This is stirring up some very fond memories. Not the least of which is you at the helm in your…nothing."

Brenda tugged his arm, stopping him. "What a wonderful idea, darling. Perhaps for our anniversary, reliving our honeymoon."

"Wow. Check out this one."

"What is that?"

"That is heaven, sweetheart." He was gazing at a gleaming white forty-six-foot luxury sport cruiser. "God, I can smell it. That beauty is brand spanking new, sweetheart. Lucky bastard."

"Darling, isn't that the one you go on and on about?"

"Yeah, my one day *Sweetheart*. How sweet will that be?"

"Very, I guess." Brenda stepped onto the fibreglass platform. "Let's find out, shall we?"

"No, no, no. Are you kidding me? You cannot do that. Get back here."

"Yes I can, darling. She was delivered yesterday."

She yanked away the silk drape covering the hand-painted *Sweetheart* on the transom, stepping through onto the social deck, Mason's rich wine splashing onto his dock shoes.

"No shit. Brenda, no shit."

"No shit, Captain." She held out her goblet in a toast. "Now take us sweethearts for a ride. She's fuelled and she's ready. So am I."

Mason stepped onboard, caressing the *Sweetheart*'s smooth lines as tenderly as he would his wife or his many clients, minutes later gliding her over the calm Atlantic a little over break-in speed. His dream had come true.

Of course, when she heard of her girlfriend's sudden lapse in good judgement, Priscilla Serra chastised Brenda severely for completely losing her mind, for being unquestionably irresponsible and insanely frivolous. The thing was exorbitantly expensive and, hello, she could not swim. But cost was not an issue, neither was swimming since the thing could practically hug the shore and was bought as much for her as for Brent. So what was the big deal? Besides, the thing came equipped with lifejackets, my darling.

The anniversary did happen in France as Mason suggested after a summer vacation in the Florida Keys and most weekends spent anchored in secluded coves wading and splashing, though never with Priscilla who made very clear that he would never see her in triangles with her very tight ass bare. Would never happen. And that after dark nudie thing? Not a chance in hell would that ever happen with him.

Then came another charitable Christmas and New Year's with the girlfriend after a profitable year and two extensive wardrobes, and September when Brenda again chartered a yacht on the romantic Riviera. Though one year later in August, Mason accommodating not far from a quarter-million in his boxes, he suggested a requisite and well-deserved week off. He needed a break. He needed to get things done with her help because he hadn't filed a tax return in three years and was fully and fearfully cognizant that shit would hit the proverbial fan in a very big way anytime soon.

"I'm done. I really need this, sweetheart. I'm thinking Miami and the Bahamas for a week."

"Darling, we'll be in Monaco very soon. Can't you wait?"

"No, that's not an option. I've been pushing my work ethic thing and a week off before our anniversary is mandatory. I'll be refreshed, the way I should be for you, not indolent the way I feel now." He smiled warmly, touching her cheek. "Fully energized for the sultry and sexy green-eyed señorita."

"Darling, can you believe three years already? I can't imagine my life if we hadn't connected, if Priscilla hadn't made me get real."

Priscilla. Fuck Priscilla. "Yeah, I suppose she did bring us together, sweetheart."

"She did. And you should love her for it, love her for me."

I'd rather drown the hateful lesbian bitch. "Won't happen. We're civil, the way I promised. At least I am because she completely rues the day she got on your case. I mean, not even a cocktail onboard the *Sweetheart*. What's up with that? I mean, really."

Brenda exhaled a deep sigh. He was right. It would never happen, though one was as bad as the other; natural, polite and needless rivals, both loving and caring and so diametrically different that never the twain shall meet. Their loss when she had the best of both worlds. Nevertheless, he did have a valid point. He did look exhausted and why not the Bahamas? They deserved.

They left on the second Saturday, plotting a course that would put them in Nassau Monday, Mason assuming the roles of captain and cabin boy while Brenda lay on the cushioned afterdeck absorbing the sun's warmth, working on an already seamless tan and loving him. Yet as deeply as she loved him, Oliver would forever have title to the most special place in her heart.

She was thirty-eight, slim, lovely and graceful. In bikinis or when sipping cocktails on the social deck at two bells in white she was an easy thirty, easy on the eyes, no one ever presuming an alarming age difference as Mason had matured since becoming who he was. Most men simply envied him, most women envying Brenda while fantasizing the impossible when studying Mason from behind dark glasses.

Though as always their time onboard was fleeting, Mason suggesting an impromptu sunset cruise as they lingered over calvados and cognac Wednesday evening. The air was pleasantly warm and the sea was agreeably calm save for a gentle breeze rippling the darkening water. An ideal evening of peaceful solitude for lovers so profoundly in love.

She thought the idea was fabulous, instructed by her captain to forego the dishes in the galley and change from her whites into a teddy or something equally appropriate for cocktails and soft music on a shimmering sea.

She obeyed, disappearing into the master stateroom while Mason brought the engines to life, freeing the *Sweetheart* from her lines and idling from the marina before easing the throttle to the three-quarter position, maintaining decent headway into deep water where dropping anchor was pointless and clearly indicative of a novice.

By the time he cut the engines, drifting on an open sea several miles offshore, the island's lights barely distinguishable against the golden backdrop of a setting sun, Brenda was straddling the transom in a silk teddy intended for private viewing.

"You are delicious, sweetheart."

"Thank you, darling." She passed Mason his wine. "I couldn't possibly imagine a more splendid evening. How deep are we?"

"Not very, about a hundred feet. Ideal for a dip before it gets dark."

"Yeah, like that'll happen. You go have a good time with that. I'll watch. Maybe take some photos."

He sat facing her, planting one foot on a cushioned seat, the other on the platform. Lost in reverie and time they talked in murmurs as though they might be overheard about Monaco and where they would vacation next, about how in love they were, their foreheads touching, kissing, Mason kneading the soft and delicate flesh of her thighs, together orchestrating their crescendo.

He put down his glass, then hers, bringing her closer; Brenda snapping open the grommets attaching the thin strips of moist silk for him, letting him tug the teddy over her head in a single fluid motion.

Laying her gently backward he swung onto the platform, stripping off his linen slacks and remounting the transom, dragging her weight closer and easing into her ready body, securing her completely with warm palms pressed to her breasts, her urgent squeals and yelps soon drowned out by the deafening silence of a darkening universe.

Her mind and her body were consumed with lust and passion. She could not in her wildest, her most titillating dreams, desire a more devoted and inexhaustible lover, pulling herself onto him, wrapping her legs and her arms tightly around his waist and his neck, squirming and twisting and gyrating, smudging her lips hard against his, wanting more, demanding more with urgent pleas and her nails digging into his tanned flesh.

Again he eased her gently backward, hovering over her, kissing her breasts and plucking teasingly at her nipples, not missing a beat; so many women's quintessential inamorato inflicting the most pleasure possible, selflessly heedless of his pounding heart, cupping her head gently in his hands, straining every fibre of his body, smothering her with an ardent and everlasting kiss.

Fixated on the delirium in her deep emerald eyes, feeling her firm breasts heaving against his chest, he panted how he would always love her, slamming her head viciously onto the transom, pausing a moment before extricating his body from hers, before catapulting her by her wide-open legs into the calm water and reaching for his wine, waiting.

He needed assurances she would be alright, that she would not suffer or awaken and cry out in terror. Then she was gone, quietly and peacefully, drifting slowly downward, lost in a hundred fathoms of black water.

*

Despite her age he was very fond of her; he could imagine that in some unique way he did love her. She was youthful enough, sexy and sensual, albeit most often when they were alone or in the company of other bons viveurs separated by anchor lines or beach beds never at par with the hedonistic and capricious Courtney.

He shrugged. More's the pity. But now they were gone and there wasn't much he could do about either one. Instead he put himself into distress mode. He first dropped Brenda's teddy into her laundry bin, taking out the tiny soiled panties she'd worn for him at dinner, reawakening the pungent scent with their love's bitter moisture still glistening on his body.

He tugged on his slacks and brought the *Sweetheart* to life, steering her a half-mile or so into deeper water, letting her drift while he tossed her glass onto the deck and spilled several ounces of amber calvados as some sort of special effect that probably happened as she went over. Why not? The same way her panties had caught on the cleat and tore away under her weight, Mason stuffing the ruined satin patch into a pocket before he switched on the *Sweetheart*'s powerful searchlight and cried "Mayday! Mayday Mayday!" into the yacht's Channel 16 VHF.

He gave his Lat and Long, choking with emotion, gulping air, gulping another rare mouthful of Rémy Martin before splashing a few drops into his eyes. He couldn't remember ever crying, or how he might even do that, but the cognac produced instant and positive results, reddening and burning his eyes, afflicting him with anguish and inconsolable grief.

Within minutes a flotilla of pleasure yachts was skimming across the sea from the marina, a mariner's brigade of the concerned and the curious; the level voice of a Defence Force Captain responding that a patrol boat was underway and that all vessels should maintain safe distance while keeping their searchlights aimed at the water. Their ETA was twelve minutes, leaving him ample time to drop a snifter of expensive cognac from his hands onto the foredeck in a moment of chilling dread and panic.

When the Defence Force ship came alongside the crew boarded quickly with not much else they could do on a dark night over dark water a thousand feet deep now some twenty minutes after the Mayday distress call. They recorded the distraught husband's statement, substantiating his account with photographs of a pristine vessel, two spilled glasses and the remnants of a romantic evening gone terribly wrong, bagging the solitary flimsy piece of evidence that would satisfy no one's curiosity or provoke anyone's suspicion before impounding the boat for further investigation by the police.

All vessels were ordered away from the area as the patrol boat began its futile search for any sign of life or worse, as the *Sweetheart* was steered to port for Mason by officers remaining onboard as he sat disconsolately begging her forgiveness in tearful whispers.

They understood. Or believed they did, giving him space, Mason reliving the horror of his evening he would recount a dozen times through the night and into Thursday when the yacht would be examined with a fine-tooth comb and patrol boats would resume searching the sea in vain. Neither search resulting in a probable cause for keeping the grieving husband in custody a moment longer.

They were celebrating, he told them, excited about their upcoming anniversary in France. She was always so effervescent. She prepared such a romantic dinner with candles, wine and music. He loved her with all his heart, dancing with her in his arms, watching completely absorbed as she swayed and danced for him, scarcely noticing darkness had taken over from a glorious sunset he would never ever forget. Until Brenda suggested he enjoy one more cocktail before bringing her heavenly evening to an end, darling.

Then she was gone. He would never see her again; he would never again feel her warmth or touch her flawless skin. When he came out from the galley with his drink refreshed she wasn't there. She wasn't anywhere. He called her name, making his way onto the foredeck, thinking she would be there gazing at the moon as always, but she wasn't. He must have screamed her name a hundred times, frantically scanning the black water with the searchlight, but she was gone. Just gone.

That's when he noticed the spilled glass and her underwear. How often had he scolded her for sitting on the gunwale without her jacket, because she couldn't swim? Still, she loved straddling the yacht's side, swinging her legs and laughing. She was always delightfully happy and playful. Now for the rest of his life he would see her drifting in a dark ocean, alone and cold, because he should have hugged her and kissed her and brought her home. Though he could never deny her, he could never disappoint her. As much as she lived for his happiness, now he couldn't imagine ever being happy again.

That's where he stopped. The cops were taking notes, probably adept at detecting flavoured bullshit. They would, however, apprise the Charleston Police who would likely interview him as a formality the moment he arrived home.

But, no. He was not returning home right away. He couldn't, not without Brenda. He would book into a resort adjacent to the marina and stay understandably royally drunk for as long as he needed. He was in no condition, nor did he have the least desire to undertake a voyage he should have enjoyed with his loving and carefree wife. Then he would sell the cursed thing she should never have bought—for him.

As he wished. He was nevertheless free to go, once at the marina preparing for three days of well-deserved relaxation and reflection at the Adults Only resort while sipping wine onboard his luxury *Sweetheart*.

That Sunday he departed Nassau for Miami, refreshed and invigorated, arriving in Charleston Monday evening at full throttle where he was met by police who weren't interested in the boat after five nights at dock, the Bahamian onboard investigation and a two-day voyage. No point. Though they had in his absence interviewed the stunned staff at the drop-in centre and devastated neighbours who together unanimously confirmed that, yes indeed, the young couple were utterly in love and inseparable. Fine and decent young folks, the Masons, charitable and community minded.

My Lord, what a terrible tragedy!

Mason was again naturally cleared as a formality late Tuesday morning. Not by virtue of indisputable innocence, rather by presumed innocence owing to the total lack of incontrovertible evidence suggesting his guilt and that Brenda Mason's disappearance occurred in an ocean 500 miles beyond their jurisdiction.

Whether she was tipsy or drunk and careless, or inconceivably thrown overboard by a sociopathic husband, was pointless conjecture when the files of so many actual murders and suspicious near misses cluttered their desks.

Case closed, the Mason File essentially forgotten the moment he walked out onto the street.

34

Arriving home tanned, rested and exonerated after an exhausting and nerve-wracking week, Mason's first surprise was seeing an unoccupied Cadillac he didn't recognize, and the Serra woman's Lexus, parked by Brenda's GranTurismo. His second was the door's polished brass lock rejecting his key.

A moment later Priscilla swung open the door with scathing candour and a complete lack of condolence or empathy.

"Understand something here, Mason. Whatever fiction you invented in your sick mind that made the Bahamians and the Charleston cops believe your pure bullshit is irrelevant. You know and I know you murdered Brenda. You killed her and discarded her beautiful body in the ocean like chum. I read the report. Pure bullshit. You murdering her was no accident."

Mason put himself into defence mode, stepping past her. He didn't trust her. "You really are a hideous bitch, Priscilla, talking that way to a grieving husband. You are so wrong, pissed because you could never score with her, could never make it under her skirt or into her bed. What can I say? Shit happens, but I loved Brenda deeply. I always will. And that you can even imagine such a terrible thing is despicable and hateful."

"You don't love shit, asshole." She slammed the door. "This woman is Ms. Darleen Jacobs, Brenda's executor. She's here to read and put into effect Brenda's precise wishes which I am very well acquainted with." She pointed toward the bottom of the stairway. "Those boxes, they're all your shit. You are done here. This is as far you get."

"Thanks, but I don't think so." He acknowledged Jacobs with a curt nod. "You women are in this house illegally, you're trespassing. This is my home until I deem otherwise. Meaning get out of here before this all turns very ugly." He sneered at Priscilla. "I would hate to see my wife's best friend arrested for breaking and entering."

"Mr. Mason, this is no longer your home," Jacobs cut in. "Nor is anything of Miss Brenda's of value or otherwise inside the house. She very succinctly expressed that wish. Ergo the lock." She passed him a copy of Brenda's will. "That's your copy. Please take your time. However, I assure you everything is in order and legally binding."

Mason accepted the guarantee of his secure and independent future nonchalantly, confident, because he knew. He knew he had become as fundamental to Brenda's life and happiness as her breathing, the crescendoing shock of his second surprise as impossible to disguise with sneers and caustic retorts as his flushed complexion and wide-eyed incredulity as he stood seething with disbelief, too stunned for words.

He didn't understand. Nothing he was reading made sense. She loved him, she adored him. How could she now be so inconsiderate and heartless? Impossible. "No way. This is not real." He waved the document. "No way this is real. She would never have done this to me. No way. I was her life as much as she was mine."

"Don't talk bullshit. She would never have wanted you to kill her either, asshole."

"This is very real in fact, Mr. Mason," Jacob replied. "Legal and binding according to Miss Brenda's considered and formal wishes."

Her investment portfolio was worth an incredible forty-five million exclusive of the home and boat; neither of which, his dead wife confirmed, were his, light years from what he had dreamed of for an eternity. A dream cruelly shattered within seconds, mocking him the more he read, ridiculing him, her notarized will proving she was as two-faced and every bit as despicable as her bitch girl-friend who was getting fifteen of those millions along with some Presley Burke he had never met, spoken with, or even seen. A staggering thirty million wasted on a frigid lesbian bitch, some de-bilitated broad she visited once a year, and another even more in-credulous ten wasted on her favourite social misfits and dregs at the centre. What the fuck!

Really! What could she have been thinking after all he had done for her, all the time he had invested in her, leaving a loving and devoted husband a paltry five and whatever might come from the immediate sale by auction or brokerage of her home, her worldly possessions, and the *Sweetheart* which he discovered was never actually his? This, she stipulated like twisting the knife in his back, after all due fees and expenses were honoured. As well he would vacate her home within the shortest possible timeframe and discontinue his enjoyment of the *Sweetheart* in order that the ex-ecutor might initiate the transactions.

He wasn't a lawyer but he understood he was royally screwed. Jacobs had absolute authority, carte blanche that had him by the balls.

"Mr. Mason," Jacobs went on, "this house and its contents will be auctioned off this coming weekend starting at three million in a blind bid. The boat as well beginning at one million, which Ms. Serra and I have agreed is very reasonable given the expressed ur-gency. You are, of course, invited to partake in the bidding."

"Are you shitting me, lady? Really? With five fucking million? Let's everyone get real here."

The issue wasn't hers to care about. "You also understand, Mr. Mason, that Miss Brenda's funeral will be paid for from these sales before any funds are disbursed to you. And that Ms. Serra has complete freedom per the wishes of Miss Brenda."

What? "What funeral? There's nothing here to bury. She is gone, lady."

"Not exactly," Priscilla cut in. "She is everywhere in this house. That was her wish, that one day I bury her by Oliver Holloway's side. You just stopped reading at the five million, asshole, which speaks volumes. Nor will Brenda or anyone else give a good shit if you stay the fuck away since you did murder her, and since your diseased mind is the reason we will never say goodbye to each other."

"You go ahead and do that. Nevertheless I'll be sitting front and centre. Bitch."

"That delusion would be in your sick dreams. Over my dead body."

He shrugged. "Okay."

"Mr. Mason, I believe we are concluded here. Ms. Serra and I will remain with you until your possessions are removed, of course. Thank you for understanding."

*

He didn't. He didn't understand a goddamn thing beyond the humiliation he suffered carrying out cartons of clothes as the supercilious bitches stood watching, smugly laughing at him.

That night Braxton Miles deliberately betrayed his taste for expensive wines with the first of several bottles of twenty-year scotch, desperately needing a quick and enduring state of well-being. He needed not to buy a gun and kill the lesbian bitch. Not that he wouldn't if he could; he fucking well would. He simply had too much at stake, relying on the euphoria of a strategic and drunken stupor to carry Brent Mason through the difficult days ahead when finally he would be rid of them all.

*

Saturday morning the luxury yacht went for 300 thousand over the start of bidding and by the close of bidding at 4:00 PM the Holloway home was sold for three and a half, that happy couple gloating as Darleen Jacobs led them inside. The Maserati, as she and Priscilla agreed, was given to a neighbour's speechless teen who often and selflessly was giving her free time at the drop-in.

Saturday night Mason finished off his fifth bottle, achieving his goal. He hadn't showered in a week, could not distinguish one day from the next while drowning in self-pity, or remember any of Braxton Miles' impetuous and sophisticated contingency plans. Irrespective of whom he was, he was too young and too focused on hostility and loathing to be of any use to himself, waking Sunday morning looking and feeling like shit.

Meanwhile Brenda's commemoration and farewell was in its final preparations, orchestrated by someone even more hostile and loathing.

The previous weekend as Mason was consoling himself in day spas and bringing the willing wives of others in the resort's Sin Room to shuddering heights without compunction or feelings of remorse, Priscilla Serra was being a good deal more diligent. She and Darleen Jacobs were meticulously removing Brenda's wardrobe, jewellery and personal effects from her home that Jacobs was adamant were never intended for sale, insisting that Priscilla take all Brenda's jewellery, artwork and photographs to share with Presley. Precisely what Miss Brenda would have emphatically wanted were she with them sharing in the moment. No argument. Everything else was 'things' no longer of value.

Although Priscilla and Jacobs, the more the women understood about Mason's charm-masked greed, did take great vindictive pleasure in squashing Mason's executive wardrobe and sundries, that Brenda for the most part had subsidized, into the fewest possible boxes.

Throughout the demanding and tireless week that ensued, Priscilla graciously forbidden by the CEO of the firm that continued boasting the Holloway name to even show herself, she worked with a single purpose at making Brenda's parting meaningful, weeping herself to sleep each night after she and Presley kissed each other's wet cheeks with fingertips on their computer screens.

She would make Sunday Brenda's best day, she promised, and she would, by laying Brenda Holloway at Oliver's side in a twenty-thousand dollar casket filled with her most special lingerie, her gowns and most treasured photos of the couple's happiest times. Each of the hundred invited couples arrived in a procession of complimentary limos, except the man who arrived last dressed in black and waited by his BMW parked in the distance; the videographer recording each arrival except his, each hug and tear and a church decorated and fragranced with thousands of carnations that were Brenda's most favourite delivered by a fleet of vans from across South Carolina.

In addition to which Mason didn't get his front and centre spotlight, a ten-grand donation to the minister's benevolent fund ensuring he was ushered to Priscilla's more preferred seating nearest the vestibule.

As Brenda would have wished the service itself was unpretentious, her friend recounting a wonderful and fruitful life from the pulpit, speaking of the youthful and loving couple they all remembered and how one day Brenda and Oliver would together confront her killer before his deserved descent into Hell, the veiled curse creasing two hundred saddened faces with alarm.

"That's right," came her final words, "our sweet and loving Brenda Holloway did not simply drown. She was murdered."

When the service ended, stoic men and mournful women tracing palms and fingers along her casket as they filed out shunning the man dressed in black seated in the corner with furrowed brows and undisguised scowls, Priscilla went alone to the cemetery with the videographer before hosting an elaborate outdoor luncheon at the Holloway home that would remain Brenda's until midnight.

Of course Mason wasn't expected or wanted. Nor did he care, eager for the coming Friday, the day before Brenda's third wedding

Doug Booth

anniversary, when he would meet the Jacobs woman at her office, not for a moment thinking Priscilla Serra would be sitting there smirking.

"Nice soliloquy last week. Tell me, isn't that sort of illegal accusing me in public of murder?"

"No."

He shrugged, sitting. "Whatever. For what it matters I won't be sticking around very long. So let's get this done so you ladies can talk more bullshit."

Darleen Jacobs slid a cheque across her desk, the eight-point-four million glaring at him like purple neon.

He coughed a laugh, flipping it over as though expecting more on the backside. "You're joking. This is a fucking sick joke, right?"

"You're the sick joke, asshole. That's what you get after all legitimate expenses and fees, each one documented. Except, of course, the two hundred grand in well-earned gratuities for everyone making Brenda's day special, that Ms. Jacobs and I agreed she and Oliver would have wished." She chortled, relishing the moment. "About one-point-four, give or take. And believe me, if I could have bankrupted you, I would have."

"You are fucking insane, Serra. I'll get a lawyer. I'll fight this. I'll fight both of you."

"We are lawyers, asshole. Good luck with that."

Darleen Jacobs stood. "Mr. Mason. Our business is again concluded. Please take the cheque and leave."

Priscilla remained seated. "That would be your business with Ms. Jacobs, Mason. Because I am not done with you, you sociopathic fuck."

272

35

11:12 AM.

"Didn't mean much at the time, Preacher. I mean, who the hell could have seen that one coming? Sure as hell I didn't. Should have though, looking back. She was one nasty conniving bitch, that one. Lots of nerve calling me sociopathic."

"Braxton, such a terrible fate for such lovely and innocent woman who loved and cherished you."

"Loved and cherished? Think so, Preacher? The woman used me from day one, letting herself be convinced and swayed, cheating me out of what was rightfully mine after all I did for her, after reigniting her passion, giving her meaning then helping her pass over without the slightest fear or pain, without a whisper or tear. And with a single purpose, Preacher, thankful I wouldn't intercede. She was happy I was letting her go, sending her away. I believe that, as good as I was for her and with her, I could never replace the pure and the perfect Oliver Holloway. So in a very real way I was reuniting them. I'm sure you can appreciate that, Preacher. And believe me, she could not have left this world any more primed and exhilarated, which was no easy task."

"The smallest of mercies, as I hope and pray."

"Yeah, a mercy of my doing. And she repaid me how? By cheating me, by helping put me in here. Yeah, Brenda was lovely alright. That's a fact, lovely and two-faced. So was the other one. Although, being honest, she has made my time here half-tolerable recalling the horrified look on her smug face that last day in court, the pure disgust in her big brown and watery eyes. Wrote her a letter detailing every inch of her body, describing how good and tight she was all those times, how she smelled like a fragrant rose by any other name, like doing a virgin, which she pretty well was. Thanked her for those arousing memories getting me through the trial…imagining her sitting there all naked and flawless. Even blew her a kiss, Preacher; inhaled a real deep breath like I was, you know, breathing in her pungent female scent, savouring her, making things more real between us." Miles snorted, grinning. "Thought the uptight bitch would pass right out. But I tell you what, she pretty fast stopped looking superior."

The dispirited preacher grimaced. "Braxton, making the woman's anguish and dolor all the deeper, her broken heart all the more shattered."

"Amen to that, Preacher. Amen. We reap what we sow, isn't that what you people believe? She screwed me over big time, not thinking for a moment of the consequences. Just one single-minded and selfish bitch. I'm not the guilty one here, not on that count. At the very worst I was an innocent accomplice, duped into becoming a facilitator and tried for a murder I didn't commit when she's the guilty one for orchestrating her own heinous crime and talking bullshit in court. The truth is, Preacher, she's as deserving of that needle as I am. And, really, let's you and me not get extra sentimental over Brenda. She would have discarded me sooner or later, the way they all did."

Reverend Emery Prisby wanted out. He was old and he was tired, trapped by his waning deep faith and obligation in Miles' death row cell so that he might bring solace to one of God's errant children, so that they might pray together for the redemption of a lost soul with mere minutes remaining in his life. Though neither would come to pass, he understood, disheartened and questioning his own life's journey more profoundly with each silent tick of the clock's second hand, afraid for what he was thinking, questioning his own worth, believing in his tormented heart that Braxton Miles' tainted soul was impervious to compassion and solace.

"If only you had chosen a different path when you truly were a child lost, my son. If you had never run from your home or met Cody Jones."

"No, Preacher. I was a backwoods dumbass hillbilly headed nowhere before I met Cody, who I believe was at the station that night for one reason, the same reason I was. He was waiting for me, the very way that finding good old mom dead in her kitchen eventually led me to Bunker and Davaux. God's will. Fate. Whatever. They were as integral to my existence as Blaire and Courtney, without whom Braxton Miles would have metamorphosed from drug courier to pimp or worse. You of all people should understand that. Each one of us connected by irreversible fate, one destiny impossible without the other, like Dick Linden and BJ Valliere. Truth be told, I truly enjoyed doing Linden the most. Took real pleasure in watching him expire, crying and moaning." Miles snorted, coughing a derisive laugh. "That piece of shit must have blubbered "Oh, God" a hundred times through that wet sock stuffed in his head, begging me with his twisted mouth and squinty wet eyes not to kill him when he was pretty well dead already, that premature round to the head an overly gracious gesture on my part given the circumstances. He didn't deserve the courtesy, but he died knowing, which I suppose was more gratifying since I promised CJ I would do things right, make things right for him and Myra. Yeah, a real pleasure."

"The devil's work is never right, Braxton. That you could somehow derive pleasure from killing another without the slightest provocation chills my heart to the core."

"A matter of perspective, Preacher. You go tell that to his wife who didn't bother playing the devastated and grieving young widow when told he was found tied-up in a ditch and seriously dead. No one goes that way for no reason. Done for clarity so that any-

one would assume the worst, that he was in deep shit with someone, which he was. Though whatever Myra might have believed,
and was truly grateful for, she kept to herself and was never implicated, returning to a better life from Mexico where she had spent a
month ostensibly being pampered, which she finally was…follow-
ing the surgery that made her exquisite again. You see Myra being
severely beaten and scarred was not her destiny, merely a requisite
and regrettable factor in his. As was I from his perspective. The
same way the ever-charming Priscilla Serra was clearly a factor in
mine. The queen of all bitches and my life's single regret."

"Braxton, I beseech you. Pray with me. Expiate these terrible
sins and free yourself."

"Free myself from what, Preacher, my imminent dispatch into a
dark eternity? Think so?"

The old man didn't know, feeling as though he was sitting closer to Hell's gate than Heaven's door. "From what I fear you have
not yet confided in me."

Prisoner Miles peered through the slot at the clock.

"Ah, yes. The young and worldly Mr. Bradley McGuire and the
enchanting Miss BJ Valliere. More precisely Bobbi-Jo, Preacher,
you know, for clarity; who, contrary to what most everyone believes, that our lives are merely sequential accidents for better or
worse, did not cross my path by any delightful serendipity. She
was put there with a purpose when I needed her. A genuine cutie,
Preacher. No question. If she wasn't delivered unto me by divine
providence nothing ever was. Sweet as honey, the colour of her
hair, and talk about scent of a woman." He peered again through
the slot. "We all have our time, don't we?"

11:19 AM.

TurnAbout

Part Four
36

The day after Brenda's funeral Priscilla Serra worked from home, making a chain of phone calls to people she trusted, people who knew other people, a chain leading to Steve Dillion who met with her that evening. When he left her, making her understand that reality was far removed from scripted theatre, that he could not guarantee she would not be disappointed, she closed the door feeling sanguine about the coming weeks and called her sister with the good news.

She was too elated to wait until the next day when the sisters would be together sharing a terribly deep sorrow, weeping and remembering their friend, Priscilla arriving near the dinner hour when several straight premium vodkas were deemed more appropriate than food; one sister reliving Sunday's heartache while the other wept copious tears at seeing her best friend being taken from her forever.

"I should have been with her, Prissy, with you, saying goodbye. The three of us together for the last time."

Priscilla kissed her sister's wet cheek, holding her close. "You know she would never want that, me losing both of you."

"Our lives will never be the same without her."

"Neither will his, I swear. I told her something was peculiar with him, never coming off too smug or self-infatuated. But he was, acting like he owned the place. Never talking about his past or his college buddies, his work or why any professor would not want a teaching post in some ancient hallowed hall. Not once, not even with Brenda. Always turning our questions smoothly into his own. And what guy in his thirties with a master's does not have a single friend? Bullshit. Everything about him, pure bullshit. I swear, Presley, he murdered her. No one falls from a boat that big in calm water. And who goes out miles into the ocean at night for no reason? No one."

"I can't imagine the terror she felt," Presley sobbed. "She couldn't swim, Prissy."

"Even if she could swim, she was not coming back." She took her sister's hands. "He killed her, no question. The shock on his smug face when he saw the cheque spoke volumes, throwing a juvenile tantrum, threatening us like he wasn't getting his full reward for a job well done. The sick bastard. But I promise, Presley; I promise Brenda. If he believes he got away with his shit, big mistake. Really big, starting this morning."

"I'm glad you didn't exclude me from Steve Dillion, Prissy. I loved that girl so much. I can't imagine our lives without her. Whatever it takes. Absolutely whatever."

"We will always love her. And she knows that. As does Steve Dillion very clearly. I like him. I feel really good about him."

Presley Burke swirled her Jean-Marc XO, gazing into the crystal snifter. "I believe in my heart I would easily kill him myself for what he did, for being such a callous monster. I do."

"No, you do not. Just be thankful you will never meet him. Because he is a monster, one with a diseased mind, one we could never trap or destroy on our own."

*

Steve Dillion was forty-three. He didn't think of himself as either debonair or charming. Never crossed his mind. Wasn't in his genes. He did not speak with a warm Southern drawl that was charming only to midwest female tourists, nor did he subscribe to the misguided factoid popular amongst the innocent of mind that most people are good. Not true.

He was polite and mannered, dressing in off-the-rack black or blue tailored suits adjusted to accommodate the monogrammed 92 FS Beretta Inox the loving wife gave him the day he made the grade. Because she loved him deeply; she was proud of the important work he would do, five years before she kicked his ass out of an uptown suburban home at the peak of a belligerent rant.

She was done with his seven-day weeks, done with her husband coming home at all hours like some drug dealer in leathers and a ponytail when he wasn't walking through the door as an indigent beggar. Or not coming home at all because—she never knew why. He never said, like he was one of the bad guys. She was done with not having a life. She wanted time-out, she told him. In fact, she wanted out for good. And she got her wish that very evening.

He didn't drink or smoke or do drugs, not anymore. That was his past, his survival on the job, though he did occasionally succumb to a polite yet meaningful fuck-you or motherfucker when called for. He was jaded and streetwise, an ex-New York gold-shield cop who relocated south within a few weeks of the break-up, setting up shop as a private investigator, doing what he wanted when he wanted without clamorous traffic, frigid winters, long hours, thankless work and a sullen wife who should have married the proverbial 'other guy'. Any other guy.

He had been that covert cop eight of the fifteen years he dedicated to a wife he once cherished and a city he once loved, bursting invisibly into hysterical laughter behind a sober expression several months later when she flew into Charleston with lots of attitude and very little choice for his signature on a deed of sale and her long-awaited declaration of divorce.

She strode last into Arrivals wearing designer jeans and heels, a button-down with the top four out of service, a blazer and a DKNY handbag à la Big Apple, making an entrance, scanning the mêlée of several hundred me-first passengers corralled by the more sea-soned herd stampeding toward taxis and limos, letting her carry-on fall from her hand, gasping. She had imagined the chinos, seer-sucker and fedora of a struggling Southern gumshoe, though her hopes could not have been more fanciful.

She stood seemingly puzzled with her mouth agape at seeing the clean-cut and tanned stranger she didn't recognize at first in a three-piece swaggering toward her, not entirely oblivious to the several other women taking favourable notice of the man she wanted signed out of her life that evening over a quiet and civil dinner. Until what left her incredibly more speechless, what left her completely unbalanced, was her husband of nearly all those fifteen years halting abruptly at arm's length, greeting her with a cool and genteel nod, not a classic airport hug or warm smile, nor offering to carry her suitcase because they were not going anywhere. At least he wasn't, especially not on her whirlwind guilt trip.

Steve Dillion was neither stunned nor speechless. He was as intimately familiar with every cubic millimetre of her brain as he was every inch of her body. He was not interested in the predicable 'if only' blame assignment of the turbulent female psyche, mean-ing 'entirely your fault'.

Instead, with a simple "Let's see them," he held out a hand. He reviewed each document, signed them without a word, wished her a pleasant flight home as any stranger might without once using her name, and walked away leaving the ex-Mrs. Dillion devastated by what she had done.

They never spoke again.

He was respected, quickly embraced by the Charleston PD who were too often hampered by politics, favours or protocol; obstacles Steve Dillion did not worry over. Nor did he worry over cheating husbands and promiscuous wives better served by less experienced and less expensive freelance cops.

His office was a desk, a couple of mismatched chairs and a filing cabinet, an answering machine he called Miss Debbie that never missed a call, and a plethora of very cool top-end PI playthings.

His life was good. Despite being single, since meeting women when abstinent by choice was pretty well an impossible dream unless sitting across from her at AA or a church social, neither of which would ever happen because he didn't need the baggage or the feigned purity. Life was already good. Good enough. He was happy. Until he clenched a fist around Miss Debbie on the last Monday of August, agreeing he would meet with her that evening once hearing Priscilla Serra's attorney-like matter-of-fact beliefs and accusations.

*

Priscilla opened her door immediately thinking no one would intentionally go up against the guy. She was impressed. He wasn't what she expected. He was well-dressed and groomed, standing straight but not at attention, his hands clasped together like he was waiting for a bus. Not really. More like he was—ready.

He wasn't exceptionally big or very tall, which surprised her. He was five-nine, ten; topping one-eighty with naturally grey hair seeming more silver against a pale tan complementing clear grey eyes, his hands free of flashy rings and gaudy jewellery. A female interpretation being: Single or divorced, though certainly not gay. And certainly not full of himself. He was smiling, but he wasn't. Not with his eyes. He was judging her, sizing her up, deciding whether or not.

From what she had gleaned from others, he was ex-NYPD, streetwise, exceptional on the job with an enviable arrest and conviction rate, and a loner. What else mattered? And whatever else he might tell her she would perforce accept at face value as well. He fit the bill, she hoped.

Once inside and seated, politely declining refreshments, Steve Dillion wasted little time with social niceties. Neither did she, making clear she preferred Ms. and Mr., which he was entirely good with.

"Let me be clear, Mr. Dillion. Brenda did not drown. She was discarded into that ocean and left in complete blackness where she died terrified and helpless."

"Yet Mason wasn't charged. Not there, not here."

"Because the Bahamians didn't give a shit and the cops here had no body, no witness. Just a very big and pristine boat after several days at dock, an obvious hosing or two, and crossing the ocean at what I'm assuming was not at full throttle. I guess they figured the motive was washed away as well. Exceptional detective work, wouldn't you say?"

"His motive being?"

"Many, many millions."

She might have said a few tens and twenties. "In the Bahamas celebrating their anniversary. That would be pretty calculated, Ms. Serra. Pretty sick, in fact."

"You got that right." She pointed to her flat screen, pressing *Play*. "That's him up close and personal at the service he did not want or want to pay for. Imagine. I've got that on tape also." She zoomed in. "Tell me he looks like a distraught husband who dearly loved his wife." She fast-forwarded, dropping the remote by her side "Nor was he at her grave. That's me saying goodbye to Brenda alone. What grieving husband, tortured with guilt for needlessly losing his loving wife, would not stand at her grave disconsolate and begging forgiveness?" She raised an open palm between them, freezing the scene. "One who's gotten away with murdering that absolutely divine girl and does not give a good shit." She opened a photo album of glossy blowups. "That's Brenda on the left, taken one year ago. My sister Presley is on the right."

"Your sister? That lady is your sister?"

"Yes. Presley."

"That is incredible, Ms. Serra. Both very lovely ladies, if I may say so."

"Thank you." She smiled, for a brief few seconds her face suffused with a warm glow. "They were always like playful girls together, as delightful on the inside as what you see. Me? Not so much. Because now one of them is dead and the other is devastated."

"What are you expecting of me, Ms. Serra? Exactly."

"I expect you to justify your reputation, everything I've been told. I want proof he is who he says he is, what he is, that all this is real. I want to know what he does, when he does it, and if what he does is consistent with someone who should be giving post-graduate lectures. Or not. Then I want him strapped on a table with a needle in his arm because he did kill her." She passed Dillion a printed sheet and a drugstore headshot. "That is all anyone knows about one Professor Brent Mason… according to Brent Mason. Whatever else he may or may not be is your job."

"You want me to track this Mason?"

"I want what is right for Brenda. I want him dead on that table and cost is not an issue."

He let that one go. Desperate hyperbole. "His background won't take long, Ms. Serra. Two, three days. But detailing his days and nights, that's another matter entirely. I work alone. It's what I do. That's why I'm sitting here and not someone else. Besides which…"

"Your concern is noted and appreciated, Mr. Dillion. Besides which," she leaned forward for affect, if not a little condescendingly, "cost is no issue. For as long as you need. What I propose is exclusivity at five thousand in cash with each weekly update plus all documented expenses. In addition, you may be interested to know, Mason is addicted to the good life. As I am sure you are." She sat back. "Are we agreed, Mr. Dillion? Or must I make further enquiries?"

"Please be aware, this could take several months. Also, cases like yours are subjective by nature, which is understandable. Still, you must be prepared for possible disappointment."

"I will not be disappointed, I assure you. Because he did kill her and you will either prove he killed her or have this case re-opened." Priscilla reached into her handbag, dropping an envelope between them. "A five grand signing bonus for taking the job, Mr. Dillion. Please start tomorrow and keep me updated." She stood, extending her hand. "Let's do this again Sunday, same time."

Steve Dillion stood, leaving the envelope where it lay, half-smirking, half-smiling. He liked her, he liked her style. "I accept the job, Ms. Serra. And we will see each other Sunday when I will accept the fee I might have possibly earned. No promises."

37

Steve Dillion sat in his office recapping the evening, curious as a single man why any woman as attractive as Priscilla Serra was a Ms. and not a Mrs. An absolute waste from a selfish standpoint.
Though he didn't see her as a career woman obsessed with proving herself. She was poised, clearly confident and soft-spoken; very soft-spoken, which he suspected she might often employ strategically in her favour, mystifying and beguiling corporate adversaries at the table. Good for her. Because all was fair in the bullshit of legalese, love, and one-sided divorces. Just too bad he hadn't met her sooner, when he might have been her client and not lost his shirt.

But that wasn't it, not that he cared. The one man gracing her album was Oliver Holloway, her home could not be more neutrally feminine, and her wall art, albeit impressive and appealing, was an exotic gallery of photos du charme and artistically abstract female nudes. Which he was also very good with. No problema. Good for her if she was, good for whomever while no doubt causing the catastrophic collapse of countless male egos.

None of that mattered, of course. Though what convinced him was the photograph of Brenda and the sister that inwardly startled him, leaving him searching for words. Putting a face and a character to Brenda gave him purpose, gave him a sense of empathy he had not felt in a very long time.

Murders happened every day, shit happened every day. In New York he had no empathy, no perspective. Wasn't needed. He was the good guy, they weren't. End of story. After his first few homicides, after puking his guts into alleyways or some dead guy's toilet, he was immune. More so from the day he went covert, from the day he began losing his wife, never caring about dead dealers, pimps and beat-up prostitutes that came with the territory.

From then on he did not need or want perspective, just a few hits at whatever hour of the night or early morning he could bury his streetwise alter ego in his closet and forget the faceless heap of big city trash.

Let them kill each other. No one's loss. However killing someone as buoyant and bubbly as Brenda—that way? No. That was not the natural order of things and, despite telling her several months, he believed several weeks was more likely. Guys like Mason, the way she described him, were easy. They were as full of shit and careless as they were full of themselves. They made mistakes, they got careless.

*

Tuesday he did the 100 miles along the I-26 corridor keeping an open mind despite an endless stream of questions riddling his mind, driving into the state capital near noon with a list of go-to names compliments of the Charleston PD Homicide boys that would get things done real quick. Although as the day and his probe progressed he regretted not bringing a suitcase, deciding with a smirk that he would not expense a new shirt, socks and underwear.

Wednesday, walking out from the four-star on an idyllic South Carolina day, his curiosity heightened, he spent the morning on the U of SC campus interviewing the dean and several professors of the Linguistics faculty. Between each meeting suffering the pangs of middle-age as giggling gaggles of young and legal co-eds passed him by in cut-offs, minis and whatever else might ensure hookups in the first semester. Something he positively needed to get serious about before fifty made him desperate, preferably someone with a cookbook and apron, someone smart and pretty with a nice body, no baggage, and good in bed.

Not too much to ask.

Driving home from Columbia, putting aside his unparalleled culinary ineptitude and personal miseries, deciding again on baked beans and wieners, he could not put Mason aside, his gut telling him that Priscilla Serra was not wrong. Brent Mason killed her best friend and he would somehow turn that well-founded suspicion into a full blown investigation.

Thursday he left home early without showering or shaving, wearing sweats, Serengetis, a ball cap and earbuds. About a quarter-mile from Mason's condo complex he sprayed exertion and fatigue onto his top and face from his water bottle, jogged the remaining few blocks, dropped onto a bench outside the building's entrance and sat breathless—waiting.

Whether Mason was coming out or already out, Dillion needed into the building, needed to situate 1015 and identify the BMW before evaluating and formulating, harbouring no doubt that Mason was dangerous, no longer believing the man would be as careless or easy as he believed Monday evening.

He was adept at biding his time, a covert cop's mantra being that all good things come to him who waits. And she was coming fast.

He sprayed his face again when she wasn't looking, wondering if she owned a cookbook and apron, wiping the sweat from his brow while ambling toward the entrance without noticing he was on a collision course with the woman slowing from a bouncy jog to a brisk walk, checking her pulse. Very trendy, very everything he didn't have in his life. She was thirty-five, tops, crashing into him at a propitious velocity.

"Whoa!" He sidestepped, twisting from his waist.

"Hey! You got a problem or what?"

"I'm sorry, miss. I didn't see you. Did I hurt you? Are you alright?"

She widened the space between them, the glare in her blue eyes softening. "No, I'm good. Besides, I guess I bumped into you. I was checking my stats."

She wasn't the only one. Tanned and trim, great legs, great everything proportioned and tight. Long and silvery platinum hair tied in a tail, a perfect button nose dotting a flawless complexion beaded with sweat. She was made for him; they were made for each other.

His imagination came alive. He was in love. And she was smiling, sort of, which was good. And single, which was better.

"I'm Steve." He checked his watch. 8:58. "I've got a nine AM with your super for a walk-through."

He was attractive enough, in decent shape, and curiously familiar. She couldn't quite put her finger on where or why, but he was clearly and obviously doing a deep scan of his own. "I'm Laura. I'm sure you'll like it here." Pig.

Dammit. Get real. Truth or consequences. No second chances here. Do not screw up. "I do already." Dammit. Could he have said anything more trite? He scrunched his face into a painful grimace. "That was not very original. I'll do better next time, when I'm more comfortable faced with incomparable beauty and charm."

Forty something and no ring, rebounding from a bad divorce. Not good and not interested. She didn't need someone else's reject. "I'll let you in." She began walking. "I hope things work out for you." Whatever.

He followed. "Well that would mean dinner this evening. Say, eightish?"

"More like, say…I don't think so."

They passed through the doors into the lobby, Dillion suitably impressed. Mason was doing okay for himself.

"Then perhaps dinner after I move in," he tried, pausing. "That is if you're free to accept a hopeful gentleman's invitation."

She turned toward the elevators, nodding toward a door by the mailroom. "That's the super. Good luck."

"Lunch. We should do lunch." He swept away his cap with one hand, his Serengetis with the other. "Bring your mother, your brother, your great aunt."

She stepped in, turning, bracing her arms against the grumbling doors. He looked pathetic, in a charming kind of way. "I'm divorced, I'm free, and in no hurry for anything more than possibly a lunch one day on condition you're approved."

Yes! "Approved by whom?"

"By my team. That would be Lieutenant Laura Peters, Charleston PD Homicide." Yeah. She nodded, understanding. "That's right, I'm a cop. Better luck next time."

His heart skipped a beat. That thunderbolt he was not anticipating. The Laura Peters whose glance had pierced his for an instant as she was hurrying somewhere, the one he had heard a whole lot about over coffee Tuesday morning while talking shop with her Homicide team about Mason and Columbia. Each one her big brother and personal bodyguard. One of them offering a, "Do not even think about it, chavo. La Chica, she is one special lady."

He stared at the elevator, transfixed by the ascending numerals. The eleventh floor flashing. What were the odds? And no way she did not misconstrue the silent shock in his eyes. She knew exactly what shot through his male brain that very second: Lady cop with a big gun and bigger issues. So been good knowin' ya.

Which didn't matter. Been good knowin' ya. He could live with that. What did matter was her being a homicide detective, drop-dead gorgeous and living one floor up from a killer with no conscience.

*

Laura Peters stepped from the elevator wishing she hadn't met him. Not that she thought he was anything special, he probably wasn't. Just another jerk who ruined her day and made her feel like shit. Anyway, she didn't care. Just another jerk she would forget before getting to Division and—"Shit!"

She couldn't be wrong. He was Dillion, the PI guy. The guy she'd seen between blinks when she was hurrying into a meeting. Who else had hair like that, like hers? Shit! He wasn't checking out condos. He was on the job; he was working Mason. Brent Mason, the case she'd filed away and forgotten. But why there? And why all that flirting bullshit?

For some irrational reason at that precise instant, practically slamming her door off its hinges, she thoroughly despised him. And she likely would have shot him had she suspected he was prowling her building while she was in her bedroom wrapped in a fleecy towel inexplicably pissed with him because, whether she wore a dress or slacks and a blouse, tap pants or a thong, a bra or camisole needing to feel like a desirable woman, they would always only see her shield and ten- millimetre Browning.

*

1015 was on the southeast corner, the door lock was common, no barrier to a pro pick-set, and the BMW tucked in a dark corner told him Mason was at home. The black Ford Taurus equipped with LED grill and dash flashers told him Laura Peters hadn't yet left for the precinct and, for the moment, he was lurking in enemy territory.

Satisfied, Steve Dillion left returning near noon looking more like a cop with his NYPD blue-gold shield and gleaming Beretta decorating his belt.

Always the gun first, never the shield. Always the same expression first: Guilt. All cops, even the good ones, played on that irreparable frailty of the human condition because they were cops and they knew. They knew most people were guilty of doing something illegal or morally wrong, something bad or indifferent. And this guy was a prime suspect.

"Yessir?"

"Charleston PD." The city's newest cop hoping a very lovely homicide detective wouldn't step out from the elevator and bust his balls. "Got a few questions about the resident in 1015. One Brent Mason."

"Nope." The super shook his head. "Not any Mason in the building. Know 'em all, all one hundred'n eight." He thought a moment. "That fellah, he's Braxton Miles. Sides which he ain't a resident. He rents by the year."

"You got a list or something official to back that up, the name?"

"Y'all got a warrant?"

"No. What I've got is Lieutenant Peters on the eleventh floor. That okay with you?"

"Y'all don't need any proof is what I'm sayin'. The fellah's name is Miles, Braxton Miles. Quiet. Has a lot of lady friends though." The man snickered. "If y'all catch my meanin'."

"Afraid I don't."

"Meanin' I wish I was him." He scratched his head. "What'd he do, hurt one of 'em gals?"

Dillion took the 5 X 7 of Mason from his jacket. "This your Braxton Miles?"

"Yep, that's him. What'd do?"

"Nothing you need to know about. Thanks."

Dillion strode out pondering what he should do next about Mason, wishing he could invite her out for a drink, and went shopping.

Very early Friday he watched Laura Peters jogging home up close and personal from a safe distance. He saw her drive out an hour later and, not long after, Brent Mason came alive on his computer as a red blinking dot until he vanished several miles north. An hour after that, give or take, Dillion was back in his car wondering how in the hell he would explain all he had learned to Priscilla Serra and what would come next apart from telling Lieutenant Peters she might have arbitrarily dismissed the Mason case too soon. Good luck with that one.

Later in the day he saw Mason return home. He watched the guy change and leave, tracking him to a chic uptown restaurant, biding his time until 10:30 when Mason drove the woman to his condo where Dillion paid more attention to the naked and deliriously happy woman than Mason. Until 2:00 AM when she left in a taxi after giving her 'darling Brent' a 'gift' that he counted out when she was gone at an even grand.

*

Saturday he took the day off. He knew Mason's schedule and he didn't need more bare ass and titties unless the one he imagined was in his bed. Besides, all work and no play? That had to stop one day.

He must have tossed the damn cell onto his sofa a dozen times, each time with an improved monologue, telling himself he should man-up, grow a pair. She was only a woman, dammit. Albeit a really gorgeous one with a gun and possibly a little pissed with him for no good reason. If she didn't already know, which he was certain she did not since he had promised her sergeant a twelve-year double malt. And she would already have shot them both. Probably with a smile on her face.

Dammit. Big mistake, he knew. Real big mistake.

"Peters."

"Hi there. Is this Lieutenant Laura Peters?"

"Yes. And you are?"

"I'm calling in a murder, Lieutenant."

"What? What murder? Who is this?"

"My murder, actually. I'm killing myself if you won't have dinner with me this evening."

She blew a burst of air from between her lips. "Assholes." She disconnected. Nice guys, but assholes. Her men were always —"Oh, shit!" She pulled to the curb, checking her Caller ID. Unknown Caller. "Shit!"

Dillion stared at his cell, pretty certain he was an asshole, very certain Laura deserved better, watching helplessly as his Judas finger pressed *Redial*.

Laura Peters stopped breathing. Shit! Unknown Caller. It was him, Dillion, and he was right. Somebody was definitely getting killed. She cleared her throat, pressing *Send*.

"Peters."

"Not very good police work, Lieutenant, hanging up on a murder victim."

"Dillion. Mr. Steve Dillion. Private Investigator Steve Dillion."

"Yes. And a self-confessed asshole for letting you close those elevator doors."

"Because I don't date. I particularly don't date liars and frauds."

"I don't particularly date drop-dead gorgeous women, but I am willing to try. Besides, I had no idea who you were till you got a little snarky about being a lady cop being that I only saw you for a split second in the squad room. And when you crashed into me the other day, you were a little out of uniform…Lieutenant Peters."

"Brent Mason."

"Yes. Mason."

"He's closed."

"Let's agree on out of sight, out of mind. Let's say Carlo's By the Sea this evening with no guns or shields or shop talk. Let's say I might actually like you and you might like me. Can we do that and put off whatever else till Monday? Or do I shoot myself?" Dammit. He expected a pause, not an eternity. "Hello? Nervous guy waiting here."

Shit! "Don't bother. I'll shoot you myself if you are an asshole and please wear a suit."

"Is that a yes? We're on?"

"We're not on anything. You know where I live and don't bother with flowers or anything else I can throw. I'll be in the lobby at eight and this is not a date, Mr. Dillion. This is strictly dinner."

Dillion's silent "Yes!" meant victory, beaming as he disconnected.

Laura Peters' was more plaintive and unsure, pressing *End*, groaning and slumping into her seat, wondering what she had done.

"You are all so dead."

38

Dillion spent his afternoon pacing, saying all the right things to her, answering her questions the way she would expect. He hadn't dated since coming to the city. In fact he had forgotten the most basic elements, certain his ex wasn't experiencing a similar dry spell.

He showered and shaved, passing on cologne. Overkill. He selected his best black suit, ironed his best button-down as crisp and sharp as he could without burning it, shined his best loafers to a rich dull lustre, completed the look with a yellow silk pocket hanky and spent the next hour admiring the single yellow rose tied with a green ribbon from a dozen different angles.

Yellow and green were her favourite colours, the rose her favourite flower. Vital information gleaned at a debt he would gladly repay Monday.

*

What the hell had she done? Laura Peters had not dated since her divorce and the prelude to her nine-year failed marriage. She didn't need the bullshit of putting herself out there, of being some jerk's interim plaything.

She was nervous with no girlfriend or sister to call, wishing Dillion would call her with some made-up excuse. She was flustered and angry for making herself vulnerable, with no idea what they would talk about because cops always talked shop, worried about what she would say when he asked for a second date. If he did, if the entire evening wasn't a complete disaster. Then what?

And could he have called any later, completely ruining her day and a peaceful evening alone?

That was on her way home. When she got home, minutes after speaking with him, she spent an hour soaking in a deep scented heat muttering and making matters worse for herself.

In her closet she pulled a bright white and pristine bra and panty set from her dresser. Not for Dillion because Hell would freeze over first. Everything she was doing she was doing for her, because she deserved, because she was a vibrant young woman, because she turned thirty-nine a week earlier and hated the thought of very soon being forty. As though he'd be thrilled.

Then she sat at her vanity for another hour making her blue eyes bluer, her unsmiling lips a deep and glossy scarlet before styling and restyling her long silver tresses, before dressing into a silky forest green curved hem and belted shirt dress, green open-toed pumps and a cute mustard yellow bucket hat that complemented her leather clutch.

Perfection. Yes, she was. As though he would notice.

At 7:58 she left her condo, carried to the lobby in seconds, her heart pounding, half-hoping he wouldn't be there. At least then she would have good reason to despise him. Until the doors opened all too soon onto the lobby, onto Steve Dillion standing there with a wide grin, Laura too late stifling a squeal erupting from nowhere, her entire body infused with a rush of heat.

She wasn't seeing some irritating guy in a track suit and ball cap, or the meddlesome PI she scarcely noticed at Division. She was seeing her date. Shit! She was on a date with a man who could not have been more handsome or elegant. She wanted to scream. This was not happening!

"Good evening, Laura. You look entirely ravishing."

"I said no flowers." Shit. I did not mean that.

"You did, which is why I brought one."

"Thank you."

She took the single yellow blossom, inhaling the fragrance. She adored yellow roses, too late realizing she was peering into his eyes. And why she was sliding her arm through his, she had no idea, mildly shocked when he held the doors and helped her into his car.

Kudos for a New Yorker, she supposed. Especially a New York cop. Even more impressed by the soft music and easy conversation that made her feel, she supposed, comfortable. Not saying she wasn't losing her mind. She was. And her sergeant was absolutely dead, righteously killed by his lieutenant Monday morning.

In the restaurant parking lot he lightly touched her arm, Laura studying him as he stepped out and crossed over to her side, opening her door and reaching for her hand while averting his eyes against all temptation. Being a gentleman once again, but not effusively, making her crazy on an evening that could not be more romantic with a full moon and a trillion sparkling stars.

Shit!

What was worse, when inside, seated across from each other like the business associates they essentially were, when other couples were sitting at right angles holding hands, caressing cheeks and whispering the same thoughts with different words, Dillion braved the possible onslaught of bullets and glares. He took the initiative and sat closer, insisting that "This does not mean we're holding hands, Laura. Way too soon for that."

She put her hands in her lap. No smile. "What are we doing here, Steve? This place is over the top for a dinner with…"

"With Laura Peters, stunning in her favourite colours. She is divorced, which means I am not the only asshole in this city. She has the most irresistible blue eyes, hair the colour of all those glistening stars she was so captivated by moments ago, a voice as warm and soft as a summer breeze, even though she can be a little snarly at times, I've noticed. And she became even more sensational last week according to public opinion." He beamed, signalling the waiter. "I'm sorry I missed the party. I heard a good time was had by all." He furrowed his brow, grinning. "As I recall, something about a lady dancing on a bar? Did I get that right?"

She was mortified, cupping her hands over her face, wondering what he wasn't saying, composing herself, regaining her dignity long enough to order a bourbon on the rocks. He ordered a JW Black with a single cube, touching his old-fashioned to hers, saluting the men of the Charleston PD Homicide Division and reigniting their lieutenant's radiant glow.

Moments later the waiter returned with his pad recommending the She-Crab Soup, which Dillion believed was appropriate, his grey eyes sparkling at the timely double entendre. Her blue eyes clearly dismissing the distinctly male humour, agreeing the Mushroom Bourguignon was an excellent choice, focused on his French cuffs and sterling silver links as her date selected the Peppercorn Salmon and a crisp Italian '88 Torre Rosazza.

She was on a date, their conversation not skipping a beat from that moment on. Until dessert that was a decadent Mudslide Soufflé, a creation of chocolat Anglaise and mocha chips over thick homemade ice cream that came with two spoons, by which time Laura Peters was lost with no idea what the hell was happening to her. Except that she was sharing a dessert with a man she first glared at, then believed was an asshole, then falsely accused, then was so cold toward even when he so thoughtfully brought her a flower practically impossible to find. And now she didn't know, too confused and too afraid to hope and wish for anything more.

"The wine was delicious, Steve. Are you an aficionado?"

"Actually my first taste since coming here. Same with the scotch. Quitting the force I took a few voluntary weeks in detox. Not getting clean, nothing like that. For me. Getting the old me back. I did my time, eight years in the dark, but somehow I stayed clean. That's the truth." He coughed a laugh, not laughing. "Guess you could say I was socially high on the job and sober at home.

Doug Booth

Until things got difficult. Then coming here, not knowing anyone, drinking alone wasn't my thing. Neither was meeting a lady who needed a drink in her hand to meet a man. That would be me." This time his smile was genuine. "Besides, I have this secret thing for women with guns and badges."

Suddenly the evening was going too quickly, ending too quickly. "I was a bitch earlier, Steve. I'm sorry." She sipped her wine, leaning into him. "Being curious, being a detective, you're what? Rejoining the living?"

"I believe I did, a few hours ago." He pressed a finger to his cheek, musing. "Or could be the moment you deliberately crashed into me, hoping I would invite you to dinner. Before you had that attitude thing happening."

The glare was completely fake. "Have you always been egomaniacal?" She put up an open palm. "Don't answer."

They were fitting in. They were having a good time, except that he couldn't put a hand to her cheek or make the evening longer, Laura casually linking her arm with his as they quietly strolled toward the car. What words could possibly make the evening anymore delightful? The gentleman pondering what she would say, the lady pondering when he would ask.

At her building, standing in the warm air under a twinkling universe caressing the petals of her flower, Laura Peters believed her heart was seconds from rupturing. She wanted to smack him or take the derringer from her purse and shoot him where he stood with his hands stuffed into his pockets being a jerk; she wanted a kiss on her cheek, a bland hug, a fateful handshake.   A n ything. Shit!

"Thank you, Steve. For my rose and a delightful evening."

"An exceptional time and exceptional company." He paused, looking left, looking right, looking up. "Anyway, I guess this is goodnight and I will see you Monday, Lieutenant." He turned toward the car, halting. "Hey, Lieutenant! I'm thinking we should do

300

this again. You up for that?"

What! The glare was real and piercing. She could not believe what she was hearing. She wanted to die, to run inside and hide. Or kill him because she was the better man.

"Let's not spoil a good thing. See you Monday. Be there at nine."

"Monday at nine. Good."He leaned against the grill, crossing his arms, waiting until her hand touched the glass door's brass handle. "Hey, Lieutenant. Hold on a minute."

She swung, fast and furious, Dillion thinking: Whoa! Female Polar Vortex!

"What?"

"Well, I remember now what I wanted to say, what I practiced saying all afternoon." He stood straight, adjusting his cuffs, walking toward her, wisely maintaining a safe distance. "This evening was incredible. You're incredible. Anyway, that was this afternoon's rehearsal. Sort of. Now I'm standing here wanting you in my arms, feeling your warmth, wanting those soft and glossy lips on mine, combing my fingers through silky strands of silver and lustrous hair. But I'll wait. I'll spend my week dreaming of you until our dinner next Saturday with dancing so I *can* have you in my arms. Getting a better sense of things."

"Really? Getting a better sense of things?" She stepped in closer, her arms akimbo. "Just so you know, Dillion, I have gun in my purse."

"I have one on my ankle. I wasn't sure how the evening would play out. Apparently you can be a little difficult at times." He jerked backward. "Apparently, Lieutenant. And, from my initial experience, completely unfounded hearsay. Absolutely."

She wanted to smack him, wipe the conceited smirk from his face. "Your initial experience? Really?" She reached out smacking him twice, like delicate feathers wafting across his cheeks. She might as well have kissed him, clenching his lapels in her fists since he wasn't doing anything, pulling him closer and pressing her soft and glossy lips into his. "How's that for your initial experience, jerk? And dream of me how?"

He caught his breath. "You know how."

"Yeah, well," she twirled, sauntering toward the doors, "that would only be in your dreams."

He wasn't so sure, but he wasn't done with her. "Laura! Lieutenant Peters. One thing more."

She halted at the doors. "Which is?"

His expression stole the sparkle from her eyes. "Brent Mason lives in this building."

39

Late Sunday afternoon, September 01st, one week after Brenda's emotional farewell and a night when Mason should have been dancing in Monaco on the eve of his adoring wife's third wedding anniversary, he sat sipping wine in his apartment staring at the cheque; the thick rolling clouds beyond his windows and balcony as dark as his mood, the muted lighting and pelting rain creating a living mural of silver rivulets.

The problem was, as worldly and streetwise as Mason believed he was, he realized he had no concept of how he might conceal his cash portfolio that was touching nine million from the ever determined crawlers at the IRS.

Far short of the fifteen he rightfully deserved, which was nevertheless beyond the capacity of any safety deposit box and even more impossible to spend freely. He needed another way. He also needed distance from Charleston, time to get his head straight and formulate a future. He needed serious help, finding himself in the peculiar position of not having a single friend or confidant in his life, save one whose friendship came at a heavy price.

He never imagined himself as solitary or socially deficient. Why would he when a constant stream of faithful and adoring women was adequately fulfilling the dual purpose of intimacy and financial reward? Which wasn't a solution, he understood. Cody Jones was.

Still, he wasn't sure. He hadn't seen the man in four years, not certain CJ would even take the call or remember him, pissed with himself for sitting there mired in self-doubt after all he had accomplished since his initial rebirth. Why? What the hell was his problem? Didn't the man say they had good history, that whenever he was needed? And Cody Jones never talked bullshit. Not one time, which didn't stop the man younger than his years from trembling as he reached for his phone, six rings later groaning a livid "Shit," sucking in air, his mind totally blank.

Then: "It's been another long while, kid, me sitting here thinking you calling me is more than a friendly what's-new thing. Is that about right, kid?"

"Shit. You kept my number, CJ?"

"Seems that way, apparently for some good reason. You calling me, that's a real twist."

"CJ, you said whenever I need you. That still stand?"

"First off, is this a phone thing or a one-on-one thing?"

"A one-on-one, I suppose. There's been some serious shit in my life. But you're right, not over the phone. Just say when, CJ. I'll be there, wherever."

"The restaurant for dinner, tomorrow. Eight sharp. You good with that?"

"Yeah, I am. Thanks, CJ. And, hey, dinner's on me."

"Well, that is how things are done down here, kid." Cody Jones chortled, pressing *End*.

He wasn't a man given to pleasantries and banter, nor did he care a whit that Braxton Miles was muttering self-praise while refilling his glass.

*

Since the three actual ladies in his life came and went all Braxton Miles understood and took for granted was first-class. He was addicted to all things superlative, landing in the Swamp late-morning Monday, booking into a suite at the Doubletree and getting a sweat on in the fitness centre before driving to Audubon Park for a favourite run he hadn't done in years.

He scarcely noticed the bright smiles of alluring young women jogging past him in check-me-out cutoffs, tank tops and bobby socks, preoccupied with his dinner meeting, deciding he would tell CJ the least possible because the man wouldn't care anyway. The man was straight-up, pragmatic. He cared about his people and getting things done right—at a price, of course. And Miles was good with that. Like he had a choice, the haunting question being at what cost or exactly how deeply in debt to the man this would put him and for how long.

The few hours until he left the hotel seemed like an eternity, much of the time spent peering across the cityscape remembering Blaire and Courtney, wondering who they were with and what they were doing at that precise moment, taking his mind off CJ, avoiding scripting his meeting. He was too urbane for that. Yet he couldn't deny that, as pumped-up as he was, he was nervous, dressing for business the way he knew CJ would. He needed the man to be impressed, appreciate how far the long-ago dumbass hillbilly had come in life, walking into Le Renard at 8:00 sharp when four years might have been as many days.

Though as sophisticated as he was Cody Jones was not in the habit of shaking hands, other than occasionally taking a lady's in his, a quirk he never saw fit to justify. He simply raised a crystal goblet inviting Miles to sit.

"Seems you have continued on your remarkable journey, kid." He sipped his wine, relishing the rich oak flavour. "I would say about as remarkable as this fine '85 Don Sebastián Rioja that I deemed appropriate for a swanky Spanish-speaking professor, which I assume is well within the young gentleman's means."

"I'm familiar with the label, CJ. Good choice. And yes, well within." Miles let the waiter fill his glass, waiting. "Good seeing you again, CJ."

"Likewise, kid. Now why are we sitting here?"

"Long story short, I got married, she died unexpectedly, and now I have a few million dollars I can't hide or spend."

If Cody Jones was shocked or surprised, his expression remained neutral. "How many is a few?"

Miles reached into his jacket pocket, framing the cheque with
his hands. "Eight and change, made out to Brent Mason."

CJ might have been looking a napkin. "Which he would prefer
not sharing with certain institutions, I presume."

"That's right. Or with himself since his future is a little unsure
at the moment." He swirled the wine, inhaling the deep bouquet,
letting the complex character settle in his mouth. Something Cody
Jones never understood. Each to their own. "And there's another
issue, CJ. One I wish I could deal with myself, but I can't without
stirring up some real serious shit."

The muted conversation continued through dinner, concluding
with one simple fix at a nominal cost of fifty thousand and a one
percent fee for the second with a shitload of one-way trust. Although not at all what he had wished for, and visibly disappointed,
he had no choice, understanding that CJ had never, and would never, murder an innocent woman. Not for any reason or anyone.

"That woman's hate for you and those white-boy blue eyes of
yours tell me she has good reason, kid. Leastways you've got serious millions and what's done is done."

"Her good reason doesn't make her less of a bitch."

"Can't tell. Never met the lady, but her being one is not reason
enough to get herself killed or your neck in a noose. She is not the
problem, you are. And you will keep your distance from her. Making things personal gets you caught. You got that? You understand
that?"

"Yeah, I do. So what are we talking here, another couple of
weeks?"

"For you specifically, about that. For the transfer, that will con-
clude by the end of business tomorrow. In the meantime you will
get yourself back to Charleston, a place you will never see again,

empty that piggybank of yours and plan a vacation abroad from which Brent Mason will never return."

Cody Jones planted his elbows on the table, pressing his hands together as though in prayer, his dark eyes penetrating Braxton's, musing on how the country cousin had metamorphosed into an educated yet wholly dispassionate and wealthy killer.

Miles put down his glass. "I remember that look, CJ. What?"

"Blaire's doing fine, kid. She remains an exemplary woman, as delightfully charming as you might remember. That said, if you had ever done her wrong in the least way, you most certainly would have been found floating face down in some dark water."

"I would never have harmed her. You know that. What's your point?"

"My point is your apparent aptitude for doing what needs taking care of, whether with a nine- millimetre or an ocean." He lowered his hands, smirking. "You up for a nighttime stroll that of necessity will require a change of attire, kid, with your millions, your fancy suits and fancy wine labels?"

He didn't hesitate. "You up for dropping a fifty K payment?"

Cody Jones signalled for the bill, passing it to Miles. "Thanks for the dinner. A good meal and good company. Now let's you and me take a walk."

Early September was good time for strolls in the Swamp, Jackson Square a perfect venue for discussions of a life-altering kind.

"He beat her that badly? How does a guy do that?"

"As easily as drowning his wife, I suppose. Not casting stones. We are what we are, what we are meant to be. Her name's Myra, Myra Linden. Paid out a goodly sum keeping the clinic from making a personal matter public. Should be naming a ward after me. She was flown to Mexico a few weeks ago by private jet, making her pretty again, and I need the husband dealt with before she gets back. Which I suppose will be whenever she's notified of being a widow."

"I'll do it, CJ. Not a problem."

*

The daytime Myra Linden was twenty-six, a mechanical engineer faced with an unexpected out-of-town family crisis that warranted an indeterminate leave of absence.

She was flawlessly beautiful like all CJ's girls. And she was married, telling Cody a week before her wedding a few years earlier that she was retiring. Thing is, the nighttime Carla Carson missed the excitement of meeting new people, of lying breathlessly beneath damp satin sheets with different and exciting lovers who adored her and wanted more of her.

That and because Dick Linden was a complete fraud. He was not the man she once believed was romantic and playful, too quickly evolving into a husband, doing her male superior most nights in less time than she took to fry an egg before falling asleep in pyjamas without ever saying he loved her. He degraded overnight, from the man who at the beginning loved seeing his topless girlfriend in thongs at the beach or getting off watching her flirting with the wind in short flighty dresses and not much else on city streets, into a predictably monotonous husband who wanted his supper at six and her after the late-night news the weeks he was home, leaving Myra feeling more like a marital receptacle than a vibrant young woman.

Until one morning she realized gazing into her bathroom mirror that she was special, that she was successful, up-and-coming; that she was as much Carla Carson as Myra Linden and that he would never be more than he was: a frustrated travelling salesman with a company credit card.

That morning she called Cody asking for part-time engagements the weeks Linden travelled out of state, always too busy to call her, never surprising her with flowers or little gifts when arriving home late most Fridays. Until a few weeks earlier when he arrived home unannounced Wednesday afternoon with liquor on his breath after being terminated, remaining awake through the night believing the worst when she didn't come home by morning but answered her phone at the office Thursday morning when she thanked him for calling as though speaking with a pollster or serviceman.

Of course she was eager for him to come home whenever his workweek was over. Whenever.

Until the Friday when she walked in near midnight with a suitcase because her reduced evening schedule no longer warranted a luxury condo, but rather five-star hotel suites. Until his hands clawed at her clothes and his fists smashed repeatedly into her face.

Though like all CJ's girls she was educated and strong-willed, not about to take shit from a loser, mere minutes after the beating opening her door to a sophisticated black man who took her away after telling the bewildered husband to make his peace with his Maker. A week later Myra was flown to another private clinic in Mexico City, while Dick Linden, maintaining a drunken stupor, had not yet made his peace with an unsympathetic God.

She was two weeks from her scheduled homecoming, placing her complete faith in CJ when he assured her all would be well and that she had no cause whatsoever for concern, Cody Jones staring at his cell's Caller ID mere moments after disconnecting from his very popular Carla Carson. He couldn't help blurting a "No shit" seconds before pressing *Send*.

Problem solved. That was his business, his entire life. He knew people. He knew the best and he knew the worst.

*

Tuesday Miles flew into Charleston, the next day enjoying a leisurely and pensive drive one notch over legal back to New Orleans, his precious Swamp. Checked-in Wednesday evening, he ordered in a light meal with a harmless glass of Chardonnay, lay in bed watching his favourite pay-per-view soft porn, and crashed early.

Thursday he did his usual hours of strength training and running, got himself photographed as an upwardly mobile gentleman for his third passport, and met CJ for instructions over a private lunch. He also learned about Braxton Miles' millions in a recently created numbered account in the Caymans and listened attentively to exactly how the evening's agenda would play out; all that before standing by the linen-draped table feeling awkward.

"You got all that, kid? We're good, and you will not fuck us up?"

"No way, CJ. I will get things done the way you want. No worry." What else could he say? Nothing. "I guess we're done? This is it, again?"

"We are done, kid. Nothing ever came from sad laments. We get on with our lives. That is what we do." He beamed a row of bright white teeth. "Most of us. And that said…"

"Yeah, I know. Get my ass out of town tomorrow. Been good seeing you, though. You know, getting things done together. Like old times, CJ." Miles sighed, his sad expression speaking volumes. "Sometimes life is shit."

"Been good seeing you too, kid. Ten years, that's real history in this short life. Know what I'm saying. Too much history to fuck with. You got that? You understand that? You be smart, kid. Be real smart. You leave that place and do not fuck with that woman or she will rain serious grief down upon you. You do things right, the way you know, the way you were taught. You be real smart about her."

He would, he promised, turning away, walking out into the bright Louisiana sunlight feeling elated and confident, studying the key to a comfortable home in suburban Mandeville north of Lake Pontchartrain. He was ready for getting things done; no way would he disappoint CJ or fail whoever Myra Linden might also be.

Checking his Rolex that Cody hadn't thought to notice he decided that, yeah, he would order in a decent Bordeaux. He had time, too much time before changing and meeting the driver three blocks north very few minutes after his phone chimed.

40

Somehow Linden managed his way home near eleven o'clock, slamming the door shut, slumping against a wall in the dark, mumbling and swearing, his last incoherent words a startled "What the fuck!" a second before a man a whole lot bigger and intense slammed his head into the wall and stepped back looking down.

"Damn if that did not feel good, kid. Damn straight." The driver kicked Linden's ribs, hard, producing a burst of phlegmy coughs, cuffing his hands behind his back with a tie-wrap and taking his wallet. "Too bad we can't keep this fucker a few days, get things done proper-like. Don't seem right somehow doin' him so quick'n easy. Not after beatin' on the poor girl the way he did so bad."

"I saw photographs. He did a real good job on her."

"Have a daughter her age. Sweet little things, both of 'em. Truth be told, I ain't particularly surprised seein' y'all here. Our Mr. CJ thinks a whole lot of you, kid. Believe that."

"Thanks. Good to hear. He's says you've got a place to put this piece of shit, somewhere he'll be found sooner than later. Mind telling me?"

"Mississippi Sound. Good bit of traffic most days; mostly quiet when things get nice'n dark. He gets done there'n left if he don't shit himself dead before we start with him. Not exactly a touristy spot, the Sound. All sorts of real bad shit out there. Not a real good place for snoozin'."

"He's pissed."

"Will be till seein' the gun, leastways. Smells like he put down half a bottle. Till seein' that big nasty gun when he'll be all wide awake'n smellin' a whole shitload worse."

"So we take his car?"

The driver's laugh was deep and throaty from three packs a day. "Don't believe so. Most men I'm familiar with would fiercely object to drivin' toward their own passin'. Some things y'all just can't rely on with any degree of certainty."

The driver reached into his pockets for more tie-wraps, doing the feet, telling Miles to find and soak a sock from the bedroom that would muffle not suffocate the hog-tied fucker, ensuring things would get done right for the girl. Then leaving Miles standing guard over the groaning body on the floor, Linden's eyes veined with fine red streaks dripping with tears, his flaring nose spitting out bubbles of clear mucous, his senses too dulled to comprehend fear, the driver went into the garage.

First smashing the lights he moved Linden's compact onto the driveway, bringing his own sedan into the cover of darkness. Too few minutes later from Linden's perspective he was summarily tumbled into the trunk by four gruff and uncaring hands, the home was darkened and locked, and they were en route to the Sound without much being said because neither man was interested in the other beyond getting the job done right for Cody Jones.

At the Sound Miles asked whether the driver might actually live thereabouts because he wasn't showing any doubt whatsoever and Miles wasn't seeing anything but black sky, black trees and a patch of brown dusty road lit by the car's dimmer lights constantly disappearing behind them every hundred feet or so.

"Folks in these parts ain't got much reason for stayin' up, kid. They're here cause they like the quiet and the dark. Besides which y'all shouldn't be walkin' out here this time of night. Can't ever tell. Like I said, all sorts of real bad shit out here."

Then about four miles down the driver pulled over, Braxton

Miles peering from his window into blackness, leaning into the driver he could scarcely make out as though saying "Fuck this."

The lights went out. "That better, city boy?"

"Thanks. Not really."

He didn't care. "Listen up, kid. We do this thing real quick. This ain't about us gettin' glory. Understand?"

"No shit."

He passed Miles a familiar A Q4 TAC. "Y'all remember?"

"Yeah, like holding an old friend. Let's just get this done and get the fuck out of here."

"Like I said, the fucker might just shit himself dead when he sees what is."

The driver went out first into the dark. Miles followed, clambering through the same door, though he did admit things weren't as black once outside, surprised all the same that Linden's body was practically indiscernible curled up in the unlit trunk.

For good reason, the driver told him. "Lights just don't ever figure into dark circumstances. Leastways not out here. Not unless y'all got a peculiar likin' for pretty blues'n reds all flashin'n some big mean fucker yellin' at y'all to get your ass down on this dusty old road."

He didn't, helping jerk Linden onto the road by his arms, dropping him onto his knees before the driver kicked him into the roadside ditch and went in after him, setting him up for Miles.

Linden was hysterical, whimpering and squirming, stretched out like he wanted to be a bigger man in his last minutes of life, which Miles thought was comical given what he had done to Myra. Until the driver began cursing in whispers and kicking his feet wildly, telling Miles as he scrambled onto the road on his hands and knees that "Y'all get things done real quick in there, kid. There is real nasty shit in that ditch. Real nasty shit y'all ain't never seen the likes of."

Miles took a hasty few steps back, thinking maybe not. Certain maybe not. "Thanks. Think I'll take care of business from here. Dead is dead. Right?"

The man shook his head. "Not this evenin'. Y'all get in that ditch'n y'all shoot that piece of shit like y'all were told. Two in the gut, one in the head after he knows what is. The fucker's got to know what is and y'all have to witness his deep desperation for that poor girl."

Miles thought back to Wally Bunker and the driver's reassuring words that made killing the dirtbag all the easier. He didn't think; he just did, half sliding, half jumping into the black trench to a frantic muffled chorus of devout praises to the Lord, thinking he might very well shit himself dead before putting down Linden.

He didn't stop skipping and dancing, shuffling his feet while telling Linden what was. "This is for Myra, asshole." Poof. Poof. Two into the gut, Miles surprised by how little the body moved. Not like Davaux who sailed halfway down the city block. "Shouldn't have beaten that pretty girl, asshole. This is for her, from her. You got that, asshole? She's the one doing this. And that God you're screaming to with your purple face and your shit-filled eyes, he doesn't give a good shit about shit like you." He leaned forward, leering, extending an arm. "This one goes into your sick head, for Myra, the way she would want in ten, nine, eight…Ah, what the fuck?"   Poof.

Done. Braxton Miles kicking and flailing and scrambling on all fours onto the road where the driver stood bent over splitting his gut with raucous laughter, aiming the narrow beam of halogen blue-white light at the corpse woefully kneeling with its damaged head bowed in unanswered prayer.

Miles turned a half-circle. "That was not fucking funny, you old shit."

"Sorry, kid. Just addin' a bit of jocularity to the fucker's de-served passin' is all. Y'all got to know there ain't nothin' much worse than some fucker hearin' mockin' laughter as he's passin' on. Got to say, though, y'all got a real talent. Wasn't expectin' no Fred Astaire."

"Still not fucking funny, you old coot." Miles side-stepped to the passenger door erupting into muted laughter, admitting that, yeah, it was kind of funny but, "Get us the fuck out of here."

*

Myra Linden received that unexpected phone call Sunday PM as a message she ignored while preoccupied sipping daiquiris poolside on a chaise-longue in a tiny string bikini rejuvenating her body, deciding she would give the matter her fullest attention when she wasn't being hit on or completely absorbed in her novel.

Dick Linden was faceless in any crowd, not deserving of a moment's consideration let alone someone actually putting three bullets into him. She could think of only one man who would do that, care that deeply about her, deciding she would call the Mandeville Precinct Monday.

She told the officer that "Dick Linden" should be buried in a pauper's grave or cremated and put in a jar at their convenience. She would of course pay any reasonable expense, however she had no interest in viewing the body or hearing the particulars. He was dead, which was good enough for her, saving her the cost of a divorce. He was a drunk and abusive; he was a loser and the worst kind of husband who somehow got himself put in a ditch. "In fact, Detective," she offered, sipping a daiquiri, "put the prick back in the ditch."

Though when she did return home as lovely and young as ever, she called CJ with an effusive and tearful thank-you for taking exquisite care of her, pausing a moment, sighing a warm breath and familiar, "You got that, CJ? For everything."

For everything. Yes, he got that, chuckling. Whatever that meant. And throughout their many more years together not another word was mentioned of Dick Linden's fortuitous and unsolved murder. He just wasn't anymore, is all, the driver reported to his boss the morning after over a breakfast as Braxton Miles was returning to Charleston, pondering when, where, and for how long with no particular purpose in life other than his immediate survival.

*

September 13th was a Friday, Hell expressing its fury with torrential rains flooding streets and a daytime darkness occluding anything of colour, drenching pedestrians and blinding drivers as Mason stood at his fogged windows impatiently cursing. He did not want to wait until Monday, practically leaping toward his door at the intercom's high-pitched squeal, meeting the courier at the elevator to sign for an express package from New Orleans.

Ripping open the plain oversized envelope, he beamed. Cody had again come through. Inside was one Mr. Bradley McGuire's birth certificate and SS card, his Master's Degree and alma mater's garnet ring along with credit cards, a passport and driver's permit McGuire would alter at a later time once determining where he would enjoy living his new life.

Without a moment's hesitation, when his date was somewhere dressing for dinner, excited and titillated about her evening's finale, Mason packed the best of his wardrobe, left the rental condo as though he was coming back and drove to the airport where he deserted the Beamer with the keys in the ignition. Not his problem. He was never coming home, simply disappearing the moment he walked out from the Aéroport Lyon-Saint-Exupéry one day later not many weeks from his thirty-third birthday with all that remained of Braxton Miles tucked into his shirt pocket.

Bradley McGuire had found himself. He had found purpose in his life and would for the next few years live a peaceful and pensive existence while in the exotic and golden nirvanas of the Côte d'Azur and Barcelona availing himself of American and British pampered daughters, lost and lonely widows, and finally-free divorcées meeting his simple criteria.

41

The Sunday when Mason was on the phone with Cody Jones, Steve Dillion was laid back in his living room sipping a JW Black alone for the first time in months. He was back on track feeling good about himself, feeling very good about Laura Peters, listening to a one-sided conversation he couldn't make sense of.

Who was CJ? What did CJ even mean? He figured Mason's serious deep shit was Brenda Holloway and that meeting CJ would somehow make things right. Question was when? Never mind when and how?

Then nothing. Mason's fixation with porn. Not his thing, Dillion planning his own when and where, making a reservation for the coming Saturday before focusing on his update meeting with Priscilla Serra that evening when he would confirm that Brenda was very likely murdered by her husband and that he was certain the Charleston PD would reopen the case with their fullest attention. The difficult part being that Professor Brent Mason, although he did exist, had no past. No one knew him, no one remembered him. The larger question being: Who was Braxton Miles?

He left with the five grand in an envelope and, when he was gone, Priscilla called her sister.

*

Very early Monday morning Steve Dillion opened his computer too late into a silent and empty condo, shrugging off the disappointment. Nothing in his world happened overnight.

Instead he left for the precinct, walking in shortly after 8:00

with a twelve-year scotch for the contented sergeant whose desk was immediately stormed by the squad, the male contingent gleefully taking their winnings from their female counterparts who demanded dinner details while the men wanted more pertinent data. Though Dillion, sparing the lady's reputation, simply replied that the evening was all he and Laura could have wished for.

Laura Peters strode into the squad room at 8:35 to standing applause and a raucous chorus of hooting and piercing whistles, her cheeks flushed with warm colour at seeing Dillion with her sergeant who seemed romantically attached to his forty-proof payoff. Both of them pitiful idiots.

All she could manage was, "Nothing happened. Whatever he said did not happen. Will not happen," which garnered her more whistles and oohs. They didn't believe her. They were cops, they recognized the signs. The instant denial and defensiveness, her sudden loss of equanimity and the pointing. Oh yeah, she was guilty as hell.

She ordered them back to work, threatening overtime and glaring at Dillion, jabbing the air with a commanding finger. "You. In my office. Now." An instant later feeling the heat searing her cheeks deepen when the sergeant put a hand to Dillion's shoulder, covered his mouth and murmured some stupid thing.

In her office she closed the blinds, shutting them out, shutting out their silly smirks, snapping at Dillion to shut the door and sit.

"That was some bombshell you laid on me."

"More of one if I hadn't told you, Laura, especially after that kiss. Because we're dining and dancing next week at The Tuxedo."

"Yeah, right. Like that'll happen. Not." Shit. She did not mean that. God, he was infuriating. "That place is ridiculously expensive, dark and," she paused, "dark. And what silly guy thing did Garcia tell you this time."

"First off, the place is upscale, subdued and romantic. And Garcia said you must like me, a lot. Said you always wear slacks and jackets on the job, unless you're on a bar dancing with your hair in a tail. But today you're in a pleated skirt, a silk blouse, and sort of a sexy updo curly thing going on because I'm here. He's very insightful. A good cop."

"Really, he said that?"

"Yes."

"Well, he's wrong."

"Then you always kiss men you don't like that way? That's a lot of men, Laura. That some type A personality thing happening with you?"

She unhooked the Browning from her waist, resting the pistol on her desk. "My personality is fine. You're the type B jerk problem telling a woman she's incredible, all that bullshit about holding her, kissing her, feeling her hair. That you'll dream of her, standing there like you're a dimwitted eunuch. I should have shot you when I had just cause."

"So you do like me, a lot. And we are on for Saturday."

"I don't know yet. I'm weighing my options. The kiss wasn't earthshaking and I really think I can do better for myself. Anyway call me this evening, convince me. Or not. Whatever. I might possibly feel sorry for you again." She reached for her phone, summoning Garcia. When the sergeant came in, leaving the banter at his desk, they got to it. "Steve, tell us all you know about Brent Mason."

He told them about Brenda, about how the couple met, how they married and how she was killed. He explained Mason's motive, Priscilla and Presley's firm convictions, and that not only did Professor Brent Mason never teach at the U of SC, no one remembered him as a postgrad student. He explained how, in fact, Mason did not exist prior to landing in the States a short time before meeting Brenda. That he had credentials, a bank account and paid taxes, but no friends, no colleagues or high school records. Then, saving the best for last, they viewed Brenda's funeral from Peters' desktop before hearing Mason's histrionics with Priscilla and Darleen Jacobs.

"He's also into porn and servicing the city's affluent and lonely older ladies. The thirties and forties, and at a pretty steep price. Strange, considering he could easily afford the younger nubile stuff. Don't you think?"

"What I think is you are a complete asshole." She leaned forward, lacing her fingers, ignoring Garcia's asinine smirk and sudden interest in the floor. "Young nubile stuff, really?"

A covert cop's first rule: Show no fear, especially with Garcia in the room. "Yes. Young women like you, Laura. Heavenly. Breathtaking beyond words."

Garcia half-stood. "Hey, you guys need some alone time here?"

She didn't look at him. "You sit down and shut up. And you, you know this how?"

"I put audio-visual into the apartment. Bedroom and living room. Did the Beamer also."

Garcia chuckled, Peters didn't. "Steve, that is illegal. You should know that. Shit!"

"Illegal for you people, not me. Different game rules. Also, he would have to report the very expert break-in first and what are the chances that will happen anytime soon? And this isn't about evidence. This is about tracking him." He passed Garcia a sheet from his notepad. "That's his tag. He also goes under Braxton Miles who also has no life prior to a degree that is real. No high school. Nothing. Just a birth certificate and dead parents. And guess what? Not only did he arrive in Charleston about the same time as Mason, living off some short-lived teaching job, they were born on the same day three years apart." He placed two headshots on the desk. "Miles and Mason. You tell me."

Peters looked to Garcia. "Call the Serra woman. Get her in here and verify Steve's findings."

He nodded. "I'm on it, boss."

Reaching out he and Dillion did that macho fist-thing, that stupid man-thing, Peters halting him at the door.

"Reynaldo. You are very welcome."

"Very welcome for what, chica?"

"For that scotch you were drooling over when I came in."

His burst of laughter was loud. "De nada, chica. We Latinos, we know these things." He turned to Dillion, beaming, giving a thumbs-up. "¡Vaya hombre!" Then he left, half-closing the door. "Hey, people…"

"No!" Laura jerked to her feet. "No vaya! No nada!" She dropped into her seat. "Not funny." Shit. She was doing it again, peering into his eyes. "What?"

"From my experience, when you're falsely accused of a major felony and found guilty, why not do the felony? I'm thinking…"

"And I'm thinking you should stop talking."

He pushed his weight from the chair. "I was thinking how stunning you are and that I can't wait until Saturday." He took her hands, brought her in close, pressed his palms to her flushed cheeks and kissed her. Then he held her by her shoulders at arm's length, absorbing every inch of her, sighing mournfully. "Very stunning. But you are right, Lieutenant Peters, not earthshaking. I really think I can do better for myself. I'll go ahead and cancel Saturday."

"In your dreams. And better than this?" She smacked him, twice, before the numbing impact of her lips crushing against his. And when she was done stealing his breath she sat palming the pleats of her new skirt. He didn't exist. "Thank you for coming in, Mr. Dillion."

"Thank you, Lieutenant." He ambled into the squad room leaving her door open, wiping red gloss onto his hanky, beaming, waving his irrefutable evidence. "Hey, guys! Raspberry."

Howls and whistles rang out, a dreamy smile forming on her pulsating lips. He'd be calling her that evening and was taking her dancing. She was going on another incredible date, and many more.

Yes!

*

Dillion kept Mason's CJ phone call to himself. The thing about homicide cops, they came off as cops, got off on looking like cops with their big black guns and shiny gold shields. Something else he defensively kept private. No offence. However there was something more to Mason than plural IDs and cops with their sense of righteous morality would simply get in the way.

At 7:30 Priscilla called thanking him. She had been with Peters and Garcia throughout the afternoon, Dillion assuring her good things would happen. Though by 8:30 Mason had not yet returned home, Dillion putting his laptop in sleep mode, thinking she'd probably suffered long enough.

They spoke for an hour, shop talk evolving quickly into their dreams and hopes and wishes, Laura realizing after disconnecting what Steve already knew, what was too premature to confess. They wanted each other and Saturday was now too many hours and lonesome evenings away, when saying "Goodnight Laura" seemed silly, Laura somehow making her whispered "Goodnight Steve" sound like an ardent kiss.

*

Tuesday Dillion sat glued to his screen, switching between Mason's apartment and a photograph of Laura seated in her office because no way would she allow any of her in bikinis or anything else that would satiate his tormented mind, Dillion slamming a fist on his desk near dinnertime. Mason was home repacking the suitcase he'd come with. A suitcase with airline tags.

Where next didn't matter. He was already packing. Land or air, whatever. What mattered was Laura. As much as he wanted her, right then he needed her more and she picked up in in blink.

"Hi."

"Hi. So listen. I've decided on Precious, for you, when we're alone. I thought Lover would be too much like a premonition, a cop's finely tuned intuition, which is for later. Right now I need one of your guys at the airport until I say so. Mason's been somewhere and he's heading out again. I may need help getting through all that security paranoia. Or not. Can you do that for me?"

"You're watching Mason now?"

"Yes. Can you do that for me?"

"It's done." Silence. "Steve, do not make me shoot you for doing something stupid before you take me dancing. Not after kissing me like that. I mean, shit. And Precious? Really? What is wrong with you?"

He chuckled. "Simple. I'm in love."

"Yeah, with yourself."

"No. I'm in love with you."

What! "What?"

"I am, with you. Now get someone over there pronto. Got to go. Bye."

"What!"

Minutes later a homicide detective was en route to the airport and Dillion was driving toward Laura Peters' condo complex with a thermos of coffee and granola bars, zooming in to her as she arrived home for a double bourbon, then another, because he could not be serious. Shit!

Yet he was, serious, spying on Mason until midnight with his suitcase in the trunk, waking on the half-hour until Mason drove from the garage at 8:00 AM, calling Garcia one hour later from the southbound I-95, believing Laura might be more female than cop at the moment and he did not need the distraction.

Vaya con Dios, amigo.

*

He kept an open mind until Mason stopped for gas in Jacksonville four hours later, thinking maybe Miami, thinking she would be

TurnAbout

fantastic in a thong, or out of one, his focus changing when he turned onto the westbound I-10 stopping again for gas in Tallahassee as Mason was pulling out. Three hours after that he was taking the Cleveland off-ramp onto Canal, tracking Mason into the French Quarter, stopping several cars behind when Mason climbed out at the Sheraton near 7:00 PM local.

Dillion checked-in at 7:15, flashing his shield, letting the twenty-something clerk be amazed by the gun on his belt, the girl confirming that Braxton Miles would be with them two nights, which gave him the night off with room service.

The next morning in jeans, a V-neck and ball cap, he watched Mason leave through the lobby all pumped-up for whatever. He wasn't interested, biding his time, tracking him near noon to a classy Bourbon Street restaurant, walking in five minutes later to see Mason sitting with some suited-up black guy who might have been an executive. Except he wasn't. The mannerisms were all wrong, Dillion recognizing a pimp cum drug dealer when he saw one.

They knew each other, but weren't friends. Neither was smiling, Mason seemingly delighted by the wine he was pouring into his glass, Dillion assuming the good stuff. Nor did they shake hands when Mason left after passing the guy an envelope, Dillion dropping a fifty on the table the moment Mason stood, walking out ahead of him.

When Mason stepped onto the sidewalk he didn't notice the businessman in a three-piece talking on his cell. Nor did the debonair black guy waiting for his Jag as Dillion was speaking with Garcia, hearing the Lieutenant was a little strung out the last couple of days, Dillion getting a taste of that himself an hour later.

"New Orleans? Really, Dillion? Are you that much of an idiot?"

He chuckled. "What's with the attitude, Lieutenant?"

"Oh, I don't know. What's with you saying you love me after

325

one date, then hanging up? I mean, really? What is wrong with you, Steve?"

"What's with assaulting me in your office, Lieutenant? I'm still drinking through straws."

"We have to talk. I mean, really, we do. You've got to be joking and I do not need shit like that in my life."

"I'm not joking. I do love you. So who is he?"

The frustrated burst of air somehow sounded sweet. "Cody Jones. Forty-one. No convictions. Not even a traffic violation. In fact he's pure as snow. A New Orleans businessman with his hands in a few pockets."

"No. He's a dealer and high-end pimp in a fancy suit."

She believed him. "Which means he's dangerous. And Mason?"

"He's not working out. Not yet."

"Meaning what exactly?"

"Meaning I can't wait to see you, to see your eyes, to see what your voice is telling me."

"Excuse me."

"You love me, Laura. Strange, but you do. You love me and you're worried about me."

Strange was an understatement. "You really are delusional, Dillion." Not on the phone, not like some giddy schoolgirl and not before she danced in his arms when she would know for sure. "Okay, so when are you coming home? And are we on for Saturday, or not?"

"Home, not back. That's good. I like that. You see, you do love me. And yes, we are."

A telling silence. "Steve, don't you dare do anything stupid to ruin my evening. My outfit cost a fortune."

She pressed *End*.

*

Dillion sat in the lobby in nondescript cords and a loose-knit raglan. He was invisible, expecting that Mason would step from an elevator for a Happy Hour cocktail, or dinner somewhere in the Quarter, or that the BMW would blink on his screen.

What happened was Mason hurrying through the lobby onto the street with a purpose at 7:30 in jeans, sneakers, and a polyester windbreaker. Not exactly the quintessential multimillionaire walking north a few blocks when he abruptly stopped.

He wasn't lost or confused or waiting for a light, he was stepping into a late model sedan and disappearing. He was doing something down and dirty, likely for Jones, Dillion believing that someone somewhere was lying dead or broken was a given when Mason hurried through the lobby near one AM minus the windbreaker, the sneakers and jeans caked with mud.

Not his problem. His day was done, though Friday he would continue tracking Mason after check-out, if not as closely, not surprised when hearing on the morning news that a body was found in some ditch or that he was on an eastbound lane and wouldn't be home until midnight.

He didn't care about another murder victim. That on-the-job disability self-corrected years earlier. He cared about his intuition, first stopping in Tallahassee minutes after Mason where he found muddy sneakers in the men's room and in Jacksonville where he found the jeans turned inside out and useless.

42

Laura Peters spent her Saturday at the spa, making herself impossibly more lovely. Dillion spent part of his morning with Priscilla Serra giving her hope, part of his afternoon bringing Garcia up to speed over a few beers before he sat watching Mason book his Sunday through Friday with six wealthy and desperate women.

Saturday evening when Laura stepped from the elevator in low-heeled silver sandals, a fitted and strapless knee-length evening gown in dusty mauve with a side slit baring her leg to her mid-thigh, a darker violet silk wrap draped over arms, her silvery straight hair seductively enhancing bare and flawless shoulders, he stood there stupefied. And she let him, torturing him with a radiant smile, because she was the epitome of elegance and grace; she felt elegant and she felt graceful, and he was in such excruciating pain.

"Close your mouth, Steve. It's not becoming. And this is where you say something nice and stop salivating."

"You are exquisite."

"Thank you. And you're very dashing." She glanced at the delicate box. "Is that a corsage for me?"

He nodded, closing the gap, adorning her wrist, adoring her. Then glancing at her sandals, "I was hoping I wouldn't be dancing with my head on your shoulder. Decidedly uncool. Thank you for that."

She kissed him, opening her clutch for a tissue, de-smudging his lips. "You really are slow at times, Steve. Please work on that for me."

He would, he promised, linking their arms.

At The Tuxedo they were in excellent company, Laura not at all perplexed about the muted lighting and romantic ambiance. She was the evening's clear winner, turning heads, garnering smiles and second glances. As for Steve, he didn't matter; he might have been invisible. But he didn't care because throughout the evening his wishes had come true, with each dance holding her in his arms and stroking her lustrous hair as her head lay dreamily against his shoulder, whispering as their last dance ended that she was precious and that he loved her. Not expecting she would ever so softly kiss his lips.

Yet what she wanted and what she would do were diametric opposites, which he understood. She needed time, more than a couple of fantastic dates in one week. Still, kissing at her elevators would seem ridiculous. Would be ridiculous. That's what she understood.

Her head was swimming. The evening was too incredible for words, a dream too wonderful to end, but she was kicking him out after their nightcap. House rules.

Inside her condo, once the requisite compliment and her gracious thank-you were exchanged, Laura pointed him into the dining room. She wanted a bourbon. She also needed a few moments, padding dreamily into her bedroom; she was in another world, stepping out long minutes later in a green silk slip and robe because, contrary to his thinking, she was not sitting curled on a sofa in her stunning gown.

Whoa! Nice. "Will you always torture me like this?"

She took her bourbon. "Steve, you are the first man I've invited into my home. You're the first man I've dated and I can't understand what's happening, why I feel this way. Meaning I will not rush into anything here and you are gone at midnight."

He pressed a fingertip to her lips. "I know that. I am good with that. We both have deep scars. Question though. This exceptional

JW Black I'm swirling came from an unopened bottle and you're a bourbon lady. Care to explain this piece of incontrovertible evidence, Lieutenant?"

She smacked him, tugging off his tie, shrugging off his jacket and taking his hand, leading him to a sofa as new as everything else in the condo.

"You're the big-city cop. You figure things out."

*

The best-laid plans of Lieutenant Detective Laura Peters did not quite evolve as she had planned that evening, waking with him in her bed the next morning naked, damp and dishevelled, feeling ravaged and enraptured, her pounding heart pressed tightly against his, her face and lips smeared with blue mascara and a deep-prune gloss.

Steve was no less marred by the same rich colour palette, firmly believing he would require a graft if not complete reconstructive surgery. She empathized, patting his cheek. Poor darling. She didn't care. And really neither did he as she clambered over him and pranced into the bathroom.

He would definitely be framing her perfect tear-drop ass in a thong on South Beach sometime very soon. Yes! And he did. Very much deserving of another ¡Vaya hombre!

Three and a half years later to the day from when he lay caressing her tanned, tight, and thong-clad body with SPF on Miami's white sand, Laura Dillion smacked him, pushing away from his toned and glistening body, reaching for her phone. Reynaldo was calling, confirming what time was good for dinner. That's what she thought until she pressed *Send*, Steve instantly feeling her smooth skin turn cold and rough, the burning love in her eyes transmuting into worry and dread.

"Laura, what is it?"

*

That Sunday, September 08th, 2002, Steve Dillion did survive without surgery.

Laura went home with him because he badly needed a change of clothes and because she was a female deeply in love with a corresponding curiosity. She believed him, of course she did, a little. However, her delirium and throbbing heart aside, she could not understand any woman her age paying for sex with any man. They were women, all things being equal. Duh.

Despite which she acquiesced. She was curious, like peeking through a window, insisting she was spotting for the all-dressed. She had also brought a small overnighter, shrugging with an impish grin when Dillion suggested Mason would likely be a few hours. What was his point?

Though when Mason did return near 10:00 with a mid-forties woman in designer everything, Dillion adjusted the volume, sat back detached with a glass of wine and notebook forewarning Laura there would be no prelude or pretence in 1015. No affection. She would not see dancing or curling on a sofa or anything remotely romantic. She would see Mason pouring premier booze while the client would strip without the slightest seduction, crawl into bed, take a swallow of whatever and simply get to it.

"How is that possible? Just like that?"

"Has been for millennia."

"You do this stuff, really?"

"Once. It's not a hobby and his encore performance is for you. I already have his client list and calendar. He's been a busy guy and will be through Sunday. All wealthy at a grand a pop and he never does freebies, like he's making them pay for something else. Check his eyes. Zero emotion. This is strictly in and out. Wham, bam, and see you next week or month or whenever. Reserved a week in advance when she'll get the biggest bang for her buck and maybe shower before taking a grand in cash from her Gucci."

"How cold is that?"

"Not cold, Laura. Pragmatic. Money for essential services rendered. The women are wealthy and don't need the hassle of a third or fourth divorce, or maybe being conned. This way they're dined at their expense, flattered by a younger man, albeit a sociopath, and they get an injection of ephemeral euphoria before going home alone. The ultimate win-win."

"That is sick shit. I was terrified when you undressed me. She's stripping so matter-of-factly."

He chuckled. "Yeah, well, you got over it pretty fast."

She smacked him, twice. "What happens now?"

"After tonight I track them. I'll put names to addresses and give you the data. No doubt I'll see this one again, so no big hurry. In the meantime I might learn more about him, Jones and Brenda when he's out for longer than a sweat."

"Do not do that. That is an order from your me. Not the cop me. Do not do that."

"No worry. Believe me, Precious. No worry at all."

She didn't believe him. "I feel sorry for her."

"Don't waste the emotion."

"I mean she's attractive, shapely, and obviously intelligent. Who would not want her? How sad is that?"

"She is not a victim, Laura."

"Yes, she is. She's afraid of whatever and she's being manipulated."

"There is no crime here." Dillion shut the computer. "Seeing him, hearing what he says and how he says it, I have a clear sense of the guy. He's very smooth and is not new at this."

"He is one sick individual and a predator. And we will get him. No shit." She eased onto his lap, straddling him, putting aside their glasses and kissing him, rapping his forehead gently with her knuckles. "No more about him. He's work. What I need is more euphoria of my own. Lots of euphoria. You have any ideas in there, Detective?"

He thought for a moment, nodding. Could be he had a few.

*

Monday Dillion drove Laura home so that Lieutenant Peters could arrive collected at Division in navy slacks and her Browning, not flustered and flushed in a green miniskirt and snug yellow sweater, after an uneventful dinner Saturday evening at some restaurant. Not earthshaking.

Not that anyone believed her. They were cops, the female contingent soon browbeating her into a full confession.

Dillion's week began where he was, across from Laura's building about the time Mason was walking in from his run, blind only when the subject went into his bank, or a restaurant, or wherever he might recall the man on the sidewalk outside Le Renard.

Mason was a sociopath, a smart one. No question. A rich one whose days never varied: Seven mornings at the gym, seven mornings running nowhere for no reason Dillion could figure; then some porn and dressing for dinner, bringing whoever back to his bed, earning his grand and sending her home in a taxi, waking late, changing the satin sheets and starting over.

A life some guys might envy. Though not him, not since that first Saturday, not since Monday when Laura had him to herself for dinner and most of the evening while Mason was working, letting him go with smudged lips near midnight when he wouldn't wait long for the lady's cab to show.

Except Friday the thirteenth when the gods had pissed torrential rains across the city all day and Laura was expecting him for the entire weekend sans his computer. He promised, spending his day monitoring Mason from across town until late afternoon when Mason rushed out with a purpose, returning in a blink with a package, his demeanour and humour visibly and curiously brighter after a day as dark as the weather.

More curious was Mason minutes later selectively packing a suitcase from a chic wardrobe in jeans and a suede jacket when he should have been dressing for dinner, stuffing the package into a zippered pocket, Dillion presuming the lady was putting out for an extra dose of rapture or that Mason had possibly fallen on someone worth more intense devotion. And that being the case, being that Mason lived one floor up, Laura would certainly understand.

He shut the screen. Mason hadn't so much as jaywalked since New Orleans, explaining as much to Priscilla when he stopped by her place en route to Laura's, reiterating the possibility of disappointment while acknowledging that he was not bringing her much hope in return for five K a week.

She allayed his concern, sliding his fee in an envelope with a cheque covering his per diem across her table, reiterating in kind that she had no timeline and that Brenda was worth every penny.

"Mr. Dillion, whatever you need. I want Mason strapped on a gurney with a needle in his arm. I want him dead and buried in a bag in a nameless grave before he does this again. Ergo any news is welcome because Mason, whoever he might be, is not merely any rich woman's bon vivant diversion. He cares nothing about assuaging loneliness or rejuvenating neglected bodies. He's evaluating them; he's waiting for an ideal match, for the next Mrs. Mason, for someone flawless, youthful and wealthy, for someone lost and alone to captivate and kill. He's waiting for a Brenda. And I want him dead. No timeline, just get this done."

She stood, thanking him. They would meet again in a week.

43

An evening shy of two weeks since Laura Peters' short-lived hissy fit brought on by dating a dimwit, before her kiss that rocked their worlds, she had Steve to herself for a weekend of home-cooked dinners, soft music and dancing, a walk in the park and canoeing on the lake with after her picnic lunch. She wanted Fred Astaire and Ginger Rogers beside her flickering fireplace; she wanted romance and scented baths, curling into him on her sofa and "What is that thing?"

"A gift."

She put aside her wine, straddling him. "No. My flowers were a gift, this is a ring box." She smacked him. "You're being stupid again."

"Just open it.

Like all women she believed coloured foil and satin ribbons were priceless keepsakes, pulling at the green ribbons as seductively as Steve would the ribbons on her panties, delicately peeling away and folding the yellow foil, staring at the green velvet box, peering into his glistening grey eyes.

And, like all women, she believed any velvet box from a man wearing a stupid grin on his face translated into 'till divorce do we part'. Shit!

Inside however, pinched in white velvet, was a gleaming sterling silver band adorned with a single sparkling emerald.

"A friendship ring. It's lovely, Steve."

"Like you. But I was thinking more like a 'She's mine' ring. So get lost."

"Really? She's mine? You think so?"

"Oh yeah, big time. Head over heals mine."

She giggled, kissing him, squirming backward, tugging him to his feet. "I'm not convinced. I think you should be telling me more about that in the bedroom."

He was certain he could do that, convince her, until she told him to stop talking.

*

Saturday morning he waited until after breakfast, until Laura was humming at the kitchen sink in a teddy, admiring her ring with every plate she put on the rack. Besides, how could she be upset with him after all that yelping and squirming and digging her fingers into him. Right?

Wrong.

She was not happy and she was not surprised. Yet she understood, grudgingly giving him fifteen minutes tops. She would monitor the GPS on his computer and call him the moment the thing started blinking, but would not step foot in Mason's condo. Nor was she ever involved and he was not to do anything stupid that would ruin her weekend, Dillion educating her for the next half-hour on the art of being a covert cop.

Nothing in Mason's apartment indicated anything more than a weekend getaway. Everything was as it should be. The office wastebasket was half-full, his computer and chequebook were on the desk with his gigolo agenda, the kitchen garbage was ready for the chute, dishes were in the rack, the fridge was full, the wine bar was stocked, his toiletries were as they should be, and his bed was ready for the next unwitting contender. Not surprised when, at quarter-past the hour, his phone chimed and Lieutenant Peters ordered him home. She wanted her picnic in the park that was everything she wished for, peering into his eyes as he paddled lazily, as she sat numbing her bum on a blanket over the ribs, wedged between the narrow gunwales and tracing ripples in the calm water.

She loved her ring, yet she could not help wondering; the peculiar form of female curiosity twinged with the duelling emotions of doubt and hope. Because when she threw him onto her bed hours earlier, when she lay sated and breathless, her breasts and her belly heaving, drifting into a deep sleep holding his hand, she was not his friend. She was his lover because she loved him. So what was her stupid problem, especially when he knew? Really? When she was already decided on Dill because that's who and what he was?

"What? What is swirling in that little cop head? We agreed not until Monday morning."

She scrunched her face. "Well, at the risk of feeding your over-inflated ego, Dill," she swallowed, "I'm in love with you."

He didn't miss a stroke. "Yes."

Silence.

The hectic stream of lake water was a direct hit. "Excuse me? Really? I just said I love you."

He lay the paddle across his lap, drying his Serengetis with his polo, his grey eyes sparkling. "You wouldn't make much of a covert operator, Laura. You've told me a thousand times with the flushed cheeks, the heated kisses, the Johnnie Walker and those dreamy eyes. And let's not forget how you practically forced me into your bed with that anesthetizing lingerie. Like that wasn't a female ploy to put us on the fast track. So of course you love me. Head over heals and entirely understandable, Precious. I mean, talk about obvious."

She wanted to smack him, really hard. "What's obvious is you being an idiot." She rested her head against the bow, closing her eyes, ignoring him, letting her hands hang over the sides, a dreamy smile creeping onto her lips. She was in love, whispering a dreamy, "I do love you, Dill."

She didn't feel the droplets of glistening water sprinkling her face, she was sleeping.

*

Saturday evening was all about romance, Dill surviving a Sunday of forties and fifties black and whites before his third culinary lesson, loving her to sleep and kissing her at Visitor Parking early Monday morning. When at Division the women noticed her ring insisting they wanted answers while her men insisted on a pirouettes, which she gave them before swaying into her office flashing a bright smile at Garcia's "¡Sí!, claro! ¡Vaya hombre!"

Meanwhile Dillion was across from her building waiting, expecting Mason would show by noon, by mid-afternoon picking his way into Mason's apartment without the slightest anxiety.

This time he wasn't relying solely on the obvious, targeting the office, searching through the credenza that proved nothing and the desk where he found Mason's phone that proved everything when he discovered that Friday evening Mason was a 'Fucker', Saturday an 'Asshole', and the previous evening a 'Total shithead'.

Mason was gone with a three-day lead and wasn't coming back. What's worse, Priscilla Serra would be devastated and Laura would be royally pissed.

"You what, Dillion?"

Dillion? That wasn't good.

"It's not a problem, Laura. He's gone and I need a quick assist finding out where. Check all flights out Friday, Mason or Miles. And you'll find a BMW in the parking lot. In the meantime I'll be doing some housecleaning."

He spent an hour debugging the condo, using another of Mason's suitcases for the equipment, the laptop and phone, the agenda and twenty bottles of exquisite wine. He would be interviewing each of the few dozen clients in the coming days, in particular the pissed-off weekend trio, the least he could do for his own client.

When he was finished he went into Laura's condo, certain that conversation would come up one day, not at all eager for the call he would make after hearing from her. Because he was right.

"Brent Mason flew one-way into Lyon-Saint-Exupéry Saturday from New York. He hasn't rented a car, registered in a hotel, or used an ATM. Nothing since La Guardia. Neither has Miles. He's gone, Steve."

"Neither one, Laura. He's someone else now. That was the package, his new ID that came from New Orleans. I'm positive."

"You couldn't have tracked him, Dill. You weren't ready. That is not on you."

"Yeah. I'll tell Serra that. Still, I'm thinking my best bet now is Braxton Miles. That must be the real him."

"We've impounded the BMW and we'll put out an alert for Miles at all airports along the East Coast. That's all I can do, Steve. This is not a case for us."

"He will be for someone someday. That's a given. Though on a brighter note, I've restocked your wine rack with some fancy stuff."

She knew better. "Dill, Garcia says you are one lucky hijo de puta. What does that mean?"

He coughed a laugh. "It means you love me."

He disconnected, deciding bad news couldn't wait, calling ahead for a meeting with Priscilla at her office.

"When and if that happens, Ms. Serra, you will be the first to know. Until then, of course, I'm of no further use to you and for that I am truly sorry. I wanted Mason for myself as much as for you and Brenda."

"No one's fault, Mr. Dillion. Following him Friday was pointless given the Charleston PD's lack of enthusiasm. That said, you're on retainer." She handed him a cheque, fifty grand. "A huge leap of faith, Mr. Dillion. One I feel is justified. Let's talk monthly, by phone. Until he makes a mistake. And he will because he's too full of himself."

Dillion placed the cheque on the table between them. "Pay me when the job's done. He's on a watchlist, Ms. Serra. Facial recognition, the whole nine yards. His big mistake will be coming back, which he likely will. This is home for him. And until that happens speaking with you for no reason serves no purpose."

Priscilla refused the cheque. "I will expect a call every month, Mr. Dillion, with very real purpose. Brenda and my sister. Do not let them down. It may well be the last day you work." She stood. "Good evening." She halted him at the door. "Mr. Dillion, please do not let us down."

*

Monday evening in Lyon, France, Bradley McGuire was sitting in a bistro feeling good about himself, feeling free, admiring his gleaming Peugeot.

Some three months from his thirty-third birthday he had found himself; he had found purpose that was the familiar Côte d'Azur a short scenic drive the next morning, the remnants of Brent Mason long since snipped into tiny pieces, flushed into sewers and scattered in trash bins.

*

Three thousand miles away Laura Peters practically barged into Dill's condo. She did not want to hear bullshit, scolding the man she would marry on Valentine's to deal with it. Shit happened. Get over it. Priscilla and her sister believed in him. The fifty K sort of proved that.

No shit.

Exactly what she blurted out Christmas morning when in baby-dolls and booty slippers she opened her second foil-wrapped box before smothering him with kisses.

TurnAbout

Part Five
44

Even with his millions vacationing Bradley McGuire was a relative pauper on the Riviera dotted with mega-yachts and Mediterranean villas he could never properly maintain, not wasting a moment initiating his business plan of bringing hope and meaning into the lives of gullible and lonely young widows or igniting latent passion in the bodies and minds of jaundiced exes that fit the profile.

Because by Christmas he still had not fully recovered from the tragic death of his adoring bride. Her name was Brenda, taken from him at such a young age by a DUI driver on his birthday two years earlier. Not long after she'd been killed by the same driver on her birthday in November and, in October, the repeat offender stole her from him on the eve of their first wedding anniversary. Nor was his grief less unbearable in September, still haunted by her dying words as he held her each time in his arms that he should never be alone, that he should find a love as deep as hers and be happy.

He could certainly commiserate with them, sharing their deep sorrow, the ones who weren't on the decadent French beaches making up for time wasted in dead-end marriages, enjoying the fruits of beneficial divorces. That was even better as he was surviving his own dirty divorce after finding his wife and best friend together weeks after their wedding, not once since his arrival making a bank transfer since their all-inclusive villas were much more comfortable and private than his frightfully incommodious hotel room that served him well enough between encounters.

Though without question Christmas was the worst day of the year without Brenda, missing her bright smiles and gleeful squeals as she would open her gifts. Yet being with BJ somehow brought him comfort and joy. They had met each other a few weeks earlier, the day after she arrived from Lafayette, Louisiana and Bradley McGuire had literally struck oil. Hallelujah!

She was forty-three going on years younger. She was drop-dead gorgeous with the help of a personal trainer, not a scalpel, and she was not on vacation. She was living a dream and was not going back because her multimillionaire husband of twenty-eight years was at long last dead of a stroke at age seventy and the very first item on her bucket list was getting herself seriously and joyfully laid by a dick that was longer than its balls that didn't hang be-tween bowed legs like a prickly lopsided pendulum.

*

In 1958 Nat Gaudier was fifteen. His pa was thirty, give or take, his ma reckoned to be one year less.

He wasn't much of anything worth looking at or wasting time thinking on. He wasn't clever or in any way gifted, working with his pa cooking up the best white brew in the county, thinking he would take over once his pa was gone to glory in forty, could be fifty years.

He had his future all laid out until the day he was poking his girl Elsie behind the shed harder than most times in a moment of fevered solitude with her trembling legs spread wide and her skirt pushed up high on her back, gripping the sawhorse for balance and shrieking her excitation across the woods, learning some months down the road that Nat had gone and planted his seed a whole lot deeper than either one intended.

The good thing was, being she was fourteen, Elsie had no fur-ther need of schooling and devoted her days from then on to mak-ing herself into a fit and ready wife as her belly grew rounder. Until some months later when, without the least hullabaloo or jubilation, Bobbi-Jo Gaudier became real and was taken straight home in a blanket, spending her first years naked and freely roaming the shed that her pa and his pa had made into a partly decent dwelling.

By the time she was fifteen BJ knew all a girl should rightly know according to her pa who wanted her gone sooner than later since she was increasingly a burden on his meagre finances and he'd been talking with a fellow down the road whose eager boy would take her on if a deal could be struck right soon.

Though BJ was one year smarter than her ma and the brightest in her class with the help of Miss Weber who was twenty and took a shine to the girl early on, giving her private attention after school when other girls were giving the boys extra attention. Despite which the kindly teacher hugged the girl with a tight embrace on the last Friday of June and sent her on her way better prepared than most because BJ could read and write beyond her grade and speak like city folks which her pa often declared would do her no good once taken on.

She was also pure and prepossessing, the young teacher told her privately, with hair the golden colour of honey, so thick and lustrous, and her wild chatoyant eyes of a wary cat. Much too lovely and alluring for the likes of any hillbilly boy and a swollen belly years before her natural time. Possibly the reason, and for the best, that no boy ever succeeded at plucking the buttons of her shirt or getting anywhere near the sweet mysteries that BJ kept well-hidden under her skirt and Sunday-go-tuh-meetin' dress that her ma stitched together and remade each year.

BJ liked her teacher very much; she liked spending time with the woman as though they were special friends, hoping that one day she would be like her, the two conspiring that BJ should find her way to the city come Monday where they would live together until BJ got herself settled. They would become best friends and do all the things that girls do together. And BJ believed her, happily surprised when Charlotte tenderly kissed her cheek at the very corner of her lips.

Still Saturday was Saturday and she helped her pa with the bottling when she wasn't washing the laundry out back, anxious for Sunday when she woke exhilarated and buoyant at the prospect of her thrilling new life, of living in the city with Charlotte.

When she was certain they were outside for a good while she sat on her mattress writing a note she would leave the next day for her pa who she knew had already spit into his calloused palm and shaken hands. Then she left home taking the few words with her because she was at the very precipice of her freedom and young Charlotte Weber told her they should not be trusted.

Thing is, Ma and Pa Gaudier weren't much on keeping company with the good Lord, except when His faithful servant would come by regularly for his jar to be filled while partaking of a swig or two with them on the porch.

Still and again Sundays were Sundays, the one day BJ could wear her dress with her bright white socks and pristine saddle shoes that her pa could scarcely afford. The one day she could sit at the five'n dime with her milkshake and straw marvelling at the rich folks in the magazines she would always put back because her pa saw no good reason for a young girl to be filling her empty head with fanciful notions. Except that particular Sunday BJ sat flipping through the glossy pages dreamily thinking of Charlotte and all the fun the girls would have together over the summer.

But when BJ was about to make her way home, stepping onto the porch, she paused awhile musing on the fancy car at the pumps and the two men paying her close attention, startled when one of them, decked out in a blue suit and cap, dark glasses and gloves, came closer telling her the man with him was requesting a few moments with her.

She hesitated, of course, being that she was a proper Southern girl, more particularly being that she was a girl. But she went over anyway because she was curious, deciding after a few minutes there wasn't any good reason why he shouldn't drive her home since judging from his demeanour and hoity-toity clothes that he was a proper gentleman. Besides, he wanted to meet her parents, wanted to congratulate them on having such an enchanting young daughter, BJ taken aback when the blue-dressed man for no reason she could fathom first opened a door for her and then for the man she had no idea about.

Unfortunately for Bobbi-Jo, what she truly wanted, why she was letting the man take her home, was for her ma and pa to hear from a real gentleman that she was enchanting and lovely.

When in fact Roche Vincent Valliere was decidedly no gentleman, despite his wealth and prominence.

*

As the limo made its way slowly along the broken lane toward the Gaudier home, oil magnate Roche Valliere was confident he would succeed. He always did, desperately wanting the girl the very moment he laid eyes on her standing on the porch with her hair radiant and golden under the sun.

He decided then and there he would at the very least occasion a judgement of her viability, taking her home no matter the cost if her entirety proved as lovely as he imagined and wished, flushing from his mind whatever doubt he may have entertained as Gaudier and the wife ambled out with their jars at the intrusion to see what the matter was.

Leaving his chauffeur leaning against the car, Valliere stepped cautiously into the ramshackle home he fully expected would collapse upon him at any moment, while allowing the place was decent enough for the rural populace. All the same he was eager to quit the loathsome habitat the very moment his business was concluded, the moment the girl's struggling father would accept Valliere's offer he could not possibly refuse.

*

"Gaudier," he began, "my name is Valliere. The oil Valliere. I'm here because I find your daughter agreeably compelling and attractive. I believe she would be a suitable companion and wife for one such as myself once she is appropriately trained and made ready."

Gaudier took a second gulp of his brew. "I'm listenin' tuh ya, mister. I've heard tell uv yer name, sure nuff. So what gives, eh? Why're y'all out uv the blue lookin' tuh take her? Seems a mite queer tuh my way uv thinkin', y'all wantin' a backwoods girl."

"I simply want her, Gaudier, and will pay handsomely for her once I approve her entirety with not the slightest interest in a protracted discourse with you or your wife. Enough said. You will either accept my offer or you will not."

"Like I said, I'm all ears."

"Indeed. What I propose is one hundred dollars in cash, here and now, if I can but view your daughter fully naked. One hundred more if her entirety is as lovely as what I see before me, and on condition I can further assess her suitability and purity in a more private situation."

Bobbi-Jo paled with shock. "No, pa! He's older than you by years. What he's suggesting isn't right. You cannot do this. Please."

Valliere turned to the girl. "What is your name, girl?"

"Bobbi-Jo. And you are not doing this to me." She swung around. "Ma!"

"Well the name will change, of course. However understand this, Bobbi-Jo. You will never in your lifetime relive this opportunity. Look around you and be smart about what will be good for you and what is decidedly not."

Gaudier stepped between them. "We ain't talkin' a good bit, mister. Not if ya poke her a good one causin' her tuh suffer on account uv yer seed cause y'all find her unfit after ya've gone'n soiled her."

"The girl will be left as you see her, I assure you. That said, should she please me as I expect she will, I will multiply our current agreement ten-fold and take her with me at once. Me with your daughter into a privileged life, you on your doorstep with two thousand, not two hundred. On my word as a Southern gentleman of unquestionable repute."

Bobbi-Jo's excited ma practically sprang across the warped floor from her corner, pushing aside her useless husband. "Shut yer hole, ya damn fool. She'll be gittin' herself goodly poked'n soiled one day soon anyways and none'll give a bugger's damn." She looked at Valliere. "We'll take ya at yer word, mister. Cause y'all won't ever find nothin' prettier'n this one anywheres."

At that Elsie stripped Bobbi-Jo buck naked fast and furious on the spot, the girl frozen rigid with fright.

She first tore at the dress BJ would no longer need, ripping away the strip of yellowed and stained bedsheet that kept the girl's developing mounds less enticing to the boys' ready hands in the schoolyard. She pushed the loose and mended underpants to BJ's ankles before she dropped onto her knees and tugged them away, spreading her daughter's legs wide apart and standing straight, wildly spinning the devastated girl whose shut-tight eyes were squeezing out trickles of warm tears.

But Elsie wasn't done, determined she would have a better life for herself since the girl would be gone in a few days anyway and a jug of brew would quell the neighbour's vexation at losing her.

"Like I told ya, mister. Ain't nothin' better'n this pretty one here. Git close in. Fill yer lungs with her smell. Sweet as honey and no doubt as tasty. Fill yer hands with her perky tits'n firm rounded backside. Ain't none better, mister. Soft'n smooth as butter on yer palms and looky here. Her gut's flat'n tight. And her cunny, well that treat ain't never bin used fer more'n passin' her water. Ain't never bin tampered with or spoiled. Pure as snow'n worth every penny of what yer offerin' tuh coat yer deservin' pecker with her sticky sweet icin'."

Valliere didn't believe he would, thanking her. Nor did he feel empathy for the petrified girl he would soon transport from poverty and despair into a pampered life of luxury and indulgence. Instead he ordered Gaudier and the vile woman from their shack, leading BJ blindly by her wrist into her room past the curtain door without preamble where without hesitation he tested his most recent acquisition.

He palmed every inch of her smooth body as though sculpting her in his mind. He cupped her soft breasts, pinched her nipples and squeezed her firm buttocks, his breathing more laboured with each new and stirring sensation before he hoisted her onto her clothes shelf and aligned her, making himself ready.

Bobbi-Jo sat terrified at what she was seeing, her face and her thighs drenched with tears. The maniacal glare in his eyes, his twisted mouth and guttural sounds wrenched her gut, making her ill, his heavy breathing making her stomach churn.

She could taste a burning bitterness rising in her throat, closing her eyes tight and grimacing as his arms wrapped around her like a slithering serpent, feeling her lithe body pulled closer and pressed against his suit, his hands clutching her buttocks and her back pushed hard against the wall. Yet strangely her sudden loud gasp shocked her more than the searing pain, her eyes flaring wide open and staring at the window until he set her down whenever Valliere had decided he was done with her.

Slumped against the wall, seeing the slick thing pointing at the floor from his trousers, she forgot she was naked and still very vulnerable, oblivious to what he had done.

She had often through her window or sitting on her swing seen her pa standing in the tub scrubbing and drying himself, the way she often saw her ma doing likewise; the way they would see her when happening by the tub on those Saturday nights, sometimes laughing and running off with her towel. But that was different, learned from her childhood since there was never the least privacy in three rooms with curtain doors and a wooden box over a hole facing the woods for their natural business that her pa would fill over and dig anew each spring. Though not one time had she seen her pa's pecker in such a curious state, swinging and bobbing, never in her memory seeing the thing looking more than when her thumbs got all shrivelled from being in dishwater too long.

The man looked silly bent over, working at shoving the sticky thing back in, telling her to clothe herself and come outside, BJ thinking she might actually giggle. Until he said he'd be taking her home, that she would adequately suit his purpose; until he was gone and she gazed between her legs at the unfamiliar trickle and retched violently as Valliere was outside nodding his approval and reassuring the dubious couple that his chauffeur would indeed arrive the next morning as agreed.

When BJ did join them after composing herself as much as a girl in her distraught condition could, after wiping herself clean and somehow dressing herself in a skirt and blouse, her mind was naturally a maelstrom of apprehension and panic, bewilderment and seething hatred.

She couldn't comprehend how such a horrific thing could happen when an hour earlier she was sipping a milkshake and dreaming the way young girls do of glamour, love and Charlotte. And now she was living in an impossible nightmare and might never see her girlfriend again.

When she stepped out, when her pa came close with wide-open arms saying nothing because he was dumbstruck with joyous elation, she stopped him with her fist at his chest and a curse. Though the wife fared much worse.

Elsie Gaudier came too close to a wounded female, thinking she should, being she was the girl's ma, her eyes all a twinkle at the thought of her incredible windfall, muttering that things would work out fine, in that instant flailing backward from a vicious punch in concert with a scathing "Fuck you. And fuck him."

Then she was gone.

45

That night Bobbi-Jo slept alone in heavenly luxury after Roche Valliere left her in peace, after he relished in a timeless state of comfort and a more pleasing ambiance that which was now his.

Strangely, when he was gone, BJ crept from her bed. She padded on tiptoes into her private bathroom where she poured a bath, where she luxuriated in heated water for the second time in her young life, cupping clouds of scented foam in her hands for the second time in her young life. Then standing alone, beaded and pink, dripping on warm tiles and studying her body, she saw for the first time in a mirror that wasn't polished tin how exceptionally pretty she was. Never before feeling the softness of a fleecy towel or the warmth of a thick fleecy robe, smiling at the girl in the mirror who wasn't afraid anymore.

Valliere wasn't handsome; neither was he was tall or dark or young like the sculpted young men in her Sunday magazines. Neither was he poor or wretched, promising her a fine wardrobe and money of her own each week that she could spend however she wanted.

Crawling into her bed, wrapped in her fleece, she pulled the duvet to her chin, tucking her knees to her chest and purring. Purring. She'd never in her life made such a soft sound, believing she would never sleep again, soon drifting into peaceful slumber and her new existence without a single tear because she'd been bought. Because she'd been sold by folks who never cared a lick about her. And if all Valliere had told her was remotely true, she would do just fine; leastways better'n 'em hillbillies.

Valliere poking her a second time wasn't as bad as the first. And if that was as horrible as her life would ever be, she would survive; she would become his sophisticated and proper wife and do just fine for herself, waking grudgingly and confused to the smell of sweetbreads and coffee, shielding her blurry eyes as the woman standing at the windows flooded the bedchamber with sunlight.

Then no sooner had the woman taken away the tray, another woman strode in carrying BJ's laundered clothes from a past life, hurrying the flustered girl into another limo for requisite spa treatments that would enhance her youthful perfection and satisfy the wishes of Valliere. Then she was off in a flurry to a fashionable ladies' boutique for a private shopping experience that did leave BJ tearful, partly believing she would be in trouble with him, partly believing she had somehow died and been delivered unto Heaven in the arms of an angel she would never love and always abhor.

She would simply live trapped in a continuum of monotonous and lonely days deprived of gaiety and her youth, deprived of Charlotte who she missed deeply and other friends her age she would never do girl things with. She would be an exquisite prisoner enveloped in luxury and comfort with no possibility of escape until the day her most fervent wish would come true.

The second day Bobbi-Jo became Roberta-Joelle for the sake of refined correctness. On day three she received her passport and opened her first bank account, gasping at the ten thousand that would be her monthly allowance; and on her fourth day she was permanently and willingly fixed, as was the previous wife, in a way that would preclude the unpleasant future possibility of unwanted spawn either of his doing or that of some unknown source. Which Roberta-Joelle very quietly viewed from an entirely different perspective in the mind of Bobbi-Jo.

On the fifth day she wed Roche Vincent Valliere in a private ceremony held at the mansion without a father to give her away or a mother to weep at the loss of a daughter.

In fact she never saw them again, never again thought of them, that evening flying with her husband in a private jet into the turquoise wonders of the South Seas where lovers lay practically naked on pearl-white sandy beaches that she never in her life imagined, wondering at the huts that gave the impression of floating on the sea while she gazed at the silvery moon from her lofty penthouse apartment while her husband was elsewhere satiating his inherent needs that bothered the young bride not at all.

She was too enthralled and infatuated, too infused with fascination and disbelief, while not unmindful that she was trapped, contemplating and planning for the day he would die and what she would do then.

*

Upon their return Valliere hired a tutor who over time educated Roberta-Joelle in keeping with the norms of his society, a governess who made her presentable for public viewing as a wealthy gentleman's discerning wife, and her personal attendant who would see to her every whim and need.

Eventually Roberta-Joelle did metamorphose into an elegant and lovely lady, though she never lost sight of Bobbi-Jo, more often breaking social circles than being caught in them, as a rule seldom accepting afternoon invitations from haughty and spoiled socialites twice her age or worse. Until they stopped inviting her into the matronly fold; unless, of course, their sycophant husbands required something of Roche Vincent Valliere.

She preferred delving into art, music and literature, the company of her personal trainer and dance instructor, her personal seamstress and driving her Bentley regularly to museums and the theatre for matinees without him. Until the afternoon she arrived home to see her staff perplexed and tearful, who believed for some reason they should feel horrified at seeing her face and eyes instantly aglow with girlish delight at hearing he was finally dead.

She didn't care, correcting them with the laugher of a prisoner set free. Their self-indulgent and pompous master who never spoke their names was at last deservedly dead and she could think of no better reason for them to rejoice and be jubilant. And, if not for him, for her, that she was at last and again Bobbi-Jo.

She didn't give a bugger's damn about anything else, especially him. Because she was set free, which she very soon after demonstrated beyond any and all doubt.

Although Valliere had lived his life as an incorrigible gambler and persistent womanizer, delighting in fine liquor and cuisine, drawn to women half his age and taking pleasure in them during frequent excursions while sparing no expense to achieve an end, he proved as tight-fisted in death as he was in life.

The will was read at Roberta-Joelle's insistence the next day. She was not wasting precious time, Valliere's attorneys depositing the relatively modest bequest into her account on the third day when, in fact, his known worth exceeded twenty-fold her twenty million. She didn't care about that either. She wanted out more than the money, leaving her wardrobe and jewellery, her possessions and car to her personal assistant, arriving in the Côte d'Azur on the day he was buried, not imagining for a moment she would meet a tall and dark, gallant and handsome gentleman on day four of her emancipation.

Nor did she imagine in her life of dreams that he would so quickly intoxicate her, discovering Bradley McGuire's personal accoutrement that evening was admirably suited to her every urgent demand. He was everything she had imagined wanting in a man, suggesting when she woke with him on her sixth day, again pungent and throbbing with sweat beaded on her back, that he check-out from his hotel and spend what remained of his vacation with her.

What was the harm since they were both searching and alone?

Nor could McGuire be more fascinated with her. She was everything he wished for at 5'6", rare yellow eyes, long honey-coloured hair, nicely shaped everything, and that she had flown in on a chartered jet didn't hurt.

Roberta-Joelle had never throughout her captivity worn a thong on a beach, or gone topless, or made love in her pool or been so heatedly ravaged on her balcony under the stars. Brad did all that for her, for Bobbi-Jo; her peaked Louisiana complexion a rich golden-brown by her first-ever fabulous Christmas Day.

"Brad, must you return home to New York? Can't you wait until your birthday? We're having such fun together." She sipped her mimosa. "For that matter, can't you stay indefinitely?"

He wasn't expecting the question, visibly taken aback, taking her hand. He liked her, he truly did, for the first time since Brenda's tragic passing feeling light-hearted and loving. Yet the hope in her eyes and in her voice shocked him. He didn't know.

"BJ, you're my first since Brenda was taken from me. I never believed I could feel this way again, that I would ever be happy again. It's just that…"

"You feel like you're cheating on her, when you are not. Brenda would want this for you, for us. She told you that."

"Two years. Two eternities. Yet sometimes her sweet smell, her soft touch, seem so real. As though she's with me still."

"Because she always will be." BJ put a warm palm to his cheek, kissing him. "I lived my own bitter eternity, Brad. Much longer than yours. I never felt the love you and Brenda shared. Now I do. My time has come to live and be happy. Please stay with me a while longer, for as long as you can. Brenda will never be gone from your heart, which is why you should feel her happiness for you, for me. And who deserves happiness more than you and me? Be my Christmas present, Brad. Please let me be yours."

He expelled a deep breath, palming his moist eyes. "You're right, BJ. I know that. And yes, I will stay with you. I will. There isn't anything I want more. Thank you...for the reality check. Thank you for finding me."

*

For his thirty-third Bobbi-Jo gave McGuire a Valentine's week in Paris. She could not believe how in a month she was falling in love with him, had fallen in love, certain he felt the same deep emotion despite their ages.

Though McGuire returning the azure Peugeot he had rented for his vacation and buying his own in bright red for the 600-km road trip very soon assured BJ of that; her second shockwave coming early in February.

A New York broker had found a buyer for his Manhattan condo. Yet he was increasingly pensive, BJ struggling with doubt and worry until she broke her silence on the fourteenth while standing under the Arc de Triomphe wrapped in his arms as Laura Dillion sat holding her husband's hands and gazing into his adoring eyes not far away on the brightly lit and enchanting Champs-Élysées.

*

Dillion had gotten over his life's second worst disappointment, as he promised Laura he would, when he was with her. He was adept at subterfuge, deceit for the sake of survival, when speaking with Priscilla each month was his worst torment; never believing in the hope he was giving her, never forgiving himself for that fateful Friday, doubting on both counts that he ever would.

The thirteenth of February, however, was not about him. That day was Laura's; Dill taking her hand and her heart, promising he would love and cherish her forever as her captain gave the bride away and Garcia stood for his friend, both men mildly pulsating from the time-honoured prelude to lifelong love and devotion that he later swore on his life did not include naked women dancing on stools or doing whirlies on a pole.

He was a pig. Absolutely disgusting. No question.

Yes, he was. As were all her men pretending meekness and innocence at the reception, with loaded Glocks under their suits. Their wives and partners, of course, acting superior as is their species' true nature.

Though in the recesses of his mind, surrounded by lovers and romance thousands of miles away the next evening, Dillion could not help pondering how close he and Mason might actually be, Laura resting her hands over his on a bistro table blanketed with crisp white linen. She knew.

"One day, Dill. I know that, I feel that. Just not on my honeymoon, Detective."

*

"Brad, you've been exceptionally reticent this past week. What ever is troubling you?"

"Introspection, I suppose. Nothing serious. Reflecting on buying the car, selling my condo and why," he pressed a palm to her cheek, "thinking that from now on I should be paying half that ten grand a month until we figure out where this is going. You and me. What I do not see is me returning stateside. I feel at home here. This is who I am." He paused, breathing in the cool evening air. "I'm moving on, Bobbi-Jo. I've decided."

She squeezed him. "I was so terribly worried, Brad, thinking you regretted the condo, the car. Me."

"No. Not for a moment, especially not you."

She stood on her tiptoes, pressing her lips hard against his. "In that case, lover, I will take that cheque on the first."

*

The second week of Laura's honeymoon they would luxuriate on the Riviera. Laura was eager for the sophistication and glamour, strutting her stuff along the shores of the Mediterranean in her newest and tiniest bikinis with casual abandon à la française while Dill was focused on other equally alluring and plentiful attractions of the exotic French playground. Though she couldn't help herself, musing quietly as she scanned the confusion of hotels and condos, the pink roofs of posh villas stuccoed in white smothering the hillside, whether Mason might well be looking down at them.

After all, why not? Mason was filthy rich.

*

In fact, as Laura was being no less admired with smiles by tourists and locals strolling the beach, McGuire and Bobbi-Jo were lounging by the pool at the villa they would share until late spring. By which time they had been lovers throughout five entirely magical months without a single pouty instance or carelessly spoken word.

The question was, what now?

The white sandy strip between the sea and the hillside dotted with lights was an idyllic setting for romance. The night air was warm, the glimmering sea was calm, a bright moon casting dark fluid shadows, and Bobbi-Jo Valliere could not have been more exquisite.

"BJ, five months. That is a long time." He took her by her shoulders. "I've already lost one phenomenal woman in my life; I cannot lose another. I cannot lose you. We loved that villa at first sight. The place could not be more perfect for us. We're perfect for each other. So why not do it? Let's buy the place."

"Eight million, lover."

"Four mill each. No big deal. We've got it, let's enjoy it." He reached into his jacket inhaling the sudden deep breath he'd practiced, easing onto one knee as he opened the velvet box, the one-karat diamond instantly glittering in the moonlight. "Roberta-Joelle, Bobbi-Jo, would you please be my wife?"

She lurched backward, smacking an open palm to her chest, another to her wide-open mouth. "Yes, Brad. Yes, I will."

She dropped to her knees, mesmerized as he slipped the titanium band onto her finger, living the moment she had believed for twenty-eight years would never happen. At that very instant remembering her hillbilly parents for the first time in as many years and dispelling them as quickly.

TurnAbout

Four weeks later Mr. and Mrs. Bradley McGuire returned from their honeymoon in Nice, the eager groom sweeping his bride across the portal of their elegant new residence high atop the French hillside, which was by no means the end of her dream.

46

BJ had often said while lying on a chaise-longue gazing at the bright white yachts drifting lazily on the sea or carving white foamy wakes at speed into the blue water that one day—maybe. But she wasn't serious. The ridiculous things cost millions.

They spent the first month of married life furnishing their home, loving and laughing, talking about the future and what they should do. They were wealthy, each now worth sixteen million, give or take, which did not mean living lackadaisical and meaningless existences. That's what he worried over and she vehemently agreed. She wanted to do something significant with her life, weeks earlier deciding she would join the world of fashion, but with everything else going on she hadn't told him she wanted her own fashionable boutiques. Not one, but three that would serve trendy tourists, borderline wealthy women like her, and the very well-heeled young enough to discriminate between fashion and frump.

He supported her at once, confessing his own kept secret that he was returning to academia in the fall, accepted by the university in Nice as head of their linguistics department and by his first day of class they were both on track. Bobbi-Jo had her boutiques whose clerks were all twenties and typically French and Braxton Miles had his exclusive pied à terre in Nice where he soon began building a loyal clientele closely mirroring his adoring wife's devotees, often over late-evening dinners hearing familiar names, as frequently during his workday complimenting the ladies on their private labels.

Although as often as he worked late, determined that his students would graduate with the highest marks, he never gave up a weekend with the woman who kept his heart beating, Bobbi-Jo believing hers would actually implode Christmas morning when she stepped onboard her gift. She was even more shocked when McGuire casually with a sheepish grin confessed his nautical prowess.

Of course the custom L550 cruiser had cut his severely damaged offshore account by half by taking yet another gamble, and clearly a good one, her expression telling him straight away that he wasn't wrong. Nevertheless, the female condition being what it is, when he asked why she was crying, she simply replied patting her eyes that he would never understand. When all he needed to know was how deeply and forever she would love him.

He didn't pursue the issue, keeping BJ completely enthralled by everything he was showing her, partly amused and partly smug as she sat at the helm nervous and in awe as he calmly and expertly maneuvered the *Elle* from the marina into blue water before easing the throttle forward to cruising speed.

Ditto for New Year's, minutes into his thirty-fourth year, celebrating amidst yachts where size always mattered, all of them bedecked with nautical flags spelling out the masters' names, BJ expressing how arrogant the protocol seemed.

He agreed. "But see how the people on the promenade enjoy the lights and the ribbons, all of them thinking what if. We all have dreams, sweet thing. Dreams beyond our reach." He kissed her, cupping her cheeks. "Or I did until I reached out and found you."

"No, lover. We found each other and I'm so marvellously happy we collided that day." She twisted from his arms. "I'll never forget how pathetic you were standing there tongue-tied and flustered."

"I was, I know. Because I had never seen anyone as breathtaking. Nor will I ever; nor will I ever stop loving you," he stroked her hair, "caring for you. Which is why this week we're seeing a lawyer about another what if, about what we should have done the day we married."

*

BJ agreed with her husband, chiding herself for not acting more responsibly earlier, considering her business and their combined assets, the couple formally indicating a few days later that, in the event of either one's death, natural or untimely, the survivor would be the sole beneficiary.

Neither one had family or lifelong friends, BJ for a brief instant lost in reverie which Brad chose not to question. They had each other, Captain BJ deciding they would cruise the coasts of Spain and Mallorca in July, by which time she was as good a navigator and mariner as McGuire. Her business and his quasi-academic career were flourishing and they could not possibly be happier. Except that McGuire was happier still that with his success in Nice he hadn't touched his offshore account since acquiring the L550, never doubting the lavish investment would one day produce an exceedingly favourable ROI.

Their third summer together they cruised the western coast of Italy through the straight of Messina and north along the country's Adriatic coast, finding marinas each night, being lovers at bistros and cafés and strolling dimly lit plazas brimming with alluring femininity and flamboyant machismo, returning home excited about the next year's extended voyage through the Greek Isles.

As in previous years, New Year's 2006 and his thirty-sixth birthday was a quiet event onboard the *Elle*, dancing and sipping champagne alone since yachtsmen were either solitary or gregarious by nature. Yin and yang, divergent extremes. The more exquisite the ship the more gregarious, which BJ understood was ostentatious and arrogant; the smaller and more quaint, as was her sleek fifty-five footer, the more solitary, which for her meant intimate, romantic and blissful.

The couple didn't have anyone they could call close friends because Brad didn't care either way and Bobbi-Jo, despite her remarkable fluency, found most French at the marina and on the hill shamefully aristocratic and monotonous, trapped in their own tight circle. Déjà-vu. She wasn't interested, which suited him perfectly well because she was forty-seven and by the time the hillbilly kid from Savannah would in fact be thirty-six she'd be seven years from sixty. Not good; McGuire increasingly aware he should confront the imminent dilemma sooner than later and move on.

His dilemma being his previous well-planned and thought-out largesse whose foredeck he was then lounging on while watching fireworks ignite the midnight sky and the sparkle in her feline eyes.

He was essentially impoverished, left with a meagre three mill in the Caymans, while BJ's portfolio had blossomed by that much beyond her original twenty and he was being forced each year to maintain a prohibitively costly ruse he had intended for the short-term.

His well-deserved Lothario-notoriety in Nice would of course sustain him for years, all things being equal. However things were far from equal and would quickly deteriorate from remediable to self-destructive if not addressed. Not that Bobbi-Jo would have cared had she known from the beginning. She more than loved him; she lived for him. Except that she did not know and the female mind would unquestionably confuse an innocent ruse borne of his deep love and fear of losing her with duplicity and subterfuge which she would never forgive.

Which to a large degree was moot since from first setting eyes on her, since first kissing and loving her, divorce was inevitable. Her destiny inescapable. No different from Davaux, Bunker or his beloved Brenda. Each one destined to cross his path, not for a moment in fourteen years losing sight of his own true nature, fully cognizant that Miles, Mason and McGuire served a singular purpose in his life: Guiding Brandon Michaels toward his destiny, wherever and whenever that might be.

And he was good with that, especially if his charmed life since delivered into the hands of CJ and Blaire was any indication, half-chuckling, half-snorting, heaving his chest—and given that he had no choice. No one did; his destiny likewise preordained and inescapable, a mere link in a chain of destinies, a cat's paw with no choice in whatever else he would accomplish or commit before his own inevitable whenever.

Destiny. Karma. Whatever.

"Hey!" Bobbi-Jo propped herself onto an elbow on the plush sun pad. "Lover, you startled me. What was that about?"

"Forgive me, sweet thing." He kissed her. "I was in a daze dreaming of you, imagining our summer in Greece and our future that I hope will last for all time."

*

July began on a Saturday, BJ the night before emptying suitcases filled with thongs, panties and muslin dresses à la Grecque that Brad was certain the attuned men of Greece would appreciate and fondly remember; BJ suggesting the ladies wouldn't do badly either.

They were the first to depart the marina stopping for lunch and fuel in Corsica, spending the night in Naples before another early start, passing through the Straight of Messina and across the Ionian Sea, arriving in Athens Sunday evening where they stayed at dock for a week.

They spent their second week dropping anchor on secluded shores, BJ eventually persuaded that no one would notice her naked. They were in Greece. Everyone got naked in Greece and by day fourteen her foredeck tan was even and deep, although she did occasionally flip over, cursing him with sensuous moans and purrs whenever various tour operators and dive boats idled by, when all he could do was lotion her back and wave, telling her she was sensational and should be proud.

He definitely was, then and at dinner each evening in charming old-world cafés.

The third week was on Mykonos, what Bobbi-Jo wanted for her birthday. A dream come true on their last evening before retracing their course to the hills of Monaco.

She was delightful and alluring in white-on-white, her tan and lustrous hair making her all the more radiant on her special evening of candlelight and dancing, of approving smiles and envious glances, a prelude to champagne and romance on the foredeck he smoothly talked her into when the marina was quiet and dark for the night.

They were leaving the next morning and they were in love. Let the entire world know, BJ within minutes forgetting they were outside under a moon and stars, not below deck under a sheet. She didn't care, she *was* in love, in the morning with a weak smile and flushed cheeks blaming the champagne for her possibly having aroused some neighbours.

"Do not say that. Do not even think that. Jesus." She took her coffee, grimacing. "Do you think? Really?"

"Oh, yeah. Big time. I know I would. You were pretty wound up. I mean, whoa!"

She punched him. "You're horrible."

"On the other hand, probably not. I mean, you all sexy and naked, sweaty and panting, all squirmy and bouncy and glistening in the moonlight? Who would want a video of that?"

She punched him again. "I feel like shit."

"And you look like…tremendous. And you were phenomenal. If someone does have a video of the very exotic and vivacious Miss Bobbi-Jo's long-awaited debut performance, good for him. Or her."

She ignored him, stepping out onto the dock and showering under a hose, realizing she was humming and smiling. So what if someone had seen her, had watched her? Good for them. In fact good for anyone seeing her white teddy effectively disappear and her body come alive under the hectic spray.

For that matter good for her. Her everything was in the right place the right way. She was spectacular and, because of Brad, she had discovered she was captivating and sensual, waiting until the twin engines groaned to life before replacing the hose, sauntering around the yacht freeing the lines and stepping onto the transom with a blasé "Got a problem, lover?"

Nope.

Monday's cruise to Athens and their passage through the Corinth Canal to the Ionian Sea was leisurely, docking in Messina by nightfall, deciding they would spend a couple of days in Naples before ending their voyage on the northern tip of Corsica an easy four-hours from their French hillside hideaway.

Thursday morning after mimosas on the transom and showers on the dock, they lingered over croissants and expressos on the marina's terrace. They weren't in a hurry, enjoying the view, the sun's warmth and holding hands, Bobbi-Jo confessing she felt tired and mildly light-headed from their evening, expecting compassion and sympathy, sneering when what she got was a patronizing smirk and gentle pats on her thigh.

She pushed his hand away, threatening him with frostbite throughout the remaining voyage if he did not very quickly revert to the gallant gentleman whose indelicate faux-pas she might conceivably forgive. Maybe. Then she stood, patting his cheek, sauntering toward the maze of gleaming yachts, smiling and turning heads. Of course he would do his best. Didn't he always?

Slouching into his seat, watching her sashay from sight exuding sexual energy and elegance, commanding attention, McGuire ordered another coffee. He couldn't help musing that not being proud of his wife was impossible. Bobbi-Jo was a remarkable woman, an exceptional gift to an ever less beautiful world.

He checked his Rolex. 9:40. Good.

The *Elle* was sturdy and fully equipped. Given the predicted light winds that would be at their backs, and a following sea at less than a half-metre, she could easily accomplish the 720-km crossing in twelve hours if they maintained speed and direction that would put them in Bastia one hour after sunset when the myriad of flickering coastal lights would create a magnificent beacon.

Giving BJ private time and space since even the biggest yacht was cramped quarters, when he stepped onto the transom he was not surprised by the water gurgling beneath his feet or that she was leaning against the helm in a trio of white triangles telling him to free the starboard lines and be quick about it. Better yet, by her expression, he was already forgiven. Of course.

*

They were in open water five minutes later, BJ reaching a forty-knot cruising speed while he was in the stateroom changing into microfibre straight-backs and a tee, bringing her chilled lemonade with aspirins.

"Thanks, lover." She swallowed the pills, sipping the sweet refreshment. "What an enchanting vacation, lover And my birthday was too special." She kissed him. "Thank you for my pendant."

"You are an enchanting lady, BJ. Thank you, for you. What would I do without you?"

She giggled. "Probably run off with one of your cute little French students, the one in tights and a beret who smokes Gitanes, drinks Calvados and is actually fascinated by the writings of Voltaire."

He shook his head. "She's not my type and she's not fascinated. She's hung-over and contrite. Besides, she has bad breath, yellow teeth, a moustache and she wears tights because she doesn't shave her legs." He sipped her drink, checking the dials and the yacht's angle of plane. "Thanks. Think I'll stay with the current model." He manoeuvred around her, kissing the nape of her neck. "You should take a nap on the deck, sweet thing. Give a man something better than blue water to marvel at."

She nodded. "I will, lover. I simply do not understand why I feel this tired."

"Sex, lady. Lots of sex. Like tonight unless I kill the engines right now." He grinned. "You think?"

"No, I do not think."

He smacked the closest of two firm and golden cheeks. "Go."

She did, clambering through the stateroom's hatch onto the foredeck sans bikini for three excellent reasons: Her lover, herself, and not marring her flawless golden glow with an eyepatch.

Crawling on all fours like the seductive feline she was, she pressed her glossy lips onto the windshield, smiling coquettishly into his lens before easing onto her sun pad where she lay motionless with her arms by her side, luxuriating under a 30° clear blue sky; the yacht's apparent wind warm and sensual, flowing over her own smooth contours like fluttering silk.

She wasn't sleeping. She was dreaming, reliving every moment of her fantasy that was her entire month of July. Until her eyes blinked open, purring and stretching, putting a hand to his body haloed by the sun glaring down from its zenith. They were drifting, floating in an endless blue sea, the faint groan of the engines as loud as her heartbeat.

"I was dreaming of you."

"Yeah, for three hours and then some. Lunch is ready."

She wiggled her way toward the hatch on her bum, feeling groggy, joining McGuire on the afterdeck in a sarong and wishing she could dive into the sea. Which he didn't believe was a very good idea, suggesting that hurling oneself into a thousand metres of water was a little too creepy.

When lunch was finished BJ didn't need much convincing, taking her aspirins like a good girl and pulling herself onto the foredeck with a Pinot Grigio where she lay resting her chin on her forearms, studying her handsome hunk at the helm.

At 5:00 McGuire first refilled her glass, gently rousing her. "Sweet thing, you should turn over. Smooth out that glorious tan, not that I don't adore your gorgeous butt. And you haven't touched your wine or your pills. Bad girl."

She rolled onto her side, sitting. "I'm sorry. I thought I did."

She sipped the chilled wine, put the pills into her mouth and sipped again, making a face.

"Another gulp, BJ. The wine won't kill you and I want you feeling better for our evening."

"You are so sweet and caring." She managed a faint smile. "I'm afraid I won't be very good company tonight, Brad. I'm sorry. I'll feel better tomorrow. I promise."

"It's my strong point, being sweet and caring. You're just coming down from a very fabulous vacation, which is not over. In fact, isn't our life a vacation?"

Bobbi-Jo smiled her answer. "What time is it?"

"Two-thirty. Now finish your wine. It'll help you relax and feel better while I keep an eye on you. A very close eye."

He eased her gently backward, leaning over her, trailing kisses from her breasts to her thighs, her intoxicating scent and seductive moans giving him pause.

Studying her as she lay drifting into another time and place, he coated her body with cream and sat for a while absorbing her, his expert fingertips bringing her to the heights of rapture one last time before leaving her in carefree slumber.

At 7:00, some 130 nautical miles from the shores of Corsica, BJ's flawless body seemingly luminescent with a glimmering evening sun, Bradley McGuire again let the yacht drift as he prepared a cocktail for his wife.

He sat for several minutes by her side remembering their years together, feeling a real love for her, patiently coaxing her into the stateroom where he helped her dress in slacks and a classic nautical cable sweater against the evening's cooling sea breeze.

"I let you sleep, BJ. Five hours. You seemed so calm and peaceful I couldn't think of waking you. Selfishly, I suppose. Until I worried you might be uncomfortable with the cooler evening air." He put a glass to her lips. "A cognac warmed by loving hands. We're still a few hours out."

"I ruined your day, Brad." Her speech was slurred, her yellow cat eyes glazed over and dull, staring blankly. She wanted his arms around her, her arms around him, to feel him, but she had no strength, completely drained of her usual effervescence. "I'm sorry."

"Don't ever be sorry for all that you brought me."

"No, lover. Each other." She sighed, resting her head against his chest. "God, what is wrong with me?"

"Nothing. You're exhausted from loving me, from our exquisite voyage. As I am from loving you." He put a palm to her cheek. "Come outside and finish your cognac. Besides I want another picture of you and the fresh air will soothe you. Then I'll lay you on the aft-lounge with a blanket and let you sink into the deep sleep you deserve."

He took her glass, and her arm, helping her onto the afterdeck where he composed a loving wife holding her glass high in a toast to the man she adored as the wind tousled her hair, which she suffered through before he lay her down and put the *Elle* back on course, clicking a final shot at speed. Some thirty minutes later easing back on the throttle to idle and stepping from the helm.

BJ had never seemed more serene, lying with her head resting upon slender hands pressed together as in prayer, McGuire sitting sidesaddle on the gunwale gazing at her, at the woman he deeply loved. Of course he loved her, the way he loved the others until his and their unalterable destinies collided and prevailed, satisfied and pleased he had done all he could for her, freeing her mind of fear and panic with the best barbiturates and finest accelerants.

Going to her, lifting her into his arms, he kissed her passionately one last time, feeling the warmth of her lips and her cheek against his as he stepped onto the transom setting her down.

Kneeling by her side he felt deeply gratified and grateful that her last breaths were soft and contented purrs, feeling her warm hands touch his face as though she understood and was saying goodbye with a thin smile on her lips. And with no further ado he eased her gently into the sea and returned to the afterdeck, hurling her snifter into the air and filling another with Courvoisier that he dropped onto the deck where it stayed rolling with the sea.

Standing at the helm, swirling his cognac, he located Bobbi-Jo fifty metres or so off the starboard side. She wasn't flailing or thrashing or screaming out in a frenzy for help. Which was good. She was leaving him peacefully, the way he wished for her, the way she deserved and faster than many would because he cared. He did right by her.

Two minutes he believed, focused on his Rolex, given her petite frame and weight, her thick woollen sweater and relaxed condition. Two minutes before he scanned the sea tinted with gold and she was gone; two minutes before he splashed cognac into his eyes and looked skyward into a fine mist of powdered jalapeño.

*

Sinking deeper into blacker depths, free at last from the lingering memories of a backwoods girl, of one husband's mean-spirited neglect and abuse, of being coolly murdered by the one man she ever loved, Bobbi-Jo McGuire née Gaudier had found everlasting peace.

47

Thursday, July 13th.

"MAYDAY! MAYDAY! MAYDAY!"

Bradley McGuire kept the dread and panic in his voice to a practiced and credible level. He knew what he should expect and what he should do, as though he had drafted a brilliant sequel to a once successful yet forgotten drama.

The French Gendarmerie Maritime responded immediately with air support, patrol vessels and high-speed launches, each in turn implementing a search pattern from the *Elle* outward in a widening circumference. Though despite their best efforts and dedication they did not stay long, an anguished and numb McGuire hearing from the armed and sombre lieutenants who came onboard the L550 long after darkness had fallen that a tragic reality must be faced, "que la Madame McGuire a été tristement perdu en mer."

Yeah. Désolé.

They were gravely sorry for the frantic husband's most unthinkable loss. However, Madame was gone, taken by the sea, and they would perforce remain onboard taking command of the *Elle* as she was being escorted to port in Bastia where local authorities would be waiting.

The interview lasted through mid-afternoon Friday as Forensics combed the yacht finding no apparent suggestion of a crime, no indication of foul play or the slightest cause for suspicion, taking photos they would forward to their colleagues in Monaco who would pursue the incident from a different perspective. Then leaving him at the port they assured him the naval officer onboard and the high-speed escort were simple courtesies given his state of mind, ensuring he would arrive without incident, McGuire understanding they were not finished with him.

He was grateful for all they had done and their swift response the previous evening, choking back his emotion as he stepped onboard, realizing in heart-shattering disbelief that Bobbi-Jo would not be with him, would never be with him again. Her laughter and warmth would never again permeate the yacht, the officer with him quietly and discreetly delighted when McGuire suggested he pilot the *Elle* from her slip.

A ship the man in several lifetimes would never afford.

*

Friday, July 14th.

In Monaco the police understood his eagerness and need to grieve alone in the quiet of his and Bobbi-Jo's home—that for him would forever be an empty shell.

Nevertheless they were cops, temporarily impounding the yacht and taking his passport as a condition. Although within forty-eight hours with no grounds for pursuing the case, with no reason to suspect Bobbi-Jo's death was not a terrible and completely plausible accident, he was neither implicated nor charged.

No one would think of wearing a PFD on a boat that size, particularly over exclusive designer fashions. And at forty knots, which they determined was accurate from the wake seen in the photographs of a loving wife who might have enjoyed one cocktail too many, possibly losing her balance upon standing too close to the transom, not only would he not have heard her, had she even screamed, within a few seconds the boat's speed would have put her beyond sight.

They were done with him, case closed; McGuire supposing the photos of a smiling and naked BJ posing on the foredeck and smudging the windshield with gloss aptly substantiated his claim

Booth

of an idyllic marriage. Certainly didn't hurt.

Throughout the weekend he tolerated shocked and mournful neighbours, meeting Monday with her overwrought and weeping employees who were given two options: Make arrangements with the bank to co-share the boutiques at half the current value or lose their lucrative jobs. That negotiation was completed by Friday bringing him a million-point-five along with her estate in excess of twenty-four million that was transferred into his account and Saturday he called a private number in New Orleans, delighted when Cody Jones picked up.

A week later the villa sold for a million over his eight and the *Elle* went on the Sunday at one-point-nine before fees, a loss he made good with her jewellery.

Thirty-seven million, transferred by the following Friday to the Caymans.

Friday, August 04th.

He was done with Monaco, three weeks after the drowning flying out on a privately chartered jet en route to JFK for refuelling and a night on the town with the female pilot he had spent nine in-flight hours charming. She was twenty-nine, single, unattached, and twice put the auto-pilot into the mile-high mode. Why not? Life was too short and who knew better than him?

She was his youngest and most vital, a definite ten-on-ten, a prelude to their late wake-up, a mid-afternoon departure and an even steamier Saturday night in New Orleans where he would begin reshaping his life with another phone call the next morning to an old friend he hadn't seen in over four years.

Monday, August 07th.
2:00 PM at Le Renard.

The pilot was in her final approach at JFK with an incredible lifelong secret as Braxton Miles was sitting with Cody Jones.

374

"It's been another long while, kid. Must say I wasn't surprised hearing from you. I did have a gut feeling we'd be sitting here again one day and I will not ask how you've been." CJ pressed Miles' lapel between his forefinger and thumb, smirking. "Two grand. And the loafers? Italian and five anyway."

"Just keeping up appearances, CJ. It's really good seeing you again."

"Likewise kid." CJ poured an '85 Chambolle-Musigny into Miles' glass. "Sorry to hear you're a grieving widower again. My condolences."

"Yeah, Bobbi-Jo. She drowned a few weeks ago in the Med. She got a little intoxicated, fell over, and by the time I noticed..." He shrugged. "She was not coming back. Too bad. She was a looker and exceedingly talented."

"I take it Miss Bobbi-Jo was what, a wealthy somebody?" He inhaled the Bourgogne's rich bouquet. "That island account still working out for you?"

"I'm doing okay. She left me comfortable."

CJ coughed a laugh, shaking his head. "And here we are again, like old times."

"The fact is I enjoy married life, having a lady of my own to love and cherish. My problem is, no lady meeting my criteria will feel good about a guy whose wife fell from a boat in the middle of the ocean, particularly if I break that newsflash to her onboard my next yacht. Unless Bryce Madison is with her."

Cody Jones slid an envelope across the table. "Bryce Madison. He's thirty-six and a bachelor, a professor emeritus of the Sorbonne Nouvelle in Paris."

Miles put down his glass. "I had the pleasure of meeting him. Wealthy from his inheritance of a family fortune. Old money, of course. Very aristocratic. His French mother, très supérieure, and his proper English father sadly died in that freak avalanche in the French Alps a few years ago." He broke the seal. "Thanks for making this happen, CJ. I owe you, big time. You know I'm there for you whenever."

"The quarter-million worked out fine. We're settled, as Madison is in every way. As you should be. You've come a long way, kid. We're talking what here, twenty mill? Twenty-five?"

"Something like that."

"Which I'm supposing translates into a shitload more. Which tells me you should buy that boat and find some Polynesian island. Get yourself lost for good. Women love that exotic shit and the source won't ever run dry. Wealthy widows, Spring Breakers gone wild. This Bryce Madison though, he might well rain serious grief down upon you one day. Greed never works. Not for very long. Meaning be smart. Do not fuck-up now. You got that, kid?"

"Precisely the reason I need Madison, CJ. Starting over, leaving behind some dirty laundry. As much as an innocuous Braxton Miles is an occasional convenience, McGuire's dead. Seems he couldn't deal with his loss. That said, I am pretty much a fatalist. Things happen the way they should. I've learned that. I'm also a realist. Shit does happen." He placed a small thank-you card by CJ's glass. "You'll pardon the sentiment."

The blank card was signed Braxton Miles at the bottom of several clearly printed numbers.

"A realist and cautious."

"I have no friends, CJ. You're it. You're the one I'll call if it ever does hit the fan." He sipped his wine. "And yes, a shitload more."

Cody Jones didn't pursue the issue, the conversation turning social as lunch was served. The man facing him was walking a dark and lonely path, too far along to ever think of turning back. Without question Bryce Madison, or whoever he might become next, would surely one day make his way blindly into that cul-de-sac and not hear the footsteps trailing behind.

48

Saturday, August 05th.

She sat straddling him, shaking her head. Adamant.

"No. Not again. And don't be pathetic. Besides, you stink."

"Hurtful. And you're what, a fragrant rose?"

"Do nor be rude." She smacked him, reaching for her phone. "Rey's calling, confirming." She pressed *Send*. "Good morning, Rey. And yes we are…What!"

Laura Dillion's heated and moist body turned cold, instinctively drawing a sheet over her breasts, her piercing eyes that seconds earlier were telling Dill there was a glimmer of hope now staring down at him with disbelief.

Steve Dillion twisted onto his elbows. "Laura, what is it?"

"Are you certain?" Laura listened for long seconds with a finger pressed to her lips. "No. It's not a case and let's you and Dill keep this shit to a minimum at dinner, Sergeant. Sixish. Love to Ercilia."

She pressed *End*.

"What was that? Keep what shit to a minimum?"

She stayed straddling him, crossing her arms. "Mason. He's in New York."

"What?" He practically toppled her, catching her. "Where?"

"He showed up on biometrics at JFK. That's it. Until he shows up somewhere else and do not spoil my dinner with this. Garcia's checking the passenger manifests."

"He won't stay in New York. He's too Southern, out of his element. He's coming home."

"Even if he does, what then? I really do not feel good about this, Dill. The guy's psychotic. You don't need this shit in your life. Or mine. And what about Priscilla?"

He shook is head, Laura clearly seeing the gears grinding. "When I have something positive to tell her."

Which wouldn't be that evening when Laura took a call from her squad telling her Mason was in New Orleans, just not on any airline manifest.

Sunday, August 06th

Steve Dillion loved his work. But Brent Mason was more than that; he was a mission, something Dillion would one day make right. That's what he years ago promised Priscilla Serra and Presley Burke.

Mason disappearing was no big surprise. People disappeared. The shock was how quickly. Thing is, most people succumb to the frailties of the human condition and the wealthy are no exception. If anything they're more susceptible. They can't let go and fuck-up, long-instilled habits transmuting from day one into inherent liabilities, like walking past a few hundred airport surveillance cameras as though he was strolling in Central Park.

"That's sure as hell him, whoever he is. Mason might have flown out, but this guy is back home. I need those manifests, Laura."

"I can do that. But Dill, this is not a case. You're solo on this. Sorry."

"Just get me those names," which Lieutenant Dillion did within mere hours after speaking with her captain who knew the right judge. A woman whose ex-brother-in-law was on death row for murdering her sister in a blind rage.

That was the extent of her involvement, arriving home with him and a few dozen boxes containing names in the tens of thousands that took him until Monday evening and several felt pens to highlight with no Brent Mason. Nothing near a Brent Mason or Braxton Miles.

Until Garcia called late Monday with a dose of reality. Dill knew where the guy was, right? "So get your ass over there, chavo. Find this hijo de puta," Garcia calling again not long after with an epiphany that was Ercilia's, a school teacher, thinking it was at least worth a try and Garcia got on it. After all, Mason was rich. Wasn't he? Duh!

"Ercilia was right, chavo. We missed this one and she is being muy pagada about it. She says we owe her a dinner."

"Meaning what, Rey?"

"Meaning Mason is one Bradley McGuire, chavo. Monaco, New York y Nueva Orleáns on a charter and I'm thinking you should be packing a bag muy pronto, amigo."

*

Tuesday, August 08th.

The earliest flight was 11:55 AM, an eternity from when he kissed Laura at eight, flashing his New York shield in the Sheraton lobby near 2:15 CDT and cursing himself for not acting sooner.

Braxton Miles had checked-out earlier that morning. No. He did not have a vehicle. However the concierge did help with his request for an airport limo. About two hours ago, which meant a flight out any minute, Laura taking the call seconds later. He need-ed a NOPD assist at the airport. Plain clothes and preferably fe-male for a 'couples' look, pleasantly shocked when a bobby-socks throwback to the fifties in jeans and a tee, a denim jacket and ponytail eased from her car in a Fire Lane and sauntered toward him minutes from three o'clock, ignoring the ten-buck-an-hour commando wannabe.

Dill was thinking she must be a Penny, a Susan or Abigail, briefing Sergeant Cerise Claret as they walked unhurried into Ad-ministration. He was all-out lovin' them Southern gals, not that he didn't have one of his own. Though more to the point, Miles likely didn't fly home for a few days to fly out. He was staying, which meant domestic, sunny and warm, which meant Miami or Tampa because Houston was neither exotic nor the nation's yachting mecca, one name standing out like a flashing purple neon, Dillion asking to see the CSAs from American's flight 4432 scheduled to depart at 4:29 with passenger Bryce Madison sitting in 3A.

The counter reps agreed. The guy in the photo was Bryce Madison, the senior rep asking if he should be denied boarding or if a sky marshal was required. Neither. What was needed was a seat in economy for Mr. Steve Dillion and a free pass through security with his 92 FS Beretta Inox.   They processed him within minutes, putting him in 6-C that would give him a clear view of Madison's head.

Shaking hands with bobby-socks Cerise, thanking her, he assured her he would keep her current, thinking some lucky guy was doing alright for himself, and when she was gone he called Laura. Garcia was getting a bottle of Patrón and not the cheap stuff. Platinum. Ercilia? He wasn't sure. Maybe flowers or a short dress or some sexy lingerie. He was at a loss, perplexed until she reminded him Garcia was Latino and big, very big and Latino, suggesting a box of chocolates and a foursome for dinner one evening would do nicely. Then she got serious and asked about Priscilla Serra.

That evening Madison and Dillion checked-in to the Marriott moments apart. They dined separately and while one was getting 500-dollar professional tenderness and devotion the other was at the mall shopping for a Miami-appropriate wardrobe.

Wednesday, August 09th.
Dillion was sitting in the lobby when Madison stepped from the elevators for a late breakfast, not the least surprised when, precisely at 11:00, Madison stepped out onto the sidewalk and into the waiting limo, elated when Madison was dropped off at a dealership

that he left sometime later in a gleaming black BMW cabriolet.

After lunch in Little Havana while Madison was meeting with a realtor, Dillion rented a mid-range American four-door that would make him invisible on any street. Next he went to a tech store, closing off the afternoon on the white sands of South Beach reminiscing before sitting through dinner in the hotel dining room seemingly disinterested in the man he was surveilling. This before quickly transforming in his room from businessman to tourist and making painful smalltalk in the dimly lit lounge as Madison casually greeted an attractive twenty-something he was clearly acquainted with, enjoyed a cocktail with, and led arm in arm toward the elevators.

Dillion musing not for the first time as he made his way to the indoor parking where he made certain Brent Mason would not disappear a second time, which gave him pause, calling Laura from his room.

He stayed with Madison through Saturday when the realtor's gleeful expression from the far end of the parking lot confirmed his expectation that Bryce Madison would not leave Miami anytime soon. And Steve Dillion was on the next flight out, this time showing his credentials and storing his Inox in a lockbox cared for by the flight crew, four hours later stepping into a candlelight dinner, soft music, and Laura in a sheer lace romper and heels because she was young, sexy and in love.

And didn't want his eventful week spoiling her romantic evening, smacking him.

Sunday, August 13th.
He slept until 9:00, waking to strumming fingers on his chest and a dishevelled naked woman straddling his legs, remaining in bed under duress until Laura wiggled her way out after 10:00, sitting on the edge asking how he felt.

"Good. Real good. Strange though, not speaking with her in

over three months. Not seeing her in over a year. Now this."

"Phone her, Dill. Now. Her timeframe. She's waited long enough, although you might want to dress first." She painted swirly circles in the air between them with a slender hand, making a face. "This seems a too little casual. And Dill, be ready for some tears. I mean, really, I feel like crying."

"Ah, yes. The Sisterhood."

She smacked him. He showered and dressed, waving away his breakfast. He wasn't hungry, calling Priscilla Serra asking for a meeting that afternoon, adding that Laura being with him was a courtesy, not official, but with information of her own obtained as an off-the-record favour.

*

Charleston being what Charleston is, being a Sunday and that Laura didn't arrive dressed like a cop with a gun and shield on her hip, the women complimented each other's ensemble.

Dillion was in a suit. So what? And in the living room Southern hospitality and graciousness preluded business, Laura commenting on the richness and bouquet of the '83 Paulliac while Dillion sat warming a snifter of Johnnie Walker Blue between his palms.

"Thank you for seeing us, Ms. Serra."

"Mr. Dillion, you've had me walking in circles and bouncing off walls since your phone call. Please cut to the chase. You've found him, haven't you? You found him."

"Mason is in Miami. He's back and he's staying put."

Dillion sipped the magical elixir twice, pausing. Priscilla put her wine down, sitting straight, clasping her hands together in her lap. Shit! Laura was right. The female psyche preconditioned to blur reality and fact with false hope and fantasy was happening. He could see the struggle in Serra's eyes.

"He's got a very swanky condo on Water Avenue."

Laura added, "Airport biometrics got him a week ago arriving from France, Priscilla. Steve's been tracking him since then."

"His name's Bryce Madison, Ms. Serra. Everything Brent Mason was and more."

"How does someone do that, Mr. Dillion, change identities on a whim without sounding an alarm?"

"Big money. Friends. Brenda's and Bobbi-Jo's kind of money, friends you don't want."

He faced Laura. She did the work, she'd get the glory.

"As Bradley McGuire he married Bobbi-Jo Valliere in Monaco not long after he disappeared, Priscilla. She was very wealthy and they were the quintessential happy couple until she drowned somewhere near Corsica a few weeks ago. She fell from her boat late at night and was never found."

"Nor will she be, because Mason killed her."

"It would appear that Braxton Miles has a unique strategy for building a fortune, Ms. Serra. Thing is, as with Brenda, no proof of wrongdoing exists. He wasn't charged and now Bradley McGuire is gone along with Mason. Whereas Bryce Madison, a French citizen travelling on a French passport, does in every way. And he can substantiate every facet of his life because bullshit does not baffle brains, if you'll pardon the expression that in itself is absolute bullshit. But a passport, a permit, a home and diplomas on the wall, that does. Have all that, which he will, and no one cares about your past. Believe in who you are, and that is who you are. That's what everyone will see and believe."

"Meaning he isn't finished."

"Probably not."

"I want you back on this exclusively, Mr. Dillion. Same terms." She passed him an envelope. "That's twenty thousand for the past week and a bonus. Invite a lovely Charleston PD Lieutenant to dinner on me." She smiled at Laura. "Off the record, of course."

"The terms are generous, Ms. Serra. Too generous. Twenty grand? That's over the top for a dinner."

She ignored him. "If need be, lease or buy a condo on Water

Avenue. Blend in. Buy a fedora and a couple of bedrooms facing the ocean would be very nice. Don't you think, Laura?"

"Steve has skills that may preclude a condo, Priscilla. And he's right. Twenty grand?"

"Skills meaning what, more audio-visual?"

"Meaning Madison in real-time twenty-four-seven." He coughed a laugh. "With strictly audio in the bedroom. I'm still recovering."

Priscilla sipped her wine. "A millionaire gigolo. Tell me that isn't completely sick."

"He's sick alright. Makes one wonder what came before Braxton Miles."

"Or will with Madison," Laura added.

"At least we know where. And if he buys another boat for a wedding present we'll know that too. Who down there with that kind of cash does not have a yacht?" Priscilla asked about refills, Steve declining. As much as they liked her, they were not friends. "Get him for me, Mr. Dillion. For me and Presley."

"He will, Priscilla. It's a matter of time and patience. Miles made a huge mistake. He changed his name a third time. We know why and we know how. The questions are who and when."

"Good. Because I want nothing more in my life than keeping the promise I made Steve."

Laura put down her glass, pointing at a framed photo. "Is that your sister and Brenda? Steve told me they were very beautiful. Like sisters."

"Thank you, Laura. That's very kind. I'll certainly pass on the compliment. They were like sisters. Crazy and crazy about each other." She stood, following Dillion's lead. "Perhaps next time you'll stay for dinner and I'll tell you about them." She turned to Dillion. "When you loosen your tie a little…Stevie."

At the door Dillion chanced a "Priscilla," garnering a warm smile.

Too little, too late. He was floating face down in Shit Creek, heading for a deep and thick pond, in the car Laura metamorphosing from homicide cop to wife. She liked Priscilla, and Dill would accept that dinner invitation. The poor woman was hurting. She wanted to talk about the closest and most important people in her life. And really, would another cocktail have been so terrible? Really?

He supposed not. He was an asshole. He didn't deserve her.

"That's right, you don't. And what promise, Dill? You never mentioned any promise."

"No. Because people say things."

"Things like what?"

He reached over, squeezing an invitingly bare thigh. "A million dollars."

*

Seven days later Dillion reported to Priscilla that Braxton Miles' condo was wired for audio-visual, the BMW was trackable, and Miles had taken out ads in the Miami Herald complete with photo and bio offering his discreet services to the city's neglected and well-heeled.

Like the lady said. Sick.

49

11:29 AM.

"BJ was indeed spectacular, Preacher. I swear she loved me more than Brenda. But she would have kicked me out sooner or later. Probably sooner. Eventually she would have wondered about Nice, about the students in tights and berets I never talked about. It's their way, they can't help themselves. And the bank account. I mean I really did not have a choice, did I? I had invested too much in her. My time, the yacht. Treating her like a princess."

"I fear for your soul, Braxton. Such an innocent and vital young woman, such a warm and loving heart. Taken for no reason but your lust for money and carnal greed."

"That's a bit harsh, Preacher. Carnal greed? I would say more like do unto others as they would do unto you. Just do it first and do it better. As for the others, they were purely business. Women I brought comfort to, women I made feel valued at a fair market value. That was honest.

Each one a cheating wife getting the best lays of her life or some young widow freed from the sagging balls and limp dick of someone's decaying granddad like Valliere."

"Desperate lives seeking comfort."

"And plenty of it. I gave them hope and dreams the way Blaire provided ephemeral escape into fantasies and better lives. And no less gifted, truth be told. You know, keep them coming back. But none was a Brenda or a BJ who served a higher purpose. I must admit though, with Bobbi-Jo, I wasn't expecting all the excitement

that night. Got a bit out of hand with helicopters, the whole goddamn navy. Practically shit myself blind. Got through it though.
Good thing was, those French cops, with all their politesse, far
more self-infatuated than brilliant." He snorted a breath, peering
through the slot. Twenty-nine minutes. "Nothing like Dillion. That
guy was one driven son of a bitch."

"Steve Dillion?"

"Talk about a quintessential cop. Fucked me up as much as that
lesbian bitch and never saw him coming."

"The orchestrator of your eventual undoing."

"A private cop. Never had a clue he was tracking me all those
years, spying on me. Makes a man truly wonder about decency in
the world. Wouldn't you say? Tell you what though, his lady, the
real cop, I would have done her gratis any number of times and
ways. Talk about a glorious treat. The lucky bastard."

The chaplain winced. "I met them yesterday, with the warden.
He harbours no malice, my son. They will however together bear
witness to your crossing over."

"Good. She'll join the party with Blaire and Courtney." Miles
chortled. "Who wouldn't wait in line for that peep show? And let's
not talk about malice. I'm the injured party here. Cheated and de-
ceived, that Mexican practically crushing my skull and mashing
my kidneys. Thing is, although neither do I bear malice, I never
gloated."

"Please speak more kindly of Detective Dillion, Braxton. She
was very nice, merely doing her job. No one here is rejoicing over
your punishment."

"Can't say that's true, Preacher. As much as I put into effect a
few destinies, I affected his big time. If anything, he should be
grateful. Those suits he wore in court didn't come from a private
dick's salary. Have to admit though, he got me. In fact if Brent Mason hadn't gone to France in a timely fashion he would probably
already be in the ground because of Dillion. So don't think for a

moment he's not gloating. He is. He's waited since taking me down for this day. Unfortunately he'll miss the grand finale."

The chaplain couldn't help himself, squeezing his cross in a clenched fist. "Preordained by God, Braxton. His destiny. Putting you in here so that you might at last atone for your sins and be free. Your destiny is what brought them together. Would that he had done so before Bobbi-Jo."

"That would be saying I'm sorry, Preacher. An execution, that's a little extreme from where I'm sitting. You know, for atonement. But do something for me, Reverend. Tell the smug son of a bitch when I'm gone. Tell him about Bunker and Davaux; tell him about good old Bill Michaels and Linden. Make his day. Make mine. Because your celestial bells, Preacher, they toll not only for me this dark and ominous day."

"Braxton?"

"Dillion put me in here, Preacher. That's true, but he didn't do so on his own. The last one, that bitch was worse than anything I ever did or could do. Her body and her mind, cold as ice. I did not kill that woman. The truth is, so help me God as you would say, I am being executed for a murder I did not commit. And what's worse, I was tried subliminally and found guilty by the human condition for two tragic accidents involving women Braxton Miles never knew, fictitious murders never substantiated in any court. Purely inadmissible cheap theatre planted as fact in the weak human mind." He checked the clock. "That is on her, Preacher, and cannot go unpunished despite my own theatrics knowing full well I was not going free. Though, as much I was not escaping this day, neither will she."

11:33.

50

Priscilla spent Thanksgiving with Presley on the West Coast, flying out again for Christmas and New Year's.

They were each other's gift, their time together more precious than boxes wrapped in pretty colours. Particularly that Christmas when Presley did have a gift, a special surprise. She had quit her job at the magazine a few days earlier and had a buyer for her condo. She was moving to Charleston. ETA: Easter.

She had done her time photographing glamorous and practically naked women day after day, her sister commiserating with the hardship. She wanted more time with Priscilla because life was too short and they missed each other despite speaking several times each week, believing Prissy would either squeeze the life out of her or smother her with kisses and tears.

"Naturally I'm driving, Prissy. They still won't let me fly."

"You look well, sweetheart."

"I am. And I'm excited. I can finally sit and talk with Brenda on warm sunny days. We can have a picnic with her and I can finally meet Steve and Laura."

"They're good people, you'll like them. Steve's a bit New Yorkish on a learning curve, but Laura's a darling...for a homicide cop. As for Mason, to-date he's keeping a low profile except for addictively fucking Miami's young and wealthy. He should be in a cage."

"He belongs in a landfill or a sewer with his own kind. And I believe Steve when he says something good will happen. I do."

Priscilla nodded. "He certainly knows enough about vermin."

Presley giggled, a heartwarming and mischievous sound that hadn't changed since her school days.

"No. I know that look, Presley. No."

*

By Thanksgiving the Dillions had been invited to dinner, Laura a little perplexed over what to take a millionaire as a hostess gift, shocked when Dill outright suggested Marcy Palmer. Really? She didn't think so, opting for a silk scarf, thinking he should get his debilitated male mind out of the gutter.

Whatever.

They reciprocated the second Saturday in January, learning more about Presley and Brenda, that they would finally meet Presley in the spring. And of Priscilla when Laura wondered out loud why such a successful and attractive woman never married, Laura shrugging a so-what, resisting the urge to smack Dill. One of her best detectives was lesbian. She was also adorable, unattached, and could put Steve on his ass in a blink.

She thanked Laura—however. That she thought fondly of them was weird enough, she didn't need her private investigator and his detective wife playing matchmaker. She was happy with her life, or very soon would be.

Still, when the quintessential day of love and romance too soon arrived, Priscilla worked late while the unattached and lonely Marcy Palmer was doing double duty for her cop buddies who were either rushing home with flowers or slipping into nylons and garters like everyone knew Laura Dillion would. She didn't care; her job was her life and her life was shit. Besides, she often wore sexy girl things alone at home with her cat Fungus that would always unconditionally love and understand her.

Easter wasn't a big thing for Priscilla, better suited to the pious and children. Except that for a week she had been tracking Presley's progress with nightly mandatory phone calls. Her sister was coming home. She was exhilarated and sleepless, with no reason to believe for a moment that within a few months her world would implode and she would want to implode with it.

Presley arrived on the world's most notable Friday; on the Sunday Laura arrived with Steve who wasn't yet comfortable with the kissy cheek thing. Especially since he was the hired hand and had never spoken with the sister.

"Hi, Laura. Steve. Thanks for coming." She hugged Laura, pressing their cheeks together, stepping back, scanning Steve from head to toe, nodding approvingly, taking the wine from him before she startled him with glossy prune lips smudging his cheeks because he had to lighten up. "My kid sister's in the kitchen. She's excited about meeting you."

Laura wasn't sympathetic, leaving him to deal with the trauma as she walked arm in arm with her hostess into the living room, because they were getting comfortable with each other; Steve followed, thinking he hadn't very often seen Priscilla smile, let alone be excited. Neither were the shorter dress and longer legs lost on him. Whoa! He was happy for her, she deserved despite what he knew was coming, feeling as though he'd been dragged into some collegiate dorm to witness a hazing ritual.

"Sit, people." She knew Laura preferred bourbon, never discussing the questionable issue. And that Steve preferred JW Black, though he would settle for the more exquisite Blue if he must. "How have you been? I am so excited about you being here, about you meeting my sister."

Steve broke in. "Your little sister a little hot in the kitchen, Priscilla? Maybe a little pissed with me?"

Laura turned to Dill, scrunching her face. "Forget him. He's not important."

With drinks served, Priscilla sat on the ottoman facing them, crossing her legs and leaning into them, as though she might be studying them.

"You are absolutely fabulous, Laura. Especially from a lesbian's perspective. Your outfit is divine. You should let Presley photograph you. You really should. She would love doing a shoot with you."

"Maybe not, but thank you." She punched Steve. "Isn't Priscilla completely fabulous today?"

"Very attractive. One could even say spectacular."

Laura punched him again. "One does say attractive. And very spectacular."

"Thanks, Steve. And yes, my sister is very hot. She's hot anywhere and no one here is pissed with you."

"Thanks. That's a relief because I'm feeling a little oppressed here."

"No worry. I promise you she isn't. She's super excited, finally sitting here with you and Laura." She leaned in closer, giggling, clinking her Jean-Marc XO to his JW Blue. "Guys, I'm the sister. I'm Presley." The stunned expressions were priceless. "Gotcha!"

From that point Priscilla's evening went south non-stop, adamant she should have stayed in the kitchen. She was the one feeling oppressed, neither Presley nor Laura exhibiting the least remorse, Steve upfront declaring he had no opinion either way. He wasn't getting involved and was quickly forgotten. Presley wanted to hear absolutely everything about Marcy Palmer, on the Friday sauntering into Division with Laura. She needed to see the to-die-for lesbo detective for herself and, when she did, no way were they not doing lunch. Her treat.

Lunch with 'the girls'. Something an unwary Marcy hadn't done in ages. Lunch in a proper restaurant, not with her feet on her desk biting into a pastrami sandwich and guzzling Coke from a can. A no brainer—until in the restaurant her survival skills kicked in, Marcy instantly on the defensive when she understood the offensive was underway from both flanks. She was not interested. No way. Uh-huh. She did not want or need some desperate middle-aged lesbian who hadn't dated in years, expelling a grim sigh when Laura leaned into her and asked how Fungus was working for her.

She sighed mournfully. She was pathetic. Her life was shit. Everyone knew her life was shit. Slouching in her chair, crossing her arms in a show of defiance like a pouty school girl being scolded, she asked for a detailed description because she was a cop, a good cop, fully resistant to bullshit.

Except that Laura simply put her hand over Presley's and said, "This one in a mirror. And she's a lawyer."

Silent glances through wide eyes met with quiet nods and self-satisfied smiles. Mission positively accomplished and no one was returning to Division. Marcy's two-woman task force was not risking failure and that evening Priscilla walked in to an unexpected and strung out guest sitting with her sister. Strung out because, hello, they had neglected to mention that Priscilla was filthy rich, living on the eighteenth floor of seventh heaven surrounded by designer everything, and that her to-die-for kitchen was the size of Marcy's entire apartment.

What was her point? More importantly from the co-conspirator's perception, the slacks and the gun were gone and she was spectacular. Which did nothing to calm a nervous Marcy Palmer visibly taken aback when she saw what had been impossible for her to believe as she was being pampered, coiffed, and made-up with her boss and Presley who she thought was too incredibly beautiful, Presley erupting into youthful giggles.

"I'm Marcy Palmer, Priscilla. I think you know about me. I'm sorry if this is embarrassing," was all she could manage.

She did. Presley's older sister by five minutes also seeing that Laura could not have painted a more perfect portrait of the woman. Marcy was adorable; she was shapely and flawless with the blackest hair and greenest eyes she had ever seen.

She also knew very well who else was to blame and Steve was by no means innocent.

Embarrassing? No. More like fucking fantastic, but how long had she stood staring?

She dropped her handbag onto a sofa, shrugging her coat from her shoulders, eyeing her sister.

"Seems to me you ladies endured a difficult day. Did they kidnap you, Marcy? Coerce you in any way?"

"I suppose they meant well."

"I can take out a bench warrant if you want. Then you can arrest them. Or maybe shoot them. No problem. Think we should talk about that?"

"Yes, I think we should."

"Good. Any chance you can stay for dinner?"

Yes! "I would like that."

"Holy mackerel! How super fast was that? Rosy cheeks and dreamy eyes. Okay, I am done here." She hugged Marcy, whispering; then she hugged her sister, whispering. "And don't thank me, guys. Or Laura. We know we did good. Buen apetito, chicas."

Presley went home, her own face glowing.

Earlier that week she had leased a corner condo in the tower opposite her sister's. Close but not in-the-way close, telling Prissy she was her sister not her shadow or an anchor. Particularly that evening when Laura was at home waiting for precise details.

*

Saturday was predictably Thank-you Day.

Marcy called Priscilla, thanking her for a lovely evening. They were joining each other for dinner downtown that evening and were excited. Then Priscilla called her sister as Marcy was speaking with her lieutenant, thanking Presley as Prissy was telling Laura how well she and Marcy hit it off. The mysterious and guarded world of the female psyche that Dillion wanted no part of.

Two of them excited and hopeful, two others shamelessly pleased with themselves and gloating, no one giving Steve even a modicum of due credit for his enlightenment months earlier which he attributed to the female tribal mood.

The following Saturday Priscilla met the furry Fungus, mildly assuaged having previously seen several selfies of the cat and mom. Though by late April the ladies' weekly goodbye kisses prefacing a lonely night evolved into heated romance and tender weekend mornings, Marcy moving into her surreal seventh heaven at the end of June with Fungus, by which time Priscilla was quite blasé about her inamorata completing her fashion du jour with a ten-millimetre Glock.

Naturally over time Marcy heard about Brenda from the sisters. She heard about Mason and Madison, always in sync with her boss that, until Madison did something really stupid, until Steve one day succeeded in cornering him, Mason and McGuire were merely guilty of being careless husbands. Each one exonerated, each one gone. And they were not coming back. However midway through July, when Detective Palmer was in Vegas attending a cops' convention and trade show, Presley invited her sister for dinner one evening, which she stipulated did not imply more lectures about her being single and alone. Because she was not alone; neither was she lonely. Besides, she had more important and much better news.

After dinner though, lounging with cognacs splashed with soda, the usual sparkle in Presley's liquid eyes disappeared. When she would often curl into her sister or rest her head in Prissy's lap, this evening she needed focus more than she did her hair being combed through with loving fingers.

"So what's this good news, if not some hunk?"

"Okay. Here's the thing, and don't get all brain-fucky on me. Because you do that. Promise me. Because you know you're the one person I love most in this miserable world. Right?"

She nodded, thinking she knew what was coming. "But promise? No guarantees."

"Yeah, well, that's a yes. You're also promising that Marcy, Laura and Steve, will never hear a word of this." She sipped her cognac. "I need those promises, Priscilla. Now."

Suddenly Priscilla was on high alert. "Yes. Yes, I promise." She put down her glass. "Now what is going on with you, sweetheart? Your heart? Because I do not like this."

"In a way, I suppose. Because in a way my heart doesn't matter anymore." She took her sister's hand. "Actually I've known for quite some time, Prissy. Why I moved here to be with my sister. Because life is too short and I love you. You know that. I kept this from you because I love you and needed to work things out, to make sense of things. Not just about me. About you and Brenda. About everything."

"Okay. Alright. Now you're not making any sense. You're scaring me. What is this secret and how long have you known about what?"

Simply put, because she had no other way, "About a year ago I was told by those experts in white frocks that the congenital defect was no longer a big issue. So go have a good time, right? Well that was the good news. And that's what I thought. Until I learned my fourth stage leukemia was sort of a bigger issue and pretty much a definitive bummer."

"What!" A bolt of ice might as well have pierced her heart, jolting the sisters apart, Priscilla losing all colour in her face, her hands losing their warmth. "What leukemia?"

"The sneaky and shitty kind, I suppose." She managed a thin smile, feeling her sister's terror. "Yeah, I know. But hey, imagine my surprise."

"No. Sweetheart, no." Priscilla's voice was plaintive, a pitiful wail. "This is not happening."

"Yeah, it is. Shit does happen. But I'm good with it, Prissy. I am. I've had a year and a bit. Believe me, I am happy. I am not faking this. Especially now that you have a wonderful someone in your life and in your loving heart."

Priscilla's eyes blurred with tears, her body convulsing, Presley pressing warm palms to her sister's wet cheeks a second before an explosion of sobs, Presley's tight embrace giving her sister time and bitter solace.

"How long do we have, sweetheart? How long?"

Presley shrugged. "Three years, maybe. Who knows? More importantly, do not speak a word of this, Priscilla. I mean it. As much as I love you, in death I would never forgive you. This thing is our secret, yours and mine. And, like I said, definitive."

"Why? That makes no sense."

"Because they'll see me differently; they'll act differently. They'll feel awkward, like a blind guy saying 'see ya around' and the closer my time comes they'll either stay away or sit staring at their watches hoping I don't fuck-up their evening. Because Laura finally caved in. She's letting me do a sexy lingerie shoot for Steve's birthday and I need her being smily and seductive in garters and teddies." She beamed, arching her eyebrows. "That's right, garters and silky stuff. How lucky am I? Oooh." The feigned cheeriness faded. "But Prissy, mostly because they are all cops and Steve works for you. That's why."

"Sweetheart, three years. No."

"Three very good years." Presley giggled. "What the hell, I might even get Laura stapled into some cop magazine. How cool would that be?"

"No. She would definitely kill you." Instant wide-eyed shock. "Oh, sweetheart, I'm sorry. I didn't…"

"See what I mean? Awkward." Presley kissed her sister, reaching for her cognac. "Just like the blind guy said."

"I'm staying the night. I am not leaving you."

"That's right, you're not. Because I am not leaving you. You're not taking this very well. Now you listen carefully and do not interrupt me because something good will come of this if you don't get all brain-fucky. That's what I promise you, Prissy. What I promised Brenda months ago. Then we'll get royally pissed." She giggled. " I can do that now."

*

Laura Dillion took the last Friday of July as a personal day. She had a ten AM at the hair salon and was sitting in Presley's upscale condo in a silk robe at noon getting her nails and makeup done.

By 1:00 she was feeling downright exposed more than an alluring temptress, pushing out and sucking in, bending and twisting this way and that for another woman. Stretched out on Presley's designer bed amidst lamps and reflectors, captured forever in heels and a thong, garters and a bustier, a teddy, and a finale sitting on a stool against a ruelle à Paris with her elbows on her knees in stay-ups and boots, a beret, a raglan sweater and her Browning held between long and open legs.

By five she was exhausted. Nevertheless, when Presley asked how she felt, she felt freaking sexy. No kidding. And very oooh. But she was not getting a preview. Wouldn't happen. And, what was worse, one week later when she went back for the finished portfolio, she was way too late. Priscilla and Marcy didn't have to deal with rush-hour traffic.

"Wow! Lieutenant!"

*

Some days later when Steve was expecting a special dinner and cake, cufflinks or a CD. What he got was Laura on white satin sheets. Lots of her and the stop-traffic Parisienne flic was going on the wall. He kissed her, squeezing her. She was fantastic; she was great, way more delicious and mouthwatering hot than dinner and cake, the French cop the next instant alive and in person reading his rights and deciding his punishment.

The next morning she called Presley who wasn't the least surprised, who called Priscilla who called Marcy who scurried into her lieutenant's office.

51

By Easter Braxton Miles' client list comprised more than two dozen of the city's wealthiest and bored wives and liberated widows. He'd struck the mother lode, puzzled yet fascinated by the endless queue of disenchanted or lost thirty-somethings eagerly paying for what hubby was no longer giving them for whatever the reason: Their own whores, a younger secretary, a hoped-for demise.

Rapture. The thrill of newness and excitation, youthful vigour and explosive titillation. That's what he brought them, what kept them coming back.

He jogged on South Beach each morning at six, maintaining his daily regimen at an upscale club since the fitness centre in his building was a danger zone swarming with incredible T and A in next-to-nothing microfibre, realizing one day that he had only dated twice in his life beyond the many. Though not once in eight months had he come across a viable candidate for something longer-term and more beneficial despite never touching his Cayman account excepting the yacht.

Those were all at the wrong end of forty or worse. Until the first weekend of August, one year into Madison's life and career, he came across Samantha Sandal and could not resist replying to her social media account with a photo, bio, and so much more to tell her in person.

He was a bachelor, thirty-seven, recently arrived from France and wasn't into the bar scene. He was a former professor, searching introspectively as well as for someone sincere and loving who would share his life. He was a yachtsman, well-travelled, decent and kind, free of emotional baggage, waiting a few days for Samantha Sandal to respond that she found him intriguing, even suggesting that perhaps they should talk.

The first night they spoke for an hour, the fourth night Bryce Madison agreeing they should meet for lunch on the Sunday. He couldn't agree more, completely charmed by her.

She was thirty-eight and sensational with everything in the right place. Her copper hair was cut in a fanciful messy bob and her impossibly dark blue eyes sparkled like sapphires belying the fact her husband's death one year earlier had left her heartbroken and lonely.

Despite not having to work she taught art at a local college and once each month in Savannah teaching inner city kids who showed promise because she adored teaching and could never have children of her own. Which was part of the problem.

Both she and her husband came from privileged families, though the parents had passed on. In fact she had no family at all, some of her more au courant students convincing her to get with the real world. She would never find the next man of her dreams sitting in a pew singing praises, aisle seven or town hall dances for the socially inept. She'd been there, done that, never feeling a synergy, none of them succeeding beyond the first date; they were all too eager and obvious.

So she thought, why not? Her students agreed and voilà, as they say. So what if she had money? Find some nice guy who had more money than love in his life. Anyhow, wasn't home where the heart was?

He understood. He endured a similar hardship: Family wealth. The few women he had dated were plainly more enamoured of the BMW M4, the fifty-foot yacht and his oceanview penthouse than him. All of them attentive and adoring until the claws came out when he perforce expressed his disappointment.

"But you're very different, Samantha. We both are, I suppose. I can't tell you how pleased I am that you suggested a luncheon."

"I'm enjoying myself immensely, Bryce. Thank you."

He checked his Rolex. Time enough. "Perhaps a stroll along the riverfront, Samantha. Simply leaving you now would seem, I suppose, final and inappropriate." The practiced smile and glint in his eyes were disarming. "And not very conclusive. Don't you agree?"

She did, inwardly thrilled. Strolling the riverfront she talked about her work, listening intently as Madison confessed his dream of creating his own private college. He had the resources and the qualifications, smirking as he suggested out of the blue a possible change of venue.

"My cherished France, of course, has the magnificent Côte d'Azur with its Mediterranean climate. And although I did admittedly choose Miami, swayed by the glamour and glitz, the beaches and Latin flavour…"

"And pretty girls in tiny bikinis, no doubt."

"And captivating women, I do find the extreme summer heat unpleasant to the same degree. In fact, seeing your charming city and its spellbinding women, I believe I will start considering a relocation. I have no ties and I like what I've seen of your city. I like what I'm seeing at this very moment."

"You mean move here?"

"I mean, may I invite you to dinner next Saturday?"

He couldn't be serious. Flying there on a whim was one thing, but twice? "Seriously?"

"Yes. I would stay the weekend again, of course. I find you enchanting, Samantha. And what's the point of excessive money if we can't occasionally indulge in self-interest?" He stopped, raising his open palms between them. "I haven't yet brought the *Indiscreet* this far north and would love for you to see her, for you to feel her sway beneath your feet."

What was he saying? This was too surreal. He was everything she could have wished for, and did. He was handsome and athletic, charming and educated, worldly with wealth of his own and had not shown the slightest interest in her many millions.

"And I thought I'd be moving to Miami, trying one of those tiny bikinis. My husband was a little conservative."

"Depriving himself and so many others." He chortled, beaming. "However, by very happy coincidence, mademoiselle, in the yachting world that very breathtaking fashion is considered not only alluring but requisite."

"I love the ocean, Bryce. But I've never been on a boat let alone a yacht. Are you serious?"

"I am. And it's a date."

*

Madison was cruising at forty knots by noon on Thursday, finding amenable companionship in Jacksonville that evening and arriving in Charleston near the dinner hour Friday. He wasn't in a hurry, wasn't eager, enjoying the leisure of the meandering Intracoastal. They had spoken twice that week and each had a good feeling.

He was thinking a month or more before condo hunting. And although he'd be docking the *Indiscreet* from then on in Charleston, he would maintain the Miami condo because once things got done Braxton Miles would again be of service.

Though he waited until relaxing dockside with a cocktail Friday evening before inviting her for lunch onboard Saturday in casual attire suitable for a laid-back dinner at the marina resort.
Keeping up appearances, exercising deliberate patience was as paramount to the cause as his increasingly deep and genuine attraction until the day he would love her and she would love him.

*

Madison waited until the Tuesday after returning home before speaking again with Samatha, as he had promised, Steve Dillion sitting for a moment quietly musing before calling Priscilla with what he termed substantive information.

He boarded the first flight out the next morning with no idea where Madison had gone that weekend or where he was going. He never mentioned the city, or how he was getting there, and Laura had no justification for involving the Miami PD. All he knew was the name. Samantha. And that Thursday Madison would take the Intracoastal north on a two-day cruise in yet another yacht.

He landed near noon, his first stop the Marriott for lunch and a change of clothes, arriving at the marina in his best casuals. He and his wife would soon take up residence; they owned a fifty-foot fly-bridge and were shopping for adequate dockage at a marina with a welcoming ambiance and social flair.

The marina's director naturally embraced the opportunity, guiding him between the marina's most magnificent prides and joys, describing many of the owners while touting the features and benefits Chuck Miller and his wife Mable would surely take pleasure in.

Chuck was impressed, agreeing the *Indiscreet* and the wife would indeed enjoy becoming members.

What? Another *Indiscreet*? Really? Do you mind, George?

"Very impressive."

"Would you care to meet the captain, Chuck. He's onboard."

Laura would smack him for even thinking about it. And she had this sixth sense thing going on. Besides, "No. That would mean shaking his hand." A pause for affect, checking his watch. "What I mean is, I'm short on time and you know how we captains are when we get talking. In any event we'll see each other in time. Possibly this evening with Mable if seven is convenient."

The rest of the day he was parked across from Braxton Miles' complex, waiting, watching an empty condo until dusk, until Madison was not coming home. Why would he when his boat was the size of a small house? At least he had seen the boat, and would throughout Thursday from every bridge crossing the waterway until Madison would choose a marina for the night that was the ritziest in Jacksonville. Not a big surprise.

That bombshell came Friday.

After Madison's and Dillion's dinners at the marina's clubhouse, Madison's departure by taxi for a probable good time and Dillion's night at a nearby Express Inn, the *Indiscreet* continued north under several more bridges until steering to port and into the Charleston Harbor where he was expected.

That Madison would choose the upscale marina resort that Dillion suspected and witnessed up close and personal through his Bushnell prisms from the parking lot was a given and, with no reason to book a room, he relaxed on the patio lingering over a glass of wine until the sun set.

At home he shocked Laura with the incredible news before he phoned Priscilla. Madison wasn't going anywhere. He was coming home, again. Count on it. Whoever Samantha was, she lived in or around Charleston and she was next. Better yet, whenever Dillion would determine the need, the marina was private detective accessible. Not a problem and if anyone was going down, Mason was. He promised.

She believed him; she had never stopped believing in him. Yet, thanking him, her voice was strangely tremulous, Priscilla reiterating very clearly at any cost. And when she disconnected she sank into her sofa and wept, explaining to an understanding Marcy Palmer that "At last."

Marcy sat beside her, taking her hand, adding what Dillion hadn't. As soon as possible the Charleston PD would be involved. That was her promise. She and Laura would be involved and South Carolina had both the death penalty and a hard-line governor who never wasted good ink granting reprieves.

She knew that; she was happy about that, swearing she would be in court everyday for Brenda, that she would tell the court the extent of his evil, and that she would watch him die.   That's what she promised for Brenda.

52

The weekend was a success beyond her wildest expectations, Samantha Sandal taking quickly to life on the open sea. She loved the adventure, the romance of lunch while drifting off the Isle of Palms, swaying in rhythm to the gentle chop, and dinner at the resort with a digestif on the patio gazing out over the vibrant cityscape under a starlit sky.

She wanted the day to go on forever. That's what she told him, kissing his cheek, reliving every moment in her bed that night, convinced she was following her heart. She could positively imagine a meaningful relationship evolving between them, quietly thrilled when he told her the yacht would stay in Charleston and that he would fly home.

He was charming, kind and attentive, not the least vain or self-infatuated. If anything he was palpably infatuated with her. They were doing breakfast at the marina before another day on the ocean that again would end too quickly, Samantha confessing a twinge of guilt for regretting her evening flight to Savannah.

He felt the same way. Nevertheless, Sunday was too premature for anything more inviting than proper shorts and a sweater. She would not send the wrong message. As eager as she was for more fabulous times with him, she would pace herself. She would be certain. Be more certain, which she was by day's end, relishing thoughts of strings and triangles and perfecting her tan for their next weekend.

Docking the yacht as late as he could Sunday, Madison

promised he would call her often. He adored her soft voice. And while he commended her week-long Savannah commitment, praising her, he did admit his coming weekend would seem selfishly interminable, fully committed to making their Labour Day weekend extra special. And from then on Madison flew in Friday and out Sunday three weeks each month, the *Indiscreet* his retreat and second love until deciding on an exclusive downtown high-rise December 01st and proposing to his first love on his thirty-eighth birthday.

Samantha suspected the day was coming, her intuition telling her something wonderful would soon happen after five months of living in a dream, wrapping her arms around him without the slightest doubt and pressing her lips to his, if not as tightly or as ardently as his clients. However as exhilarated and excited as she was, he would not move in until they were husband and wife. And Madison expected nothing less.

She wanted her wedding in June and her honeymoon in the Bahamas, planning her perfect day and their idyllic life together that included her attorney drawing up a will making each other their sole beneficiary, Madison practically losing a lung when realizing her wealth approached fifty million. Conversely, when he divulged his net worth, she scarcely batted an eye. She wasn't marrying him for his money.

They were married at city hall by a justice of the peace, a few of Samantha's colleagues from academia standing as witnesses, select dock friends later joining in the celebration at the resort until the small hours, the delirious bride and proud groom the next morning cruising the well-travelled Intracoastal she'd never been on, Bahamas bound, Samantha Madison returning a couple of weeks later tanned and adored.

Both his second BMW M4 and her Alpha Romeo Giulia blinking onto Dillion's split screen Monday morning.

*

What Dillion couldn't fathom was how Madison continued returning guiltlessly to Miami each week Samantha Sandal was doing
her thing. He had often seen her from afar at the marina resort and
could easily imagine what he couldn't see.

Miami? He got that. The place was Braxton Miles' base, his
escape route. What he didn't get was the constant stream of women
and the inverse flow of money.

What the four women didn't get and found sickening as
women, since Laura and Marcy could not yet officially be involved, wasn't that Miles continued remorselessly sleeping with a
different woman in Miami the times his enchanting wife was in
Georgia making the world a better place. Or even that they paid
him because any half attractive woman contravening the natural
order of things obviously had serious issues.

No. What was undeniably more appalling was that for months
he'd been living his perverse life in Charleston with wild abandon
and that a week after their Bahamas honeymoon he was back in the
gutter.

Bastard.

A streetwise Dillion had no comment, the last week in June
strolling along the marina resort's docks and onto the *Indiscreet*
where he worked at obviating the need to spy on a married couple
from inside their home. Then he wired Braxton Miles' Charleston
high-rise rental where the emeritus professor of Romance tongues
was ostensibly elevating business types beyond the charm of a
southern drawl. This before showering and going home to his loving bride fully sanitized.

Although one week later, relaxing with a scotch at home as
Samantha Madison was sunning on the bow in some sparsely pop-
ulated cove wearing a thong, he dutifully reminded Laura she was
not involved. Which was unfortunate because "Oh, yeah. Exceptional."

She smacked him, squirming in beside him, daring him to say

something male. She was on a stakeout with probable cause; Steve chortling, asking with a smirk what that cause would be—exactly?

*

Laura and Steve were never told of Presley's conditions. She didn't need the pity and they had become Priscilla's friends, not hers. Neither was Marcy Palmer aware, not until the evening she came home to find Priscilla sobbing inconsolably, herself then sworn to secrecy, her own face streaked with tears.

They did see her occasionally, when Steve had a significant up-date, and she did speak with her sister each week, often joining her and Marcy for dinner. Or inviting them. Either way, she always looked perfect and perfectly well, insisting privately with Prissy that she would leave the world with dignity looking exquisite. She was determined, because when she wasn't being poked and prod-ded at the clinic she was at the gym maintaining her strength most mornings and the spa most afternoons maintaining her vanity. All she wished for, all she desired and prayed for, was that Brent Ma-son would fuck-up first and very soon.

"I mean, shit, Prissy. She's been with him two years, married fifteen months. What is he waiting for? It's time. I mean, is it?"

"Steve didn't say, sweetheart. I'm sorry. You know how he is."

"Well we know he doesn't love her, out everyday fucking the phone book. I mean, how much longer does she have to suffer with him? And it's pretty obvious she's not the spellbound bride any-more."

"Sweetheart, we know him. He's predictable. It will happen."

"No way will I die first, Prissy. I won't let myself die first."

"No, you won't. And do not talk like that. Do not ever talk like that."

"You know what, I should kill him. I could do that. I should do that." She sipped her wine. "A few months in prison for what he did to Brenda? Boohoo. I could positively do that. Kill him."

"No, you won't. Because then you would never be with Brenda. You would forever struggle in turmoil by his side. Besides," she glanced at her watch, "Steve and Laura will be here in a few minutes with Marcy."

"I like Steve. I do. And Laura's a doll. But seven years? And five K a week for watching home movies? Maybe we should have sweetened the pot with another million."

"That's not appropriate, Presley. I haven't paid him since the wedding. He refuses. He's doing this on his own dime because he wants Mason as much as we do. And the million? I doubt he ever believed me."

She held out her glass for a refill, sighing, her gaze distant. "I can't imagine being dead, Prissy, not being with you. I think about that."

"Not exactly how things work, sweetheart. And not what I need to hear," the very moment the door opened.

Priscilla sauntered toward Marcy and Laura kissing their cheeks, smacking Dillion. Everyone liked smacking Steve and she could tell by the women's bright eyes she should hurry with their cocktails. Except when she peered into Steve's eyes—nothing. Which didn't disturb her; she had come to understand him, wondering at that precise moment how many animals like Mason he'd put down in the dark alleys of New York that no one ever heard about.

As drinks were being served Presley's mood quickly turned too volatile for her to bother with social correctness. In short, she no longer cared. She didn't have the privilege of time. In fact she had very little time and seeing the four of them smiling made her angry.

"Steve, despite what my sister believes about me, I am killing that fucking deviant myself. I am. In fact I'm killing him tomorrow because I am through with all this bullshit."

Silence.

Dillion leaned forward, very calm, very collected. "No need,

Presley. And not because you wouldn't be extremely popular in prison. I'm sure you'd be very well received. More because he's doing Samantha a week Sunday off Folly Beach. And we're ready. Meaning these ladies and Charleston Homicide. Sorry I couldn't tell you sooner."

Presley gripped her sister's hand. "What! No!" Her liquid brown eyes burst into a flood of tears. "This soon?"

Not quite what he expected. Unmoved, he turned to Priscilla. "What am I missing here? Are we having one of those proverbial bad days?"

Her full attention was on her sister. "No, Steve. You hit us with an unexpected shockwave. You might have been a little more delicate. You might have told us you have some good news. Some very good news."

A distraught Presley fought to compose herself, her sister and Marcy gently calming her as Laura sat glaring at her husband who stood his ground, waiting.

Presley patted her eyes dry, palming her thighs. She was fine. She was, she insisted. "I'm sorry, Steve. It's been such a long time. I'm sorry."

Priscilla knew otherwise. "Are you certain? Can you be properly prepared this quickly?"

"He called Cody Jones yesterday. Seems a grieving Bryce Madison will soon disappear in France as Briand Moire takes up residence in Monaco. He said divorcing her that Sunday would lend an extra special meaning to their separation, making their two-year anniversary especially memorable. His going away present for her." He shook his head. "The sonofabitch was actually laughing."

"What!" Presley twisted free. "He said what? He was laughing about killing her? A divorce? Are you fucking kidding me?"

Dillion's tone remained deadpan. He had been expecting a little more enthusiasm, perhaps a little more joy. Cause for celebration, somehow striking a raw nerve. "Understand something here, Presley. People like Braxton Miles, their blood runs cold. Miles was born emotionless and would likely forget her the moment she's gone. Divorce, murder, bye-bye, whatever. She would simply be gone."

"Which will not happen," Laura cut in.

Dillion nodded. "Though what he expects is that their division of assets, as it were, will be promptly and amicably concluded. After which he'll meet Jones in New Orleans." He sipped the JW Blue. "He also went shopping today. Came back with a whack of serious drugs he's probably not using to entice the redhead he's entertaining as we speak."

"Meaning what, exactly?" Priscilla asked.

"Meaning he'll put her to sleep and dunk her after dark. Or thinks he will. I checked with one of Laura's men, Garcia. He says the beach is pretty popular. We'll fit in and we'll be very close."

Marcy added, "We're very good at this, Presley. He is done."

Presley practically snarled, "Let's get fucking real here, people. Can we? How does anyone gets murdered at a crowded beach? How does that happen?" She needed to know. "I mean, how is that even remotely possible?"

Steve answered. This was his long-awaited hour as much as the sisters' requital. "My best guess is that he'll serve her increasingly spiked drinks, numbing her, obviating any chance of an incriminating struggle, and bide his time until dark because he has no choice. Then he'll put her over, possibly gently, possibly letting her stumble and fall on her own in a stupor, getting himself quickly and believably royally drunk, falling asleep, waking the next morning disoriented and confused without her, and putting out a frantic Mayday call." He sipped his Blue. "He's done this twice before that we're aware of, an accomplished actor devoid of guilt and humanity, switching from hot to cold as easily as he flips from late-night news to porn."

"Except we won't let that happen," Marcy added.

"No. We will not."

53

After Steve and Laura were gone Marcy sat with the sisters listening and commiserating. She had nothing to add that would assuage their grief or deepen their sense of relief. Of closure. And later that night, when Priscilla went home with Presley for the weekend, she understood. She had come to understand they were more than sisters; they were each other in their bodies and in their souls, needing, cherishing what precious little time was left to them, grieving privately, consoling and comforting each other. As she would very soon console and comfort the one person she would forever love in her life.

Presley's sweet and caring guardian angel had infused her with the inner strength and resolve to endure unimaginable pain and strife. A kind yet enervating reprieve until Braxton Miles would very soon be taken down and punished, before she would soon after be carried into a peaceful eternity that would forever be forbidden to the darkest of creatures such as Miles; Marcy Palmer praying, as she knew Dillion fervently wished, that he would do something extremely stupid— extremely deserving of a more immediate justice.

*

Steve and Laura:
Dillion's weekend began with a cold shoulder, which he attributed to the collective female mood,
Laura seemingly miffed about his abrupt relapse into New York-speak Friday evening, scolding him that Priscilla and Presley were

Southern ladies.

"They're not accustomed to your insensitive male squad room parlance. Dunking and doing. Really? What is wrong with you?"

He stood musing for a moment, his brow furrowed. "Yeah, I suppose I was thoughtless. I'm sorry. Forgive me. I see now that Miles will most certainly take Samantha lovingly by the hand. He'll fondly kiss her farewell, courteously assisting her down the ladder and into the sea, where he'll remain by her side, comforting her until she's ready to drown because she's a Southern lady and he's a Southern gentleman. You're right, of course. What was I thinking?"

Really? She wanted to smack him, hard. That self-satisfied signature smirk was so incredibly irritating. "Really, Dill? "She turned, sauntering away, shaking her head. "I have better things to do than talk with an idiot. And Sunday, none of your New York dark alley macho bullshit. I mean it, Dill. Or I will seriously hurt you. Not some little love tap."

Her ass was fantastic. "I know. Because you love me." Of course she did.

She kept walking. "Who else would?"

Laura understood that male and female cops were wired differently. The men in her squad often saw humour in death, or were casually indifferent; where the women often internalized homicides, bringing the job home with them, and somehow being close to Priscilla and working with Palmer made Miles personal. They had no room for error. Samantha was not being killed; nor was Miles transmuting into a Frenchman. He would do serious time for attempted murder and very possibly, hopefully, be executed for the murders of Brenda and Roberta-Joelle.

Failure was not an option.

Through Friday Dillion's week was theoretical, reliving the adrenalin rush of his years on New York's darker side, perfecting a takedown, spending hours at Folly Beach with Laura, Garcia and

Palmer, the Charleston PD Dive Team that would lay low and the Harbor Patrol that would appear unremarkable Sunday evening in their linens, raglans, and ten-millimetres. Each team leader at day's end briefing the others with strategy updates.

They didn't bother with Miles. They had him on-demand on full-screen at home servicing his clients each day, Garcia commenting on the Friday that not having visuals inside the seemingly blissful Madison home was like sitting deaf and blind at a movie.

He had a point, Dillion allowed. Nevertheless, doing Samantha at home did not fit Miles' profile. Wasn't his MO. He needed deep water as a stage, drugs and booze as props because he was also making a point: That he was masterful.

What they did know about Samantha was that she usually left home near 8:00, returning near 6:00, and that she wasn't in imminent danger. Sunday, however, from the moment she left home until zero hour, she wouldn't for a second be alone with him.

The teams would assemble again early Saturday AM for a final run-through, everyone in civvies before boaters would begin dropping anchors and being curious since binoculars weren't strictly for spotting navigational aids and hazards.

Friday evening, however, required suits and ties, pretty dresses and champagne. The four detectives, Priscilla and Garcia's Ercilia were the guests of Presley Burke who hurried first to Steve, hugging him, her brown eyes glistening with happy tears. She was truly sorry. Then she smacked him, evoking smiles across the room.

Actually they were both sorry, Steve pleasantly surprised when she took his hand.

*

Priscilla & Presley:
Saturday morning the sisters woke side by side holding hands, their noses touching.

"I was rude last night, Prissy. I shouldn't have acted that way. And I've been thinking, lying here staring at my sexy and sensational sister. I'm good with what you said. Steve does deserve the extra million. I can't believe he didn't take the envelope."

"You haven't been with him very often, sweetheart. Laura told me he was constantly talking about doing this for you. For me and Brenda, angry with himself for disappointing us. She told me he was so excited he actually kissed Garcia…and my girlfriend in the middle of the squad room. He couldn't wait to get here."

"I spoiled that for him. I ruined his special moment."

"You spoiled nothing. Steve's a big boy."

"Eight days, Prissy. That's why I cried. Hearing what he said, the way he said it. Like death was nothing, like he was being cruel. He made me angry and frightened, thinking how little time I have left with you."

"Steve doesn't know you're dying, sweetheart. He wasn't being cruel." She patted Presley's warm cheek. "But Marcy does. I got a little emotional one night awhile ago because I was angry and frightened. I needed a shoulder to cry on and she was available, meaning no more pretence with us. We'll all cry together whenever we feel like it and we'll drink too much. Good deal?"

"Good deal." Presley propped herself onto an elbow. "I'm not afraid anymore, Prissy. I'm happy. You have Marcy and I'm going to Brenda." She kissed her sister's cheek. "I am so happy for you, and for Marcy. Please both of you be happy for me."

A tear trickled onto Priscilla's pillow. "Life is absolute shit. You're too beautiful to die."

She lay back. "Yeah, life is shit. Now let's get a cry on, make ourselves gorgeous, and let's go see Marcy. She's probably feeling alone and worried."

First though, while they were dressing and doing what flawless ladies feel they must, Presley outlined her coming week.

She wanted every day with her sister; she wanted walks in the park and strolls on the beach; she wanted no more tears or morbid talk about dying; she wanted a spa day together on Friday when they would be the most gorgeous women in Charleston for the party she was throwing Friday evening. That's what she wanted, because who knew anything? She was tired, depleted, tired of pretending she wasn't; tired of her daily regimen, an arduous ruse when she felt like shit more each day.

"You just make sure when I'm gone they get him killed, Prissy. And whatever the cost you make sure they incinerate the corpse and put it in with the worst possible garbage. A million, whatever. You do that for me, for me and Brenda. Please do that."

"I will, I promise. Whatever the cost. I promise."

"Now, one thing more. And here's why. So don't get all mushy on me."

Priscilla listened, too depleted herself with sorrow to cry more than she had. Besides, she promised. No morbid talk. Strictly happy tears from then on and thereafter. She was not dying. She was moving on, like when she lived on the West Coast, always in her sister's heart; her sister always in hers.

And that would never change, Marcy greeted by smiling faces at her door she didn't believe. She was a cop, and that would never change, still shocked when Presley stepped in suggesting a glass of wine, which she didn't think would hurt so early in the day, particularly being a Saturday and she was dying.

They spent the entire day together until late that evening when Presley went home. She would see them the next day, insisting that being with them all week did not mean moving in, joining them for lunch the next day. Each day after spending precious hours with her sister until her spa day when they went with Marcy to the restaurant looking more like ravishing twins than they had in years.

When Garcia walked in with his wife he filled the room with his stature and presence, embracing the three ladies tightly, holding each one at arm's length with effusive Latin flattery. When Laura and Steve walked in he put rank aside, twirling his lieutenant, telling her mournfully she could do better than a gringo.

She believed him, commenting as he pulled out her chair that Latinos were so much more gallant, that next time she would make better choices.

"¡Ojalá! This gives me hope, chica."

She patted his hand. "And I'm sure your very lovely Ercilia feels the way I do. Now sit and behave." She glanced toward Steve and Presley speaking near the entrance. "Because if you and the gringo start with shop talk I'll shoot both of you. ¿Comprendes, amigo?"

He did, sadly, eyeing Dill with a smirk who Presley had cornered and was hugging at the door.

Though Steve was viewing his situation differently, forewarned by Laura that he deserved whatever. What's worse, once Presley released her tight grip, tears were welling. The female condition: Never understood by the rational mind, yet forever anticipated and faced with when least expected.

"You are delightful this evening, Presley. So why the wet eyes? This should be a very happy occasion for you."

"Don't worry, Steve. You're safe. I won't hurt you. My tears are happy tears." She took the silk square from his pocket, patting the corners of her eyes. "I'm sorry for last week. I wasn't myself."

"Don't be. I was in the wrong. Too many years with callous cops and bad guys. Not enough time in the company of lovely ladies."

"I wasn't expecting the end coming this quickly."

He chuckled. "I was also a little tactless, less genteel than my usual charming self. However, believe me when I say I was severely and duly punished."

Her eyes brightened. "Oh, that's right. I forgot. I was having one of those bad days." She smacked him, giggling. "Now we're even. And we're friends again?"

"Always friends."

"Good. And they're watching us."

She took his hand, guiding him to their seats, thanking him graciously as she sat, commenting on how handsome the gentlemen were, and garnering genteel nods, Steve wondering aloud at the empty seat between him and Presley.

"Who else is expected, Presley? Hopefully another dazzling young lady who would make Rey's evening and mine even more enjoyable?"

She glanced at Laura. "Oh, he's good. I think maybe you should keep him after all." She faced Steve. "Yes. In fact a very dazzling young woman. Brenda is joining us this evening and she very much wanted to sit between Steve Dillion and me. She told me that,Steve, and she thanks you from the bottom of her heart. We both do."

"¡Vaya! hombre. I believe we will all need more napkins this evening." Garcia stood, Steve followed, raising their glasses. "Señoras, Dill, a toast to our enchanting hostess y la muy preciosa Miss Brenda. May their incomparable beauty and charm endure forever."

Garcia was right about the napkins, he and Dillion quietly letting the flood subside; both men flushed and floored when Presley then blurted to the accompaniment of high-pitched giggles, "Hey, Dill. Good for you and Rey for finally coming-out. Heard about that."

*

Madison & Samantha:
Saturday Bryce Madison came home later than expected, walking in near midnight, which wasn't particularly unusual. His Miami flight was often delayed, which Samantha never questioned, for which he never apologized. That part of their life had become the norm, as was not being greeted at the door, or having a cocktail waiting for him, or Samantha not wearing anything silky or satiny, or letting him see her in the shower or the bath. And sex? Basic high school manoeuvres. He could hold his breath longer than she

took climaxing and falling asleep.

Whenever the last time was.

Leaving his luggage at the door, he poured a deep scotch, dropped onto a sofa and called out her name, asking about her week in Savannah when she came in as he was pouring his second glass.

Not that he cared. He loathed hearing about her students and the college, her tales and her workweek life painfully mundane. Truth was, he was finding her increasingly difficult to live with. She had become self-absorbed and moody and he hadn't touched her in months, realizing that since the wedding, and compared with his clients, she was a serious disappointment. A virtual Ice Queen. Never curious, never the least inventive, Madison believing the first husband must have died from some massive attack of boredom.

As hard as he often tried he couldn't remember a single memorable event and for whatever the reason she had most clearly metamorphosed into 'the wife'.

Even onboard the yacht she was remote, spending more time with neighbours than with him. And thongs? Topless? Not for months despite him always playing the quintessential husband. Whatever had soured between them was in her head. He didn't understand. He'd done everything right. He never put restrictions on her, always giving her free rein, always encouraging her work with dead-end inner city kids going nowhere except the county jail or prison. Applauding her.

If anyone should be righteously pissed, he had every right. He also had every right to fully enjoy a wife that was stop-traffic appealing, irrespective of frost bite. And he would, very soon teach her what it means to abandon him.

When she finally stopped talking, "I'm thinking the marina tomorrow. We'll at least have one full day."

"I can't, Bryce. I'm doing an extra session with my students, doing a theme day in the park."

"It's summer, Samantha. And Sunday. What the fuck?"

"With no rain in the forecast two weeks before the summer semester exams. We're talking about one day, Bryce. I'm sure you'll survive on your own." She stood. She was tired and did not need or want his bullshit. "I mean, why not go yourself? You deserve and you're exhausted. It'll be good for you. We'll do next weekend together. But right now I need sleep more than salt air. I'll see you in the morning."

"Yeah. I'll do that. Sweet dreams." Bitch. "I'm staying down for a few more hits."

Good. "Enjoy yourself."

Samantha climbed the stairway to her bedroom. She had never asked about what he actually did in Miami. In part, she supposed, because in the beginning she was waiting for him to tell her. Then she lost interest, in Miami and in his private college scheme that had clearly become a faded dream.

Teaching executives in a tiny downtown office was completely without merit; he'd lost his fervour, becoming too reticent, never talking about their future, and complacent, too comfortable with their shared richesse. And that she had taken a lover was not her fault. That was wholly on him. She'd lost respect for him.

Climbing into her bed, pulling the cool satin sheets to her chin, she was happy, content, her entire being infused with warmth for the one she did love. She was doing what was right for her, and for him. They were never meant to be together, each one fulfilling the other's ephemeral need. She was simply saying the words first, divorcing him first, fully anticipating he would react badly and with good reason. He loved the thought of her wealth as much as he once pretended as deep a love for her. In fact she believed she could have multiple lovers and he wouldn't care. As smooth and debonair as he was, and he was, as loving and caring, his icy blue eyes betrayed him more each day. Meaning the time had very definitely come before he made a complete fool of her, stealing her dignity before one day taking her money.

She would tell him on the weekend, suppress her usual gay laughter at initiating the divorce, at shocking him. Then she would leave him with her dignity intact and be with the one eagerly waiting to be with her forever, closing her eyes and drifting into peaceful slumber until waking to a pleasantly warm and bright August day, pleased he hadn't come to her bed.

Even better was that he was gone and, an hour later, she was being hugged and kissed and adored. Bryce Madison completely forgotten.

The couple were together everyday, because there was no summer semester, speaking of the future over intimate dinners and loving each other, Samantha neither doubting nor losing her resolve for a moment, confronting her husband Friday morning after a week of his late evenings that she didn't believe were all about work. Nor would her Friday be, stopping him at the door.

"I won't be home this evening, Bryce. A last-minute thing. Yesterday a colleague asked if I could join her for a dinner and the theatre. Her girlfriend backed out and she asked me. I won't be home because it's in Myrtle Beach. We booked a room."

"Another fucked-up weekend? That's what you're saying?"

"No. That is not what I'm saying. I'm suggesting you stay onboard this evening and I'll join you tomorrow. We'll be at Folly before noon. I promise."

"You know what? Do whatever you want, Samantha. Just make fucking sure you're with me tomorrow."

"Bryce, don't have a stroke. And watch your mouth. I said I'll be there."

"I didn't buy that yacht so I could sit alone in an empty marina. And this weekend, let's see some ass. I mean it, Samantha. I didn't marry a nun."

He didn't say another word, Samantha watching as he climbed

into the M4, slammed the door, and sped off like a pouty teenager whose girlfriend wasn't taking her panties off after the prom.

When he was gone she closed her door gently, leaning against the plate glass, mildly angry, mildly amused, pondering the weekend, of finally making her life meaningful again. If he was that pissed about one night without her, what about an entire lifetime? Because he didn't marry a nun; he married her. Huge mistake.

She pushed her weight from the door. He was no longer an issue, nor would he ever again set foot in her home that was never truly theirs. She was adamant. She was done with him, moving on to a better place in her life with a hectic day ahead of her and an even fuller evening and night that had nothing to do with theatre. The day was all about her, her evening all about tender moments, beginning a few minutes later when she left home elated, stopping by the marina before crossing over the city.

She didn't bother bringing a weekend wardrobe she had no intention of wearing; instead she poured a chilled Chardonnay and sat at the helm musing. Why not enjoy the moment? She had an hour; she would never again be alone onboard and was determined she would make their last day together his most memorable.

She couldn't help herself, chortling at the thought of his wide-eyed stunned expression, of his utter disbelief, of how he would forever despise her.

Saturday

The day ensured that lovers would stroll in the parks, that dads would fly kites with their boys on the shores, that moms and daughters would enjoy quality time together in their gardens, and that Team Indiscreet would have perfect conditions for their run-through. And Sunday's forecast promised an equally idyllic day for the takedown of a sociopathic serial killer.

Laura and Steve began the day with an early breakfast at the marina resort, talking about the party, about how impossibly identical the twins were, yet how diametrically opposite. Priscilla serious and reserved, Presley full of life and bubbly, Laura commenting on the marked difference in Marcy. As though being with Priscilla had breathed life into her, Laura smacking him at the table when he added with an exaggerated smile and his eyes too bright, "Who would not want a front row seat for that?"

"Really, Dill? You are so sad and pitiful."

He chuckled, "It's a guy thing. The pretty ones, naturally."

She shook her head, checking her watch. Time for wearing off the weekend special with a leisurely stroll along on the docks, as if they belonged, supposing when they ambled past the *Indiscreet* that Samantha was below deck, Laura remarking that for someone as dangerous as Miles to seem so innocuously mainstream was creepy. She could actually feel her skin crawling, Dill welcoming her to the dark side.

She had never worked undercover, had never experienced a stakeout or gurgling bowels not uncommon at a takedown. Being a homicide detective was all about after the fact, cleaning up the mess instead of making one.

She thanked him for that, reminding him that Lieutenant Laura Dillion who was, in fact, in charge of the operation would not have a mess to cleanup because Steve Dillion who was, in fact, a guest of the Charleston PD would not make one, waving at Palmer and Garcia as the stepped onto the public gas dock.

With no mention of the previous evening they were underway, Laura titillated minutes later skimming over the surface a few miles out at thirty knots on a calm sea, three unmarked PD harbor patrol boats racing to close that distance between them heightening the adrenaline surge. Until Garcia and Dillion agreed with eager nods that bikinis would certainly make the team less conspicuous, two slender and synchronized middle fingers jabbing the air.

The men shrugged, exchanging smirks, because they knew, raucous male laughter erupting when Garcia yelled over the rush of wind that Sunday would be a balmy thirty degrees with no apparent wind on a white boat.

¡Vaya!

*

Priscilla and Marcy woke early, gently stirring Presley from a blissful dream in their guest room.

It's what she wanted, asking Prissy while lounging with a nightcap after her party what was the point of being a lesbian if she wanted to sleep with her straight sister? Hello. And looking at Marcy, was anything sadder than a lonely lesbian? She would be fine. She would. Like she said, no more tears, only happiness for her. They would all be fine after Sunday. And hey, Marcy, about those handcuffs?

Watching her sister and Marcy at the door Presley was happy for Prissy who for too long had been alone. They were fabulous together and no way was Marcy a hard-ass cop, not in flared retro shorts, her long tanned legs and nautical V-neck. No way. She was warm and she was loving, Presley hugging her tightly before she left, kissing her cheek, telling her to always take care of her sister.

Please always take care of her because we never know. Because life is shit. And, are you sure?

Yes. She was certain. Despite a successful dinner party, despite their persistent pleas, the sisters were not invited to Laura Dillion's beach party. Wouldn't happen, Marcy promising a full recap that evening and on Sunday videos of the takedown taken from onboard the *Indiscreet* and the patrol boats. That's what Laura promised; that's what Marcy would take care of.

When she left the sisters lay back on the sky-high patio sipping coffees and holding hands the way Presley wanted, a quiet morning with the most special person in her life. She saw no point in shopping for outfits she would never wear, no point in crushing into so little time the lifetime of special memories that fate had stolen from them. This was the memory she wanted for Prissy.

Then she would go home, she would rest, and make herself lovely for her evening with them when she would tell them again how much she loved and adored them. Because all too soon—

Which was too much for Priscilla, sweeping Presley into her arms and sobbing, not at all comforted by her sister's gentle strokes and kisses.

*

Bryce Madison took advantage of his Friday bachelor status to service a needful client, arriving at the marina near midnight in a dark mood that would not abate anytime soon.

He was eager for Sunday, for the day he could sell the yacht, return to Miami where he would disappear, where Braxton Miles would dispose of his holdings and Briand Moire could at last live the life he richly deserved on the French Côte d'Azur.

She had become unpredictable, as though she was intentionally provoking him, when for two entire and difficult years he had done nothing but devote himself to her, care for her and love her.

Then, on the eve of his success, telling him she had made other plans, believing she was fucking with his brain, mocking him when she was the one totally fucked.

He fell asleep on the afterdeck seething, the old-fashioned tightly gripped in his hand. She could not imagine.

When he woke he had nothing to do except dress for the day and plan his evening with her as he paced the dock and afterdeck watching the marina empty, watching minutes turn into hours, morning into afternoon. He was livid, thinking he should right then take her out to sea and dump the bitch. Screw the plan. Improvise. He could do that.

Three-thirty, six unanswered messages, and she was sauntering along the dock as though she was on a catwalk dressed for a photo shoot, as though she hadn't completely ignored his wishes.

"You cannot fucking be serious. The day's finished. We'll never find decent anchorage and what the hell is with that? We're at a fucking marina, Samantha, not some fashion show."

She stepped onboard, not bothering with her sandals. "Please stop acting like a petulant child. And I told you to watch your mouth. I stopped by the house for a change of fashion because I need to look better than I feel. Do you have a real problem with that, Bryce?"

He poured a chilled Pinot Grigio, for himself. "Fine. Except I've been waiting and worried since breakfast. You didn't answer one call. Where the hell were you?"

No. Not then. She wanted the greatest shock value possible when she would tell him that evening after a day of digging the knife deeper. She wanted total victory.

"We'll talk this evening. I'm not feeling well right now. Meaning we're staying at dock. But I'll be fine by tomorrow," because what's making me nauseous is you. "However I would like one of those. Thank you for offering. A petulant child and inconsiderate. How wonderful. I'll be on the foredeck."

She was pushing the limit, being a supreme bitch.

Watching her walk away he couldn't imagine hating any woman more. This one he would absolutely enjoy, he mused, pouring the wine and taking it to her, studying her staring across the marina, across the city. She was ignoring him, smirking; Madison pondering how good he would feel when he stood smirking as she disappeared into a dark ocean without the compassion he showed the others.

When actually she wasn't ignoring him or smirking. She was

remembering the days onboard in her thongs, sunning. Good for them, seeing her. Why not? She was young and attractive with a body to die for. Still he couldn't take the bullshit. She knew that and when he was finally gone, preferring the marina patio to anymore time than he needed with her, she went to the afterdeck for more wine.

By six she was feeling good, very good. And by seven when he came back anticipating an uncomfortable dinner at the restaurant she was feeling even better after several more glasses of wine, telling him she wasn't interested in dinner, or in sitting with him, that he should dine alone. She was feeling worse and didn't trust herself in public, thinking a restful evening would serve her better. Besides, she had a phone call to make, thanking her friend for a wonderful evening.

Whatever.

He did precisely that, changing into required evening casual, telling her to take it easy on the booze. Because pissed or sober he'd be fucking his wife for dessert. He didn't care which. He'd had it with her bullshit and if he had to strip her naked on deck the next day at Folly he would.

If he actually believed that, good for him. And when he was gone, stomping away like the pettish child he was, she turned off the power. She didn't need the distraction of music or the irritating squawking over Channel 16.

Saturday Evening

As Dill was telling Laura he wouldn't half-mind putting a round in the bastard's smug face, his computer screen went black the instant he watched Samantha switch off the yacht's power.

The good thing was, she was at the marina. She would be alone for most of the evening and she was safe. Not a big deal. Miles would never be that stupid and the teams would be in place in less than ten hours.

*

As the minute hand on her watch was touching nine, as Samantha watched Madison swaggering like King Shit along the deserted dock she kissed her phone with tender passion, disconnecting, promising she would not be long. Fifteen minutes, tops. Then she poured another and deeper Rémy Martin, dropped the vial under her seat and stood flipping a switch at the helm. For what was a divorce without music?

"Shit. Seriously? You're still drinking?"

"No. I'm still celebrating, asshole."

He coughed a laugh. "Celebrating what? Finally spreading your legs and being a wife?"

"That won't happen. You want it so badly? Go fuck yourself."

"You get those clothes off now, or I will. I swear."

"I'm divorcing you."

"You're drunk." He jerked his head toward the companionway. "Get your ass downstairs."

"Not that drunk. Not yet." She downed the cognac, bracing herself strategically against the gunwale. "Last night I wasn't in Myrtle Beach. I was having a romantic dinner with another man." She paused. "Oh, I'm sorry. What I meant was, a man. Then breakfast at his place. So yes, you are gone. Your bags are on the doorstep. Just don't bother with the doorbell. You won't like who opens the door."

*

At 8:55 Marcy was beside herself. She didn't understand the one-sided conversation; she didn't understand the sobbing and the clenched hands. As much as she pleaded, Priscilla wouldn't say. She didn't know what to tell her lieutenant, except, "Laura, you and Steve, get there now. No red lights. Go."

And as the big hand of her watch was touching nine Priscilla Serra was speeding past traffic and through red lights too overcome with emotion to be nervous, watching Marcy speak with Garcia as calmly as though she was having a coffee. She was still being reticent, Dill and Laura
 on the other side of town racing toward the same location; Steve, though, wishing he was at the wheel, albeit seeing a different side of his wife.

A man-thing.

*

By 9:10 the quarrel onboard the *Indiscreet* had escalated, a composed and determined Samantha relieved the marina was empty. She didn't need a crowd witnessing his tantrum.

"That's right. You're embarrassing, a failure. Emeritus professor, my ass. You're a loser, a gigolo with a wedding band. I mean really, except for this thing, how much have you ever put out? I didn't see that at first." She stung his face and her hand with a vicious slap. "Now I see that you're disgusting, a shallow joke."

He gripped her by the throat, his other hand slicing through the buttons of her blouse. "You arrogant bitch. You're all alike. I knew this would happen."

"Fuck you."

She broke free, slashing his face with her fingers, mocking him, rejoicing in his rage, scarcely feeling his fist slam into her face, closing her eyes against a second savage blow, at peace with herself and resolute. Then or never, tearing away her hat and her glasses, staring into the lens. Bright blue eyes now liquid brown, piercing and unafraid; her copper hair now chocolate brown and lustrous.

Braxton Miles stood frozen in time, his blood ice cold. "Serra!"

She loved her sister so very much, but Brenda was waiting. She knew Brenda was waiting to carry her away. With all her remaining strength she screamed "Prissy, be happy for me!" And she went over into the marina's dark and deep water, grasping at the yacht's fender, her face bright with triumph and jubilation, her chilling whisper guttural and strong. "You're Braxton Miles. You killed me tonight the way you murdered Brenda and Bobbi-Jo. They know who you are and they're watching you. You're done, asshole."

And she let go, gazing up unblinking for as long as she could, dragged down quickly and mercifully by the weights at her ankles.

*

9:14.

Steve Dillion blurted, "What the fuck!" lurching forward as though he might have saved her.

Marcy and Laura stood helplessly horrified witnessing the young woman, who the evening before was bantering and giggling, being murdered in real time, staring at Priscilla trembling between them, her lips quivering, her eyes blurred with a flood of tears.

Garcia crossed himself, murmuring a prayer no one heard.

"What just happened here?" Dillion demanded, his voice urgent. "Priscilla, that was Presley."

She inhaled a calming breath, wiping her palms across her face. "Yes. That's who Braxton Miles murdered, my sister, because Samantha Sandal does not exist. She never did. Her papers were all fake and they're gone. The mansion I rented from a friend for my own convenience and, if you care to check, all traces of Bryce Madison and Samantha Sandal have been removed."

Laura cut in. "Why would she possibly have done that, marry him? Let herself be murdered? How could you?"

"It was a gamble, one I fought. You see Presley was dying, enduring terrible pain. She didn't have much time and wanted the man we believed was Brent Mason in Charleston as much for Steve as for you, the Charleston PD. We both did. Though how we lured him has no bearing. He got here on his own for his own purpose. That's what happened. But they were never married. The JOP and the lawyer who drew up the wills were Presley's actor friends from the West Coast. Everything was staged including the college colleagues at the wedding, all West Coast actors and friends whose real names I've forgotten. Nor did she ever teach art or travel to Savannah. Those weeks were Presley's time with me, with all of you." She turned to Marcy. "She came home to be with me for the little time she had left and for this. This is what she wanted. She wanted Miles. She wanted the man who killed Brenda and she wanted death with dignity. But she did not suffer. What she threw under the bench was a very strong paralytic drug with his fingerprints on the vial. She went onboard yesterday, making a switch and I doubt she even felt his fists. That's what your lab will find in her blood. And yes, your divers will find weights that she was wearing for the sole purpose of toning her beautiful legs. Right, Marcy?"

Laura answered for her. "What ankle weights? Our divers found no such thing. Now Rey, cut the lights. Marcy, I want Presley out of that water tonight. Pronto. And Priscilla, you will not see that happen. Steve, stop recording. Put it back to when that piece of shit boarded. We've got company coming."

Within minutes PD divers were en route, a tearful Priscilla explaining why Saturday, why she couldn't tell Marcy. In a word, them. Difficult to get yourself murdered when surrounded by cops and your girlfriend is one of them.

Marcy Palmer wrapped Priscilla tightly in her arms, Laura gently squeezing her thigh; Dillion and Garcia instinctively checked their weapons by the door. Neither was comfortable with the unfamiliar emotion and the usual après-murder banter did not apply.

Laura didn't have that issue. "There is no guilt here, Priscilla. No recrimination. What you will do is always remember that you did what was best for Presley. She believed in her heart she would be with Brenda and she is. That's what you must believe. You and Marcy. Because I do."

Garcia added, "What La Chica says is true, Priscilla. This you must believe, always."

Dillion added, "And she got the sick bastard. Good for her. She's a hero. Good for both of you."

*

Braxton Miles switched off the power, literally springing from the yacht the instant he realized. He had time, screeching into the driveway soon after, stumbling inside the foyer at seeing the empty living and dining rooms, bounding up the stairway into the empty bedroom and walk-in for the first time in years hearing his heart pound with dread.

He no longer had the luxury of time, a hunted man driving as normally as he could a few blocks over, leaving the car with the engine running and the driver's door ajar, flagging a cab and stepping out a block from his condo that he stepped into as PD divers were stepping onto the *Indiscreet.*

A nanosecond later a 6'6" angry Latino cop had him pinned to the floor, telling Dill no hurry with the lights, neither Laura nor Marcy hearing the crushing thuds or pained gasps coming from somewhere in the dark.

"For Presley, hijo de puta. For Brenda."

And however Steve lost his balance, however the toe of his

shoe accidentally crashed into Miles' side, was not his problem. He wasn't a cop, simply an interested party—and clumsy.

He flicked the light switch.

"Braxton Miles. Nice little classroom you've got here. Nice list of private students also. My personal favourite was Miss Elouise. Nice ass, nice everything. Got to love those squeals. Good job."

Garcia jerked Miles to his feet, patting him down, clamping the cuffs as tightly as he could, grabbing hold of the links between the steel bracelets with a gloved hand. "You are done, asshole."

Dillion pointed to vents and furniture. "That's right. Peekaboo, I see you. I've got quite the library, Miles. And no question that Deidre is Miss Miami, the one who likes the doggie thing. So how did that work for her? You are quite the man, with women. Though this bedroom unfortunately was always strictly sound."

Miles wasn't listening. He was staring at the screen, at Priscilla, watching as he pushed her over, smirking. "Your twin. No shit. But things aren't always what they appear. I was reaching out to her. She was drunk. She slipped and I panicked. I ran here to call the police."

Laura stopped him. "Brenda and Roberta-Joelle. And now you're under arrest for murdering Presley Burke."

"I don't think so. My wife's name was Samantha Sandal and I want a lawyer."

"There was no Samantha Sandal. We also tracked your car this evening to a home rented by Ms. Serra. Explain that one. And your clothes by the way are in a garbage bin. Not that you'll ever need them."

"That's right," Priscilla added. "Exactly where you're going the day they execute you for murdering my sister. Know that. Believe that."

He coughed a snide laugh, sneering. "What I know is what it's like to fuck you. I know every inch of you; I know the smooth texture of your warm flesh, the scent of your breath and your skin."

He sniffed the air. "Sweet like honey. That's what you should know."

A thick fist smashed into his back. "¡Cállate!, motherfucker."

56

Presley Burke was located by several divers and carried in caring arms to the surface by 10:30 and by midnight, by Lieutenant Dillion's instructions, she was ready to be with her sister for the last time; the forensic pathologist promising Priscilla that she went peacefully without the least indication of fear or torment.

Priscilla stayed alone by Presley's side for an hour before Laura and Marcy pulled her away, saying their own goodbyes before Dill and Garcia arrived after booking her killer.

She was laid to rest Tuesday afternoon alongside her lifelong friend, attended by many from Division in full dress and her friends from the West Coast who had played such a crucial role, who Priscilla had flown in so that they might say goodbye and for her to thank them.

Wednesday, under the warmth and muted glow of an early evening sun, Priscilla returned with Marcy, sitting for awhile by the stone that was inscribed *Together Forever With Brenda*.

Her final gift to her sister.

*

Braxton Miles did not have an enviable time in lockup through Monday morning. As much as Division liked Dill, they loved Laura and Marcy and that made Priscilla family.

Monday Laura's captain agreed Dillion should be permitted certain privileges, given his ties to the force and his dedication to bringing down Miles.

"You've got one call, Miles. Make it a good one. There is no charity here."

"I should have had that call Saturday."

"We forgot you were here."

"I didn't kill her. You know I didn't."

"What I know, smart guy, is Sunday. What I know is drugs on the boat. What I know is Briand Moire won't be delighting lonely ladies in Monaco for a thousand Euros a pop. What I know is Cody Jones. What I know is New Orleans and Le Renard. You don't remember me standing on the sidewalk years back, smart guy?"

A telling pause, betraying eyes.

"No. I don't pay much attention to certain demographics. No offence."

"None taken. I am curious, though. How do you suppose CJ will thank you for screwing with him? What is he, a hundred K out of pocket? One-fifty? And what is that favour? He got you by the balls, smart guy?"

"Who's Cody Jones?"

Dillion shrugged. "You've got one call. Make it a good one."

*

Miles was cuffed and shackled, waddling his way toward the phone at the end of the hall as Dillion and the uniform with him waited at the holding cell. Cody Jones picked up on the third ring, waiting.

"CJ, you there? It's. me, Braxton."

"I heard, kid. Tough luck."

"I'm sorry, CJ. I disappointed you."

"She has rained the most serious grief down upon you, kid. The way I warned you she would. You were good to go. You should have gone, should have been satisfied with the many bountiful fruits of your labours and your many women."

"Destiny, CJ. What can I say? Truthfully, I got screwed over. I did not kill that woman. I did not, which isn't why I'm calling. You keep names, you keep numbers. Do you have mine from the Garden District?"

"Yes."

"Well, the thing is, my gut tells me I am not getting out of this and that number completes what I gave you at the restaurant. My gift to you, CJ, for all that you've done for me. I ask only one favour. If this thing turns out badly for me, which will happen, when I go down, that day you make things right for me with that PS bitch."

"Meaning?"

"Meaning this phone isn't clean. Meaning the driver. An easy forty and change with a whole lot of zeros for a simple favour whenever the needle goes in, which I don't have a real big issue with. I had a good run and shit happens. The way I want for her. Do unto others, right?" He coughed a hoarse laugh. "You got that? You understand that?"

"Yeah, kid. I do. We had good history together, you and me. Might even have had a favour for you this time around. I'll miss you. Now you listen up. You be smart. Before you go making serious enemies, and you will, you make friends. You take care of business first. You got that?"

"Thanks, CJ. You tell Blaire goodbye for me if you ever see her. That's my one regret. And now I guess this is goodbye."

"You stand tall, kid. Consider the favour done."

Click.

*

Thursday evening Priscilla went alone to visit with Laura and Steve. She and Presley had unfinished business with him and the twenty-dollar Merlot would do very well.

"Thank you, Steve. We did have every confidence in you. What we did we did for Presley. At the time she had a few years, at the end a few days. She told me what she hoped to say at the end, what I believe she did because despite the drug she was focused." She smiled, reaching into her handbag. "The words don't matter. We all saw the fright on his face."

"He'll be put down, Priscilla. That's a given. He'll have his turn on the gurney one day very soon and I'll be there."

"With me."

"No. Not with you," Laura cut in. "With me. You do not want to see that and Marcy will tell you why."

She understood, however—

"At any cost, Steve. I made my sister a promise."

"And one you will keep. That's my promise."

"Good. Now, a few years ago I made *you* a promise." She passed him an envelope. "Except that Presley suggested a slight change I fully agreed with, which can never express how we feel."

"What is this?"

"What do you think?" She looked at Laura. "For dinner with a lovely homicide cop."

Two Years Later

11:46

"Seems like yesterday, Preacher, seeing Courtney and Serra sitting so close together yet so far apart. Makes me wonder if they might have met up, swapping stories. Which certainly would have been a little one-sided, the two of them bitching on me. Especially the sister laughing at me, Courtney agreeing I was shit, probably now not giving a shit. Like I had a choice." He shifted in his seat. "Like any of us have a choice. Imagine the catastrophic brain-fuck, hearing I was never married to the slut. That's what she was, all that work for nothing. Talk about feeling cheated. And how was that tidbit never mentioned in court?" He snorted, smirking. "Then again, I suppose if I had, I'd likely still be in the nuthouse instead of being put down in about fourteen minutes for a murder I didn't commit."

The good reverend leaned in closer. "Braxton, at this late hour I see hatred festering in your eyes, my son. Fourteen minutes is time enough for us to pray and find peace."

"Not hatred, Preacher. I mean, what was in her head that she was so intent on murdering me that she went ahead and killed herself? Tell me that wasn't pure insanity, pure hatred. Tell me that wasn't a complete fucking cover-up. So not hatred, Preacher. Disappointment I suppose for not listening to CJ. He warned me that serious grief would rain down upon me. Told me a hundred times and it sure as hell did. You know, I called him this morning."

"Bidding farewell to a friend?"

"Sort of. Not that I ever doubted him. CJ is very big on disap-

pointment. Because Serra is sitting somewhere smugly sipping champagne and gloating, staring at the clock, waiting for twelve noon."

"When I will be at your side, Braxton."

"For what purpose, Preacher?"

"By your side bringing you comfort as you cross over into your salvation, praying for your soul."

At that Miles chortled. "Salvation, Preacher? Do you think so? Really? Now if you'd like to stand-in for me we can sure as hell talk about that. But comfort? I'll get that by imagining Blaire all naked and sweaty on one side and Courtney on the other in my final minutes. Not a man of the cloth who hates his own reality. Sorry, but that's what I see in your eyes. "

Emery Prisby bowed his head, clasping his hands in prayer, startled by the door clanging open, looking up to see Braxton Miles smiling.

11:50

Warden Booker Mudd stepped in with humourless guards, a matching set standing ready in the corridor by the door.

"Inmate Miles, we gonna have us a problem here, boy? You and me?"

Miles stared at the warden's hand, at the familiar ring he hadn't worn in two years, smirking. "No sir, Warden. Everything's good."

His feet and hands were matter-of-factly unshackled as though he was going to the latrine and not his death, the reverend's eyes beseeching him.

"Your salvation is at hand, Braxton. Believe in me, believe in Him. He will not forsake you."

"Think He already has, Preacher." Standing tall the way CJ told him, he looked down at the old man. "Reverend Prisby. Go home. No one on this row gives a shit what you believe. We're all going to the same place for the same reasons. But first do me a favour. Tell them the moment I'm gone. Tell Dillion and his cop wife. Do that for me."

"Tell them what exactly, my son?"

He leaned forward. "Tell them exactly that Priscilla Serra is dead. Will you do that for me, Preacher?" He turned to the warden. "Let's do this thing."

The old man paled; the warden didn't care. He'd heard the rhetoric all too often. More importantly he had an inmate to execute, tickets for the Saturday game with his son, and Miles was taken away, the warden leading the procession, giving the routine event no thought. Miles would be his eleventh in the chamber

Inside Miles had no expression seeing technician and gurney, the coloured liquids in glass cylinders and the rubber tubes, as if he was indeed on the verge of timeless slumber, climbing onto the vinyl mattresses unaided. Though when the warden drew back the curtain into the viewing room, he sat sneering, a row of bright teeth gleaming as he saw through the window Dillion and his cop wife bolting from the room.

"Thank you, CJ? Thank you."

"Say what, boy?"

"I said let's get this done."

Those were his last words, Braxton Miles reclining on his own, once again strapped in place and ready for sleep, freeing his mind of pinches and words, inviting two alluring and adoring women into his eternity.

"Braxton Miles, by authority vested in me by the state of South Carolina…"

*

11:56

Priscilla Serra was sitting with Marcy Palmer waiting for noon, waiting for absolute closure, not expecting the intercom's buzz, wondering who would challenge such a dark and threatening day.

Thick rain was slashing at their windows, bolts of yellow-white lightening highlighting the creases and curves of rolling black clouds, the cacophony of ceaseless thunder shaking the building and their nerves, Marcy Palmer commenting on how magnificent the day was for an execution.

"Yes, hello?"

"Miss Serra, good morning. My name is Cody Jones. I'm here on business regarding you and your sister, Presley, on behalf of Mr. Braxton Miles. You may know of me and I do assure you I mean you no harm. May I come up? Or would you prefer a meeting in your lobby with your doorman and security person? I have no preference."

She turned to Marcy who was reaching into her purse for her phone, an instant later reaching for her weapon, nodding.

"Eighteen-twelve, Mr. Jones."

Precisely at noon Cody Jones was greeted by Priscilla at the open door; stepping in he was greeted by Marcy whose ten-millimetre was held in her hands at her waist.

Laying his wet coat and hat across a chair by the door, she invited him into her living room.

"Thank you for seeing me, Miss Serra." He acknowledged the other woman with scarcely a twinge, tilting his head. "Madam."

"I do know who you are, Mr. Jones. And I cannot imagine what business you would have with me."

"You have a lovely home, Miss Serra. May we sit?" He noticed the wine bar. "And at the risk of appearing inexcusably gauche, may I impose upon you for a curative taste of one of those excellent vintages? I've had a long and miserable drive." He pointed to the weather, grinning. "As you can appreciate. And we New Orleanians tend to ignore the customary five PM rule." He turned to Marcy, deliberately opening his jacket. "I assure you, madam, I intend you no harm."

Priscilla selected an '87 Côtes de Bergerac, inviting him to sit, scarcely believing she had Miles' facilitator in her home.

She poured a generous amount into a crystal goblet, excited and nervous. She knew exactly what he was, yet he had the appearance and manner of a Wall Street businessman, pouring a deep one for herself and joining them.

"He killed my sister, Mr. Jones. So you can understand my partner's apprehension. She's a cop. Sergeant Palmer."

"A very lovely policewoman, I would add. And more precisely, Miss Serra, Braxton would have killed your sister the next day. We both know that to be true. Don't we?" He accepted the long-stemmed goblet, thanking her, silently appreciating the rich bouquet, checking his watch. "As I understand the due process Braxton is now in his final minute of life, which is why he entrusted me with coming here. You see, he fervently wished for you to expire with him." He sipped the deep-scarlet wine, savouring the velvet smoothness. "You need not worry, Miss Palmer. And I assure you I am reaching for a simple envelope." He did, passing it to Priscilla. "You see, when Braxton was arrested he foresaw this day; he likely always did. He and I had history dating back to 1992 when we first met. He had a destiny, what he believed above all else, which included Brenda Holloway, Bobbi-Jo Valliere and Miss Burke, the first two ladies making him very wealthy, which was his life's single ambition apart from a singularly distasteful diversion."

"He was worse than psychotic, Mr. Jones. I would say diseased."

"That would certainly be difficult to argue. Braxton was indeed damaged goods and what he did was entirely without merit, walking his own path, making his own way as we all must, a dark path that he ensured would continue beyond his passing. In short, Miss Serra, he paid me very handsomely to be here, to carry out his final and decidedly vindictive wish. He paid me what has amounted to forty-three million dollars and in that envelope is a cashier's cheque for half that amount. So please, Miss Palmer, relax. I warned Braxton that one day a grievous rain would fall down upon him. You and your sister were that rain, Miss Serra. You were the destiny he deeply believed in."

The faint distant wail of sirens crescendoed quickly into a cacophony, tires screeching. Then quiet, Cody Jones smiling. "Miss Palmer's reinforcements, I presume."

"Marcy, put that thing away and please meet them at the door. Mr. Jones, Steve and Laura Dillion with Marcy were the arresting detectives."

"I am fully aware of their considerable involvement, Miss Serra. And given their well-timed arrival perhaps we should wait for them and Miss Palmer. I have a great deal more to tell you, if I may."

*

Moments later introductions were made, more exquisite wine was served, Dill and Laura were brought up to speed, and nervous tension evolved into relaxed curiosity.

"That brings us to the current day, as the man you have known as Braxton Miles and others journeys into a deserved place. But now may I tell you what you do not know? May I tell you of a sixteen-year-old Brandon Michaels and a very fateful night at a New Orleans bus station?"

TurnAbout

Other Mystery - Suspense - Thriller Novels
By Doug Booth:

Split Verdict

The 4th Man

The Madam

Family Lies

Mother of Pearl

From Inside Her Bedroom

The Feast of Tombola

Deferred Prejudice

The Hunt for Gilligan Rose

The Fatal Diners' Club

Silent Conviction

A Christmas Killer, Comfort and Joy

Pariah In the Mirror

Girl on the Corner

Turnabout

***

No One to Tell (Creative Non-fiction)

www.ingramcontent.com/pod-product-compliance
Lightning Source LLC
Chambersburg PA
CBHW021121260626
47169CB00005B/1379